AMERICAN SCHOOL TEXTBOOK

VOCABULARY KEY

GRADE **4**

Michael A. Putlack

FÜN學美國英語課本

各學科關鍵英單 二版+ Workbook

MP3

寂天雲 APP

如何下載 MP3 音檔

❶ 寂天雲 APP 聆聽：掃描書上 QR Code 下載「寂天雲－英日語學習隨身聽」APP。加入會員後，用 APP 內建掃描器再次掃描書上 QR Code，即可使用 APP 聆聽音檔。

❷ 官網下載音檔：請上「寂天閱讀網」（www.icosmos.com.tw），註冊會員／登入後，搜尋本書，進入本書頁面，點選「MP3 下載」下載音檔，存於電腦等其他播放器聆聽使用。

FÜN學美國英語課本

各學科關鍵英單 GRADE 4

AMERICAN SCHOOL TEXTBOOK
VOCABULARY KEY

二版

作者簡介

Michael A. Putlack

專攻歷史與英文，擁有美國麻州 Tufts University 碩士學位。

作　　　者	Michael A. Putlack
	Zachary Fillingham／Shara Dupuis（Workbook B 大題）
翻　　　譯	歐寶妮
編　　　輯	王婷葦／歐寶妮
校　　　對	王婷葦
封 面 設 計	林書玉
內 頁 排 版	林書玉
製 程 管 理	洪巧玲
發 行 人	黃朝萍
出 版 者	寂天文化事業股份有限公司
電　　　話	+886-(0)2-2365-9739
傳　　　真	+886-(0)2-2365-9835
網　　　址	www.icosmos.com.tw
讀 者 服 務	onlineservice@icosmos.com.tw
出 版 日 期	2023 年 9 月　二版二刷　（寂天雲隨身聽 APP 版）

郵 撥 帳 號　1998620-0 寂天文化事業股份有限公司
訂書金額未滿 1000 元，請外加運費 100 元。
〔若有破損，請寄回更換，謝謝。〕

國家圖書館出版品預行編目資料

Fun 學美國英語課本：各學科關鍵英單 Grade. 4 (寂天隨身聽 APP 版)/
Michael A. Putlack
著；歐寶妮譯 . -- 二版 . -- [臺北市]：寂天文化 , 2023.09
　　面；　公分

ISBN　978-626-300-208-1（菊 8K 平裝）

1.CST: 英語 2.CST: 詞彙

805.12　　　　　　　　　　　　　　　112014126

FUN學美國英語課本：各學科關鍵英單

進入明星學校必備的英文單字

　　用美國教科書學英文是最道地的學習方式，有越來越多的學校選擇以美國教科書作為教材，用全英語授課（immersion）的方式教學，讓學生把英語當成母語學習。在一些語言學校裡，也掀起了一波「用美國教科書學英文」的風潮。另外，還有越來越多的父母優先考慮讓子女用美國教科書來學習英文，讓孩子將來能夠進入明星學校或國際學校就讀。

　　為什麼要使用美國教科書呢？TOEFL 等國際英語能力測驗都是以各學科知識為基礎，使用美國教科書不但能大幅提升英文能力，也可以增加數學、社會、科學等方面的知識，因此非常適合用來準備考試。即使不到國外留學，也可以像在美國上課一樣，而這也是使用美國教科書最吸引人的地方。

以多樣化的照片、插圖和例句來熟悉跨科學習中的英文單字

　　到底該使用何種美國教科書呢？還有如何才能讀懂美國教科書呢？美國各州、各學校的課程都不盡相同，而學生也有選擇教科書的權利，所以單單是教科書的種類就多達數十種。若不小心選擇到程度不適合的教科書，就很容易造成孩子對學英語的興趣大減。

　　因此，正確的作法應該要先累積字彙和相關知識背景。我國學生的學習能力很強，只需要培養對不熟悉的用語和統合教學（Cross-Curricular Study）的適應能力。

　　本系列網羅了在以全英語教授社會、科學、數學、語言、藝術、音樂等學科時，所有會出現的必備英文單字。只要搭配書中真實的照片、插圖和例句，就能夠把這些在美國小學課本中會出現的各學科核心單字記起來，同時還可以熟悉相關的背景知識。

四種使用頻率最高的美國教科書的字彙分析

　　本系列套書規畫了 6 個階段的字彙學習課程，本套書搜羅了 McGraw Hill、Harcourt、Pearson 和 Core Knowledge 等四大教科書中的主要字彙，並且整理出各科目、各主題的核心單字，然後依照學年分為 Grade 1 到 Grade 6。

　　本套書的適讀對象為「準備大學學測指考的學生」和「準備參加 TOEFL 等國際英語能力測驗的學生」。對於「準備赴美唸高中的學生」和「想要看懂美國教科書的學生」，本套書亦是最佳的先修教材。

《FUN學美國英語課本：各學科關鍵英單》 系列的結構與特色

1. 本套書中所收錄的英文單字都是美國學生在上課時會學到的字彙和用法。

2. 將美國小學教科書中會出現的各學科核心單字，搭配多樣化照片、插圖和例句，讓讀者更容易熟記。

3. 藉由閱讀教科書式的題目，來強化讀、聽、寫的能力。透過各式各樣的練習與題目，不僅能夠全盤吸收與各主題有關的字彙，也能夠熟悉相關的知識背景。

4. 每一冊的教學大綱（syllabus）皆涵蓋了社會、歷史、地理、科學、數學、語言、美術和音樂等學科，以循序漸進的方式，學習從基礎到高級的各科核心字彙，不僅能夠擴增各科目的字彙量，同時還提升了運用句子的能力。（教學大綱請參考第 8 頁）

5. 可學到社會、科學等的相關背景知識和用語，也有助於準備 TOEFL 等國際英語能力測驗。

6. 對於「英語程度有限，但想看懂美國教科書的學生」來說，本套書是很好的先修教材。

7. 全系列 6 階段共分為 6 冊，可依照個人英語程度，選擇合適的分冊。

   Grade 1 美國小學 1 年級課程　　　　**Grade 2** 美國小學 2 年級課程

   Grade 3 美國小學 3 年級課程　　　　**Grade 4** 美國小學 4 年級課程

   Grade 5 美國小學 5 年級課程　　　　**Grade 6** 美國小學 6 年級課程

8. 書末附有關鍵字彙的中英文索引，方便讀者搜尋與查照（請參考第 14 頁）。

強烈建議下列學生使用本套書：

1. 「準備大學學測指考」的學生

2. 「準備參加以全英語授課的課程，想熟悉美國學生上課時會用到的各科核心字彙」的學生

3. 「對美國小學各科必備英文字彙已相當熟悉，想朝高級單字邁進」美國學校的七年級生

4. 「準備赴美唸高中」的學生

MP3

收錄了本書的「Key Words」、「Power Verbs」、「Word Families」單元中的所有單字和例句，和「Checkup」中 E 大題的文章，以及 Workbook 中 A 大題聽寫練習文章。

How to Use This Book

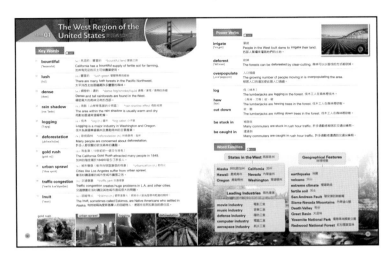

Key Words
熟記和主題有關的10個關鍵字彙，同時也記下該字的例句，並且瀏覽相關補充用語。搭配MP3反覆聽三遍，一直到熟悉字義和發音為止。

Power Verbs
熟記和主題相關的高頻率核心動詞和動詞片語。片語是用簡單的字來表達複雜的涵義，常在TOEFL等國際英語能力測驗中的題目出現，所以要確實地將這些由2–3個字所組成的片語記熟。

Word Families
將容易聯想在一起的字彙或表現形式，以獨特的圈組方式來幫助記憶。這些字就像針線一樣，時常在一起出現，因此要熟知這些字的差異和使用方法。

Checkup

A Write｜練習寫出本書所學到的字彙，一方面能夠熟悉單字的拼法，一方面也能夠幫助記憶。

B Complete the Sentences｜將本書所學到的字彙和例句，確實背熟。

C Read and Choose｜透過多樣化的練習，熟悉本書所學到的字彙用法。

D Look, Read, and Write｜透過照片、插畫和提示，加深對所學到的字彙的印象。

E Read and Answer｜透過與各單元主題有關的「文章閱讀理解測驗」，來熟悉教科書的出題模式，並培養與各學科相關的背景知識和適應各種考試的能力。

Review Test
每5個單元結束會有一回總複習測驗，有助於回想起沒有辦法一次就記起來或忘記的單字，並且再次複習。

Table of Contents

Introduction
How to Use This Book

Workbook 聽力閱讀試題本

Syllabus Vol. 4

Subject	Topic & Area	Title
Social Studies • **History and Geography**	Geography and Culture	The West Region of the United States
	Geography and Culture	The Southwest Region of the United States
	Geography and Culture	The Southeast Region of the United States
	Geography and Culture	The Northeast Region of the United States
	Geography and Culture	The Midwest Region of the United States
	Geography and Culture	The Mountain States of the United States
	World Geography	Mountains, Rivers, and Deserts of the World
	World History	Asian Cultures
	World History	Europe in the Middle Ages
	American History	The Civil War
Science	What Is Science?	Inquiry Skills and Science Tools
	Life Science	Classifying Living Things
	Life Science	Heredity
	Earth Science	The History of the Earth
	Earth Science	The Weather and Water Cycle
	Physical Science	Changes in Matter
	Physical Science	Light and Heat
	Life Science	Circulation and Respiration
	Physical Science	Electricity
	Physical Science	Motion and Forces
Mathematics	Fractions and Decimals	Fractions and Decimals
	Geometry	Lines, Rays, Angles, and Figures
	Geometry	Kinds of Polygons, Circles, and Triangles
	Data and Graphs	Data and Graphs
Language and Literature	Mythology	Norse Mythology
	Language Arts	Learning about Sentences
Visual Arts	Visual Arts	The Art of the Middle Ages
	Visual Arts	The Art of Islam, Africa, and China
Music	A World of Music	The Elements of Music
	A World of Music	Understanding Music

CHAPTER 1

Social Studies •
History and Geography ①

The West Region of the United States 美國西部地區

Key Words

🔊 001

01	**bountiful** [ˋbaʊntəfəl]	*(a.)* 充足的；豐富的　*bountiful land 富饒之地 California has a **bountiful** supply of fertile soil for farming. 加州有充足的沃土可供農業使用。
02	**lush** [lʌʃ]	*(a.)* 豐富的　*lush green 鬱鬱蔥蔥的綠地 There are many **lush** forests in the Pacific Northwest. 太平洋西北地區蘊藏許多豐富的森林。
03	**dense** [dɛns]	*(a.)* 稠密的；濃的　*dense fog/smoke/liquid 濃霧／濃煙／濃稠的液體 **Dense** and tall rainforests are found in the West. 稠密高大的雨林分佈於西部。
04	**rain shadow** [ren ˋʃædo]	*(n.)* 雨影（山脊背風面的少雨區）　*rain shadow effect 雨影效應 The area within the **rain shadow** is usually warm and dry. 雨影地區通常溫暖乾燥。
05	**logging** [ˋlɔgɪŋ]	*(n.)* 伐木　*log (n.) 圓木　*log cabin 小木屋 **Logging** is a major industry in Washington and Oregon. 伐木為美國華盛頓州及奧勒岡州的主要產業。
06	**deforestation** [ˌdɪfɔrəsˋteʃən]	*(n.)* 砍伐森林　*reforestation (n.) 林地復育；造林 Many people are concerned about **deforestation**. 許多人都很關切砍伐森林的議題。
07	**gold rush** [gold rʌʃ]	*(n.)* 淘金潮（19世紀的一個文化特色） The California **Gold Rush** attracted many people in 1849. 加州的淘金潮於1849年吸引了許多人。
08	**urban sprawl** [ˋɝbən sprɔl]	*(n.)* 城市擴張（都市向郊區擴張的現象）　*urbanization (n.) 都市化 Cities like Los Angeles suffer from **urban sprawl**. 像洛杉磯這樣的城市受城市擴張之苦。
09	**traffic congestion** [ˋtræfɪk kənˋdʒɛstʃən]	*(n.)* 交通壅塞　*traffic jam 交通堵塞 **Traffic congestion** creates huge problems in L.A. and other cities. 交通壅塞在洛杉磯及其他城市造成很大的問題。
10	**Inuit** [ˋɪnuɪt]	*(n.)* 因紐特人　*Eskimo (n.) 愛斯基摩人（被部分人認為是帶有貶義的稱呼） The **Inuit**, sometimes called Eskimos, are Native Americans who settled in Alaska. 有時被稱為愛斯基摩人的因紐特人，是居住在阿拉斯加的原住民。

gold rush

urban sprawl

logging

deforestation

🔊 002

irrigate
[ˈɪrəˌget]

灌溉

People in the West built dams to **irrigate** their land.
西部人築壩來灌溉他們的土地。

deforest
[ˈdifɔrəst]

砍掉

The forests can be **deforested** by clear-cutting. 森林可以以皆伐的方式被砍掉。

overpopulate
[ˌovəˈpɑpjəˌlet]

人口過盛

The growing number of people moving in is **overpopulating** the area.
移居人口的增加使此區人口過盛。

log

伐（林木）

The lumberjacks are **logging** in the forest. 伐木工人在森林裡伐木。

hew
[hju]

（用斧、刀等）砍、劈

The lumberjacks are **hewing** trees in the forest. 伐木工人在森林裡砍樹。

cut down

砍、劈

The lumberjacks are **cutting down** trees in the forest. 伐木工人在森林裡砍樹。

be stuck in

被困在

Many commuters **are stuck in** rush hour traffic. 許多通勤者被困於交通尖峰期。

be caught in

遭遇到

Many commuters **are caught in** rush hour traffic. 許多通勤者遭遇到交通尖峰期。

Word Families

🔊 003

States in the West 西部各州

Alaska 阿拉斯加州	**California** 加州
Hawaii 夏威夷州	**Nevada** 內華達州
Oregon 奧勒岡州	**Washington** 華盛頓州

Leading Industries 領先產業

movie industry	電影工業
music industry	音樂工業
defense industry	國防工業
computer industry	電腦工業
aerospace industry	航太工業

Geographical Features 地理特徵

earthquake 地震

volcano 火山

extreme climate 極端氣候

fertile soil 沃土

San Andreas Fault 聖安德烈斯斷層

Sierra-Nevada Mountains 內華達山脈

Death Valley 死谷

Great Basin 大盆地

Yosemite National Park 優勝美地國家公園

Redwood National Forest 紅衫國家森林

Checkup

A

Write l 請依提示寫出正確的英文單字和片語。

1　充足的；豐富的 ＿＿＿＿＿＿＿＿＿＿
2　豐富的 ＿＿＿＿＿＿＿＿＿＿
3　稠密的；濃的 ＿＿＿＿＿＿＿＿＿＿
4　雨影 ＿＿＿＿＿＿＿＿＿＿
5　伐木 ＿＿＿＿＿＿＿＿＿＿
6　砍伐森林 ＿＿＿＿＿＿＿＿＿＿
7　淘金潮 ＿＿＿＿＿＿＿＿＿＿
8　交通壅塞 ＿＿＿＿＿＿＿＿＿＿

9　城市擴張 ＿＿＿＿＿＿＿＿＿＿
10　因紐特人 ＿＿＿＿＿＿＿＿＿＿
11　灌溉 ＿＿＿＿＿＿＿＿＿＿
12　砍掉 d＿＿＿＿＿＿＿＿＿
13　伐（林木） l＿＿＿＿＿＿＿＿＿
14　砍、劈 c＿＿＿＿＿＿＿＿＿
15　被困在 ＿＿＿＿＿＿＿＿＿＿
16　人口過盛 ＿＿＿＿＿＿＿＿＿＿

B

Complete the Sentences l 請在空格中填入最適當的答案，並視情況做適當的變化。

bountiful congestion	urban sprawl rain shadow	lush dense	deforestation gold rush	logging Inuit

1　California has a ＿＿＿＿＿＿＿＿ supply of fertile soil for farming.
　加州有充足的沃土可供農業使用。

2　There are many ＿＿＿＿＿＿ forests in the Pacific Northwest.
　太平洋西北地區蘊藏許多豐富的森林。

3　The area within the ＿＿＿＿＿＿ ＿＿＿＿＿＿ is usually warm and dry.
　雨影地區通常溫暖乾燥。

4　Many people are concerned about ＿＿＿＿＿＿＿＿.
　許多人都很關切砍伐森林的議題。

5　＿＿＿＿＿＿＿＿ is a major industry in Washington and Oregon.
　伐木為美國華盛頓州及奧勒岡州的主要產業。

6　Cities like Los Angeles suffer from ＿＿＿＿＿＿ ＿＿＿＿＿＿.
　像洛杉磯這樣的城市受城市擴張之苦。

7　The California ＿＿＿＿＿＿ ＿＿＿＿＿＿ attracted many people in 1849.
　加州的淘金潮於1849年吸引了許多人。

8　Traffic ＿＿＿＿＿＿＿＿ creates huge problems in L.A. and other cities.
　交通壅塞在洛杉磯及其他城市造成很大的問題。

C

Read and Choose l 閱讀下列句子，並且選出最適當的答案。

1　People in the West built dams to (irrigate｜irrigation) their land.
2　The forests can be (forested｜deforested) by clear-cutting.
3　Many commuters are (stuck｜congestion) in rush hour traffic.
4　The lumberjacks are (logging｜cutting) down trees in the forest.

D

1 ► an area of a mountain that is dry because precipitation falls on the other side

_____

3 ► a large number of vehicles unable to move or moving very slowly

_____

2 ► a situation in which people go quickly to a place where gold has been discovered

_____

4 ► a member of a Native American people who live in the cold northern areas

_____

E

Earthquakes and Forest Fires

California is one of the richest states in America. It has a large amount of land. And it also has more people than any other state. It has plenty of natural resources, too. But everything is not perfect there. California has two major problems: earthquakes and forest fires.

The San Andreas Fault runs through California. Because of it, the state gets many earthquakes. Some of them are very powerful. For example, there was a strong earthquake in San Francisco in 1906. It destroyed many buildings. And it started numerous fires. Over 3,000 people died after it. There have also been many other strong earthquakes. Some people fear that the "big one" will hit someday. They think an earthquake will cause a huge amount of damage.

During summer and fall, much of California is dry. So forest fires, or wildfires, often start. These fires can spread rapidly. They burn many forests. But they also can burn people's homes and buildings. They often kill people before firefighters can put them out.

Fill in the blanks.

1　California has more _____ than any other state.
2　There was a strong _____ in San Francisco in 1906.
3　California is often dry in the _____ and fall.
4　_____ can burn forests, homes, and buildings.

Key Words
🔊 005

01	**Sunbelt** [ˋsʌn͵bɛlt]	*(n.)* 陽光地帶（美國南部與西南部）　*Frostbelt (n.) 霜凍地帶（美國北部）
		The **Sunbelt** is a region that has a warm and sunny climate all year.
		陽光地帶是指氣候整年溫暖且陽光充足的地區。

02	**precious** [ˋprɛʃəs]	*(a.)* 寶貴的；貴重的　*precious metal 貴金屬　*precious stone 寶石
		In the dry Southwest, water is a **precious** resource.
		在乾燥的西南部，水是很寶貴的資源。

03	**aquifer** [ˋækwəfɚ]	*(n.)* 含水土層　*confined/unconfined aquifer 受壓／非受壓含水層
		Aquifers with groundwater supply much water to the Southwest.
		蘊藏地下水的含水土層供給西南部大量的水。

04	**aqueduct** [ˋækwɪ͵dʌkt]	*(n.)* 溝渠　*Roman aqueduct 羅馬渠道　*ditch (n.) 溝渠；壕溝
		People build **aqueducts** to carry water from place to place.
		人們建造溝渠讓水通往每個地方。

05	**petroleum** [pəˋtroliəm]	*(n.)* 石油（= oil）　*refined petroleum 精煉石油　*petroleum jelly 凡士林
		The **petroleum** industry provides many jobs in Oklahoma and Texas.
		石油工業為美國奧克拉荷馬州及德州帶來許多就業機會。

| 06 | **refinery** [rɪˋfaɪnərɪ] | *(n.)* 精煉廠　*oil/sugar refinery 石油精煉廠／製糖廠 |
| | | A **refinery** is a factory where oil is refined. 精煉廠是提煉石油的工廠。 |

07	**ranch** [ræntʃ]	*(n.)* 大牧場　*ranch house 牧場式住宅　*ranch dressing 田園沙拉醬
		There are huge **ranches** with thousands of cows in the Southwest.
		西南部有許多飼養數以千計母牛的大片牧場。

08	**cattle drive** [ˋkætḷ draɪv]	*(n.)* 驅趕牛群　*cattle grid 攔畜溝柵（車輛可以通行但牲畜無法通過的柵欄）
		A **cattle drive** is usually led by cowboys on horses.
		驅趕牛群的工作通常由騎著馬的牛仔來執行。

09	**reservation** [͵rɛzəˋveʃən]	*(n.)* 保留區域　*conservation (n.) 保育；保護　*preservation (n.) 維護；保護
		The Hopi and Apache live on **reservations** in the Southwest.
		霍皮族和阿帕契族生活在西南部的保留區域。

| 10 | **adobe** [əˋdobɪ] | *(n.)* 泥磚　*adobe house 土坯房 |
| | | **Adobe** is a sun-dried brick of clay that the Hopi people make homes with. 泥磚是一種曬乾的黏土磚塊，霍皮人利用它來建造房子。 |

Roman aqueduct

oil refinery

cattle drive

adobe houses

Power Verbs 🔊 006

herd — 驅趕
Cowboys used to herd cattle from Texas to the markets in the north.
牛仔以往將牛群從德州驅趕至北方的市場。

drive — 驅趕
Cowboys used to drive cattle from Texas to the markets in the north.
牛仔以往將牛群從德州驅趕至北方的市場。

drill — 鑽；鑽除
The company is drilling for oil in the desert. 那家公司在沙漠裡鑽地取油。

refine — 提煉；精煉
Crude oil is refined in a refinery. 原油在精煉廠裡被提煉。

preserve — 維護；保護
Many Native Americans try to preserve their traditional way of life.
許多印地安人試圖維護他們傳統的生活方式。

carry on — 延續
The Hopi carry on the traditions of their ancestors.
霍皮人延續他們祖先的傳統。

Word Families 🔊 007

cowboy — 牛仔
A cowboy works on a ranch and helps drive cattle.
牛仔在牧場工作並且幫忙驅趕牛群。

vaquero [vɑˋkɛrə] — （西南部的）牧人；牧童
A vaquero works on a ranch and helps drive cattle.
牧人在牧場工作並且幫忙驅趕牛群。

herder — 牧人
Cattle herders drive cows to the market. 牧牛人將母牛驅趕至市場。

crude oil — 原油
Crude oil can be used to make gasoline and other products.
原油可以用來製造汽油及其他產品。

petrochemical [pɛtroˋkɛmɪkl] — 石油化學的
The petrochemical industry is very important in the Southwest.
石化工業對西南部非常重要。

States in the Southwest 西南部各州

- **Arizona** 亞利桑納州
- **New Mexico** 新墨西哥州
- **Oklahoma** 奧克拉荷馬州
- **Texas** 德州

Geographical Features 地理特徵

- **plateau** 高原
- **canyon** 峽谷
- **desert** 沙漠
- **mesa** 臺地；平頂山
- **butte** 孤山；孤峰
- **Grand Canyon** 大峽谷
- **Four Corners** 四角落
- **Painted Desert** 彩色沙漠
- **Sonoran Desert** 索諾蘭沙漠

Checkup

A

Write | 請依提示寫出正確的英文單字和片語。

1	陽光地帶	_____	9 精煉廠	_____
2	貴重的；寶貴的	_____	10 泥磚	_____
3	含水土層	_____	11 驅趕	h_____
4	溝渠	_____	12 鑽；鑽除	_____
5	石油	_____	13 提煉；精煉	_____
6	大牧場	_____	14 （西南部的）牧人；牧童	_____
7	驅趕牛群	_____	15 原油	_____
8	保留區域	_____	16 石油化學的	_____

B

Complete the Sentences | 請在空格中填入最適當的答案，並視情況做適當的變化。

petroleum reservation	aqueduct refinery	Sunbelt cattle drive	precious adobe	aquifer ranch

1   In the dry Southwest, water is a _____ resource.
在乾燥的西南部，水是很寶貴的資源。

2   People build _____ to carry water from place to place.
人們建造溝渠讓水通往每個地方。

3   _____ with groundwater supply much water to the Southwest.
蘊藏地下水的含水土層供給西南部大量的水。

4   The _____ industry provides many jobs in Oklahoma and Texas.
石油工業為美國奧克拉荷馬州及德州帶來許多就業機會。

5   A _____ _____ is usually led by cowboys on horses.
驅趕牛群的工作通常由騎著馬的牛仔來執行。

6   The Hopi and Apache live on _____ in the Southwest.
霍皮族和阿帕契族生活在西南部的保留區域。

7   A _____ is a factory where oil is refined. 精煉廠是提煉石油的工廠。

8   _____ is a sun-dried brick of clay that the Hopi people make homes with.
泥磚是一種曬乾的磚瓦黏土，霍皮人利用它來建造房子。

C

Read and Choose | 閱讀下列句子，並且選出最適當的答案。

1   Cowboys used to (carry | herd) cattle from Texas to the markets in the north.
2   Crude oil is (refined | drilled) in a refinery.
3   The company is (refining | drilling) for oil in the desert.
4   The Hopi (preserve | carry) on the traditions of their ancestors.

D

Look, Read, and Write | 看圖並且依照提示，在空格中填入正確答案。

 ▶ the southern and southwestern states of the US

_____

 ▶ a large farm on which animals are kept

_____

 ▶ a factory where oil in their natural state is made pure

_____

 ▶ an area of land made available for a particular group of people to live in

_____

E

Read and Answer | 閱讀並且回答下列問題。 ⊙ 008

The Southwest

The American Southwest covers a very large area. But it only has a few states. It includes the states Arizona, New Mexico, Texas, and Oklahoma. Most of the land in these states is very dry. In fact, there are many deserts in these areas. Because of that, the people must practice water conservation all the time. But not all of the land there is desert. The Colorado River flows through Arizona. And the Rio Grande River flows through Texas. Also, the Rocky Mountains go through parts of Arizona and New Mexico. Arizona itself has a very diverse geography. Much of its land is desert. But the Grand Canyon is in the northern part of the state. Much of the northern part of the state has mountains. Also, there are many forests in this area. Texas is also a part of the Southwest. Much of the land is very dry. But many parts of Texas are rich with oil. The oil industry is a huge business in Texas. It's one of the biggest oil-producing states in the entire country.

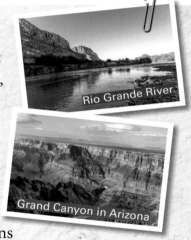

Rio Grande River

Grand Canyon in Arizona

What is NOT true?
1   There are many deserts in the Southwest.
2   Oklahoma and New York are in the Southwest.
3   The Grand Canyon is in Arizona.
4   Texas has a lot of oil.

The Southeast Region of the United States 美國東南部地區

Key Words 🔊 009

01 delta
[ˈdɛltə]

(n.)（河口的）三角洲　*the Nile Delta 尼羅河三角洲

The Mississippi River **Delta** is where the river empties into the Gulf of Mexico.
密西西比河三角洲位於密西西比河注入墨西哥灣處。

02 wetland
[ˈwɛtˌlənd]

(n.) 溼地；沼地　*marshland (n.) 沼澤地　*swamp (n.) 沼澤

The Everglades in Florida is a huge **wetland** area.
佛羅里達的大沼澤地是一個巨大的溼地區域。

03 bayou
[ˈbaɪu]

(n.)（美國南部）水流緩慢的小河　*creek (n.) 小溪；小河

Alligators live in the **bayous** in Mississippi. 鱷魚生活在密西西比的小河。

04 agriculture
[ˈægrɪˌkʌltʃɚ]

(n.) 農業　*shifting agriculture 輪墾　*horticulture (n.) 園藝

Agriculture is how many Southerners make a living.
農業是許多南方人賴以為生的方式。

05 cash crop
[kæʃ krɑp]

(n.) 經濟作物　*subsistence crop 自給作物

Cotton and tobacco are important **cash crops** in the South.
棉花和菸草是南方重要的經濟作物。

06 irrigation
[ˌɪrəˈgeʃən]

(n.) 灌溉　*under irrigation 在灌溉

Farmers use **irrigation** methods to bring water to their crops.
農夫利用灌溉的方式為他們的作物帶來水分。

07 Bible Belt
[ˈbaɪbl̩ bɛlt]

(n.) 聖經地帶　*Great Awakening 大覺醒運動（美國基督教的數次復興運動）

People call the Southeast the **Bible Belt** because many people there are very religious. 人們稱東南部為聖經地帶，因為那裡有很多人都非常虔誠。

08 segregation
[ˌsɛgrɪˈgeʃən]

(n.) 隔離；分開　*racial/religious segregation 種族／宗教隔離

Segregation is the dividing of people because of race or gender.
隔離是指將人們根據種族或性別加以分隔。

09 civil rights
[ˈsɪvl̩ raɪts]

(n.) 民權；公民權　*civil liberties 公民自由　*civil law 民法

Many blacks fought for their **civil rights** in the 1960s.
許多黑人於1960年代為他們的民權抗爭。

10 boycott
[ˈbɔɪˌkɑt]

(n.) 聯合抵制；杯葛　*a boycott against/on sth. 對某物的抵制

During a **boycott**, people refuse to buy or use a company's products or services. 在聯合抵制期間，人們拒絕購買或使用某家公司的產品或服務。

delta

wetland

bayou

agriculture

flow into　流入
The Mississippi River flows into the Gulf of Mexico. 密西西比河流入墨西哥灣。

empty into　流入；注入
The Mississippi River empties into the Gulf of Mexico. 密西西比河流入墨西哥灣。

segregate　隔離
['sɛɡrɪ,ɡet]
Blacks and whites were segregated in the past. 過去黑人與白人間實行種族隔離。

integrate　整合
['ɪntə,ɡret]
Blacks and whites are integrated today. 今日黑人與白人間已經整合。

boycott　聯合抵制；杯葛
Many blacks boycotted the buses in Montgomery, Alabama in the 1950s.
許多阿拉巴馬州蒙哥馬利的黑人，於 1950 年代聯合抵制公車。

Word Families　● 011

tributary　支流
['trɪbjə,tɛrɪ]
The Mississippi River has many smaller tributaries that flow into it.
密西西比河有許多的小支流注入其中。

source　源頭
A river's source is the place where it starts. 水源是指河流發源的地方。

mouth　河口
The mouth of the Mississippi River is in the Gulf of Mexico.
密西西比河的河口位於墨西哥灣。

States in the Southeast
東南部各州

Arkansas 阿肯色州	**Louisiana** 路易斯安那州
Mississippi 密西西比州	**Tennessee** 田納西州
Kentucky 肯塔基州	**Alabama** 阿拉巴馬州
Georgia 喬治亞州	**Florida** 佛羅里達州
South Carolina 南卡羅來納州	
North Carolina 北卡羅來納州	
Virginia 維吉尼亞州	
West Virginia 西維吉尼亞州	

Geographical Features
地理特徵

mountain range 山脈

river 河流

wetland 溼地

fertile soil 沃土

Mississippi River 密西西比河

Tennessee River 田納西河

Potomac River 波托馬克河

Okefenokee Swamp 奧克弗諾基沼澤

Checkup

A

Write | 請依提示寫出正確的英文單字和片語。

1 （河口的）三角洲 _____	9 民權；公民權 _____
2 溼地；沼地 _____	10 聯合抵制；杯葛 _____
3 水流緩慢的小河 _____	11 流入；注入 _____
4 農業 _____	12 隔離(v.) _____
5 經濟作物 _____	13 整合 _____
6 灌溉 _____	14 支流 _____
7 聖經地帶 _____	15 源頭 _____
8 隔離；分開(n.) _____	16 沃土 _____

B

Complete the Sentences | 請在空格中填入最適當的答案，並視情況做適當的變化。

civil rights	bayou	segregation	delta	agriculture
cash crop	irrigation	boycott	wetland	Bible Belt

1 The Everglades in Florida is a huge _____ area.
佛羅里達的大沼澤地是一個巨大的溼地區域。

2 The Mississippi River _____ is where the river empties into the Gulf of Mexico.　密西西比河三角洲位於密西西比河注入墨西哥灣處。

3 Alligators live in the _____ in Mississippi. 鱷魚生活在密西西比的小河。

4 Cotton and tobacco are important _____ _____ in the South.
棉花和菸草是南方重要的經濟作物。

5 Farmers use _____ methods to bring water to their crops.
農夫利用灌溉的方式為他們的作物帶來水分。

6 _____ is how many Southerners make a living.
農業是許多南方人賴以為生的方式。

7 Many blacks fought for their _____ _____ in the 1960s.
許多黑人於1960年代為他們的民權抗爭。

8 _____ is the dividing of people because of race or gender.
隔離是指將人們根據種族或性別加以分隔。

C

Read and Choose | 閱讀下列句子，並且選出最適當的答案。

1 The Mississippi River (grows | empties) into the Gulf of Mexico.

2 Blacks and whites were (integrated | segregated) in the past.

3 Blacks and whites are (integrated | segregated) today.

4 Many blacks (vetoed | boycotted) the buses in Montgomery, Alabama in the 1950s.

D

Look, Read, and Write | 看圖並且依照提示，在空格中填入正確答案。

 ▸ an area of very wet, muddy land with wild plants growing in it

_____

 ▸ a crop that is grown to be sold rather than for use by the farmer

_____

 ▸ the rights of people to be treated equally whatever their race or gender

_____

 ▸ to refuse to buy a product or take part in an activity as a way of expressing strong disapproval

_____

E

Read and Answer | 閱讀並且回答下列問題。 🔊 012

The Civil Rights Movement

For many years, people in the South owned black African slaves. In the 1860s, the United States fought the Civil War because of slavery. During the war, all of the slaves were freed. But there were still many problems between blacks and whites. There was a lot of discrimination against blacks. This means they were not treated fairly. Also, blacks and whites in the South were segregated. So they ate at separate restaurants. They went to separate schools. And they even sat in separate places on buses.

But in the 1950s, the Civil Rights Movement began in the South. Blacks began demanding equal treatment. The most famous leader of the movement was Martin Luther King, Jr. Blacks often organized boycotts of different places. They had sit-ins at restaurants where they weren't allowed to eat. King tried to use nonviolence. But the police and others often used violence against blacks. Still, in 1964, the Civil Rights Act was passed. It guaranteed equal rights for people of all colors.

Fill in the blanks.

1 The _____ was fought because of slavery.
2 In the South, blacks and whites were often _____.
3 The Civil Rights Movement began in the _____.
4 _____ was a famous leader of the Civil Rights Movement.

Key Words 🔊 013

01 coastal plain
['kostl plen]
(n.) 沿海平原
The Atlantic Coastal Plain runs up the entire American east coast.
大西洋沿海平原分布於美國整個東海岸。

02 mountain range
['mauntn rendʒ]
(n.) 山脈（= mountain chain = range/chain of mountains）
There are many mountain ranges in the Northeast. 東北部有許多山脈。

03 foliage
['folɪdʒ]
(n.) 葉子；葉　 * foliage plant 觀葉植物
Colorful foliage is a well-known feature of the Northeast's forests during fall. 在秋天期間，東北部森林以色彩鮮豔的葉子著稱。

04 bog
[bɑg]
(n.) 沼澤；泥塘　 *peat bog 泥炭沼澤　 *bog-standard (a.) 極其普通的
People in the Northeast grow cranberries in bogs.
東北部的人們在沼澤中種植蔓越莓。

05 seaway
['si,we]
(n.) 海上航道（= sea lane = shipping lane）　 *trade route 貿易路線
Most ships follow a seaway to help them get to port.
大部分的船沿著海上航道行走以便於抵達港口。

06 heritage
['hɛrətɪdʒ]
(n.) 遺產；遺留物；傳統　 *heritage-listed building 列入文物保護範圍的建築
Heritage is the history and culture that is passed on from our ancestors. 遺產是我們祖先流傳下來的歷史與文化。

07 descendant
[dɪ'sɛndənt]
(n.) 子孫；後裔　 *descendant of ……的後裔　 *ancestor (n.) 祖先
The descendants of Native Americans still preserve their heritage.
印地安人的子孫至今仍保留他們的傳統。

08 metropolitan
[,mɛtrə'pɑlətn]
(a.) 大都會的　 *Metropolitan Museum of Art 大都會美術館
A city and its surrounding towns make up a metropolitan area.
都市與其周邊城市形成一個大都會區。

09 metropolis
[mə'trɑplɪs]
(n.) 大都市；首都　 *a bustling/modern metropolis 繁忙的／現代化的大都市
A metropolis is a very large city with over a million people.
大都市是指人口超過一百萬的大型城市。

10 megalopolis
[,mɛgə'lɑpəlɪs]
(n.) 都會區；人口稠密地帶　 *megacity (n.) 巨型都市
The area from Boston to New York to Washington, D.C. is one big megalopolis. 自波士頓、紐約至華盛頓這整個區域是一個巨大的都會區。

coastal plain

golden autumn foliage

seaway

bog

stretch 延伸；伸縮
The Appalachian Mountains **stretch** from Maine to Maryland and all the way south to Alabama. 阿帕拉契山由緬因州延伸至馬里蘭州，南至阿拉巴馬州。

live off 依……為生
The Native Americans **lived off** the land by fishing, hunting, and farming. 印地安人依靠捕魚、打獵以及務農為生。

commute 通勤
People in the suburbs must **commute** to their downtown jobs every day. 住在郊區的人每天都必須通勤前往市中心工作。

Word Families 🔊 015

coast 海岸
There are many cities along the Atlantic **coast** in the Northeast.
東北部的大西洋沿岸有許多城市。

harbor 港灣
Many ships sail into Boston **Harbor** every day. 每天都有許多船航行至波士頓海港。

bay （海或湖泊的）灣
A **bay** is a small gulf that goes in toward the land. 灣是指深入內地的小海灣。

canal 運河；水道
The Erie **Canal** helped connect New York to the Great Lakes.
伊利運河幫助紐約連接五大湖。

lock 水閘（= lock gate）
The canal's **locks** help ships move to higher or lower elevations.
運河的水閘幫助船升降高度。

States in the Northeast 東北部各州

Pennsylvania 賓夕法尼亞州

Vermont 佛蒙特州 **Delaware** 德拉威州

Connecticut 康乃迪克州 **Maine** 緬因州

New Jersey 紐澤西州 **New York** 紐約州

Maryland 馬里蘭州

New Hampshire 新罕布夏州

Massachusetts 麻薩諸塞州

Rhode Island 羅德島州

Geographical Features 地理特徵

coast 海岸 **bay** 灣 **river** 河流

mountain 山

seasonal climate 季節性氣候

metropolitan area 都會區

Appalachian Mountains 阿帕拉契山

St. Lawrence River 聖勞倫斯河

Cape Cod 科德角 **Hudson River** 哈德遜河

Catskill Mountains 卡茨基爾山

Checkup

Write | 請依提示寫出正確的英文單字和片語。

1	沿海平原	_____	9	葉子；葉 _____
2	山脈	_____	10	沼澤；泥塘 _____
3	海上航道	_____	11	延伸；伸縮 _____
4	遺產；遺留物；傳統	_____	12	依……為生 _____
5	子孫；後裔	_____	13	通勤 _____
6	大都會的	_____	14	運河；水道 _____
7	大都市；首都	_____	15	（海或湖泊的）灣 _____
8	都會區；人口稠密地帶	_____	16	水閘 _____

B

Complete the Sentences | 請在空格中填入最適當的答案，並視情況做適當的變化。

descendant	coastal plain	seaway	bog	megalopolis
metropolitan	mountain range	heritage	foliage	metropolis

1 The Atlantic _____ _____ runs up the entire American east coast.
大西洋沿海平原分布於美國整個東海岸。

2 Colorful _____ is a well-known feature of the Northeast's forests during fall.
在秋天期間，東北部森林以色彩鮮豔的葉子著稱。

3 People in the Northeast grow cranberries in _____.
東北部的人們在沼澤中種植蔓越莓。

4 Most ships follow a _____ to help them get to port.
大部分的船沿著海上航道行走以便於抵達港口。

5 There are many _____ _____ in the Northeast. 東北部有許多山脈。

6 A city and its surrounding towns make up a _____ area.
都市與其周邊城市形成一個大都會區。

7 The area from Boston to New York to Washington, D.C. is one big
_____. 自波士頓、紐約至華盛頓這整個區域是一個巨大的都會區。

8 _____ is the history and culture that is passed on from our ancestors.
遺產是我們祖先流傳下來的歷史與文化。

C

Read and Choose | 閱讀下列句子，並且選出最適當的答案。

1 The Appalachian Mountains (locate | stretch) from Maine to Maryland and all the way south to Alabama.

2 The Native Americans (lived | grew) off the land by fishing, hunting, and farming.

3 The (ancestors | descendants) of Native Americans still preserve their heritage.

4 People in the suburbs must (commute | communicate) to their downtown jobs every day.

Look, Read, and Write | 看圖並且依照提示，在空格中填入正確答案。

1 ▶ a series of hills or mountains

_____

2 ▶ features belonging to the culture that still have historical importance

_____

3 ▶ the people in later generations; the opposite of ancestor

_____

4 ▶ a very large city; often the most important city in a large area or country

_____

E

Read and Answer | 閱讀並且回答下列問題。 🔊 016

Washington Irving

Short Stories from the Northeast

Many of the first settlers from Europe went to the Northeast part of the United States. Most of them were English. They lived in New York and Pennsylvania. A lot of them lived in the Hudson River Valley area in New York. Some great American literature comes from this area.

The writer Washington Irving wrote many stories about this area. One of the most famous was *Rip van Winkle*. It takes place in the Catskill Mountains in New York. In the story, Rip goes off in the mountains by himself. After meeting some ghosts, he sleeps for twenty years. Then he wakes up, returns to his village, and sees how life has changed.

Another famous story by Irving was *The Legend of Sleepy Hollow*. It was also set in upstate New York. It involved the Headless Horseman, who was the ghost of a man with no head. Instead, he had a jack-o'-lantern for a head.

These stories and others by Irving became important in American culture. They depicted early life in the Northeast. And millions of children and adults have read them ever since.

What is NOT true?

1 Many English lived in the upstate New York area.
2 Washington Irving lived in the Catskill Mountains.
3 *Rip van Winkle* was a story about early American life.
4 The Headless Horseman had a jack-o'-lantern for a head.

Unit 05

The Midwest Region of the United States 美國中西部地區

Key Words 🔊 017

| 01 | **prairie** [ˈprɛrɪ] | *(n.)* 牧場；大草原　　*prairie dog 草原犬鼠（土撥鼠）*
 A **prairie** is a large, flat area covered with grasses.
 牧場是指廣大平坦且覆蓋著牧草的地區。 |

01 prairie [ˈprɛrɪ]
(n.) 牧場；大草原　　*prairie dog 草原犬鼠（土撥鼠）*
A **prairie** is a large, flat area covered with grasses.
牧場是指廣大平坦且覆蓋著牧草的地區。

02 lake effect [lek ɪˈfɛkt]
(n.) 大湖效應　　*lake effect snow 大湖效應降雪*
The effect of the Great Lakes on the climate of the Midwest is called a **lake effect**. 中西部氣候受五大湖的影響稱為大湖效應。

03 breadbasket [ˈbrɛdˌbæskɪt]
(n.) 產糧地區；糧倉　　*the breadbasket of the world 世界糧倉*
The Midwest is called the **breadbasket** of the U.S. since so much grain is grown there. 由於中西部盛產大量的穀物，此地被稱為美國的糧倉。

04 grain [gren]
(n.) 穀物；穀類　　*grains of wheat/rice 麥／米粒　　*wholegrain (a.) 全穀物的*
Grains like wheat, rye, and barley are often grown in the Midwest.
像小麥、黑麥以及大麥這樣的穀物，通常生長在中西部。

05 livestock [ˈlaɪvˌstɑk]
(n.) 家畜　　*livestock farming 畜牧業（= animal husbandry）*
Midwest farmers raise **livestock** like cattle, pigs, and sheep.
中西部地區的農夫飼養牛、豬以及羊等的家畜。

06 frontier [frʌnˈtɪr]
(n.) 邊境　　*the frontier between/with sth. 某處的邊界*
At one time, the Midwest was a part of the American **frontier**.
中西部地區曾是美國邊境的一部分。

07 pioneer [ˌpaɪəˈnɪr]
(n.) 拓荒者；先驅者　　* a pioneer of/in sth. 某物的先驅*
Early American **pioneers** moved around the Midwest to settle in the West. 早期美國拓荒者搬離中西部地區，移居西部地區。

08 assembly line [əˈsɛmblɪ laɪn]
(n.) 生產（裝配）線　　*assembly-line workers 生產線上的工人*
The **assembly line** is a fast way of manufacturing certain products.
生產線是大量製造產品的一種快速方式。

09 industrialization [ɪnˌdʌstrɪələˈzeʃən]
(n.) 工業化　　*Industrial Revolution 工業革命*
The building of factories in the 1800s led to the **industrialization** of the U.S. 1800年代工廠的建造，導致了美國的工業化。

10 reclamation [ˌrɛkləˈmeʃən]
(n.) （對土地的）再造；再生　　*land reclamation 填海造陸*
Reclamation is restoring land to its previous state after it has been mined. 再造是指在土地開墾後將其恢復成原本的狀態。

breadbasket

grain

livestock

industrialization

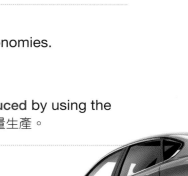

cultivate
[ˋkʌltəˌvet]

栽培
The farmers are cultivating wheat and corn in their fields.
農夫在他們的農地上栽培小麥和玉米。

industrialize
[ınˋdʌstrɪəlˌaɪz]

使工業化
Today, many countries are trying to industrialize their economies.
現今有許多國家試圖使它們的經濟工業化。

mass-produce

大量生產
Today, cars and many other products can be mass-produced by using the assembly line. 藉由生產線，現今汽車和許多其他產品都能大量生產。

assemble
[əˋsɛmbl]

裝配
Many companies assemble automobiles in Detroit.
許多公司在底特律裝配汽車。

manufacture
[ˌmænjəˋfæktʃ⋅]

製造
Many companies manufacture automobiles in Detroit.
許多公司在底特律製造汽車。

compete with

與……競爭
American automakers compete with Japanese and Korean companies.
美國的汽車製造業者與日本以及韓國的公司競爭。

compete against

與……競爭
American automakers compete against German and Italian companies.
美國的汽車製造業者與德國以及義大利的公司競爭。

States in the Midwest
中西部各州

Michigan 密西根州　**Ohio** 俄亥俄州
Indiana 印地安納州　**Illinois** 伊利諾州
Wisconsin 威斯康辛州
Missouri 密蘇里州　**Kansas** 堪薩斯州
Nebraska 內布拉斯加州
South Dakota 南達科他州
North Dakota 北達科他州
Minnesota 明尼蘇達州
Iowa 愛荷華州

Geographical Features
地理特徵

inland climate 內陸性氣候
lake effect 大湖效應
farming 農業
mining 礦業
the Great Lakes 五大湖
the Badlands 惡地
the Great Plains 北美大平原
Mount Rushmore National Memorial
拉什莫爾山國家紀念公園

Checkup

A

Write | 請依提示寫出正確的英文單字和片語。

1	牧場；大草原	_____	
2	大湖效應	_____	
3	產糧地區	_____	
4	穀物；穀類	_____	
5	家畜	_____	
6	邊境	_____	
7	拓荒者；先驅者	_____	
8	生產（裝配）線	_____	
9	工業化	_____	
10	（對土地的）再造；再生	_____	
11	栽培	_____	
12	使工業化	_____	
13	大量生產	_____	
14	裝配	_____	
15	製造	_____	
16	與……競爭	_____	

B

Complete the Sentences | 請在空格中填入最適當的答案，並視情況做適當的變化。

breadbasket	livestock	lake effect	reclamation	grain
industrialization	frontier	assembly line	pioneer	prairie

1 The effect of the Great Lakes on the climate of the Midwest is called a _____ _____. 中西部氣候受五大湖的影響稱為大湖效應。

2 The Midwest is called the _____ of the U.S. since so much grain is grown there. 自從大量的穀物被種植於中西部後，此地就被稱為美國的糧倉。

3 _____ like wheat, rye, and barley are often grown in the Midwest. 像小麥、裸麥以及大麥這樣的穀物通常生長在中西部。

4 Midwest farmers raise _____ like cattle, pigs, and sheep. 中西部地區的農夫飼養牛、豬以及羊等的家畜。

5 At one time, the Midwest was a part of the American _____. 中西部地區曾是美國邊境的一部分。

6 The _____ _____ is a fast way of manufacturing certain products. 生產線是大量製造產品的一種快速方式。

7 The building of factories in the 1800s led to the _____ of the U.S. 1800年代工廠的建造導致了美國的工業化。

8 Early American _____ moved around the Midwest to settle in the West. 早期美國拓荒者搬離中西部地區，移居西部地區。

C

Read and Choose | 閱讀下列句子，並且選出最適當的答案。

1 The farmers are (cultivating | covering) wheat and corn in their fields.

2 Today, many countries are trying to (industrialization | industrialize) their economies.

3 Many companies (restore | manufacture) automobiles in Detroit.

4 American automakers (complete | compete) with Japanese and Korean companies.

D

Look, Read, and Write | 看圖並且依照提示，在空格中填入正確答案。

1 ▸ a large, mostly flat area of land that has few trees and is covered in grasses
_____

3 ▸ a border between two countries
_____

2 ▸ the effect of the Great Lakes on the climate of the Midwest
_____

4 ▸ the attempt to make land suitable for building or farming again
_____

E

Read and Answer | 閱讀並且回答下列問題。 🔊 020

The Midwest

lighthouse of Lake Erie

The American Midwest covers an enormous amount of land. It starts with Ohio, Michigan, and Indiana. It goes as far west as North and South Dakota, Nebraska, and Kansas. There are a total of twelve states in the Midwest.

Actually, the Midwest is in the east and central part of the country. But, a long time ago, the United States was much smaller. The only states in the country were beside the Atlantic Ocean. So people called the lands west of them the Midwest.

The land in the Midwest is almost completely identical. It is full of plains and prairies. The Midwest is very flat land. There are no mountains in it. Most hills only rise a few hundred feet high. However, the Great Lakes are in the Midwest. These are five huge lakes located between the U.S. and Canada.

Nowadays, people in the Midwest often work in industry or agriculture. In Detroit and other cities, making automobiles is a huge business. However, there are also many farmers. They grow corn, wheat, and other grains. And they also raise pigs and cows.

Answer the questions.

1 How many states are in the Midwest? _____
2 What is the land in the Midwest like? _____
3 What are the Great Lakes? _____
4 What city in the Midwest makes automobiles? _____

Review Test 1

A

Write | 請依提示寫出正確的英文單字和片語。

1	雨影	_____	11	灌溉(v.)	_____
2	伐木	_____	12	砍掉	_____
3	石油	_____	13	提煉；精煉	_____
4	保留區域	_____	14	原油	_____
5	（河口的）三角洲	_____	15	隔離(v.)	_____
6	經濟作物	_____	16	整合	_____
7	遺產；遺留物；傳統	_____	17	依……為生	_____
8	大都會的	_____	18	通勤	_____
9	牧場；大草原	_____	19	工業化	_____
10	拓荒者；先驅者	_____	20	（對土地的）再造；再生	_____

B

Choose the Correct Word | 請選出與鋪底字意思相近的答案。

1 Many commuters are stuck in rush hour traffic.

   a. rushed   b. caught   c. worked

2 The Mississippi River empties into the Gulf of Mexico.

   a. locates   b. flows   c. carries

3 A vaquero works on a ranch and helps drive cattle.

   a. Hopi   b. farmer   c. cowboy

4 The lumberjacks are logging in the forest.

   a. building   b. cutting down trees   c. planting

C

Complete the Sentences | 請在空格中填入最適當的答案，並視情況做適當的變化。

bountiful	civil rights	aqueduct	mountain range

1 California has a _____ supply of fertile soil for farming.
加州有充足的沃土可供農業使用。

2 People build _____ to carry water from place to place.
人們建造溝渠讓水通往每個地方。

3 Many blacks fought for their _____ _____ in the 1960s.
許多黑人於1960年代為他們的民權抗爭。

4 There are many _____ _____ in the Northeast.
東北部有許多山脈。

2

Social Studies •
History and Geography ②

Key Words 🔊 021

01 Continental Divide
[ˌkɑntəˈnɛntl̩ dəˈvaɪd]

(n.) 北美大陸分水嶺　*drainage divide 分水嶺

The Continental Divide runs north to south along the peaks of the Rocky Mountains. 北美大陸分水嶺沿著落磯山脈由北向南延伸。

02 elevation
[ˌɛləˈveʃən]

(n.) 高度；海拔（= altitude）　*at high/low elevations 在高／低海拔

The elevation of Mount Elbert, the highest point in the Rocky Mountains, is 14,433 feet. 埃爾伯特山是落磯山脈的最高峰，高度為14,433英尺。

03 peak
[pik]

(n.) 山峰；山頂　*to climb/scale a peak 登上頂峰　*a mountain peak 山巔

The highest mountain peaks in the Rockies are usually covered with snow. 落磯山脈中最高的山峰通常都覆蓋著雪。

04 timberline
[ˈtɪmbɚˌlaɪn]

(n.) 林木線（= tree line）　*timber (n.) 樹木；木材；樹木倒下前的叫喊

On mountains, no trees grow above the timberline.
在高山上，樹木無法在林木線以上的地方生長。

05 gorge
[gɔrdʒ]

(n.) 峽谷　*Three Gorges Dam 長江三峽大壩

A gorge is a small canyon with a stream running through it.
峽谷是指有一條溪流貫穿的小山谷。

06 wildfire
[ˈwaɪldˌfaɪr]

(n.) 野火；大火災　*spread like wildfire 迅速傳播開來；（消息）不脛而走

Wildfires occur every year during the dry season.
每年的乾季會發生大火災。

07 transcontinental
[ˌtrænskɑntəˈnɛntl̩]

(a.) 橫貫大陸的　*transcontinental railroad/flight 橫貫大陸的鐵路／飛行

The transcontinental railroad crosses the Rocky Mountains.
橫貫大陸的鐵路穿越了落磯山脈。

08 ghost town
[gost taʊn]

(n.) 鬼鎮　*ghost ship 幽靈船

Ghost towns in the Mountain States are abandoned mining towns where no one lives. 位於山嶽州的鬼鎮是無人居住的廢棄礦業城鎮。

09 whitewater
[ˌhwaɪtˈwɑtɚ]

(n.) 急流　*whitewater rafting 急流泛舟

Some people enjoy whitewater rafting on swiftly moving rivers.
有些人喜愛在急流中泛舟。

10 mountain chain
[ˈmaʊntn̩ tʃen]

(n.) 山脈（= mountain range）

The Rocky Mountains are a mountain chain that runs through many parts of the Mountain States.
落磯山脈是一座山脈，它貫穿了山嶽州的許多部分。

peak

gorge

ghost town

whitewater

Power Verbs 🔊 022

rise 高出
The Rocky Mountains rise high above the Great Plains. 落磯山脈聳立於北美大平原之上。

span 橫跨
The Rocky Mountains span a wide range of land. 落磯山脈橫跨一片幅員遼闊的土地。

climb 攀登
People enjoy climbing Pikes Peak in Colorado. 人們喜愛攀登科羅拉多州的派克斯峰。

hike up 攀登
People enjoy hiking up Pikes Peak in Colorado. 人們喜愛攀登科羅拉多州的派克斯峰。

affect 影響
Elevation affects climate, temperature, and plant life in the Rocky Mountains.
海拔影響了落磯山脈的氣候、溫度以及植物的生活。

Word Families 🔊 023

cliff dwelling 懸崖居所
[klɪf `dwɛlɪŋ]
There are many Native American cliff dwellings in the Mountain States.
西部山區有許多印地安人的懸崖居所。

cliff dweller 懸崖居民
[klɪf `dwɛlɚ]
Cliff dwellers lived in Mesa Verde for hundreds of years.
懸崖居民住在梅薩維德已數百年。

sparse 稀少的
Wyoming has a sparse population, so few people live there.
懷俄明州人口稀少，因此很少人居住在那裡。

deserted 無人居住的
[dɪ`zɝtɪd]
Some towns in the Mountain States are completely deserted.
有些西部山區的城鎮完全無人居住。

States in the Mountain States
西部山區各州

Montana 蒙大拿州
Idaho 愛達荷州
Wyoming 懷俄明州
Utah 猶他州
Colorado 科羅拉多州

Geographical Features
地理特徵

mountain range 山脈
The Rocky Mountains 落磯山脈
Bingham Canyon Mine 賓漢谷銅礦場
Mesa Verde National Park 梅薩維德國家公園
Yellowstone National Park 黃石國家公園
Glacier National Park 冰川國家公園

Checkup

A

Write | 請依提示寫出正確的英文單字和片語。

1 北美大陸分水嶺 _____	9 急流 _____
2 高度；海拔 _____	10 山脈 _____
3 山峰；山頂 _____	11 高出 _____
4 林木線 _____	12 橫跨 _____
5 峽谷 _____	13 攀登　c_____
6 野火；大火災 _____	14 懸崖居所 _____
7 橫貫大陸的 _____	15 稀少的 _____
8 鬼鎮 _____	16 無人居住的 _____

B

Complete the Sentences | 請在空格中填入最適當的答案，並視情況做適當的變化。

mountain chain	timberline	transcontinental	gorge	wildfire
Continental Divide	whitewater	ghost town	peak	elevation

1 The _____ _____ runs north to south along the peaks of the Rocky Mountains. 北美大陸分水嶺沿著落磯山脈由北向南延伸。

2 The highest mountain _____ in the Rockies are usually covered with snow. 落磯山脈中最高的山峰通常都覆蓋著雪。

3 The _____ of Mount Elbert, the highest point in the Rocky Mountains, is 14,433 feet. 埃爾伯特山是落磯山脈的最高峰，高度為14,433英尺。

4 The Rocky Mountains are a _____ _____ that runs through many parts of the Mountain States. 落磯山脈是一座山脈，它貫穿了山嶽州的許多部分。

5 The _____ railroad crosses the Rocky Mountains. 橫貫大陸的鐵路穿越了落磯山脈。

6 On mountains, no trees grow above the _____. 在高山上，樹木無法在林木線以上的地方生長。

7 Some people enjoy _____ rafting on swiftly moving rivers. 有些人喜愛在急流中泛舟。

8 _____ _____ in the Mountain States are abandoned mining towns where no one lives. 位於山嶽州的鬼鎮是無人居住的廢棄礦業城鎮。

C

Read and Choose | 閱讀下列句子，並且選出最適當的答案。

1 The Rocky Mountains (span | rise) high above the Great Plains.

2 The Rocky Mountains (span | rise) a wide range of land.

3 Elevation (climbs | affects) climate and temperature in the Rocky Mountains.

4 Wyoming has a (sparse | deserted) population, so few people live there.

D

Look, Read, and Write | 看圖並且依照提示，在空格中填入正確答案。

 ▶ an imaginary line on a mountain that marks the level above which trees do not grow

_____

 ▶ a fire in a wild area that is not controlled and can burn a large area very quickly

_____

 ▶ a small canyon with a stream running through it

_____

 ▶ a town where few or no people now live

_____

E

Read and Answer | 閱讀並且回答下列問題。 024

Yellowstone National Park

One of the most beautiful places in the U.S. is Yellowstone National Park. It is located mostly in Wyoming. But parts of it are in Montana and Idaho, too.

For many years, people had heard about a beautiful land in the west. But few ever saw it. Then more people began visiting the area in the 1800s. Also, the artist Thomas Moran visited Yellowstone. He made many beautiful landscapes of the region. This helped Yellowstone to become the first national park in 1872.

Many different animals live in Yellowstone. Bison, wolves, elk, eagles, and lots of other animals live there. Much of the land is forest. But there are also plains. And there are even geysers there. Geysers shoot hot water into the air. The most famous geyser is called Old Faithful. It has this name because it erupts on a regular schedule all the time.

What is true? Write T(true) or F(false).

1   Yellowstone National Park is only in Wyoming.   _____

2   Thomas Moran was a photographer.   _____

3   Yellowstone became the first national park in the U.S.   _____

4   Old Faithful is the name of a geyser in Yellowstone.   _____

Mountains, Rivers, and Deserts of the World 世界的山、河和沙漠

Key Words
🔊 025

01	**summit** [ˈsʌmɪt]	(n.) 峰頂 （= peak） *the summit of sth. 某物的巔峰 A mountain's **summit** is its highest point. 一座山的峰頂就是它的最高點。
02	**rugged** [ˈrʌgɪd]	(a.) 崎嶇不平的；粗糙的 *rugged landscape/hill 崎嶇的地貌／陡峭的山丘 **Rugged** mountains have cliffs and are very rocky. 崎嶇不平的山充滿懸崖峭壁和岩石。
03	**majestic** [məˈdʒɛstɪk]	(a.) 雄偉的；崇高的 *majestic view/scenery/beauty 壯闊的美景 The Himalayas look very **majestic** as they rise into the sky. 喜馬拉雅山脈看起來非常雄偉，如高聳入天一般。
04	**backbone** [ˈbækˌbon]	(n.) 主（山）脈；骨幹（= spine） *to the backbone 徹頭徹尾地 The Andes Mountains are the **backbone** of South America. 安地斯山脈是南美洲的主山脈。
05	**extend** [ɪkˈstɛnd]	(v.) 延伸；擴展 *to extend beyond sth. 延伸至超過某物 The Rocky Mountains **extend** from Canada down into Mexico. 落磯山脈由加拿大往下延伸至墨西哥。
06	**sea level** [si ˈlɛvl]	(n.) 海平面 *above/below sea level 海拔以上／海平面以下 **Sea level** is the average level of the oceans in the world. 海平面是指世界上海的平均高度。
07	**river system** [ˈrɪvɚ ˈsɪstəm]	(n.) 水系（= drainage system） *drainage (n.) 排水能力；排水系統 The Mississippi **River system** includes the river and its tributaries. 密西西比河水系包含它的河流以及支流。
08	**silt** [sɪlt]	(n.) 泥沙；淤泥 *to silt (sth.) up 使淤塞 Rivers carry **silt**, which is fine sand or mud, with them as they flow. 河流流動時會挾帶成分為細沙或淤泥的泥沙。
09	**arid** [ˈærɪd]	(a.) 乾燥的；乾旱的 *arid land/region 乾燥的不毛之地 The weather in most deserts is both hot and **arid**. 大部分沙漠的氣候既熱又乾。
10	**nomadic** [noˈmædɪk]	(a.) 游牧的 *nomad (n.) 遊牧民族（= nomadic people） Some **nomadic** people live in the desert and wander through it. 有些游牧民族居住在沙漠，並游徙於沙漠之中。

backbone

silt

arid

nomadic

attempt
試圖
Many different climbers have **attempted** to climb K2.
許多不同的登山者試圖要攀登 K2。

be attempted by
被……嘗試
The ascent of K2 has **been attempted by** many different climbers.
一直以來有許多登山者都嘗試要挑戰 K2 的上坡路。

be accompanied by
[bɪ əˈkʌmpənɪd baɪ]
伴隨著
Edmund Hilary **was accompanied by** a Sherpa guide when he climbed Mount Everest.
艾德蒙‧西拉瑞登上聖母峰時，身旁有一位雪巴的嚮導陪同。

dehydrate
[diˈhaɪˌdret]
脫水
The heat of the desert can cause people to **dehydrate** quickly.
沙漠的炎熱天氣可能會造成人們快速脫水。

Word Families 027

Earth's Highest Mountains 地球上最高的山

Mount Everest 聖母峰；珠穆朗瑪峰
(8,848 m)
Mt. Everest is the highest mountain in the world and is located in the Himalaya range. 聖母峰位於喜馬拉雅山脈，是世界第一高山。

K2 K2
(8,611 m)
K2 is the second highest mountain in the world and is a part of the Himalaya range. K2 屬於喜馬拉雅山脈的一部分，是世界第二高山。

Kanchenjunga 肯欽真加峰
(8,586 m)
Kanchenjunga is the third highest mountain in the world and is located on the border of India and Nepal.
肯欽真加峰位於印度和尼泊爾的邊界，是世界第三高山。

Lhotse 洛子峰
(8,516 m)
Lhotse is the fourth highest mountain on Earth and is located on the border of Tibet and Nepal. 洛子峰位於西藏和尼泊爾的邊界，是世界第四高山。

Earth's Longest Rivers
地球上最長的河

Nile River (Africa) 尼羅河（非洲）
Amazon River (South America) 亞馬遜河（南美洲）
Yangtze River (Asia) 長江（亞洲）
Mississippi River (North America) 密西西比河（北美洲）

Earth's Biggest Deserts
地球上最大的沙漠

Sahara Desert (Africa) 撒哈拉沙漠（非洲）
Arabian Desert (Asia) 阿拉伯沙漠（亞洲）
Gobi Desert (Asia) 戈壁沙漠（亞洲）
Rub' al Khali (Asia) 魯卜哈利沙漠（亞洲）

Checkup

A

Write | 請依提示寫出正確的英文單字和片語。

1	峰頂 _____	9	崎嶇不平的；粗糙的 _____
2	雄偉的；崇高的 _____	10	水系 _____
3	主（山）脈；骨幹 _____	11	試圖 _____
4	延伸；擴展 _____	12	被……嘗試 _____
5	海平面 _____	13	伴隨著 _____
6	泥沙；淤泥 _____	14	脫水 _____
7	乾燥的；乾旱的 _____	15	聖母峰 _____
8	游牧的 _____	16	撒哈拉沙漠 _____

B

Complete the Sentences | 請在空格中填入最適當的答案，並視情況做適當的變化。

sea level	rugged	majestic	silt	backbone
river system	nomadic	summit	arid	extend

1   _____ mountains have cliffs and are very rocky.
    崎嶇不平的山充滿懸崖峭壁和岩石。

2   The Himalayas look very _____ as they rise into the sky.
    喜馬拉雅山脈看起來非常雄偉，如高聳入天一般。

3   The Rocky Mountains _____ from Canada down into Mexico.
    落磯山脈由加拿大往下延伸至墨西哥。

4   The Andes Mountains are the _____ of South America.
    安地斯山脈是南美洲的主山脈。

5   The Mississippi _____ _____ includes the river and its tributaries.
    密西西比河水系包含它的河流以及支流。

6   _____ _____ is the average level of the oceans in the world.
    海平面是指世界上海洋的平均高度。

7   Rivers carry _____, which is fine sand or mud, with them as they flow.
    河流流動時會挾帶成分為細沙或淤泥的泥沙。

8   Some _____ people live in the desert and wander through it.
    有些游牧民族居住在沙漠並游徒於沙漠之中。

C

Read and Choose | 閱讀下列句子，並且選出最適當的答案。

1   The ascent of K2 has been (attempt | attempted) by many different climbers.

2   The heat of the desert can cause people to (dehydrate | hydrate) quickly.

3   Edmund Hilary was (companied | accompanied) by a Sherpa guide when he climbed Mt. Everest.

4   (Mount Everest | K2) is the second highest mountain in the world.

D

Look, Read, and Write | 看圖並且依照提示，在空格中填入正確答案。

1 ▶ the highest point of a mountain; the top of a mountain

_____

3 ▶ wild and not even; not easy to travel over

_____

2 ▶ the average height of the sea where it meets the land

_____

4 ▶ very dry; having very little rain or water

_____

E

Read and Answer | 閱讀並且回答下列問題。 028

Climbing Mount Everest

Mount Everest is in the Himalaya Mountains. It is located near the border of Nepal, Tibet, and China. At 8,848 meters high, it is the highest mountain in the world. People call it "The Top of the World."

For years, people wanted to be the first to climb the mountain. But no one could get to the top. Many people tried, but none of them succeeded. Some of them even died.

But, in 1953, at last two men were successful. They were Sir Edmund Hilary and Tenzing Norgay. Hilary was from New Zealand. Norgay was a Sherpa. Sherpas are expert mountain climbers from Tibet and Nepal. They are often employed as guides for mountaineering expeditions in the Himalayas, particularly Mt. Everest.

There were nine people on the team. They also had hundreds of porters and twenty Sherpas. It took them several days to get near the top. Some men came very close. But they couldn't get there. Finally, on May 29, 1953, Hilary and Norgay got to the top of the mountain. They were the first people to stand on top of the world!

What is true? Write T(true) or F(false).

1   Mount Everest is the highest mountain in the world.   _____
2   Sir Edmund Hilary climbed Mount Everest in 1953.   _____
3   Sherpas come from New Zealand.   _____
4   Sir Edmund Hilary climbed Mount Everest all by himself.   _____

Asian Cultures 亞洲文化

Key Words
🔊 029

01	**Hinduism** [ˈhɪnduˌɪzəm]	*(n.)* 印度教　*Hindu (n.) 印度教徒

Hinduism was a religion with many gods that began in India.
印度教是一個多神教，起源於印度。

02	**caste** [kæst]	*(n.)* （印度社會的）種姓；種姓制度　*caste system 種姓制度

The people in India have been divided into four different **castes**.
印度人一直以來都被分為四種不同的種姓。

03	**Brahmin** [ˈbrɑmɪn]	*(n.)* 婆羅門（= Brahman）　*Brahmanism (n.) 婆羅門教（印度教的前身）

The **Brahmins** are the highest caste in Indian society.
婆羅門在印度的社會中屬於最高階層的種姓。

04	**Buddhism** [ˈbʊdɪzəm]	*(n.)* 佛教　*Buddhist (n.) 佛教徒　*Buddha 佛，佛陀；佛像

Buddhism was founded in India by Buddha. 佛教由佛陀於印度創立。

05	**Confucianism** [kənˈfjuʃəˌnɪzm]	*(n.)* 儒學　*Confucius 孔子　*Confucius Institute 孔子學院

Confucianism was taught by the Chinese philosopher Confucius.
儒學由中國的思想家孔子所講授。

06	**Taoism** [ˈtaʊˌɪzəm]	*(n.)* 道教　*Taoist (n.) 道教徒　*Chuang Tzu 莊子

Taoism was the philosophy of Lao Tzu. 道教是老子的人生哲學。

07	**meditation** [ˌmɛdəˈteʃən]	*(n.)* 打坐；冥想　*to practice meditation 靜坐冥想

Meditation is a way to relax one's mind and body.
打坐是舒緩個人身心的一種方式。

08	**dynasty** [ˈdaɪnəstɪ]	*(n.)* 王朝；朝代　*to establish/overthrow a dynasty 建立／推翻一個王朝

There were several **dynasties** that ruled China over the years.
歷年來有許多王朝統治過中國。

09	**gunpowder** [ˈgʌnˌpaʊdər]	*(n.)* 火藥　*to sit on a keg of gunpowder 危如累卵

The Chinese were the first to invent **gunpowder**. 中國人率先發明火藥。

10	**Silk Road** [sɪlk rod]	*(n.)* 絲路　*Maritime Silk Road 海上絲路

The **Silk Road** was a trade route from China to Europe.
絲路是中國通往歐洲的貿易路線。

Krishna, a major Hindu god

Buddha

meditation

gunpowder

make up one's mind
下定決心
Siddhartha **made up his mind** to leave his easy, comfortable life.
希達多下定決心離開他安逸的生活。

determine
[dɪˋtɝmɪn]
決定
Siddhartha **determined** to leave his easy, comfortable life.
希達多決定離開他安逸的生活。

set off
啟程；出發
He **set off** to try to understand why there was suffering.
他啟程去試圖瞭解為何會有苦難。

be enlightened
[bɪ ɪnˋlaɪtn̩d]
獲得覺悟 （= become enlightened）
Buddha **was enlightened** through all of his meditation.
佛陀透過禪定獲得覺悟。

attain enlightenment
[əˋten ɪnˋlaɪtn̩mənt]
得到覺悟
Buddha **attained enlightenment** through all of his meditation.
佛陀透過禪定得到覺悟。

meditate
[ˋmɛdə͵tet]
沉思；冥想
A philosopher **meditates** to try to clear his mind.
哲學家試圖透過沉思來釐清他的思緒。

sacred
神聖的；不可侵犯的
For Hindus, the cow is the most sacred animal.
對印度教徒來說，牛是最神聖的動物。

holy
神聖的；供神用的
For Hindus, the Ganges is a holy river. 對印度教徒來說，恆河是一條神聖的河。

| **Asian Religions** 亞洲的宗教 | **Buddhism** 佛教
Hinduism 印度教
Confucianism 儒學
Zen Buddhism 禪宗 | **Caste System in India** 印度的種姓制度 | **Brahmin** 婆羅門（祭司）
Kshatriya 剎帝利（武士、王宮貴族）
Vaisya 吠舍（庶民）
Sudra 首陀羅（奴隸） |
| **Chinese Philosophers** 中國的思想家 | **Confucius** 孔子
Mencius 孟子
Lao Tzu 老子
Sun Tzu 孫子 | **Four Chinese Inventions** 中國四大發明 | **paper** 紙
printing 印刷術
gunpowder 火藥
compass 羅盤 |

Checkup

A

Write | 請依提示寫出正確的英文單字和片語。

1	印度教	_____	
2	種姓；種姓制度	_____	
3	婆羅門	_____	
4	佛教	_____	
5	儒學	_____	
6	道教	_____	
7	打坐；冥想(n.)	_____	
8	王朝；朝代	_____	
9	火藥	_____	
10	絲路	_____	
11	下定決心	_____	
12	決定	_____	
13	啟程；出發	_____	
14	得到覺悟	a _____	
15	羅盤	_____	
16	神聖的；不可侵犯的	_____	

B

Complete the Sentences | 請在空格中填入最適當的答案，並視情況做適當的變化。

meditation	Confucianism	Buddhism	Taoism	caste
Hinduism	gunpowder	Brahmin	dynasty	Silk Road

1 _____ was a religion with many gods that began in India.
印度教是一個多神教，起源於印度。

2 The people in India have been divided into four different _____.
印度人一直以來都被分為四種不同的種姓。

3 _____ was founded in India by Buddha. 佛教由佛陀於印度創立。

4 _____ was the philosophy of Lao Tzu. 道教是老子的人生哲學。

5 The _____ are the highest caste in Indian society.
婆羅門在印度的社會中屬於最高階層的種姓。

6 _____ was taught by the Chinese philosopher Confucius.
儒學由中國的思想家孔子所講授。

7 _____ is a way to relax one's mind and body.
打坐是舒緩個人身心的一種方式。

8 There were several _____ that ruled China over the years.
歷年來有許多王朝統治過中國。

C

Read and Choose | 閱讀下列句子，並且選出最適當的答案。

1 Siddhartha (determined | made) up his mind to leave his easy, comfortable life.

2 Buddha was (enlightened | enlightenment) through all of his meditation.

3 A philosopher (attains | meditates) to try to clear his mind.

4 For Hindus, the cow is the most (sacred | secrete) animal.

D

Look, Read, and Write ┃ 看圖並且依照提示，在空格中填入正確答案。

▶ the system of dividing people into different social classes in a Hindu society
_____

▶ a religion based on the ideas of the Chinese philosopher Confucius
_____

▶ the main religion of India which include the worship of many gods
_____

▶ an ancient trade route from China to Europe
_____

E

Read and Answer ┃ 閱讀並且回答下列問題。 🔊 032

Marco Polo and the Silk Road

China and Europe are very far from each other. Today, people can fly between the two in a few hours. But in the past, it took months or years to go from one place to the other. When people traveled from China to Europe, they went on the Silk Road.

The Silk Road was not a real road. It was a large group of trade routes. But, by following it, people could get from the Mediterranean Sea to the Pacific Ocean. It was called the Silk Road because the Chinese transported silk to the west on it.

The Silk Road became very famous because of Marco Polo. He was an Italian  adventurer. With his father and uncle, he left Italy and returned twenty-four years later. He had taken the Silk Road to China. He had many adventures. He even became an advisor to the emperor. When he came back, he wrote a book, *The Travels of Marco Polo*, about his travels and became very famous.

Answer the questions.

1   How did people go from China to Europe in the past?

2   What was the Silk Road?

3   Who transported silk on the Silk Road?

4   Who was Marco Polo?

Europe in the Middle Ages 中世紀的歐洲

Key Words 🔘 033

01 Byzantine Empire
[bɪˈzæntɪn ˈɛmpaɪr]

(n.) 拜占庭帝國（= Eastern Roman Empire）　*byzantine (a.) 錯綜複雜的

The capital of the **Byzantine Empire** was Constantinople.
拜占庭帝國的首都是君士坦丁堡。

02 medieval
[ˌmɪdɪˈivəl]

(a.) 中世紀的　*Middle Ages 中世紀

Another name for the Middle Ages is the **medieval** period.
中世紀的另一個名稱為中古時期。

03 feudalism
[ˈfjudḷɪzəm]

(n.) 封建制度　*a feudal lord/kingdom/society 封建領主／國家／社會

Feudalism was a social system in the Middle Ages.
封建制度是中世紀的一種社會制度。

04 manor
[ˈmænɚ]

(n.) 莊園；領地　*manorialism (n.) 莊園制度

The lord lived in a large **manor** and managed his estate from it.
領主住在寬大的莊園裡，並從中管理他的財產。

05 knight
[naɪt]

(n.) 騎士　*knight errant 遊俠騎士　*the Knights of the Round Table 圓桌騎士

Knights swore loyalty to their lord. 騎士向他們的主人宣誓忠誠。

06 chivalry
[ˈʃɪvḷrɪ]

(n.) 騎士精神　*the knight's code of chivalry 騎士精神

Chivalry was the code of honor that medieval knights lived by.
騎士精神是騎士賴以維生的榮譽準則。

07 noble
[ˈnobḷ]

(n.) 貴族　*noblesse oblige 位高應不負重望　*noble (a.) 高尚的；高貴的

Dukes, earls, and barons were all **nobles**.
公爵、伯爵以及男爵全都是貴族。

08 cathedral
[kəˈθidrəl]

(n.) 大教堂　*cathedral ceiling 大教堂天花板（屋頂挑高，且兩邊斜度對稱）

Cathedrals are enormous churches that rise high in the sky.
大教堂是指高聳入天的巨大教堂。

09 Dark Ages
[dɑrk edʒz]

(n.) 黑暗時代

The **Dark Ages** began in Europe after the fall of the Roman Empire.
羅馬帝國瓦解後，歐洲就進入了黑暗時代。

10 Crusade
[kruˈsed]

(n.) 十字軍　*crusader (n.) 十字軍戰士　*to go on a crusade 參加聖戰

Many Europeans went on the **Crusades** to the Holy Land.
許多歐洲人加入十字軍，前往聖地。

manor

knight

cathedral

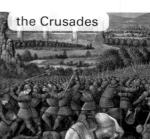
the Crusades

collapse
[kəˈlæps]
瓦解
The Middle Ages began when the Roman Empire collapsed.
羅馬帝國一瓦解，中古時代即來臨了。

split
分裂；使分裂
The Roman Empire was split in two: the Western Roman Empire and the Eastern Roman Empire. 羅馬帝國一分為二：西羅馬帝國與東羅馬帝國。

last
持續
The Eastern Roman Empire, also known as the Byzantine Empire, lasted until 1453. 東羅馬帝國又被稱為拜占庭帝國，持續到 1453 年才結束。

reign
當政
Charlemagne reigned for more than 45 years. 查理曼大帝當政超過 45 年。

swear an oath
宣誓
Vassals, lords, and kings swore oaths to observe certain rules.
封臣、領主以及國王都要宣誓遵守特定的規則。

take an oath
宣誓
Knights took an oath to be faithful to their lord and their king.
騎士宣誓會對他們的領主及國王忠誠。

Word Families 🔊 035

lord
領主
The lord was the owner of all the land in an area.
領主是指特定區域內全部土地的所有人。

vassal
封臣
A vassal swore loyalty to his lord. 封臣向他的主人宣誓忠誠。

fief
封地
A vassal was given a fief, which was land that he owned.
封臣被賜予一塊封地，這塊地會歸他所有。

serf
奴隸
Serfs were people with few rights and who had to work on manors owned by lords.
擁有少數權利且必須在領主莊園裡工作的人稱為奴隸。

Famous Kings in the Middle Ages
中世紀著名的國王

Famous Events in the Middle Ages
中世紀的重大事件

Justinian the Great 查士丁尼大帝

Charlemagne 查理曼大帝

William the Conqueror 征服者威廉

Henry II 亨利二世

Richard I the Lionhearted 獅心王理查一世

the Crusades 十字軍東征

the signing of the Magna Carta 大憲章的簽署

the Black Death 黑死病

the Hundred Years' War 百年戰爭（英法戰爭）

the Norman Invasion of England 諾曼人征服英格蘭

Checkup

A

Write | 請依提示寫出正確的英文單字和片語。

1	拜占庭帝國	_____	9	黑暗時代	_____
2	中世紀的	_____	10	十字軍	_____
3	封建制度	_____	11	瓦解	_____
4	莊園；領地	_____	12	分裂	_____
5	騎士	_____	13	當政	_____
6	騎士精神	_____	14	宣誓	s_____
7	貴族	_____	15	封臣	_____
8	大教堂	_____	16	封地	_____

B

Complete the Sentences | 請在空格中填入最適當的答案，並視情況做適當的變化。

cathedral	Dark Ages	noble	chivalry	manor
Crusade	feudalism	knight	medieval	vassal

1   Another name for the Middle Ages is the _____ period.
中世紀的另一個名稱為中古時期。

2   _____ was a social system in the Middle Ages.
封建制度是中世紀的一種社會制度。

3   The lord lived in a large _____ and managed his estate from it.
領主住在寬大的莊園裡，並從中管理他的財產。

4   _____ was the code of honor that medieval knights lived by.
騎士精神是騎士賴以維生的榮譽準則。

5   Dukes, earls, and barons were all _____. 公爵、伯爵以及男爵全都是貴族。

6   The _____ _____ began in Europe after the fall of the Roman Empire.
羅馬帝國瓦解後，歐洲就進入了黑暗時代。

7   _____ swore loyalty to their lord. 騎士向他們的主人宣誓忠誠。

8   Many Europeans went on the _____ to the Holy Land.
許多歐洲人加入十字軍東征，前往聖地。

C

Read and Choose | 閱讀下列句子，並且選出最適當的答案。

1   The Middle Ages began when the Roman Empire (collapsed | split).

2   The Roman Empire was (collapsed | split) in two: the Western Roman Empire and the Eastern Roman Empire.

3   Charlemagne (lasted | reigned) for more than forty-five years.

4   Vassals, lords, and kings (swore | wore) oaths to observe certain rules.

Look, Read, and Write | 看圖並且依照提示，在空格中填入正確答案。

1 ▶ a different name for the Eastern Roman Empire

_____

3 ▶ a social system that existed in Europe during the Middle Ages

_____

2 ▶ the system of values that knights in the Middle Ages were expected to follow

_____

4 ▶ the period occurred in Europe following the end of the Roman Empire

_____

E

Read and Answer | 閱讀並且回答下列問題。　● 036

The Middle Ages

The Roman Empire fell in 476. It was conquered by Germanic invaders. In the east, there was still the Byzantine Empire. It was the eastern part of the Roman Empire. It lasted for almost 1,000 more years. It was finally defeated in 1453.

But in Western Europe, after the fall of the Western Roman Empire, the Dark Ages began. This term is sometimes applied to the first 300 years after the fall of Rome and sometimes to the whole Middle Ages. During this time, only a few people could read and write. The people had hard lives. They often just struggled to survive. Most people farmed the land. Their lives were very simple then.

Throughout the Middle Ages, there were very slow improvements in people's lives. Some kings ruled their lands fairly. Others were very harsh. They treated their people like slaves. And they taxed them very much. Many people died of starvation. Others died because of diseases. The Black Death killed almost half of the people in Europe in the fourteenth century. The Middle Ages were a very difficult time for most people.

What is NOT true?

1　The Roman Empire fell in 476.
2　The Byzantine Empire was in Western Europe.
3　The Dark Ages happened after the fall of the Roman Empire.
4　Many people had difficult lives in the Middle Ages.

Unit 10 The Civil War 南北戰爭

01 slavery
['slevərı]

(n.) 奴隸制　*the abolition of slavery 奴隸制的廢止

Many Southern states permitted **slavery** before the Civil War.
南北戰爭前，許多南方州允許奴隸制的存在。

02 secession
[sɪ'sɛʃən]

(n.) 脫離聯邦　*the secession from sth. 自……脫離

The **secession** of several Southern states led to the start of the war.
許多南方州脫離聯邦導致戰爭的開始。

03 Union
['junjən]

(n.)（美國）聯邦（= United States of America）

The **Union** was made up of the Northern states. 聯邦由北方各州組成。

04 Confederacy
[kən'fɛdərəsɪ]

(n.)（美國）邦聯（= Confederate States of America）

The **Confederacy** was made up of the Southern states.
邦聯由南方各州組成。

05 rebellion
[rɪ'bɛljən]

(n.) 反抗；反對　*a rebellion against sth. 對……的反抗

The South was in **rebellion** against the North. 南方各州反抗北方各州。

06 emancipation
[ɪ,mænsə'peʃən]

(n.) 解放　*Emancipation Proclamation《解放奴隸宣言》

The **emancipation** of the slaves by Abraham Lincoln freed them.
亞伯拉罕‧林肯使奴隸獲得自由，因此他們得到了解放。

07 blockade
[blɑ'ked]

(n.) 封鎖；包圍　*air/sea blockade 空中／海上封鎖

A **blockade** is the closing of a port so that no ships can get in or out.
封鎖是指將港口關閉，而使船隻無法進出。

08 attrition
[ə'trɪʃən]

(n.) 損耗；磨損　*war of attrition 消耗戰　*attrition rate 損耗率

The Civil War was a war of **attrition**, and both sides suffered greatly.
南北戰爭是一場損耗戰，雙方都損傷慘重。

09 ironclad
['aɪən,klæd]

(a.) 裝甲的　*ironclad warship 裝甲艦

The first **ironclad** ships in the world fought during the war.
世界上的第一艘裝甲船於戰爭期間進行作戰。

10 assassination
[ə'sæsə,neʃən]

(n.) 暗殺　*assassin (n.) 暗殺者　*character assassination 人身攻擊；誹謗

The **assassination** of President Lincoln happened days after the war ended. 戰爭過後幾天，林肯總統即遭暗殺。

Union and Confederate flags from the Civil War
Confederacy　Union

slavery

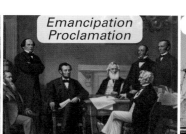
Emancipation Proclamation

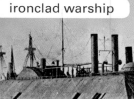
ironclad warship

Power Verbs 🔊 038

secede
[sɪˈsid]
脫離
South Carolina was the first state to secede from the Union.
南卡羅來納州是第一個脫離聯邦的州。

break away
脫離
South Carolina was the first state to break away from the Union.
南卡羅來納州是第一個脫離聯邦的州。

rebel
反抗
The South rebelled against the rest of the country. 美國南方各州反抗其餘各州。

blockade
封鎖；包圍
Union ships blockaded most Southern ports. 聯邦的船封鎖了南方大部分的港口。

emancipate
[ɪˌmænsəˈpet]
解放
The Emancipation Proclamation emancipated all of the slaves.
《解放奴隸宣言》解放了所有的奴隸。

surrender
[səˈrɛndɚ]
投降
General Lee surrendered to General Grant at Appomattox Court House. 李將軍在阿波馬托克斯法院向格蘭特將軍投降。

Word Families 🔊 039

Famous Battles of the Civil War
南北戰爭著名的戰役

Bull Run 牛奔河之役
Antietam 安提坦耶之戰
Shiloh 賽羅之役
Gettysburg 蓋茲堡之役
Vicksburg 維克斯堡之役

Union Leaders
聯邦的領導人

President Abraham Lincoln
亞伯拉罕・林肯總統

General Ulysses S. Grant
尤利賽斯・S・格蘭特將軍

General William Sherman
威廉・謝爾曼將軍

General George Meade
喬治・米德將軍

Confederate Leaders
邦聯的領導人

President Jefferson Davis
傑佛遜・戴維斯總統

General Robert E. Lee
羅伯特・E・李將軍

General Thomas "Stonewall" Jackson
湯瑪士・「石牆」・傑克森將軍

General Jeb Stuart
傑布・斯圖爾特將軍

Abraham Lincoln

Jefferson Davis

Grant
Lee
General Lee surrendering to General Grant

Checkup

Write | 請依提示寫出正確的英文單字和片語。

1	奴隸制	_____	9	裝甲的	_____
2	脫離聯邦	_____	10	暗殺	_____
3	（美國）聯邦	_____	11	脫離	s _____
4	（美國）邦聯	_____	12	脫離	b _____
5	反抗；反對	_____	13	反抗	_____
6	解放(n.)	_____	14	封鎖；包圍(v.)	_____
7	封鎖；包圍(n.)	_____	15	解放(v.)	_____
8	損耗；磨損	_____	16	投降	_____

B

Complete the Sentences | 請在空格中填入最適當的答案，並視情況做適當的變化。

Union	Confederacy	rebellion	attrition	secession
blockade	emancipation	ironclad	slavery	assassination

1 Many Southern states permitted _____ before the Civil War.
南北戰爭前，許多南方州允許奴隸制的存在。

2 The _____ was made up of the Southern states. 邦聯由南方各州組成。

3 The _____ was made up of the Northern states. 聯邦由北方各州組成。

4 The South was in _____ against the North. 南方各州反抗北方各州。

5 The Civil War was a war of _____, and both sides suffered greatly.
南北戰爭是一場損耗戰，雙方都損傷慘重。

6 The _____ of several Southern states led to the start of the war.
許多南方州脫離聯邦導致戰爭的開始。

7 The _____ of the slaves by Abraham Lincoln freed them.
亞伯拉罕·林肯使奴隸獲得自由，因此他們得到了解放。

8 The _____ of President Lincoln happened days after the war ended.
戰爭過後幾天，林肯總統即遭暗殺。

C

Read and Choose | 閱讀下列句子，並且選出最適當的答案。

1 South Carolina was the first state to (break | secede) from the Union.

2 The South (rebelled | rebellion) against the rest of the country.

3 The Emancipation Proclamation (blockaded | emancipated) all of the slaves.

4 General Lee (surrendered | lost) to General Grant at Appomattox Court House.

D

Look, Read, and Write | 看圖並且依照提示，在空格中填入正確答案。

 ▶ the activity of having slaves or the condition of being a slave

_____

 ▶ the process of giving people social or political freedom and rights

_____

 ▶ an act in which one country stops people or supplies from entering or leaving another country

_____

 ▶ the murder of someone famous or important

_____

E

Read and Answer | 閱讀並且回答下列問題。 🔊 040

The American Civil War

The Civil War was the bloodiest war in American history. It was fought for many reasons. One big reason was slavery. The South had slaves. The North did not.

The Civil War began after Abraham Lincoln became president. It started in 1861. The North had more men. It also had more railroads and more industries. But the South had better generals than the North. There were many battles during the war. At first, the South seemed to be winning the war. But, in 1863, General Robert E. Lee lost at Gettysburg. The next day, the South lost the Battle of Vicksburg. The North began winning after that.

Two Union generals were very important. General William T. Sherman cut through the South. His March to the Sea from Atlanta to the port of Savannah destroyed much of the South's will to fight. General Ulysses S. Grant led the Union forces. He finally defeated the South, so General Lee surrendered to him. Five days later, John Wilkes Booth assassinated President Lincoln.

Fill in the blanks.

1 Abraham Lincoln was president when the _____ started.
2 The South had better _____ than the North.
3 General Sherman went on the _____ to the Sea.
4 _____ killed President Lincoln after the war ended.

A

Write | 請依提示寫出正確的英文單字和片語。

1 林木線 _____	11 稀少的 _____
2 高度；海拔 _____	12 無人居住的 _____
3 雄偉的；崇高的 _____	13 崎嶇不平的；粗糙的 _____
4 海平面 _____	14 水系 _____
5 種姓；種姓制度 _____	15 沉思；冥想(v.) _____
6 儒學 _____	16 神聖的；不可侵犯的 _____
7 中世紀的 _____	17 十字軍 _____
8 封建制度 _____	18 瓦解 _____
9 奴隸制 _____	19 封鎖；包圍(n.) _____
10 脫離聯邦 _____	20 解放(v.) _____

B

Choose the Correct Word | 請選出與鋪底字意思相近的答案。

1 For Hindus, the cow is the most sacred animal.

   a. precious   b. holy   c. important

2 Siddhartha made up his mind to leave his easy, comfortable life.

   a. determined   b. set off   c. enlightened

3 Knights took an oath to be faithful to their lord and their king.

   a. reigned   b. swore   c. made

4 South Carolina was the first state to secede from the Union.

   a. rebel   b. blockade   c. break away

C

Complete the Sentences | 請在空格中填入最適當的答案，並視情況做適當的變化。

Hinduism	river system	manor	Continental Divide

1 The _____ _____ runs north to south along the peaks of the Rocky Mountains. 北美大陸分水嶺沿著落磯山脈由北向南延伸。

2 The Mississippi _____ _____ includes the river and its tributaries.
密西西比河水系包含它的河流以及支流。

3 _____ was a religion with many gods that began in India.
印度教是一個多神教，起源於印度。

4 The lord lived in a large _____ and managed his estate from it.
領主住在寬大的莊園裡，並從中管理他的財產。

3

Science ①

Unit 11 Inquiry Skills and Science Tools 探究技術與科學工具

Key Words
🔊 041

01 inquiry
[ɪn'kwaɪrɪ]

(n.) 探究；調查　　*to make an inquiry about/into sth. 調查某事

In science, the process of asking and answering questions is called **inquiry**. 在科學中，提出和解決問題的過程稱作探究。

02 scientific method
[ˌsaɪən'tɪfɪk 'mɛθəd]

(n.) 科學方法　　*scientific revolution 科學革命

The **scientific method** is what scientists use to ask and answer questions about science. 科學家用科學方法提出和解決科學問題。

03 observation
[ˌɑbzɝ've∫ən]

(n.) 觀察；觀測　　*to keep sb./sth. under observation 監視某人／某事物
*powers of observation 觀察力

A scientist should engage in **observation** to learn about a topic.
科學家應該要致力於觀察來瞭解某一主題。

04 inference
['ɪnfərəns]

(n.) 推論；推斷　　*by inference 通過推理

An **inference** is an untested conclusion based on observations or information. 推論是一個未經檢驗的結論，主要以觀察或資料為基礎。

05 infer
[ɪn'fɝ]

(v.) 推斷；推論　　*to infer from sth. 從……推斷　　*to infer that . . . 推斷為……

We can **infer** from facts or observations to solve a problem.
我們可以經由對事實或觀察的推斷來解決問題。

06 investigation
[ɪnˌvɛstə'ge∫ən]

(n.) 研究；調查　　*under investigation 在調查中

Plan an **investigation** to find out what you want to know.
計畫一個研究來找出你想知道的事情。

07 hypothesis
[haɪ'pɑθəsɪs]

(n.) 假說；前提　　*to formulate hypotheses 制定假說

A **hypothesis** is a guess about what is going to happen.
假說是對可能發生的事進行猜測。

08 experiment
[ɪk'spɛrəmənt]

(n.) 實驗；試驗　*(v.)* 進行實驗　　*to experiment on sb./sth. 用某人／某物做實驗

A scientist tests a hypothesis by conducting an **experiment**.
科學家藉由進行實驗來檢驗假說。

09 conclusion
[kən'kluʒən]

(n.) 結論　　*to reach/draw a conclusion 得出結論
*to jump/leap to conclusions 匆忙下結論

When the data is analyzed, a scientist can reach a **conclusion** about it.
科學家分析資料以得出結論。

10 microscope
['maɪkrəˌskop]

(n.) 顯微鏡　　*to put sth. under the microscope 仔細檢查

Microscopes let people see small things very clearly.
顯微鏡讓人們能清楚看見微小的東西。

Science Tools 科學工具

 microscope 顯微鏡　　 scale 天平　　 dropper 滴管　　 beaker 燒杯　　 magnifying glass 放大鏡

inquire
[ɪnˋkwaɪr]

調查
Scientists often inquire about what they observe.
科學家時常會調查他們所觀察到的事情。

investigate
[ɪnˋvɛstə͵get]

研究
When scientists want to answer a question, they investigate and conduct tests. 當科學家想解決問題，他們會研究並進行實驗。

observe
[əbˋzɝv]

觀察
A good hypothesis must be based on what you observe.
一個好的假說必須以你所觀察到的事情為基礎。

hypothesize
[haɪˋpɑθə͵saɪz]

假設；假定
Scientists hypothesize about what they think will happen.
科學家對他們認為會發生的事進行假說。

form a hypothesis

形成假說
Scientists form a hypothesis about what they think will happen.
科學家對他們認為會發生的事形成假說。

predict
[prɪˋdɪkt]

預測
When you predict, you say what you think will happen next.
當你預測，表示你假設了接下來可能會發生的事。

analyze
[ˋænḷ͵aɪz]

分析
Analyze data to answer questions or to solve a problem.
分析數據來回答或是解決問題。

interpret
[ɪnˋtɝprɪt]

解釋
Interpret data to answer questions or to solve a problem.
解釋數據來回答或是解決問題。

conclude
[kənˋklud]

推斷出
Did you conclude anything from the results?
你能夠從這個結果中推斷出任何事情嗎？

draw a conclusion

得出結論
Did you draw a conclusion from the results? 你能夠從這個結果中得出結論嗎？

Word Families 🔊 043

data

數據；資料
Data is the information a scientist collects from research.
數據是科學家從實驗中蒐集而來的資訊。

information

資料；資訊
A scientist gathers information by doing research. 科學家藉由做研究來蒐集資料。

Science Tools
科學工具

forceps
鑷子

test tube
試管

thermometer
溫度計

litmus paper
石蕊試紙

Bunsen burner
本生燈

Checkup

A

Write | 請依提示寫出正確的英文單字和片語。

1 探究；調查(n.) _____	9 結論 _____
2 科學方法 _____	10 顯微鏡 _____
3 觀察；觀測 _____	11 調查(v.) _____
4 推論；推斷(n.) _____	12 研究(v.) _____
5 推論；推斷(v.) _____	13 假設；假定 _____
6 研究；調查(n.) _____	14 分析 _____
7 假說；前提(n.) _____	15 解釋 _____
8 實驗；試驗 _____	16 推斷出 _____

B

Complete the Sentences | 請在空格中填入最適當的答案，並視情況做適當的變化。

observation	inference	conclusion	scientific method	infer
hypothesis	experiment	microscope	investigation	inquiry

1 In science, the process of asking and answering questions is called _____.
在科學中，提出和解決問題的過程稱作探究。

2 A scientist should engage in _____ to learn about a topic.
科學家應該要致力於觀察來瞭解某一主題。

3 An _____ is an untested conclusion based on observations or information.
推論是一個未經檢驗的結論，主要以觀察或資料為基礎。

4 We can _____ from facts or observations to solve a problem.
我們可以經由對事實或觀察的推斷來解決問題。

5 A _____ is a guess about what is going to happen.
假說是對可能發生的事進行猜測。

6 A scientist tests a hypothesis by conducting an _____.
科學家藉由進行實驗來檢驗假說。

7 Plan an _____ to find out what you want to know.
計畫一個研究來找出你想知道的事情。

8 When the data is analyzed, a scientist can reach a _____ about it.
科學家分析資料以得出結論。

C

Read and Choose | 閱讀下列句子，並且選出與舖底字意思相近的答案。

1 Scientists form a hypothesis about what they think will happen.
   a. inquire   b. predict   c. hypothesize

2 Analyze data to answer questions or to solve a problem.
   a. Infer   b. Observe   c. Interpret

3 Did you draw a conclusion from the results?
   a. predict anything   b. conclude anything   c. investigate anything

D

Look, Read, and Write | 看圖並且依照提示，在空格中填入正確答案。

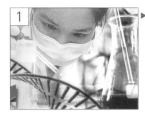
1 ▸ the process that is used by scientists for testing ideas and theories

_____

3 ▸ an idea or explanation that is based on known facts but has not yet been proved

_____

2 ▸ a guess that you make based on the information that you have

_____

4 ▸ a device used for producing a much larger view of very small objects

_____

E

Read and Answer | 閱讀並且回答下列問題。 🔊 044

The Scientific Method of Inquiry

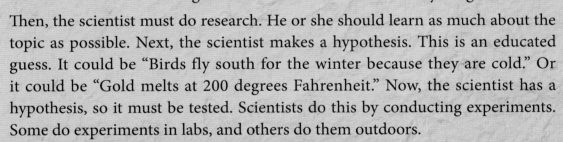

Scientists have a method they use when they are trying to learn something new. It is called the scientific method of inquiry.

The first step is to ask a question. It could be "Why do birds fly south for the winter?" Or it could be "How much heat does it take for gold to melt?" It could be about anything.

Then, the scientist must do research. He or she should learn as much about the topic as possible. Next, the scientist makes a hypothesis. This is an educated guess. It could be "Birds fly south for the winter because they are cold." Or it could be "Gold melts at 200 degrees Fahrenheit." Now, the scientist has a hypothesis, so it must be tested. Scientists do this by conducting experiments. Some do experiments in labs, and others do them outdoors.

After the experiments are complete, the scientist must analyze the data. Then he should compare it with the hypothesis. Was the hypothesis right or wrong? Even with a wrong hypothesis, scientists can still learn a lot. Finally, they should write about their results. That way, other people can learn, too.

Fill in the blanks.

1 Scientists use the scientific _____ of inquiry to learn.

2 A _____ is an educated guess.

3 Scientists conduct experiments in _____ or outdoors.

4 Scientists _____ data after they finish their experiments.

Key Words 🔊 045

01	**organism** [ˋɔrgənˏɪzəm]	*(n.)* 有機體;生物　*living organism 生物;活體生物 Anything that is living is called an **organism**. 任何有生命的事物都稱作有機體。
02	**microorganism** [ˏmaɪkro ˋɔrgənˏɪzəm]	*(n.)* 微生物　*microbe (n.) 微生物;(尤指致病的)細菌　*microbiology (n.) 微生物學 **Microorganisms** like viruses and bacteria are so small that you need a microscope to see them. 像病毒和細菌這麼小的微生物,你必須用顯微鏡才能看見它們。
03	**protist** [ˋprotɪst]	*(n.)* 原生生物　*prokaryote (n.) 原核生物(指細胞沒有細胞膜與核膜的生物) **Protists** are simple one-celled organisms. 原生生物是單細胞生物。
04	**bacteria** [bækˋtɪrɪə]	*(n.)* 細菌(複數)　*bacterium (n.) 細菌(單數) **Bacteria** are one-celled organisms which often cause diseases. 細菌是單細胞生物,常會造成疾病。
05	**fungus** [ˋfʌŋgəs]	*(n.)* 真菌;真菌類植物　*fungi (n.) 真菌(複數)(= funguses) Mushrooms and yeasts are two kinds of **fungus**. 蘑菇和酵母是兩種真菌。
06	**vascular plant** [ˋvæskjələ plænt]	*(n.)* 維管束植物　*vascular bundle 維管束 **Vascular plants** have tubes that carry water and nutrients to all of their parts. 維管束植物擁有攜帶水分和營養至全身各部位的管狀器官。
07	**cell** [sɛl]	*(n.)* 細胞　*cell count 細胞數　*cell division 細胞分裂 The basic unit of all organisms is the **cell**. 細胞是所有有機體的基本單位。
08	**membrane** [ˋmɛmbren]	*(n.)* 薄膜　*biological membrane 生物膜　*mucous membrane 黏膜 The outer covering of a cell is its **membrane**. 細胞的外層是一層細胞膜。
09	**nucleus** [ˋnjuklɪəs]	*(n.)* 細胞核　*the nucleus of sth. 某物的核心 The **nucleus** of a cell contains the parts which control its growth and reproduction. 細胞核包含了控制生長與生殖的部分。
10	**cytoplasm** [ˋsaɪtəˏplæzəm]	*(n.)* 細胞質　*cytology (n.) 細胞學 **Cytoplasm** is located between the cell membrane and nucleus. 細胞質介於細胞膜與細胞核之間。

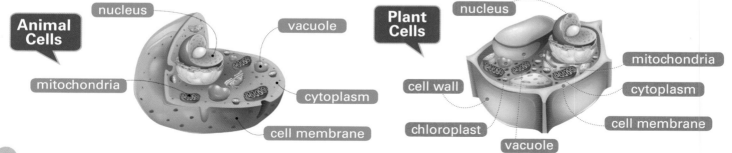

Animal Cells: nucleus, vacuole, mitochondria, cytoplasm, cell membrane

Plant Cells: nucleus, mitochondria, cytoplasm, cell wall, chloroplast, vacuole, cell membrane

classify
[ˋklæsəˌfaɪ]

分類;歸類
There are many ways to classify organisms. 有很多方式可以分類有機體。

group

分類;分組
There are many ways to group organisms. 有很多方式可以分類有機體。

divide
[dəˋvaɪd]

分裂;分割
Multi-celled organisms grow as their cells divide.
當細胞分裂時,多細胞有機體開始長大。

split

分裂;使分裂
Multi-celled organisms grow as their cells split.
當細胞分裂時,多細胞有機體開始長大。

reproduce
[ˌriprəˋdjus]

複製;生殖
Some cells reproduce by splitting into two parts.
有些細胞利用一分為二的方式複製個體。

replicate
[ˋrɛplɪˌket]

複製
Some organisms can replicate themselves. 有些有機體可以自行複製個體。

duplicate
[ˋdjupləkɪt]

複製
Some organisms can duplicate themselves. 有些有機體可以自行複製個體。

one-celled organism

單細胞生物
Amoebas are one-celled organisms. 變形蟲是單細胞生物。

single-celled organism

單細胞生物
All single-celled organisms have a cell membrane.
所有單細胞生物有機體都有細胞膜。

multi-celled organism

多細胞生物
Multi-celled organism, like humans, are very complicated creatures.
像人們這樣的多細胞生物是非常複雜的生物。

Plant Cells
植物細胞

nucleus 細胞核　　**cytoplasm** 細胞質　　**cell membrane** 細胞膜
cell wall 細胞壁　　**chloroplast** 葉綠體　　**vacuole** 液泡
mitochondria 粒線體

Animal Cells
動物細胞

nucleus 細胞核　　**cytoplasm** 細胞質　　**cell membrane** 細胞膜
vacuole 液泡　　**mitochondria** 粒線體

Checkup

A

Write | 請依提示寫出正確的英文單字和片語。

1 有機體；生物	_____	9 細胞核 _____
2 微生物	_____	10 細胞質 _____
3 原生生物	_____	11 分類；歸類 c _____
4 細菌	_____	12 分裂；分割 d _____
5 真菌；真菌類植物	_____	13 分裂；使分裂 s _____
6 維管束植物	_____	14 複製 r _____
7 細胞	_____	15 單細胞生物 s _____
8 薄膜	_____	16 多細胞生物 _____

B

Complete the Sentences | 請在空格中填入最適當的答案，並視情況做適當的變化。

single-celled	organism	microorganism	protist	cell
membrane	nucleus	vascular plant	fungus	cytoplasm

1 Anything that is living is called an _____.
任何有生命的事物都稱作有機體。

2 _____ are simple single-celled organisms. 原生生物是單細胞生物。

3 _____ like viruses and bacteria are so small that you need a microscope to see them.
像病毒和細菌這麼小的微生物，你必須用放大鏡才能看見它們。

4 _____ _____ have tubes that carry water and nutrients to all of their parts. 維管束植物擁有攜帶水分和營養至全身各部位的管狀器官。

5 Bacteria are _____ organisms which often cause diseases.
細菌是單細胞生物，常會造成疾病。

6 The _____ of a cell contains the parts which control its growth and reproduction. 細胞核包含了控制生長與生殖的部分。

7 Mushrooms and yeasts are two kinds of _____. 蘑菇和酵母是兩種真菌。

8 _____ is located between the cell membrane and nucleus.
細胞質介於細胞膜與細胞核之間。

C

Read and Choose | 閱讀下列句子，並且選出與鋪底字意思相近的答案。

1 There are many ways to classify organisms.
   a. divide   b. carry   c. group

2 Multi-celled organisms grow as their cells divide.
   a. replicate   b. duplicate   c. split

3 Amoebas are one-celled organisms.
   a. multi-celled   b. single-celled   c. two-celled

D

Look, Read, and Write | 看圖並且依照提示，在空格中填入正確答案。

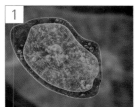 1 ▶ a simple one-celled organism

_____

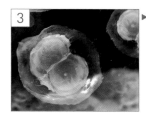 3 ▶ the smallest basic unit of a plant or animal

_____

 2 ▶ a plant that has tubes to carry water and nutrients

_____

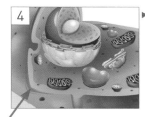 4 ▶ the thin, limiting covering of a cell or cell part

_____

E

Read and Answer | 閱讀並且回答下列問題。 ⊙ 048

Organisms

There are millions of types of organisms on the Earth. An organism is any creature that is alive. These include animals, plants, fungi, and microorganisms. All organisms are made of cells. Some have just one cell. Others have billions and billions of them.

Microorganisms are very, very small. In fact, you can't even see them without a microscope. Bacteria and protists are microorganisms. These are often one-celled organisms. So everything they need to survive is in a single cell. How do they reproduce? They simply divide themselves in half. This is called asexual reproduction.

But most organisms are multi-celled. So they may have a few cells. Or they could have trillions of them. Multi-celled organisms have specialized cells. These cells often do one specific thing. They could be used to defend the organism from disease. They could be used for reproduction. They could be used for digestion. Or they could be used for many other purposes.

What is true? Write T(true) or F(false).

1 There are one million organisms on the Earth.   _____
2 You need a microscope to see a microorganism.   _____
3 Multi-celled organisms have only one cell.   _____
4 Cells have many different uses.   _____

Key Words 🔊 049

01	**evolution** [ˌɛvəˈluʃən]	(n.) 演化；進化 *Darwin's theory of evolution 達爾文的進化論 The **evolution** of a species can take generations to occur. 物種的演化可能耗時數世代才會發生。
02	**adaptation** [ˌædæpˈteʃən]	(n.) 適應；適合 *to make an adaptation to sth. 適應某物 **Adaptations** are the changes animals make to get used to a new environment. 適應是動物使本身習慣新環境的改變。
03	**behavior** [bɪˈhevjɚ]	(n.) 行為；舉止 *behavioral patterns 行為模式 **Behavior** is how animals act in certain situations. 行為是指動物面對特定情況時的反應。
04	**species** [ˈspiʃiz]	(n.) 種；物種 *a species of sth. 某物的品種 *an endangered species 瀕危物種 There are millions of **species** of animals on the planet. 地球上有數以百萬計的動物物種。
05	**gene** [dʒin]	(n.) 基因；遺傳因子 *gene pool 基因庫 *gene expression 基因表現 **Genes** are what determine which traits an animal inherits from its parents. 基因決定了動物會從親代遺傳到何種特徵。
06	**genetic** [dʒəˈnɛtɪk]	(a.) 遺傳的；基因的 *genetic defect/disease 基因缺陷／遺傳疾病 Animals pass on **genetic** material to their babies. 動物傳遞遺傳物質給下一代。
07	**inherited** [ɪnˈhɛrɪtɪd]	(a.) 遺傳的 *inherited disease/disorder 遺傳疾病 Some traits are **inherited**, so they are passed down from the parents. 有些特徵是遺傳的，所以它們從親代傳遞下來。
08	**heredity** [həˈrɛdətɪ]	(n.) 遺傳；遺傳特徵 *congenital (a.) 先天的 **Heredity** is the passing of certain characteristics from parents to their offspring. 遺傳是指從親代傳遞至子代的某些特徵。
09	**sperm cell** [spɝm sɛl]	(n.) 精細胞 *sperm (n.) 精子；精液 *spermatozoon (n.) 精液 Genes are transferred when a **sperm cell** and an egg cell join. 精細胞與卵細胞結合時，基因就會改變。
10	**egg cell** [ɛg sɛl]	(n.) 卵細胞 *egg (n.) 卵子 *egghead (n.)（尤指男性）學究；書呆子 **Egg cells** are the reproductive cells found in females. 卵細胞是雌性的生殖細胞。

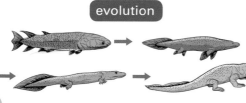

evolution

gene model

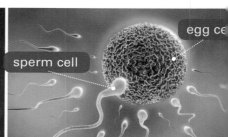

sperm cell

egg ce

evolve 進化
Animals evolve by developing new characteristics that help them survive.
動物經由發展能幫助牠們生存的新特徵來進化。

adapt 適應
An animal that cannot adapt to its environment will quickly die.
無法適應新環境的動物將會快速死亡。

inherit 經遺傳獲得
Babies inherit traits from their parents. 嬰兒經遺傳獲得父母的特徵。

pass on 傳遞
Parents pass on traits to their babies. 父母傳遞特徵給他們的嬰兒。

transfer 轉移
Genes are transferred from parents to their offspring.
基因會由親代轉移到他們的下一代。

behave 行為舉止
Animals behave differently according to their situation.
動物的行為舉止會因情況而異。

Word Families ● 051

feature 特徵；特色
One feature of the wolf is its fur. 狼的特徵之一是牠的軟毛。

characteristic 特性；特色；特徵
[ˌkærəktəˋrɪstɪk]
One characteristic of a dog is its loyalty. 狗的特性之一是牠的忠心。

trait 特徵；特點；特性
One trait of the penguin is its black and white color.
企鵝的特徵之一是牠黑與白的顏色。

learned behavior 學習行為
Learned behavior is taught to an animal.
學習行為是動物被教導而來的。

instinctive behavior 本能行為
Instinctive behavior comes naturally to an animal.
本能行為是動物與生俱來的。

learned behavior

instinctive behavior

Checkup

A

Write | 請依提示寫出正確的英文單字和片語。

1 演化;進化(n.)	_____	9 精細胞	_____
2 適應;適合(n.)	_____	10 卵細胞	_____
3 行為;舉止	_____	11 進化(v.)	_____
4 種;物種	_____	12 適應(v.)	_____
5 基因;遺傳因子	_____	13 經遺傳獲得	_____
6 遺傳的;基因的	g_____	14 轉移	_____
7 遺傳的	i_____	15 行為舉止(v.)	_____
8 遺傳(n.)	_____	16 特性;特色;特徵	c_____

B

Complete the Sentences | 請在空格中填入最適當的答案,並視情況做適當的變化。

adaptation	egg cell	evolution	behavior	gene
heredity	sperm cell	genetic	inherited	species

1 The _____ of a species can take generations to occur.
物種的演化可能耗時數世代才會發生。

2 _____ is how animals act in certain situations.
行為是指動物面對特定情況時的反應。

3 _____ are the changes animals make to get used to a new environment.
適應,是動物使本身習慣新環境的改變。

4 There are millions of _____ of animals on the planet.
地球上有數以百萬計的動物物種。

5 _____ are what determine which traits an animal inherits from its parents.
基因決定了動物會從親代遺傳到何種特徵。

6 _____ is the passing of certain characteristics from parents to their offspring.
遺傳是指從親代傳遞至子代的某些特徵。

7 Animals pass on _____ material to their babies.
動物傳遞遺傳物質給下一代。

8 Genes are transferred when a _____ _____ and an egg cell join.
精細胞與卵細胞結合時,基因就會改變。

C

Read and Choose | 閱讀下列句子,並且選出最適當的答案。

1 Animals (behave | evolve) by developing new characteristics that help them survive.

2 Animals (behave | inherit) differently according to their situation.

3 Genes are (transferred | learned) from parents to their offspring.

4 (Instinctive | Learned) behavior comes naturally to an animal.

Look, Read, and Write | 看圖並且依照提示，在空格中填入正確答案。

1  ▶ the way in which living things change and develop over millions of years
_____

3 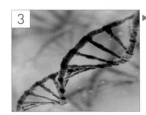 ▶ a part of a cell that controls or influences the appearance, growth, etc., of a living thing
_____

2  ▶ the passing of certain characteristics from parents to their offspring
_____

4 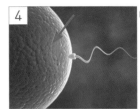 ▶ a cell that is produced by the female sexual organs
_____

E

Read and Answer | 閱讀並且回答下列問題。 🔊 052

Heredity

People often look very similar to their parents. They might have the same face. Or they have the same color hair or eyes. They might be tall or short like their parents. Why do they look this way? The answer is heredity.

Heredity is the passing of traits from a parent to his or her offspring. This happens because of genes. Genes contain DNA. DNA is the basic building block for life. Both parents pass on their genes to their offspring. So the offspring may resemble the mother, father, or both.

There are dominant and recessive genes. Dominant genes affect the body more than recessive genes. Recessive genes exist in a body. But they do not affect it. Dominant genes, however, affect the organism.

Genes do not just determine an organism's physical characteristics. They also determine the organism's mental characteristics. This can include intelligence. And it may even affect personality, too.

Answer the questions.

1   Why do children often look like their parents?   _____

2   What do genes have?   _____

3   What kind of genes are there?   _____

4   Which genes affect an organism?   _____

The History of the Earth

Key Words

🔊 053

01 eon
[ˈiən]

(n.)（地質）宙／元；萬古　*eternity (n.) 永恆；無窮

An eon is an extremely long period of time that can be more than a billion years. 宙是一段極久的時間，它有可能超過十億年。

02 era
[ˈɪrə]

(n.)（地質）代；紀元；年代　*Christian era 西元
*epoch (n.)（地質）世；紀元

An era is an important time period in history.
代是歷史上很重要的一段時間。

03 formation
[fɔrˈmeʃən]

(n.) 形成；構成　*the formation of sth. 某物的形成　*rock formation 岩石結構

The formation of the Earth took billions of years to occur.
地球的形成耗時數十億年發生。

04 dating
[ˈdetɪŋ]

(n.) 年代；時期　*radiocarbon dating 放射性碳定年法　*date back（時間）追溯

Carbon dating is one method scientists use to determine how old something is. 碳定年法是一種用來測定某物年歲的科學方法。

05 geology
[dʒɪˈɑlədʒɪ]

(n.) 地質學　*the geology of somewhere（某地區的）地質（情況）

Geology is the study of the Earth, rocks, and the changes that have occurred to the Earth.
地質學是指對地球、岩石以及地球發生的改變所做的研究。

06 topography
[təˈpɑɡrəfɪ]

(n.) 地形；地勢；地貌　*topographer (n.) 地誌作者；地形測量員

Topography is the shape of landforms in an area.
地形是指某個地貌的形狀。

07 plate
[plet]

(n.) 板塊　*plate boundary 板塊邊界　*Eurasian Plate 歐亞板塊

The Earth's crust is made up of many pieces of plates.
地殼由許多板塊所組成。

08 fault
[fɔlt]

(n.) 斷層　*fault line 斷層線　*San Andreas Fault 聖安德列斯斷層

A fault is a boundary line where two plates meet one another.
斷層是指兩個板塊彼此接觸的邊界線。

09 continental drift
[ˌkɑntəˈnɛntl̩ drɪft]

(n.) 大陸漂移　*continental crust 大陸地殼

The Earth's continents move around very slowly because of continental drift. 由於大陸漂移，地球的陸地移動地非常緩慢。

10 collision
[kəˈlɪʒən]

(n.) 碰撞　*in a collision with sth. 與某物相撞

A collision between two plates can cause earthquakes.
兩個板塊間的碰撞可能會造成地震。

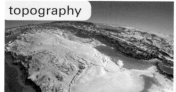
topography

plate boundary

fault line

continental drift

elapse
[ɪˈlæps]
（時間）過去；消逝
A long time elapsed while the Earth was being formed.
地球形成的同時，很長的一段時間也隨之過去。

pass
（時間）推移；流逝
A long time passed while the Earth was being formed.
地球形成的同時，很長的一段時間也隨之推移。

date
確定年代
Scientists try to date the various layers of rocks on the planet.
科學家試圖去確定地球上不同岩石層的年代。

strike
碰撞
Two plates striking each other cause an earthquake.
兩個板塊彼此碰撞會造成地震。

collide with
碰撞
Two plates colliding with each other cause an earthquake.
兩個板塊彼此碰撞會造成地震。

crash into
碰撞
Two plates crashing into each other cause an earthquake.
兩個板塊彼此碰撞會造成地震。

shake
搖動
Some earthquakes shake the ground very violently. 有些地震會使地面猛烈地搖動。

tremor
[ˈtrɛmɚ]
震動
After the big earthquake, there were some minor tremors.
大地震過後，會有一些較小的餘震。

seism
[saɪˈzəm]
地震（較少用）
The seism shook the ground and caused a lot of damage.
地震使地面搖動並造成許多損害。

tsunami
[tsuˈnɑmi]
海嘯
A tsunami is a very large wave often caused by an earthquake.
海嘯是一個非常大的巨浪，通常由地震造成。

tidal wave
海嘯
A tidal wave is a huge wave that happens very close to shore.
海嘯是發生在非常靠近岸邊的巨浪。

Geologic Eras
地質年代

the Precambrian Era 前寒武紀
the Mesozoic Era 中生代

the Paleozoic Era 古生代
the Cenozoic Era 新生代

Checkup

A

Write | 請依提示寫出正確的英文單字和片語。

1	宙／元；萬古	_____	
2	代；紀元；年代	_____	
3	形成；構成	_____	
4	年代；時期	_____	
5	地質學	_____	
6	地形；地勢	_____	
7	板塊	_____	
8	斷層	_____	

9	大陸漂移	_____	
10	碰撞(n.)	_____	
11	（時間）過去；消逝	e _____	
12	確定年代	_____	
13	碰撞	s _____	
14	碰撞(v.)	c _____	
15	搖動	_____	
16	震動	_____	

B

Complete the Sentences | 請在空格中填入最適當的答案，並視情況做適當的變化。

collision	era	eon	geology	topography
formation	plate	dating	fault	continental drift

1 An _____ is an extremely long period of time that can be more than a billion years.
宙是一段極久的時間，它有可能超過十億年。

2 An _____ is an important time period in history. 代是歷史上很重要的一段時間。

3 Carbon _____ is one method scientists use to determine how old something is.
碳定年法是一種用來測定某物年歲的科學方法。

4 _____ is the shape of landforms in an area.
地形是指一地地貌的形狀。

5 A _____ is a boundary line where two plates meet one another.
斷層是指兩個板塊彼此接觸的邊界線。

6 The _____ of the Earth took billions of years to occur.
地球的形成耗時數十億年發生。

7 The Earth's continents move around very slowly because of _____
_____. 由於大陸漂移，地球的陸地移動地非常緩慢。

8 A _____ between two plates can cause earthquakes.
兩個板塊間的碰撞可能會造成地震。

C

Read and Choose | 閱讀下列句子，並且選出最適當的答案。

1 A long time (elapsed | caused) while the Earth was being formed.

2 Scientists try to (pass | date) the various layers of rocks on the planet.

3 Two plates (crashing | colliding) with each other cause an earthquake.

4 After the big earthquake, there were some minor (tremors | seism).

Look, Read, and Write | 看圖並且依照提示，在空格中填入正確答案。

1

▶ a science that studies rocks, layers of soil, etc., to learn about the Earth and its life

_____

3

▶ a break in the Earth's crust

_____

2

▶ one of the large pieces of the surface of the earth that move separately

_____

4

▶ an extremely large wave caused by a movement of the earth under the sea

_____

Read and Answer | 閱讀並且回答下列問題。 ◉ 056

The Formation of the Earth

Billions of years ago, the sun formed. There was a huge disk of rocks and gases in the solar system. Eventually, these rocks and gases began to form planets. This was about 4.5 billion years ago. Earth was the third planet from the sun. At first, the Earth was extremely hot. But, over millions of years, it began to cool down.

As the Earth cooled, water vapor started forming in the atmosphere. This caused the creation of clouds all over the planet. Soon, the clouds began dropping huge amounts of water all over the planet. This caused the creation of the Earth's oceans, seas, rivers, and lakes.

But the Earth 4.5 billion years ago looked different from the Earth of today. Today, there are seven continents. In the past, this was not true. There have been different numbers of continents. Once, there was just one continent on the whole planet. Why? One clue is the theory of plate tectonics. There are many plates that make up the Earth's crust. These plates are huge pieces of land. And they are constantly moving. As the Earth ages, the plates slowly move around. Today, there are seven continents. In the future, perhaps there will be more or less.

Fill in the blanks.

1   The Earth started to form about _____ years ago.
2   Water _____ started forming when the Earth cooled.
3   There are seven _____ on the Earth today.
4   Because of _____, the plates in the crust are constantly moving.   Unit 14   69

Unit 15 The Weather and Water Cycle 天氣與水循環

Key Words
🔊 057

01 evaporation
[ˌɪˌvæpəˋreʃən]
(n.) 蒸發；發散　*evapotranspiration (n.) 蒸發散
In hot weather, **evaporation** happens quickly as water becomes water vapor. 天氣炎熱時，蒸發的現象在水變為水蒸氣時迅速發生。

02 condensation
[ˌkɑndɛnˋseʃən]
(n.) 凝結；凝聚　*cloud condensation nucleus 雲凝結核
Condensation is the process that lets water vapor form into clouds in the atmosphere. 凝結是指水蒸氣在大氣中形成雲的過程。

03 weather map
[ˋwɛðɚ mæp]
(n.) 天氣圖　*weatherman/weathergirl (n.) 男／女天氣預報主持人
A **weather map** shows the different kinds of weather a region is having. 天氣圖顯示了一個地區所擁有的不同天氣情況。

04 humidity
[hjuˋmɪdətɪ]
(n.) 濕度　*absolute/relative humidity 絕對／相對濕度
The **humidity** level measures the amount of moisture in the air. 濕度能顯示出空氣中的水分含量。

05 air mass
[ɛr mæs]
(n.) 氣團　*tropical marine air mass 熱帶海洋氣團
　　　*continental polar air mass 極地大陸氣團
A large body of air that has the same characteristics is an **air mass**. 一群龐大且擁有相同性質的空氣稱為氣團。

06 cold front
[kold frʌnt]
(n.) 冷鋒　*frontal surface 鋒面（冷暖氣團相遇的交界面）
A **cold front** often brings colder and drier weather.
冷鋒通常帶來較寒冷且乾燥的天氣。

07 warm front
[wɔrm frʌnt]
(n.) 暖鋒　*stationary front 滯留鋒（冷暖氣團實力相當）
A **warm front** often brings warmer and more humid weather.
暖鋒通常帶來較溫暖且潮濕的天氣。

08 isobar
[ˌaɪsəˋbɑr]
(n.) 等壓線　*isotherm (n.) 等溫線　*isohyet (n.) 等雨量線
An **isobar** is a line on a weather map that connects places with equal air pressure. 等壓線是指天氣圖中連接氣壓相同地區的線。

09 wind speed
[wɪnd spid]
(n.) 風速　*wind gauge 風力計；風速計
Hurricanes are categorized by their **wind speed**.
颶風通常由它們的風速來分級。

10 runoff
[ˌrʌnˋɔf]
(n.) 降雨徑流　*surface runoff 地表逕流
　　　*precipitation (n.)（雨或雪的）降落；降水
Rain that does not soak into the soil becomes **runoff**.
沒有滲入泥土的雨成為降雨徑流。

Weather Map

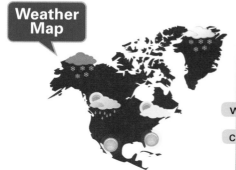

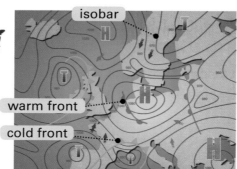
isobar / warm front / cold front

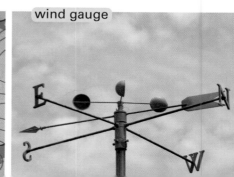
wind gauge

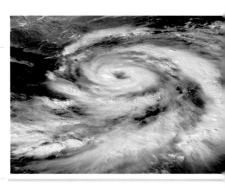

move up 上升
When water vapor **moves up** in the air, it becomes cooler.
當水蒸氣上升到空氣中，天氣變得較涼爽。

rise into 上升
When water vapor **rises into** the air, it becomes cooler.
當水蒸氣上升到空氣中，天氣變得較涼爽。

soak into 滲入
Some precipitation **soaks into** the ground. 有些降水會滲入土壤。

seep into 滲入
Some precipitation **seeps into** the ground. 有些降水會滲入土壤。

rate 劃分等級
Hurricanes are **rated** on a scale of 1 to 5. 颶風被劃分為一到五等級。

Word Families ● 059

storm surge 暴潮
A **storm surge** can cause flooding. 暴潮會帶來洪水。

eye 風眼
The center of a tropical storm is called the **eye**. 熱帶風暴的中心稱為風眼。

raindrop 雨滴
How does a **raindrop** form? 雨滴如何形成？

droplet 小滴
When the water **droplets** become too heavy to stay in the air, they become raindrops that fall to the earth.
一旦水滴重得無法待在空氣中，就會成為雨滴降落在地面。

high pressure 高氣壓
High pressure systems can cause sunny weather. 高氣壓系統帶來晴天。

low pressure 低氣壓
Low pressure systems can cause stormy weather. 低氣壓系統帶來暴風雨。

The Layers of the Atmosphere 大氣層

thermosphere 熱氣層／增溫層

mesosphere 中氣層

stratosphere 平流層

troposphere 對流層

Checkup

A

Write | 請依提示寫出正確的英文單字和片語。

1	蒸發;發散	_____	
2	凝結;凝聚	_____	
3	天氣圖	_____	
4	濕度	_____	
5	氣團	_____	
6	冷鋒	_____	
7	暖鋒	_____	
8	等壓線	_____	
9	風速	_____	
10	降雨徑流	_____	
11	上升	r_____	
12	滲入	_____	
13	劃分等級	_____	
14	暴潮	_____	
15	小滴	_____	
16	高氣壓	_____	

B

Complete the Sentences | 請在空格中填入最適當的答案,並視情況做適當的變化。

cold front	condensation	evaporation	runoff	air mass
warm front	weather map	wind speed	humidity	isobar

1 In hot weather, _____ happens quickly as water becomes water vapor.
天氣炎熱時,蒸發的現象在水變為水蒸氣時迅速發生。

2 _____ is the process that lets water vapor form into clouds in the atmosphere. 凝結是指水蒸氣在大氣中形成雲的過程。

3 The _____ level measures the amount of moisture in the air.
濕度能顯示空氣中的水分含量。

4 Rain that does not soak into the soil becomes _____.
沒有滲入泥土的雨成為降雨徑流。

5 A large body of air that has the same characteristics is an _____ _____.
一群龐大且擁有相同性質的空氣稱為氣團。

6 A _____ _____ often brings colder and drier weather.
冷鋒通常帶來較寒冷且乾燥的天氣。

7 An _____ is a line on a weather map that connects places with equal air pressure. 等壓線是指天氣圖中連接氣壓相同地區的線。

8 Hurricanes are categorized by their _____ _____.
颶風通常由它們的風速來分級。

C

Read and Choose | 閱讀下列句子,並且選出最適當的答案。

1 Some precipitation (evaporates | seeps) into the ground.

2 Hurricanes are (rated | connected) on a scale of 1 to 5.

3 When water vapor (moves | runs) up in the air, it becomes cooler.

4 (Low | High) pressure systems can cause sunny weather.

D

Look, Read, and Write | 看圖並且依照提示，在空格中填入正確答案。

 ▸ a map that shows what the current and future weather in an area

_____

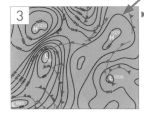 ▸ a measurement of how much water there is in the air

_____

 ▸ a line on a weather map joining all the places that have the same air pressure

_____

 ▸ the center of a tropical storm

_____

E

Read and Answer | 閱讀並且回答下列問題。 ⏺ 060

The Water Cycle

There is a limited amount of water on the Earth. In fact, for billions of years, the amount of water has not changed. However, water can often appear in many different forms. These all make up the water cycle.

The first stage is evaporation. This happens when the sun's heat on rivers, lakes, seas, and oceans causes water to turn into water vapor. The water vapor then rises into the air.

The second stage is condensation. As water vapor rises, the air gets colder. This causes the water vapor to turn into tiny water droplets. These droplets come together to form clouds.

The third stage is precipitation. The water droplets fall to the ground in some form. The most common kind of precipitation is rain. But, in cold weather, snow, sleet, or ice may fall instead.

The final stage is collection. When water falls to the ground, it may flow into rivers, lakes, seas, or oceans. Or it may go down into the ground. There, it becomes groundwater. But the water cycle goes on and on.

What is true? Write T(true) or F(false).

1   The amount of water on the Earth is always changing.   _____
2   Evaporation is the first stage of the water cycle.   _____
3   Water vapor is a form of ice.   _____
4   Rain, sleet, and snow are all kinds of precipitation.   _____

Review Test 3

A

Write | 請依提示寫出正確的英文單字和片語。

1. 探究；調查(n.) _____
2. 推論；推斷(n.) _____
3. 微生物 _____
4. 原生生物 _____
5. 演化；進化(n.) _____
6. 遺傳(n.) _____
7. 板塊 _____
8. 斷層 _____
9. 天氣圖 _____
10. 氣團 _____
11. 假說；前提 _____
12. 分析 _____
13. 細胞核 _____
14. 細胞質 _____
15. 經遺傳獲得 _____
16. 轉移 _____
17. 大陸漂移 _____
18. 碰撞(v.) _____
19. 滲入 _____
20. 劃分等級 _____

B

Choose the Correct Word | 請選出與鋪底字意思相近的答案。

1 Scientists form a hypothesis about what they think will happen.
   a. inquire　　　　　b. predict　　　　　c. hypothesize

2 Analyze data to answer questions or to solve a problem.
   a. Infer　　　　　b. Observe　　　　　c. Interpret

3 Multi-celled organisms grow as their cells divide.
   a. split　　　　　b. duplicate　　　　　c. replicate

4 A long time elapsed while the Earth was being formed.
   a. dated　　　　　b. passed　　　　　c. happened

C

Complete the Sentences | 請在空格中填入最適當的答案，並視情況做適當的變化。

fungus	collision	runoff	gene

1 Mushrooms and yeasts are two kinds of _____. 蘑菇和酵母是兩種菌類植物。

2 _____ are what determine which traits an animal inherits from its parents.
   基因決定了動物會從親代遺傳到何種特徵。

3 A _____ between two plates can cause earthquakes.
   兩個板塊間的碰撞可能會造成地震。

4 Rain that does not soak into the soil becomes _____.
   沒有滲入泥土的雨成為降雨徑流。

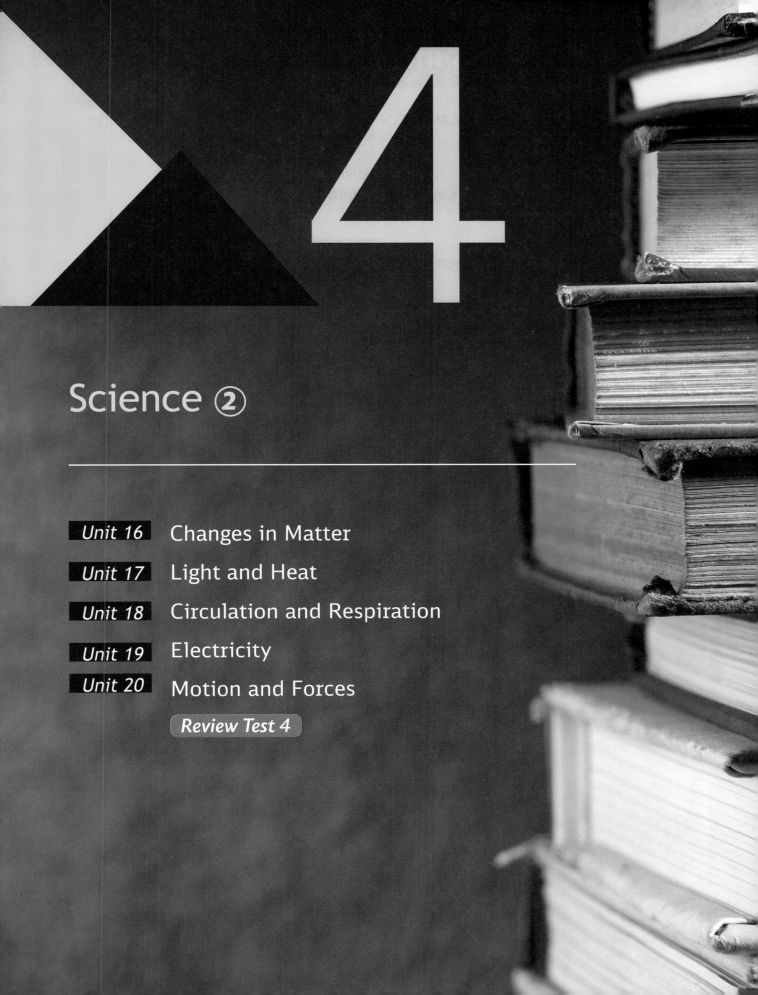

4

Science ②

Key Words 🔊 061

01 matter
[ˋmætɚ]
(n.) 物質　*inert/organic/inorganic matter 惰性／有機／無機物質
Matter is made up of atoms. 物質由原子組成。

02 element
[ˋɛləmənt]
(n.) 元素　*chemical element 化學元素　*periodic table 元素週期表
Elements are the basic substances that make up all matter.
元素是構成所有物質的基本要件。

03 property
[ˋprɑpɚtɪ]
(n.) 特性　*medicinal property 藥用特性
Matter can be described by **properties**. 物質可以經由特性來描述。

04 atom
[ˋætəm]
(n.) 原子　*atom bomb 原子彈　*atomic number 原子序
An **atom** is the smallest unit of an element. 原子是元素的最小單位。

05 molecule
[ˋmɑləˏkjul]
(n.) 分子　*molecular weight 分子量
A **molecule** is created when two or more atoms join together.
兩個以上的原子結合在一起產生分子。

06 particle
[ˋpɑrtɪkḷ]
(n.) 粒子；質點　*particle accelerator 粒子加速器
An atom is the smallest **particle** of a substance.
原子是物質中的最小粒子。

07 compound
[ˋkɑmpaʊnd]
(n.) 混合物；化合物　*carbon compounds 碳化合物
A **compound** is a substance that is formed by the chemical
combination of two or more elements.
混合物是兩種以上元素經由化學結合而形成的物質。

08 solubility
[ˏsɑljəˋbɪlətɪ]
(n.) 溶解度　*water-soluble vitamins/compounds 水溶性維生素／化合物
An object's **solubility** is how easily it dissolves in water.
物體的溶解度是指其在水中溶解的程度。

09 physical change
[ˋfɪzɪkḷ tʃendʒ]
(n.) 物理變化
A **physical change** is a change that does not make a new substance.
物理變化是指不會產生新物質的變化。

10 chemical reaction
[ˋkɛmɪkḷ rɪˋækʃən]
(n.) 化學反應
When atoms become new substances, they undergo a **chemical
reaction**. 當原子變成一種新物質，表示它們經過了化學反應。

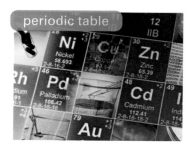
periodic table

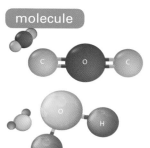
molecule

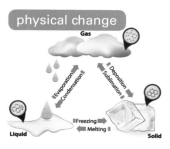
physical change

chemical reaction

🔊 062

take up	佔據
	Everything that has mass and **takes up** space is matter.
	物質為擁有質量且佔有空間的事物。
take place	發生
	When water boils, some physical changes **take place**.
	水沸騰時會發生一些物理變化。
occur	發生
	When water boils, some physical changes **occur**. 水沸騰時會發生一些物理變化。
dissolve [dɪˋzɑlv]	溶解
	Oil does not **dissolve** in water. 油不溶於水。
break down	分離
	It is possible to **break down** a compound into separate elements.
	將混合物分離為單獨的元素是有可能的。
break up	分離
	It is possible to **break up** a compound into separate elements.
	將混合物分離為單獨的元素是有可能的。
combine [kəmˋbaɪn]	結合
	Hydrogen and oxygen **combine** to form water. 氫氣與氧氣結合形成水。
join with	與……結合
	Hydrogen **joins with** oxygen to form water. 氫氣與氧氣結合形成水。
react	做出反應
	Elements **react** differently to one another. 元素對彼此做出不同的反應。

Word Families

🔊 063

substance [ˋsʌbstəns]	物質
	All physical matter is **substance**. 所有的實體物都是物質。
material [məˋtɪrɪəl]	材料
	The substance that things are made of is their **material**. 形成事物的物質稱為材料。
matter	物質
	The Earth is made of many kinds of solid **matter**. 地球由許多種固體物質組成。

Common Elements and Their Symbols
常見元素及其代號

hydrogen (H) 氫氣 [ˋhaɪdrədʒən]
nitrogen (N) 氮氣 [ˋnaɪtrədʒən]
iron (Fe) 鐵
silver (Ag) 銀

oxygen (O) 氧氣 [ˋɑksədʒən]
helium (He) 氦氣 [ˋhilɪəm]
gold (Au) 金

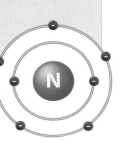

Checkup

A

Write | 請依提示寫出正確的英文單字和片語。

1 元素	_____	9 化學反應 _____
2 特性	_____	10 物質 m_____
3 原子	_____	11 佔據 _____
4 分子	_____	12 發生 t_____
5 粒子；顆粒	_____	13 溶解 _____
6 混合物；化合物	_____	14 分離 _____
7 溶解度	_____	15 結合 _____
8 物理變化	_____	16 做出反應 _____

B

Complete the Sentences | 請在空格中填入最適當的答案，並視情況做適當的變化。

matter	physical change	particle	element	atom
compound	chemical reaction	property	solubility	molecule

1 _____ are the basic substances that make up all matter.
元素是構成所有物質的基本要件。

2 _____ is made up of atoms. 物質由原子組成。

3 An _____ is the smallest unit of an element. 原子是元素的最小單位。

4 A _____ is created when two or more atoms join together.
兩個以上的原子結合在一起產生分子。

5 An atom is the smallest _____ of a substance. 原子是物質中的最小粒子。

6 When atoms become new substances, they undergo a _____
_____. 當原子變成一種新物質，表示它們經過了化學反應。

7 A _____ is a substance that is formed by the chemical combination of two
or more elements. 混合物是兩種以上元素經由化學結合而形成的物質。

8 Matter can be described by _____. 物質可以經由特性來描述。

C

Read and Choose | 閱讀下列句子，並且選出最適當的答案。

1 Everything that has mass and (takes | makes) up space is matter.

2 When water boils, some (chemical | physical) changes take place.

3 Oil does not (combine | dissolve) in water.

4 Elements (react | occur) differently to one another.

D

Look, Read, and Write | 看圖並且依照提示，在空格中填入正確答案。

1  ▸ the smallest unit of any chemical element

_____

3 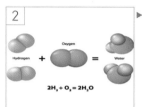 ▸ the ability of being dissolved in a liquid

_____

2  ▸ a chemical that combines two or more elements

_____

4  ▸ a usually reversible change in the physical properties of a substance

_____

E

Read and Answer | 閱讀並且回答下列問題。 🔊 064

Physical and Chemical Changes

Matter often undergoes many changes. There are two main types of changes. They are physical and chemical changes.

There are a lot of physical changes. They can often involve changing a substance into a solid, a liquid, or a gas. For instance, melting ice to get water is a physical change. And boiling water to get water vapor is another one. But it is also possible to make physical changes in other ways. For instance, put some sugar in water and then stir it. The sugar dissolves. That is a physical change. Or, simply tear up a piece of paper. That is another physical change.

Chemical changes are different. Chemical changes involve the forming of a new compound. For instance, if sodium and chlorine come together, they undergo a chemical reaction. The result is the creation of salt. Photosynthesis is another chemical reaction. Water and carbon dioxide change into sugar and oxygen.

What is NOT true?

1   Matter can undergo physical or chemical changes.
2   Ice melting to become water is a chemical change.
3   Sugar dissolving in water is a physical change.
4   Photosynthesis is a chemical change.

Key Words
🔊 065

01 light wave
[laɪt wev]

(n.) 光波　*light meter 曝光表；測光儀　*light year 光年
Light waves are a form of energy that moves faster than anything else in the universe.
光波是能量的一種形式，它行進的速度比宇宙中的任何事物都來得快。

02 reflection
[rɪ`flɛkʃən]

(n.) 反射　*reflected ray 反射光（線）　*incident ray 入射光（線）
Reflection is the bouncing back of light when it hits a surface.
反射是指光線撞擊到某一表面時所產生的光線反彈。

03 refraction
[rɪ`frækʃən]

(n.) 折射　*index of refraction 折射率　*angle of refraction 折射角
Refraction is the bending of light when it goes through an object or surface. 折射是指光線通過一物體或表面時，所產生的光偏折現象。

04 thermal
[`θɝml̩]

(a.) 熱的；熱量的　*thermal energy 熱能　*thermal imaging 熱成像
Thermal energy measures the heat of an object.
熱能用來度量物體的溫度。

05 conduction
[kən`dʌkʃən]

(n.) （物）傳導　*thermal conduction 熱傳導
The transfer of heat by matter to carry it is called conduction.
經由物體傳送的方式來傳熱，稱為傳導。

06 convection
[kən`vɛkʃən]

(n.) （物）對流　*convection heater 對流加熱器（=convector）
The transfer of heat by moving through a heated liquid or gas is called convection. 經由受熱液體或氣體的流動來傳熱，稱為對流。

07 radiation
[ˌredɪ`eʃən]

(n.) 輻射　*microwave/ultraviolet radiation 微波／紫外線輻射
The transfer of heat without matter to carry it is called radiation.
不需靠物體傳送的方式來傳熱，稱為輻射。

08 conductivity
[ˌkɑndʌk`tɪvətɪ]

(n.) 傳導性　*thermal conductivity 導熱係數
An object's conductivity is its ability to transfer heat.
物質的傳導性是指其傳熱的能力。

09 radiate
[`redɪˌet]

(v.) 散發；輻射　*to radiate from sth. 從某物散發出；從某物向四周輻射狀發散
Heat can radiate from objects like the sun.
熱能可以從像太陽這樣的物體散發出來。

10 thermogram
[`θɝməˌgræm]

(n.) 溫度自記曲線　*thermostat (n.) 恆溫器
Scientists use thermograms to detect infrared rays.
科學家利用溫度自記曲線來探測紅外線。

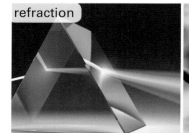
refraction

conduction

convection

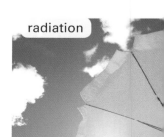
radiation

Power Verbs
🔊 066

conduct　傳導
Some objects conduct heat very well. 有些物體導熱良好。

transfer　轉換
It is possible to transfer heat from one substance to another.
將熱能由一個物質轉換至另一個物質是有可能的。

pass through　通過
Light passes through glass. 光線通過玻璃。

see through　看穿
You can see through glass. 你可以看穿玻璃。

reflect　反射
A mirror reflects light by making it bounce back. 鏡子經由反彈的方式來反射光線。

refract　折射
Water refracts light by bending light waves. 水經由彎曲光波的方式來折射光線。

Word Families
🔊 067

transparent
[træns`pɛrənt]　透明的
It is possible to easily see through a transparent object.
看穿透明的物體很容易。

translucent
[træns`lusnt]　半透明的
It is difficult to see through a translucent object.
看穿半透明的物體很困難。

opaque
[o`pek]　不透明的
It is impossible to see through an opaque object.
看穿不透明的物體是不可能的。

convex lens
[`kɑnvɛks lɛnz]　凸透鏡
A convex lens curves outward. 凸透鏡的曲線向外。

concave lens
[`kɑnkev lɛnz]　凹透鏡
A concave lens curves inward. 凹透鏡的曲線向內。

transparent

translucent

opaque

convex lens

concave lens

Checkup

A

Write | 請依提示寫出正確的英文單字和片語。

1 光波	_____	9 散發；輻射(v.)	_____
2 反射(n.)	_____	10 溫度自記曲線	_____
3 折射(n.)	_____	11 轉換	_____
4 熱的；熱量的	_____	12 通過	_____
5 （物）傳導(n.)	_____	13 看透	_____
6 （物）對流	_____	14 透明的	_____
7 輻射(n.)	_____	15 半透明的	_____
8 傳導性	_____	16 不透明的	_____

B

Complete the Sentences | 請在空格中填入最適當的答案，並視情況做適當的變化。

refraction	reflection	light wave	conduction	radiation
radiate	convection	thermogram	thermal	conductivity

1 _____ _____ are a form of energy that moves faster than anything else in the universe. 光波是能量的一種形式，它行進的速度比宇宙中的任何事物都來得快。

2 _____ is the bending of light when it goes through an object or surface.
折射是指光線通過一物體或表面時所產生的光偏折現象。

3 _____ is the bouncing back of light when it hits a surface.
反射是指光線撞擊到表面時所產生的光線反彈。

4 The transfer of heat by matter to carry it is called _____.
經由物體傳送的方式來傳熱，稱為傳導。

5 The transfer of heat by moving through a heated liquid or gas is called
_____. 經由受熱液體或氣體的流動來傳熱，稱為對流。

6 _____ energy measures the heat of an object. 熱能用來判斷物體的溫度。

7 Heat can _____ from objects like the sun. 熱能可以從像太陽這樣的物體散發出來。

8 Scientists use _____ to detect infrared rays.
科學家利用溫度自記曲線來探測紅外線。

C

Read and Choose | 閱讀下列句子，並且選出最適當的答案。

1 Some objects (conduct | pass) heat very well.

2 You can (see | pass) through glass.

3 A mirror (refracts | reflects) light by making it bounce back.

4 It is difficult to see through a (transparent | translucent) object.

Look, Read, and Write | 看圖並且依照提示，在空格中填入正確答案。

1  ▶ the process by which heat or electricity goes through a substance

_____

3  ▶ the flow of heat through a gas or a liquid

_____

2  ▶ energy from heat or light that you cannot see

_____

4  ▶ the ability to move heat or electricity from one place to another

_____

E

Read and Answer | 閱讀並且回答下列問題。 ⊙ 068

Conduction, Convection, and Radiation

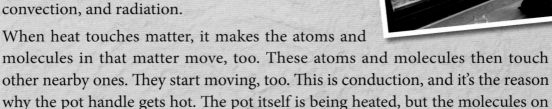

Heat is a form of energy. It can move from place to place. There are three ways it can move: conduction, convection, and radiation.

When heat touches matter, it makes the atoms and molecules in that matter move, too. These atoms and molecules then touch other nearby ones. They start moving, too. This is conduction, and it's the reason why the pot handle gets hot. The pot itself is being heated, but the molecules on the pot touch those on the handle. They make the handle hot, too.

Convection is the second way that heat moves. Convection happens when something that can move becomes heated in gravity. This can be air, water, or some other liquid. Ovens work by convection. Coils in the oven heat the air. The air rises, where it cooks the food. The air then cools, so it goes down. Then the coils heat it again, so it rises once more.

Radiation is the third way that heat moves. This occurs when heat moves as waves. The sun heats the Earth by radiation. The sun sends out heat in the form of waves. The waves reach the Earth, where they provide heat.

Fill in the blanks.

1 Heat is a kind of _____.

2 _____ explains why pot handles get hot.

3 Most ovens cook food because of _____.

4 The Earth is heated by the sun through _____.

Key Words 🔊 069

01 artery
['artərɪ]

(n.) 動脈　*carotid artery 頸動脈　*coronary artery 冠狀動脈
Arteries are the tubes that carry blood from your heart to the rest of your body. 動脈是指從心臟攜帶血液至身體其他部分的血管。

02 vein
[ven]

(n.) 靜脈　*jugular vein 頸靜脈　*varicose vein 靜脈曲張
Veins are blood vessels that move blood around the body.
靜脈是指運送血液來回全身的血管。

03 aorta
[e'ɔrtə]

(n.) 主動脈　*aortic valve 主動脈瓣（分隔大動脈和左心室的瓣膜）
The aorta is the main artery and the biggest blood vessel of all.
主動脈是大動脈，也是最粗大的血管。

04 blood vessel
[blʌd 'vɛsl̩]

(n.) 血管　*to burst a blood vessel 十分生氣；大動肝火
Blood circulates throughout the body in blood vessels.
血液在體內的血管中循環。

05 blood cell
[blʌd sɛl]

(n.) 血球　*corpuscle (n.) 血細胞；血球　*blood count 血球數
There are three types of blood cells in your body: red blood cells, white blood cells, and platelets. 你的體內有三種血球：紅血球、白血球以及血小板。

06 platelet
['pletlɪt]

(n.) 血小板　*platelet aggregation 血小板聚集
Platelets help stop bleeding when you get a cut or are wounded.
當你割傷或受傷時，血小板能幫你止血。

07 blood pressure
[blʌd 'prɛʃɚ]

(n.) 血壓　*take the blood pressure 測量血壓
　　　　　 *high/low blood pressure 高／低血壓
Blood pressure is the force with which blood flows around your body.
血壓是指血液流動於體內所造成的壓力。

08 heart rate
[hɑrt ret]

(n.) 心率　*heartbeat (n.) 心跳　*pulse (n.) 脈搏
A person's heart rate is the number of times the heart beats in a minute. 心率是指一個人心臟一分鐘跳動的次數。

09 respiration
[,rɛspə'reʃən]

(n.) 呼吸　*respiration rate 呼吸速率　*artificial respiration 人工呼吸
The act of breathing is called respiration. 呼出吸入氣體的行為稱為呼吸。

10 immune system
[ɪ'mjun 'sɪstəm]

(n.) 免疫系統　*immune response 免疫反應
The body's immune system fights diseases and keeps people healthy.
身體的免疫系統會對抗疾病並保持人體健康。

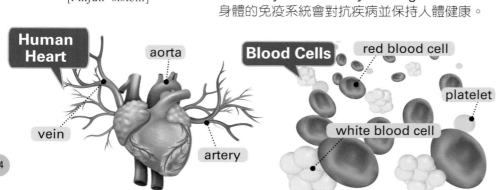

Human Heart — aorta, vein, artery
Blood Cells — red blood cell, platelet, white blood cell

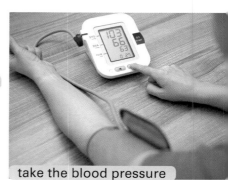

take the blood pressure

🔊 070

circulate [ˈsɝkjə‚let]	循環 Blood circulates by moving through the body. 血液經由流動全身來循環。
inhale [ɪnˈhel]	吸氣 When you inhale, you breathe in. 當你吸氣，表示你吸入氣體。
exhale [ɛksˈhel]	吐氣 When you exhale, you breathe out. 當你吐氣，表示你呼出氣體。
respire	呼吸 When you breathe in and out together, you respire. 當你吸氣與吐氣時，表示你在呼吸。
resist	抵抗；抗拒 The immune system tries to resist diseases. 免疫系統試圖去抵抗疾病。
be immune to	對……免疫 Thanks to vaccinations, some people are immune to certain viruses. 由於接種疫苗，有些人得以對特定病毒免疫。

Word Families 🔊 071

atrium [ˈɑtrɪəm]	心房 Blood enters the heart in the atrium. 血液從心房進入心臟。
ventricle [ˈvɛntrɪkl]	心室 Blood leaves the heart from the ventricles. 血液自心室離開心臟。
chamber [ˈtʃembɚ]	腔；室 There are four chambers in the heart. 心臟內有四個腔室。

The Four Chambers of the Heart
心臟的四個腔室

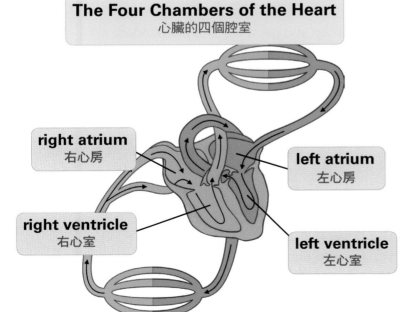

right atrium 右心房
left atrium 左心房
right ventricle 右心室
left ventricle 左心室

Cardiovascular System
心血管系統

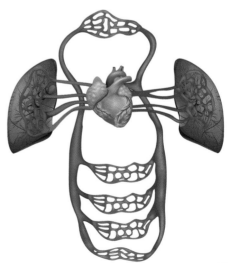

Checkup

Write | 請依提示寫出正確的英文單字和片語。

1	動脈	_____	
2	靜脈	_____	
3	主動脈	_____	
4	血管	_____	
5	血球	_____	
6	血小板	_____	
7	血壓	_____	
8	心率	_____	

9　呼吸(n.)　_____
10　免疫系統　_____
11　吸氣　_____
12　吐氣　_____
13　對……免疫　_____
14　抵抗；抗拒　_____
15　心室　_____
16　心房　_____

B

Complete the Sentences | 請在空格中填入最適當的答案，並視情況做適當的變化。

artery	aorta	respiration	immune system	blood cell
platelet	vein	heart rate	blood pressure	blood vessel

1 _____ are blood vessels that move blood around the body.
靜脈是指運送血液來回全身的血管。

2 _____ are the tubes that carry blood from your heart to the rest of your body.
動脈是指從心臟攜帶血液至身體其他部分的血管。

3 Blood circulates throughout the body in _____ _____.
血液在身體內的血管中循環。

4 There are three types of _____ _____ in your body.
你的體內有三種血球。

5 _____ help stop bleeding when you get a cut or are wounded.
當你割傷或受傷時，血小板能幫你止血。

6 _____ _____ is the force with which blood flows around your body.
血壓是指血液流動於體內所造成的壓力。

7 The act of breathing is called _____. 呼出吸入氣體的行為稱為呼吸。

8 The body's _____ _____ fights diseases and keeps people healthy.
身體的免疫系統會對抗疾病並保持人體健康。

C

Read and Choose | 閱讀下列句子，並且選出最適當的答案。

1 When you (inhale | exhale), you breathe in.
2 When you (inhale | exhale), you breathe out.
3 When you breathe in and out together, you (resist | respire).
4 There are four (atriums | chambers) in the heart.

D

Look, Read, and Write | 看圖並且依照提示，在空格中填入正確答案。

1  ▶ one of the thick tubes that carry blood from the heart to other parts of the body

_____

3 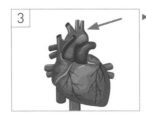 ▶ the large artery that brings blood from the heart to the rest of the body

_____

2  ▶ a tube that carries blood to the heart from the other parts of the body

_____

4 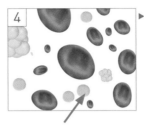 ▶ a blood cell that helps blood to stop bleeding by becoming thick and sticky

_____

E

Read and Answer | 閱讀並且回答下列問題。 🔊 072

The Circulatory System

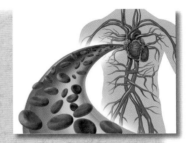

The circulatory system is the part of the body that controls the flow of blood. It has many parts. The most important is the heart. However, there are also arteries and veins that send blood throughout the body.

The heart has four chambers. They are the left and right atria and the left and right ventricles. First, blood flows into the right atrium. Then it goes to the right ventricle and into the lungs. In the lungs, oxygen is added to the blood. Then the blood returns to the heart. It goes into the left atrium and then into the left ventricle. From there, it leaves the heart by going to the aorta.

The aorta is the body's main artery. It feeds blood to the rest of the body. The body has both arteries and veins. Together, they are called blood vessels. These blood vessels take oxygen-rich blood and transport it everywhere in the body. The body then uses the blood, which loses its oxygen. Then, other veins and arteries take the oxygen-depleted blood back to the heart, and the cycle begins again.

What is NOT true?

1   The circulatory system controls the flow of blood.
2   The heart has four ventricles.
3   The main artery in the body is the aorta.
4   Blood vessels move blood throughout the body.

Unit 19 Electricity 電

Key Words 🔊 073

01	**static electricity**	*(n.)* 靜電 *electrostatic discharge 靜電放電
	[ˈstætɪk ˌɪlɛkˈtrɪsətɪ]	Static electricity is an electric charge that builds up on an object by rubbing or friction. 靜電是一種電荷，會經由摩擦物體而增大。

02	**current electricity**	*(n.)* 電流 *voltage (n.) 電壓（= electric pressure）
	[ˈkɜənt ˌɪlɛkˈtrɪsətɪ]	The flow of electric charge through a wire is **current electricity**. 電荷透過金屬線來流動稱為電流。

03	**series circuit**	*(n.)* 串聯電路
	[ˈsiriz ˈsɜkɪt]	A **series circuit** is a circuit that has only one path for the current to follow. 串聯電路是指電流只有單一路徑可以行進的電路。

04	**parallel circuit**	*(n.)* 並聯電路
	[ˈpærəˌlɛl ˈsɜkɪt]	A **parallel circuit** is a circuit that has more than one path for the current to follow. 並聯電路是指電流有一條以上的路徑可以行進的電路。

05	**charge**	*(n.)* 電荷 *charged particle 帶電離子
	[tʃɑrdʒ]	Electricity can have both positive and negative **charges**. 電可分為正電荷和負電荷。

06	**conductor**	*(n.)* 導體 *lightning rod/conductor （美／英）避雷針 *semiconductor (n.) 半導體
	[kənˈdʌktə]	A **conductor** is material that lets electricity easily move through it. 導體是能讓電流易於通過的材料。

07	**insulator**	*(n.)* 絕緣體（= nonconductor） *insulating tape 絕緣膠帶
	[ˈɪnsəˌletə]	Material that does not conduct electricity well is an **insulator**. 無法讓電流順利通過的材料稱為絕緣體。

08	**electromagnet**	*(n.)* 電磁體 *electromagnetic field 電磁場
	[ɪˈlɛktrəˌmægnɪt]	A metal surrounded by a coil becomes an **electromagnet** when an electric current runs through the coil. 當電流通過線圈，被線圈環繞住的金屬會變成電磁體。

09	**generator**	*(n.)* 發電機 *substation (n.) 變電站；配電室 *power plant 發電廠
	[ˈdʒɛnəˌretə]	A **generator** is a machine that can produce electricity. 發電機是可以產生電力的機器。

10	**hydroelectric**	*(a.)* 水力發電的 *wind power 風力發電 *solar power 太陽能發電
	[ˌhaɪdroɪˈlɛktrɪk]	**Hydroelectric** power is created from water. 水力發電用水進行發電。

Conductors

copper   gold   silver

Insulators

glass   paper   rubber

conduct 傳導
Gold and silver **conduct** electricity very well. 金和銀導電良好。

insulate 絕緣
Glass and porcelain **insulate** electricity. 玻璃與瓷器與電絕緣。

charge 將（某物）充電
You must **charge** an electrical device to use it. 你要將電器裝置充電才能使用它。

recharge 再充電
You must **recharge** a battery when it runs out of electricity.
當電池沒電時，你要幫它再充電。

Word Families 🔊 075

closed circuit 閉路
A closed circuit lets electricity flow. 閉路讓電流流動。

open circuit 開路；斷路
An open circuit does not allow electricity to flow.
開路無法讓電流流動。

potential energy 位能；勢能
Energy not being used is potential energy.
未被使用的能量稱為位能。

kinetic energy 動能
[kɪ`nɛtɪk `ɛnədʒɪ]
Energy in the process of being used is kinetic energy.
能量被使用的過程稱為動能。

geothermal energy 地熱能
[,dʒio`θɝml `ɛnədʒɪ]
Geothermal energy comes from beneath the ground.
地熱能來自地底。

solar energy 太陽能
Solar energy comes from the sun. 太陽能來自太陽。

chemical energy 化學能
Chemical energy comes from chemical reactions.
化學能來自化學反應。

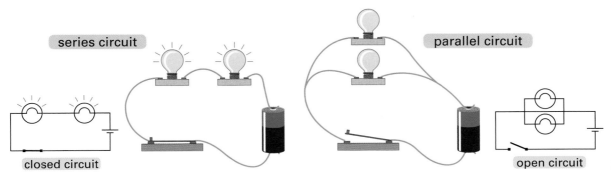

series circuit   parallel circuit

closed circuit   open circuit

Checkup

Write | 請依提示寫出正確的英文單字和片語。

1	靜電	_____	9	發電機 _____
2	電流	_____	10	水力發電的 _____
3	串聯電路	_____	11	傳導 _____
4	並聯電路	_____	12	絕緣 _____
5	電荷	_____	13	將（某物）充電 _____
6	導體	_____	14	閉路 _____
7	絕緣體	_____	15	位能；勢能 _____
8	電磁體	_____	16	動能 _____

B

Complete the Sentences | 請在空格中填入最適當的答案，並視情況做適當的變化。

parallel circuit	charge	static electricity
generator	current electricity	insulator
hydroelectric power	electromagnet	

1 Electricity can have both positive and negative _____.
電可分為正電荷和負電荷。

2 _____ _____ is an electric charge that builds up on an object by rubbing or friction. 靜電是一種電荷，會經由摩擦物體而增大。

3 The flow of electric charge through a wire is _____ _____.
電荷透過金屬線來流動稱為電流。

4 A _____ _____ is a circuit that has more than one path for the current to follow. 並聯電路是指電流有一條以上的路徑可以行進的電路。

5 Material that does not conduct electricity well is an _____.
無法讓電流順利通過的材料稱為絕緣體。

6 A metal surrounded by a coil becomes an _____ when an electric current runs through the coil. 當電流通過線圈，被線圈環繞住的金屬會變成電磁體。

7 A _____ is a machine that can produce electricity.
發電機是可以產生電力的機器。

8 _____ _____ is created from water. 水力發電用水進行發電。

C

Read and Choose | 閱讀下列句子，並且選出最適當的答案。

1 Glass and porcelain (conduct | insulate) electricity.

2 Gold and silver (conduct | insulate) electricity very well.

3 You must (recharge | build) a battery when it runs out of electricity.

4 A (open | closed) circuit lets electricity flow.

D

Look, Read, and Write | 看圖並且依照提示，在空格中填入正確答案。

1 ▶ a material or object that allows electricity or heat to move through it

_____

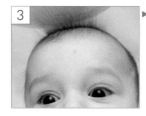
3 ▶ electricity that collects on the surface of something and does not flow as a current

_____

2 ▶ a material that allows no heat, electricity, or sound to go into or out of something

_____

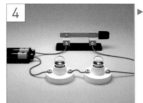
4 ▶ a circuit in which the electric current passes through each of the connected parts in turn

_____

E

Read and Answer | 閱讀並且回答下列問題。 ⊙076

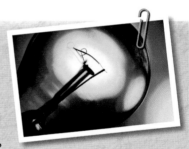

Conductors and Insulators

Electricity can move thanks to conductors. These are materials that let electricity move freely. Gold and silver are very good conductors. Some people make wires out of them. But they are both expensive. So, people often use other conductors to make wires. Most electrical wires are made from a conducting metal, such as copper.

What are some other conductors? Lots of metals are conductors. So is graphite. Water is an excellent conductor. That's why it's a bad idea to go swimming in thunderstorms. Lightning can strike the water and hurt or even kill a person. The human body is also a conductor. That's why people need to be careful around electricity.

Of course, people may want to stop the flow of electricity. To do this, people use insulators. They prevent electricity from moving from place to place. What are some of them? Plastics are very good insulators. Paper and rubber are also insulators. And glass and porcelain are two more insulators. These materials are all useful for stopping the flow of electricity.

Answer the questions.

1   What are some conductors?

_____

2   What does a conductor do?   _____

3   What does an insulator do?   _____

4   What are some insulators?   _____

Unit 20 Motion and Forces 運動與力

01 force
[fɔrs]

(n.) 力　*the force of gravity 地心引力

Force is anything that affects another body and causes it to react in some way. 任何影響另一物體並造成其某些狀態改變稱為力。

02 motion
[ˈmoʃən]

(n.) 運動　*slow motion 慢動作　*motion picture 電影；影片

Motion is a change of position of an object. 運動是指物體的位移。

03 position
[pəˈzɪʃən]

(n.) 位置　*to be in position 就位　*to take up a position 佔據位置

Position is the location of an object. 位置是指物體的所在。

04 velocity
[vəˈlɑsətɪ]

(n.) 速率　*to gain/lose velocity 加速／減速　*high/low velocity 高／低速

Velocity measures the rate of speed of an object.
速率測量出物體運動的速度。

05 acceleration
[æk͵sɛləˈreʃən]

(n.) 加速度　*accelerator (n.) 加速器；油門　*acceleration time 加速時間

Acceleration measures the rate that something increases in speed.
加速度測量出某物在速度上的增加率。

06 inertia
[ɪnˈɝʃə]

(n.) 慣性　*inertial sensor 慣性感測　*inertia reel seat belt 慣性捲筒安全帶

The law of inertia says that the state of motion of an object does not change until a force is applied to it.
慣性定律說明，除非受到外力影響，物體的運動狀態不會改變。

07 gravity
[ˈgrævətɪ]

(n.) 重力；地心引力　*center of gravity 重心　*zero gravity 零重力；失重狀態

Gravity is the force of attraction between Earth and other objects.
重力是指地球與其他物體間的吸引力。

08 gravitation
[͵grævəˈteʃən]

(n.) 萬有引力　*gravitational field 重力場

Gravitation is the force that acts between any two objects and makes them attract one another.
萬有引力作用於任兩物體間，並使它們互相吸引。

09 friction
[ˈfrɪkʃən]

(n.) 摩擦力　*to reduce/lessen friction 減少摩擦力

Two bodies rubbing against each other cause friction.
兩物體互相摩擦會產生摩擦力。

10 fulcrum
[ˈfʌlkrəm]

(n.) 支點；支軸　*lever rule 槓桿原理

The fixed point of a lever is the fulcrum.
槓桿中固定不動的一點稱為支點。

motion

gravity

friction

fulcrum

accelerate 加速
Rockets can accelerate very quickly. 火箭能迅速加速。

decelerate 減速
[diˈsɛləˌret]
Jets can decelerate very quickly. 噴射機能迅速降低速度

attract 吸引
Because of gravitation, every object in the universe attracts each other.
因為萬有引力，宇宙間每個物體都會互相吸引。

pull 吸引
Because of gravitation, every object in the universe pulls each other.
因為萬有引力，宇宙間每個物體都會互相吸引。

fall 墜落
Because of gravity, objects fall to the ground when you drop them.
因為重力，當你將物體丟下，它們會墜落至地面。

Word Families 🔊 079

Newton's Law of Motion 牛頓運動定律

the first law of motion 牛頓第一運動定律
Newton's first law of motion is also called the *law of inertia*.
牛頓第一運動定律又稱為「慣性定律」。

the second law of motion 牛頓第二運動定律
Newton's second law of motion is called the *law of acceleration*.
牛頓第二運動定律稱為「加速度定律」。

the third law of motion 牛頓第三運動定律
Newton's third law of motion is called the *law of action and reaction*. 牛頓第三運動定律稱為「作用與反作用定律」。

Simple Machines 簡單機械

| **lever**
槓桿；控制桿 | **pulley**
滑輪組 | **wheelbarrow**
手推車 | **wheel and axle**
轆轤 | **screw**
螺絲 |

Checkup

A

Write | 請依提示寫出正確的英文單字和片語。

1	力	_____	9	速率	_____
2	運動	_____	10	重力；地心引力	_____
3	位置	_____	11	萬有引力	_____
4	加速度	_____	12	減速	_____
5	慣性	_____	13	吸引	a _____
6	摩擦力	_____	14	吸引	p _____
7	支點	_____	15	墜落	_____
8	加速(v.)	_____	16	運動定律	_____

B

Complete the Sentences | 請在空格中填入最適當的答案，並視情況做適當的變化。

force	motion	velocity	inertia	acceleration
gravity	fulcrum	friction	position	gravitation

1 _____ is anything that affects another body and causes it to react in some way.
任何影響另一物體並造成其某些狀態改變稱為力。

2 _____ is the location of an object. 位置是指物體的所在。

3 _____ measures the rate of speed of an object.
速率測量出物體運動的速度。

4 The law of _____ says that the state of motion of an object does not change until a force is applied to it.
慣性定律說明，除非受到外力影響，物體的運動狀態不會改變。

5 _____ is the force of attraction between Earth and other objects.
重力是指地球與其他物體間的吸引力。

6 _____ is the force that acts between any two objects and makes them attract one another. 萬有引力作用於任兩物體間，並使它們互相吸引。

7 Two bodies rubbing against each other cause _____.
兩物體互相摩擦會產生摩擦力。

8 _____ measures the rate that something increases in speed.
加速度測量出某物在速度上的增加率。

C

Read and Choose | 閱讀下列句子，並且選出最適當的答案。

1 Rockets can (affect | accelerate) very quickly.

2 Jets can (decelerate | attract) very quickly.

3 Because of gravitation, every object in the universe (drops | attracts) each other.

4 Because of gravity, objects (fall | pull) to the ground when you drop them.

D

Look, Read, and Write | 看圖並且依照提示，在空格中填入正確答案。

1 ▸ the act or process of moving, or a particular action or movement

_____

3 ▸ the rate at which the speed of a moving object increases over time

_____

2 ▸ the speed at which an object is travelling

_____

4 ▸ the support on which a lever moves when it is used to lift something

_____

E

Read and Answer | 閱讀並且回答下列問題。 ⊙ 080

Sir Isaac Newton

Sir Isaac Newton lived in the seventeenth and eighteenth centuries. He was one of the greatest scientists who ever lived. He worked with light. He invented calculus. And he also discovered gravity and the three laws of motion.

Supposedly, Newton was sitting under an apple tree one day. An apple fell and hit him on the head. So he started thinking about gravity. He realized that it was gravity that caused objects to fall to the ground.

Newton's three laws of motion are incredibly important to physics. The first law says that the state of motion of an object does not change until a force is applied to it. It is often called the *law of inertia*.

The second law of motion is called the *law of acceleration*. It is often written as F = ma. That means "force equals mass times acceleration." This is the most important of the three laws.

The third law says that for every reaction, there is an equal and opposite reaction. The third law means that all forces are *interactions*.

What is true? Write T(true) or F(false).

1 Sir Isaac Newton lived in the twentieth century.   _____

2 Newton discovered gravity.   _____

3 The first law of motion is F = ma.   _____

4 Newton came up with three laws of motion.   _____

A

Write ┃ 請依提示寫出正確的英文單字和片語。

1	元素	_____	11	佔據	_____
2	原子	_____	12	溶解	_____
3	（物）傳導	_____	13	半透明的	_____
4	（物）對流	_____	14	不透明的	_____
5	動脈	_____	15	心室	_____
6	靜脈	_____	16	心房	_____
7	串聯電路	_____	17	發電機	_____
8	並聯電路	_____	18	水力發電的	_____
9	慣性	_____	19	速率	_____
10	摩擦力	_____	20	重力；地新引力	_____

B

Choose the Correct Word ┃ 請選出與舖底字意思相近的答案。

1 It is possible to break down a compound into separate elements.

   a. break up   b. dissolve   c. make up

2 When water boils, some physical changes take place.

   a. take up   b. occur   c. circulate

3 Some objects conduct heat very well.

   a. inhale   b. transfer   c. react

4 Hydrogen joins with oxygen to form water.

   a. combines with   b. goes with   c. strikes with

C

Complete the Sentences ┃ 請在空格中填入最適當的答案，並視情況做適當的變化。

thermal	matter	blood vessel	charge

1 _____ is made up of atoms. 物質由原子組成。

2 _____ energy measures the heat of an object. 熱能用來判斷物體的溫度。

3 Blood circulates throughout the body in _____ _____.
血液在體內的血管中循環。

4 Electricity can have both positive and negative _____.
電可分為正電荷和負電荷。

5

Mathematics

Unit 21 Fractions and Decimals 分數與小數

Key Words 🔊 081

01	**improper fraction** [ɪmˈprɑpɚ ˈfrækʃən]	*(n.)* 假分數　*proper fraction 真分數　*numerator (n.) 分子 *denominator (n.) 分母 Improper fractions have numerators that are the same or greater than the denominator. $\frac{4}{4}$ and $\frac{5}{3}$ are improper fractions. 假分數中的分子等於或大於分母。$\frac{4}{4}$ 和 $\frac{5}{3}$ 是假分數。
02	**mixed number** [mɪkst ˈnʌmbɚ]	*(n.)* 帶分數　*decimal fraction 十進位分數（分母為10的次方的分數） A mixed number is a combination of a whole number and a fraction. 帶分數是一個整數和一個分數的組合。
03	**equivalent fraction** [ɪˈkwɪvələnt ˈfrækʃən]	*(n.)* 等值分數 $\frac{2}{3}$ and $\frac{4}{6}$ are equivalent fractions since they have the same value. 因為 $\frac{2}{3}$ 與 $\frac{4}{6}$ 數值相等，所以稱它們為等值分數。
04	**unit fraction** [ˈjunɪt ˈfrækʃən]	*(n.)* 單位分數（分子為1，分母是整數的分數）　*reciprocal (n.) 倒數 A unit fraction has a numerator of 1. The fraction $\frac{1}{5}$ is a unit fraction. 單位分數的分子為1。分數 $\frac{1}{5}$ 就是一個單位分數。
05	**common factor** [ˈkɑmən ˈfæktɚ]	*(n.)* 公因數（= common divisor）　*common multiple 公倍數 A common factor is a number that the numerator and the denominator can be divided by. 3 is a common factor of $\frac{3}{9}$. 公因數是能同時除分子與分母的數。3是 $\frac{3}{9}$ 的公因數。
06	**greatest common factor** [ˈgretɪst ˈkɑmən ˈfæktɚ]	*(n.)* 最大公因數（GCF）　*least common multiple 最小公倍數（LCM） In the fraction $\frac{12}{18}$, 6 is the greatest common factor of 12 and 18. 在分數 $\frac{12}{18}$ 中，6是12和18的最大公因數。
07	**common denominator** [ˈkɑmən dɪˈnɑməˌnetɚ]	*(n.)* 公分母 The fractions $\frac{2}{7}$, $\frac{3}{7}$, and $\frac{5}{7}$ have a common denominator of 7. 分數 $\frac{2}{7}$、$\frac{3}{7}$ 與 $\frac{5}{7}$ 的公分母為7。
08	**lowest term** [ˈloɪst tɝm]	*(n.)* 最簡分數　*coprime (a.) 互質的（= relatively prime）　*prime number 質數 Put $\frac{3}{9}$ in its lowest term. 將 $\frac{3}{9}$ 化為最簡分數。
09	**simplest form** [ˈsɪmplɪst fɔrm]	*(n.)* 最簡式　*reduction of a fraction 約分 The simplest form of $\frac{6}{10}$ is $\frac{3}{5}$. $\frac{6}{10}$ 的最簡式為 $\frac{3}{5}$。
10	**thousandth** [ˈθaʊzņdθ]	*(n.)* 千分之一；千分位　*per mille 千分率；千分比 The third place to the right of the decimal point is the thousandth's place. 小數點右邊第三位為千分位的位置。

improper fraction	$\frac{4}{3}$, $\frac{8}{6}$	mixed number	$1\frac{2}{3}$, $5\frac{4}{6}$	proper fraction	$\frac{1}{2}$, $\frac{4}{7}$
equivalent fraction	$\frac{2}{3} = \frac{4}{6}$	unit fraction	$\frac{1}{5}$, $\frac{1}{20}$	lowest term	$\frac{9}{11}$, $\frac{3}{5}$

Power Verbs ● 082

reduce to one's lowest term	化最簡式 Reduce the fractions to their lowest terms. 將分數化為它們的最簡式。
put in one's lowest term	化最簡式 Put $\frac{6}{8}$ in its lowest term. 將 $\frac{6}{8}$ 化為它的最簡式。
round	四捨五入 Round to the nearest tenth. 四捨五入至小數點第二位。
round up	進位 Round up numbers ending from 5 to 9. 末位數為 5 到 9 則進位。
round down	捨去 Round down numbers ending from 0 to 4. 末位數為 0 到 4 則捨去。
be equivalent to	等於 $\frac{1}{2}$ is equivalent to $\frac{2}{4}$. $\frac{1}{2}$ 等於 $\frac{2}{4}$。

Word Families ● 083

Fractions and Decimals 分數與小數

Fraction	$\frac{1}{10}$	$\frac{1}{100}$	$\frac{1}{1000}$
Decimal	0.1	0.01	0.001
Read	one-tenth	one-hundredth	one-thousandth

Reading and Writing Fractions
分數的讀法與寫法

Write(寫法)	Read(讀法)
$\frac{5}{11}$	five-elevenths five out of eleven five divided by eleven
$\frac{13}{200}$	thirteen two-hundredths thirteen out of two hundred thirteen divided by two hundred

Reading and Writing Decimals
小數的讀法與寫法

Write(寫法)	Read(讀法)
0.1	zero point one one-tenth
0.28	zero point two eight
4.18	four point one eight
15.14	fifteen point one four
600.25	six hundred point two five

Place Value of Decimal 小數的位值

Ones	.	Tenths	Hundredths	Thousandths
0	.	3	5	7

Checkup

A

Write | 請依提示寫出正確的英文單字和片語。

1 假分數	_____	9 最簡分數	_____
2 帶分數	_____	10 千分之一；千分位	_____
3 等值分數	_____	11 化最簡式 r	_____
4 單位分數	_____	12 化最簡式 p	_____
5 公因數	_____	13 四捨五入	_____
6 最大公因數	_____	14 進位	_____
7 公分母	_____	15 捨去	_____
8 最簡式	_____	16 等於	_____

B

Complete the Sentences | 請在空格中填入最適當的答案，並視情況做適當的變化。

common factor	improper fraction	mixed number	greatest
unit fraction	common denominator	simplest form	thousandth's

1 _____ _____ have numerators that are the same or greater than the denominator. 假分數中的分子等於或大於分母。

2 A _____ _____ is a combination of a whole number and a fraction. 帶分數是一個整數和一個分數的組合。

3 A _____ _____ has a numerator of 1. 單位分數的分子為1。

4 A _____ _____ is a number that the numerator and the denominator can be divided by. 公因數是能同時除分子與分母的數。

5 In the fraction $\frac{12}{18}$, 6 is the _____ common factor of 12 and 18.
在分數 $\frac{12}{18}$ 中，6是12和18的最大公因數。

6 The fractions $\frac{2}{7}$, $\frac{3}{7}$, and $\frac{5}{7}$ have a _____ _____ of 7.
分數 $\frac{2}{7}$ 、 $\frac{3}{7}$ 與 $\frac{5}{7}$ 的公分母為7。

7 The _____ _____ of $\frac{6}{10}$ is $\frac{3}{5}$. $\frac{6}{10}$ 的最簡式為 $\frac{3}{5}$ 。

8 The third place to the right of the decimal point is the _____ place.
小數點右邊第三位為千分位的位置。

C

Read and Choose | 閱讀下列句子，並且選出最適當的答案。

1 (Replace | Reduce) the fractions to their lowest terms.

2 Put $\frac{6}{8}$ in its (lowest | highest) term.

3 Round (down | up) numbers ending from 5 to 9.

4 $\frac{1}{2}$ is (round | equivalent) to $\frac{2}{4}$.

D

Look, Read, and Write | 看圖並且依照提示，在空格中填入正確答案。

1
$$\frac{7}{5}, \frac{13}{11}$$
▸ a fraction in which the number below the line is smaller than the number above it

_____

3
$$\frac{9}{15} \dashrightarrow 3$$
▸ a number that a set of two or more different numbers can be divided by exactly

_____

2
$$\frac{1}{3}, \frac{1}{7}$$
▸ a fraction that has a numerator of 1

_____

4
$$\frac{2}{10} = \frac{1}{5}$$
▸ fractions that have the same value

_____

E

Read and Answer | 閱讀並且回答下列問題。 ⊙084

Reading and Writing Fractions and Decimals

You can write both fractions and decimals as numbers and words. There are many ways to do this. For example, write the fraction two-thirds as $\frac{2}{3}$. However, there are other ways to say fractions. You can say that $\frac{1}{6}$ is one-sixth or one out of six. And the fraction $\frac{5}{8}$ could be five divided by eight.

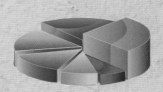

As for decimals, usually just say the individual numbers to the right of the decimal point. For example, 1.1 is one point one. 2.45 is two point four five. However, for some decimals, you can say them as fractions. 0.1 is zero point one or one-tenth. 0.7 is zero point seven or seven-tenths.

Sometimes, you can write a fraction in easier terms. This is called its simplest form. For instance, think about the fraction $\frac{4}{8}$. In its simplest form, it is $\frac{1}{2}$. And the simplest form of $\frac{3}{9}$ is $\frac{1}{3}$.

Finally, you can sometimes write fractions as decimals. The fraction $\frac{2}{10}$ can be 0.2. The fraction $\frac{9}{10}$ can be 0.9. This is why you can read the decimal 0.1 as one-tenth.

Answer the questions.

1 How do you write one-sixth? _____

2 How can you read 2.45? _____

3 What is the simplest form of $\frac{4}{8}$? _____

4 What is $\frac{2}{10}$ in decimal form? _____

Lines, Rays, Angles, and Figures 線、射線、角度與圖形

Key Words 🔊 085

01	**plane** [plen]	(n.) 平面　*an inclined plane 斜面　*horizontal/vertical plane 水平面／垂直面 A **plane** is a flat surface that keeps going without end in all directions. 平面是一個可以往四周無限延伸的平坦表面。
02	**two-dimensional** [ˌtudaɪˈmɛnʃən!]	(a.) 二維空間的；平面的　*three-dimensional (a.) 三維空間的；3D A rectangle is an example of a **two-dimensional** figure. 長方形是一個二維空間圖形的例子。
03	**segment** [ˈsɛgmənt]	(n.) 線段（= line segment） A line goes on forever in both directions, but a **segment** has a beginning and ending point. 線可以往兩端無限延伸，但線段有起點和終點。
04	**ray** [re]	(n.) 射線　*vector (n.) 向量　*scalar (n.) 純量 A **ray** is a part of a line that has one endpoint and continues without end in one direction. 射線屬於線的一部分，它有一個端點並往某一方向無限延伸。
05	**endpoint** [ˈɛndˌpɔɪnt]	(n.) 端點　*midpoint (n.) 中點 The place where a line segment stops is its **endpoint**. 線段中斷的地方稱為端點。
06	**degree** [dɪˈgri]	(n.) 度　*an angle of 90° 直角90度　*a latitude/longitude of degrees 經／緯度 The size of an angle is measured in **degrees**(°). 一個角的大小以度 (°) 來測量。
07	**acute angle** [əˈkjut ˈæŋg!]	(n.) 銳角 An **acute angle** measures greater than 0° and less than 90°. 銳角的角度大於 0°且小於 90°。
08	**obtuse angle** [əbˈtus ˈæŋg!]	(n.) 鈍角 An **obtuse angle** measures greater than 90° and less than 180°. 鈍角的角度大於90°且小於180°。
09	**right angle** [raɪt ˈæŋg!]	(n.) 直角 A **right angle** measures 90°. 直角的角度為90°。
10	**straight angle** [stret ˈæŋg!]	(n.) 平角 A **straight angle** measures 180°. 平角的角度為180°。

plane

line

line segment

ray

B　　C

A　　　　B

C　　D

Power Verbs 🔊 086

intersect
[ˌɪntɚˈsɛkt]

相交
When two perpendicular lines **intersect**, they form four right angles.
當兩條垂直線相交，它們會形成四個直角。

classify

將……分類
Classify each triangle by the lengths of its sides. 根據邊長將三角形分類。

be classified by

進行分類
Triangles can **be classified by** their features.
三角形可以根據它們的特點進行分類。

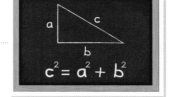

parallel
[ˈpærəˌlɛl]

平行
The two lines **parallel** each other. 這兩條線彼此平行。

run parallel to

平行
The length lines of a square **run parallel to** one another. 正方形的長互相平行。

Word Families 🔊 087

protractor
[ˈproˌtræktɚ]

量角器
A **protractor** is a tool that is marked 0° to 180°.
量角器是一種被標記上 0° 到 180° 的工具。

compass

圓規
A **compass** is a tool used to construct circles. 圓規是一種繪製圓形的工具。

Types of Lines
線的種類

Types of Angles
角的種類

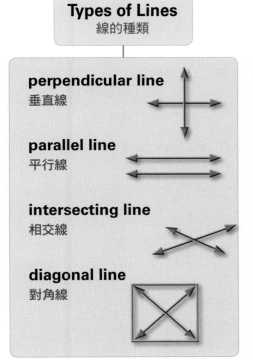

perpendicular line
垂直線

parallel line
平行線

intersecting line
相交線

diagonal line
對角線

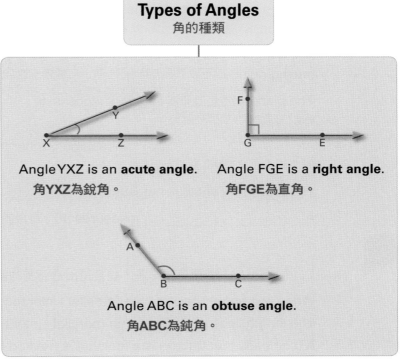

Angle YXZ is an **acute angle**.
角YXZ為銳角。

Angle FGE is a **right angle**.
角FGE為直角。

Angle ABC is an **obtuse angle**.
角ABC為鈍角。

Checkup

A

Write | 請依提示寫出正確的英文單字和片語。

1	平面	_____	9	直角	_____
2	二維空間的	_____	10	平角	_____
3	線段	_____	11	相交	_____
4	射線	_____	12	平行	p_____
5	端點	_____	13	量角器	_____
6	度	_____	14	圓規	_____
7	銳角	_____	15	垂直線	_____
8	鈍角	_____	16	對角線	_____

B

Complete the Sentences | 請在空格中填入最適當的答案，並視情況做適當的變化。

acute angle	obtuse angle	plane	two-dimensional	segment
right angle	straight angle	endpoint	degree	ray

1 A _____ is a flat surface that keeps going without end in all directions.
평면是一個可以往四周無限延伸的平坦表面。

2 A rectangle is an example of a _____ figure.
長方形是一個二維空間圖形的例子。

3 A _____ is a part of a line that has one endpoint and continues without end in one direction. 射線屬於線的一部份，它有一個端點並往某一方向無限延伸。

4 A line goes on forever in both directions, but a _____ has a beginning and ending point. 線可以往兩端無限延伸，但線段有起點和終點。

5 The place where a line segment stops is its _____.
線段中斷的地方稱為端點。

6 An _____ _____ measures greater than 0° and less than 90°.
銳角的角度大於0度且小於90度。

7 The size of an angle is measured in _____(°). 一個角的大小以度 (°) 來測量。

8 A _____ _____ measures 90°. 直角的角度為90度。

C

Read and Choose | 閱讀下列句子，並且選出最適當的答案。

1 When two perpendicular lines (parallel | intersect), they form four right angles.

2 The length lines of a square run (parallel | intersect) to one another.

3 A (compass | protractor) is a tool that is marked 0° to 180°.

4 A (compass | protractor) is a tool used to construct circles.

104

D

Look, Read, and Write | 看圖並且依照提示，在空格中填入正確答案。

1
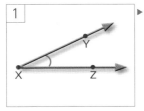
▶ an angle whose measure is between 0° and 90°

_____

3
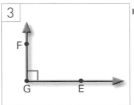
▶ an angle that is 90°

_____

2
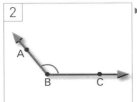
▶ an angle greater than 90° but less than 180°

_____

4
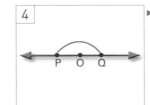
▶ an angle that is 180°

_____

E

Read and Answer | 閱讀並且回答下列問題。 ⊙088

Angles

When two line segments meet at the same endpoint, they form an angle. The size of an angle is measured in degrees. An angle can measure anywhere from 0 to 180 degrees. There are four different kinds of angles. What type they are depends on how many degrees they have.

A straight angle measures 180°. A straight angle forms a line.

The next kind of angle is an acute angle. This angle measures more than 0° but less than 90°. All triangles have at least one acute angle, and many have three of them.

A right angle occurs when two perpendicular lines intersect. These two lines form a ninety-degree angle. This is called a right angle. All of the angles in a square or rectangle are right angles. Some triangles have one right angle, so they are called right triangles.

The last kind of angle is an obtuse angle. An obtuse angle is more than 90° but less than 180°. Some triangles have obtuse angles, but a triangle can never have more than one obtuse angle.

What is NOT true?

1   A straight angle forms a line.
2   An acute angle is between 0° and 90°.
3   A right angle is greater than an obtuse angle.
4   An obtuse angle is greater than an acute angle.

Key Words 🔊 089

| 01 | **polygon**
[ˋpɑlɪˌgɑn] | (n.) 多邊形　*polyhedron (n.) 多面體
Any closed object with three or more sides is a **polygon**.
任何三邊以上的封閉圖形稱為多邊形。 |

| 02 | **quadrilateral**
[ˌkwɑdrɪˋlætərəl] | (n.) 四邊形 (a.) 四邊形的　*quadrangle (n.) 四角形
A **quadrilateral** is any polygon that has four sides.
四邊形是指任何有四個邊的多邊形。 |

| 03 | **parallelogram**
[ˌpærəˋlɛləˌgræm] | (n.) 平行四邊形
Both squares and rectangles are **parallelograms**.
正方形和長方形都是平行四邊形。 |

| 04 | **diagonal**
[daɪˋægənḷ] | (n.) 斜線 (a.) 對角線的　*be diagonal to sth. 與某物呈斜角的
A **diagonal** is a line that goes at an angle.
斜線是指沿著一個角度延伸的線。 |

| 05 | **chord**
[kɔrd] | (n.) 弦　*to strike a chord 觸動心弦　*arc (n.) 弧
The line segment between two points on a circle is a **chord**.
圓上任意兩點連接的線段稱為弦。 |

| 06 | **diameter**
[daɪˋæmətɚ] | (n.) 直徑　*. . . in diameter 直徑為……
Diameter is a chord that passes through the center of a circle.
直徑是通過圓心的弦。 |

| 07 | **radius**
[ˋredɪəs] | (n.) 半徑　*a radius of sth. 某物半徑
The **radius** of a circle is half the length of the diameter.
圓的半徑是直徑長度的一半。 |

| 08 | **equilateral**
[ˌikwɪˋlætərəl] | (a.) 等邊的 (n.) 等邊形　*equiangular (a.) 等角的
All three sides of an **equilateral** triangle are the same length.
等邊三角形的三邊等長。 |

| 09 | **transformation**
[ˌtrænsfɚˋmeʃən] | (n.) 變換　*transformation progress 變換過程
Transformation is the movement of a figure by translation, rotation, or reflection. 變換是指圖形經過平移、旋轉以及反射後的移動。 |

| 10 | **formula**
[ˋfɔrmjələ] | (n.) 公式　*mathematical/chemical formula 數學／化學公式
A **formula** is a way of writing a mathematical rule by using numbers.
公式是指用數字來表示數學規則的書寫方式。 |

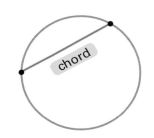

chord

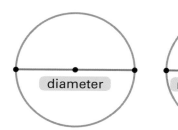

diameter

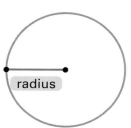

radius

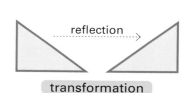

reflection

transformation

Power Verbs

🔊 090

construct	建構;組成	
	Use a compass to **construct** circles. 利用圓規繪製圓形。	
draw	畫	
	Use a compass to **draw** circles. 利用圓規畫圓。	
figure out	算出	
	Use a ruler to **figure out** the length of a line. 用直尺算出線的長度。	
calculate ['kælkjə,let]	計算	
	Use a ruler to **calculate** the length of a line. 用直尺計算線的長度。	
measure	估量	
	Measure a rectangle's area by multiplying the length and the width 將長和寬相乘來估量出長方形的面積。	

Word Families

🔊 091

length	長度	The **length** of a line segment measures how long it is. 長度測量出線段有多長。
width	寬度	The **width** of a square measures how wide it is. 寬度測量出正方形有多寬。
height	高度	The **height** of a cube measures how high it is. 高度測量出立方體有多高。

Types of Triangles 三角形的種類	**acute triangle** 銳角三角形	**right triangle** 直角三角形	**obtuse triangle** 鈍角三角形

	equilateral triangle 等邊三角形	**isosceles triangle** 等腰三角形	**scalene triangle** 不等邊三角形

Kinds of Quadrilaterals 四邊形的種類	**parallelogram** 平行四邊形	**rectangle** 長方形	**square** 正方形	**rhombus** 菱形	**trapezoid** 梯形;不規則四邊形

Checkup

A

Write | 請依提示寫出正確的英文單字和片語。

1	多邊形	_____	9	變換；變式	_____
2	四邊形	_____	10	公式	_____
3	平行四邊形	_____	11	建構；組成	_____
4	斜線	_____	12	算出	_____
5	弦	_____	13	長度	_____
6	直徑	_____	14	寬度	_____
7	半徑	_____	15	高度	_____
8	等邊形	_____	16	直角三角形	_____

B

Complete the Sentences | 請在空格中填入最適當的答案，並視情況做適當的變化。

parallelogram	polygon	quadrilateral	chord	formula
transformation	diameter	equilateral	radius	diagonal

1　Any closed object with three or more sides is a _____.
　任何三邊以上的封閉圖形稱為多邊形。

2　A _____ is any polygon that has four sides.
　四邊形是指任何有四個邊的多邊形。

3　Both squares and rectangles are _____.
　正方形和長方形都是平行四邊形。

4　The line segment between two points on a circle is a _____.
　圓上任意兩點連接的線段稱為弦。

5　_____ is a chord that passes through the center of a circle.
　直徑是通過圓心的弦。

6　All three sides of an _____ triangle are the same length.
　等邊三角形的三邊等長。

7　_____ is the movement of a figure by translation, rotation, or reflection. 變換是指圖形經過平移、旋轉以及反射後的移動。

8　A _____ is a way of writing a mathematical rule by using numbers.
　公式是指用數字來表示數學規則的書寫方式。

C

Read and Choose | 閱讀下列句子，並且選出最適當的答案。

1　Use a compass to (calculate | construct) circles.
2　The (width | length) of a square measures how wide it is.
3　The (width | length) of a line segment measures how long it is.
4　The (area | height) of a cube measures how high it is.

D

Look, Read, and Write | 看圖並且依照提示，在空格中填入正確答案。

1 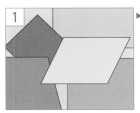 ▶ a flat shape with four straight sides

_____

2 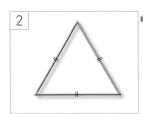 ▶ a triangle that has three sides that are the same length

_____

3 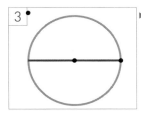 ▶ a straight line from one side of a circle to the other side that passes through the center point

_____

4 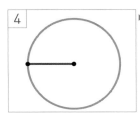 ▶ a straight line from the center of a circle or sphere to any point on the outer edge

_____

E

Read and Answer | 閱讀並且回答下列問題。 🔊 092

Triangles

Triangles are geometrical figures that have three sides. There are several kinds of triangles. They depend on the type of angles in the triangles and the lengths of the sides of the triangles.

The first three types of triangles are acute, right, and obtuse triangles. An acute triangle is one where all three angles in the triangle are acute. So each angle is less than 90°. A right triangle has one angle that is 90°. And the other two angles are acute. Finally, an obtuse triangle has one angle that is more than 90° but less than 180°. The other two angles in it are acute.

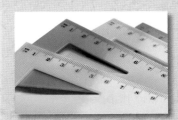

Next, there are three types of triangles that are characterized by the length of the triangles' sides. They are equilateral, isosceles, and scalene triangles. Equilateral triangles have three sides that are the same length. All three angles are always 60°, so they are also acute triangles. Isosceles triangles have two sides with equal length. And all three sides in a scalene triangle are of different lengths.

Fill in the blanks.

1 Triangles have _____ sides.
2 Every angle in an _____ triangle is less than 90°.
3 A _____ triangle has one angle that is 90°.
4 The sides of an equilateral triangle are all the _____ length.

Data and Graphs 數據與圖表

Key Words 🔊 093

01	**elapsed time** [ɪˈlæpst taɪm]	*(n.)* 實耗時間　*time lag（兩個事件之間的）時間差 **Elapsed time** is how much time has passed from a certain point. 實耗時間是指某個點所經過的時間。
02	**survey** [səˈve]	*(n.)* 調查；測量　*to conduct/carry out/do a survey 進行調查 　　　　　　　　　　*a geological/an aerial survey 地質／航空測量 People conduct **surveys** to try to get information from many different sources. 人們進行調查來試圖獲取許多不同來源的資訊。
03	**diagram** [ˈdaɪəˌgræm]	*(n.)* 圖表；圖解　*tree diagram 樹狀圖　*scatter diagram 散佈圖 People use **diagrams** to display data they have collected. 人們利用圖表來展示他們所搜集的數據。
04	**chart** [tʃɑrt]	*(n.)* 圖；圖表　*bar chart 柱狀圖　*pie chart 圓餅圖 A **chart** is a way to display data or information. 圖表是展示數據或資料的一種方法。
05	**graph** [græf]	*(n.)* （曲線）圖；圖表　*line graph 折線圖　*infographic (n.) 資訊圖表 Circle **graphs** can be used to show percentages in picture form. 圓形圖適用於以圖形的方式來顯示百分比。
06	**mean** [min]	*(n.)* 平均數（= average）　*mean value 平均值　*Golden mean 中庸之道 The **mean** is the average value of a group of numbers. 平均數是一組數字中的平均值。
07	**median** [ˈmidɪən]	*(n.)* 中位數 The middle number in a sequence is the **median**. 一串數字中位置居中的數稱為中位數。
08	**mode** [mod]	*(n.)* 眾數 The **mode** is the number found most often in the data. 眾數是指數據中出現最頻繁的數字。
09	**frequency** [ˈfrikwənsɪ]	*(n.)* 頻率　*high/low frequency 高／低頻率　*in order of frequency 依頻率順序 **Frequency** is the rate at which something happens. 頻率是指某件事情發生的比率。
10	**probability** [ˌprɑbəˈbɪlətɪ]	*(n.)* 機率　*in all probability 很有可能；十之八九　*likelihood (n.) 可能；可能性 **Probability** is the likelihood that something will happen. 機率是指某件事情發生的可能性。

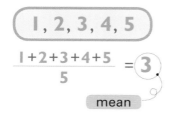

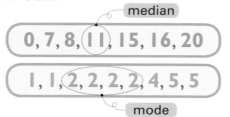

🔊 094

take 進行
You can **take** a survey to get information. 你可以進行調查來獲取資料。

conduct 進行
You can **conduct** a survey to get information. 你可以進行調查來獲取資料。

make a prediction 進行預測
Researchers often **make predictions** based on their data.
研究員常根據他們的數據來進行預測。

predict 預測
Researchers often **predict** results based on their data.
研究員常根據他們的數據來預測結果。

order 排序；整理
Order the data from the least to the greatest values.
將數據依數值最小至最大來排序。

organize 整理；安排
People **organize** data by putting it in graphs or charts.
人們藉由圖表來整理數據。

Word Families
🔊 095

coordinate grid 座標 A coordinate grid is a grid formed by an x-axis and a y-axis.
[koˈɔrdn̩et grɪd] 座標是由 X 軸和 Y 軸形成的網格。

x-axis X 軸 The horizontal line on a coordinate grid is called the **x-axis**.
[ˈɛksˈæksɪs] 座標中的水平線稱為 X 軸。

y-axis Y 軸 The vertical line on a coordinate grid is called the **y-axis**.
[ˈwaɪˈæksɪs] 座標中的垂直線稱為 Y 軸。

Kinds of Graphs and Diagrams
圖表的種類

bar graph
直條圖

circle graph
圓形圖

line graph
折線圖

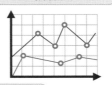

Venn diagram
文氏圖

flow diagram
流程圖

Coordinate Grid
座標

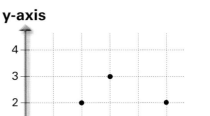
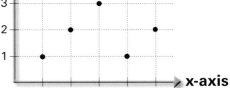

Checkup

A

Write | 請依提示寫出正確的英文單字和片語。

1	實耗時間	_____	9	頻率	_____
2	調查；測量	_____	10	機率	_____
3	圖表；圖解	d_____	11	預測	_____
4	圖；圖表	c_____	12	進行	c_____
5	（曲線）圖；圖表	_____	13	進行預測	_____
6	平均數	_____	14	整理；安排	_____
7	中位數	_____	15	排序；整理	_____
8	眾數	_____	16	座標	_____

B

Complete the Sentences | 請在空格中填入最適當的答案，並視情況做適當的變化。

frequency	mode	diagram	median	chart
elapsed time	mean	probability	survey	graph

1 _____ _____ is how much time has passed from a certain point.
實耗時間是指某個點所經過的時間。

2 People use _____ to display data they have collected.
人們利用圖表來展示他們所搜集的數據。

3 The _____ is the number found most often in the data.
眾數是指數據中出現最頻繁的數字。

4 The middle number in a sequence is the _____.
一串數字中位置居中的數稱為中位數。

5 _____ is the rate at which something happens.
頻率是指某件事情發生的比率。

6 The _____ is the average value of a group of numbers.
平均數是一組數字中的平均值。

7 People conduct _____ to try to get information from many different sources.
人們進行調查來試圖獲取許多不同來源的資訊。

8 A _____ is a way to display data or information.
圖表是展示數據或資料的一種方法。

C

Read and Choose | 閱讀下列句子，並且選出與鋪底字意思相近的答案。

1 You can take a survey to get information.
   a. conduct   b. form   c. use

2 Researchers often make predictions based on their data.
   a. conduct results   b. predict results   c. show results

3 People organize data by putting it in graphs or charts.
   a. interpret   b. order   c. display

D Look, Read, and Write | 看圖並且依照提示，在空格中填入正確答案。

1 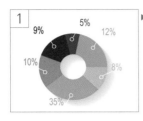 ▶ a graphic representation by means of a circle divided into sectors

_____

3  ▶ a measure of how often a particular event will happen if something

_____

2 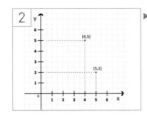 ▶ a grid formed by an x-axis and a y-axis

_____

4 $$\frac{1+2+3+4+5}{5} = 3$$ ▶ an average number

_____

E Read and Answer | 閱讀並且回答下列問題。 🔊 096

Collecting and Organizing Data

People often conduct research. They may research a topic and find as much information as they can about it. Perhaps they want to know the daily temperature in a region for an entire year. Or maybe they want to know how many books students read during a semester. First, they decide what information they want. Then they collect the data.

But the raw data they collect could be useless by itself. So they need to organize it. One common way to organize data is to use charts and diagrams. This lets people see the visual results of their data. For example, perhaps the researchers have some data on how many books each student reads. They can put that data onto a bar graph. This will let them analyze it more easily. Or, maybe they know the average temperature for each day of the year. They can organize it into a circle graph. This will show them the percentage of hot, warm, cool, and cold days the area gets. By using these visual aids, they can interpret their data much more easily.

What is NOT true?

1 Data is information that people collect.
2 People use charts to organize their information.
3 Bar graphs use circles to show the data.
4 Diagrams are visual aids.

Review Test 5

A

Write | 請依提示寫出正確的英文單字和片語。

1	假分數	11	化最簡式 p
2	公因數	12	等於
3	最大公因數	13	垂直線
4	銳角	14	對角線
5	鈍角	15	量角器
6	直角	16	變換
7	四邊形	17	公式
8	等邊的	18	直角三角形
9	平均數	19	頻率
10	眾數	20	機率

B

Choose the Correct Word | 請選出與鋪底字意思相近的答案。

1 Use a compass to construct circles.
   a. calculate   b. take   c. draw

2 The length lines of a square run parallel to one another.
   a. equal   b. intersect   c. parallel

3 You can take a survey to get information.
   a. conduct   b. form   c. use

4 Researchers often make predictions based on their data.
   a. conduct results   b. predict results   c. show results

C

Complete the Sentences | 請在空格中填入最適當的答案，並視情況做適當的變化。

parallelogram	two-dimensional	common denominator	diagram

1 A rectangle is an example of a _____ figure.
長方形是一個二度空間圖形的例子。

2 The fractions $\frac{2}{7}$, $\frac{3}{7}$, and $\frac{5}{7}$ have a _____ _____ of 7.
分數 $\frac{2}{7}$、$\frac{3}{7}$ 與 $\frac{5}{7}$ 的公分母為7。

3 Both squares and rectangles are _____.
正方形和長方形都是平行四邊形。

4 People use _____ to display data they have collected.
人們利用圖表來展示他們所搜集的數據。

6

Language •
Visual Arts • Music

Unit 25 Norse Mythology 北歐神話

Key Words 🔊 097

01 **Norse**
[nɔrs]

(a.) 古代斯堪地那維亞的 *(n.)* 古北歐人 *Nordic (a.)* 來自北歐的；北歐國家的

Norse mythology tells stories from Scandinavian countries.
北歐神話中的故事來自古代斯堪地那維亞國家。

02 **Asgard**
['æsgɑrd]

(n.)（北歐神話）諸神國度 *Midgard (n.)*（北歐神話）人類國度

The Norse gods all lived in the land called **Asgard**.
北歐眾神都居住在稱為諸神國度的土地上。

03 **Odin**
['odɪn]

(n.)（北歐神話）奧丁

Odin was the greatest of all the gods in Norse mythology.
奧丁是北歐神話中最偉大的神。

04 **Ragnarok**
['rɑgnə'rɑk]

(n.)（北歐神話）諸神的黃昏

Ragnarok was the end of the world in Norse myth.
諸神的黃昏是北歐神話中的世界末日。

05 **trickster**
['trɪkstər]

(n.) 騙子；魔術師 *con artist* 騙子 *fraud (n.)* 騙子；詐騙

Tricksters like Loki constantly tried to fool people.
像洛基這樣的騙子一直試圖去欺騙人們

06 **troll**
[trol]

(n.)（北歐神話）山精；巨怪 *giant (n.)* 巨人

Trolls were huge monsters that lived underground.
山精是住在地底下的巨大怪獸。

07 **dwarf**
[dwɔrf]

(n.) 侏儒；小矮人 *elf (n.)* 精靈

A **dwarf** was a very small person who lived underground.
侏儒是居住在地底下的小矮人。

08 **Valkyrie**
['væl‚kɪrɪ]

(n.) 瓦爾基麗（女武神）

Valkyries were female winged messengers that collected the souls of dead warriors. 瓦爾基麗是女性，擁有翅膀的使者，她們會接走戰亡將士的靈魂。

09 **Valhalla**
[væl'hælə]

(n.) 瓦爾海拉（英靈殿）

The souls of warriors who died in battle lived in **Valhalla**.
戰亡將士的靈魂會住在瓦爾海拉。

10 **Edda**
['ɛdə]

(n.) 埃達經 *Poetic Edda* 詩體埃達
Prose Edda 散文埃達（此二者並稱埃達經）

The tales of Norse mythology were told in *Eddas*.
《埃達經》講述北歐神話中的故事。

troll　dwarf　Valkyrie

Valhalla

dead warrior

Power Verbs 🔊 098

trick
欺騙；欺詐
Loki often tried to **trick** others. 洛基常常試圖欺騙他人。

fool
欺騙；愚弄
Loki often tried to **fool** others. 洛基常常試圖欺騙他人。

swing
擺動；搖動
When Thor **swung** his hammer, thunderbolts flew and rain fell.
索爾一擺動他的錘子，就會打雷下雨。

name after
以……命名
Four of the days of the week are **named after** Norse gods: Tuesday, Wednesday, Thursday, and Friday.
一星期中有四天是以北歐諸神命名：星期二、星期三、星期四以及星期五。

reincarnate
[ˌriɪmˈkɑrˌnet]
轉生
Every day, the warriors in Valhalla fight and die, and then they are **reincarnated** to fight the next day.
每一天瓦爾海拉中的戰士奮戰並死去，隔天他們又轉生繼續戰鬥。

SCANDINAVIA

Word Families 🔊 099

Scandinavian Countries
古代斯堪地那維亞（北歐的）國家

Sweden 瑞典	**Denmark** 丹麥
Norway 挪威	**Finland** 芬蘭

Norse Gods
北歐諸神

Odin the chief god 奧丁（主神）
Thor Odin's oldest son; the god of thunder 索爾（奧丁之長子；雷神）
Loki half god and half giant; the trickster 洛基（半神半巨人；狡詐之人）
Frigg the wife of Odin 弗麗嘉（奧丁之妻）
Freya the goddess of love and beauty 芙蕾雅（掌管愛與美之女神）
Hel the goddess of the dead 海爾（掌管死亡之女神）

Odin's two ravens

Odin

Thor   Loki

Freya

Checkup

Write | 請依提示寫出正確的英文單字和片語。

1	古代斯堪地那維亞的 _____	9	瓦爾海拉（英靈殿） _____
2	諸神國度 _____	10	埃達 _____
3	奧丁 _____	11	欺騙；欺詐 _____
4	諸神的黃昏 _____	12	欺騙；愚弄 _____
5	騙子；魔術師 _____	13	擺動；搖動 _____
6	山精；巨怪 _____	14	以……命名 _____
7	侏儒；小矮人 _____	15	轉生 _____
8	瓦爾基麗 _____	16	索爾 _____

B

Complete the Sentences | 請在空格中填入最適當的答案，並視情況做適當的變化。

Ragnarok	trickster	Norse	Asgard	troll
Valkyrie	dwarf	Valhalla	Odin	Edda

1 _____ mythology tells stories from Scandinavian countries.
   北歐神話中的故事來自古代斯堪地那維亞國家。

2 The Norse gods all lived in the land called _____.
   北歐眾神都居住在稱為諸神國度的土地上。

3 _____ was the end of the world in Norse myth.
   諸神的黃昏是北歐神話中的世界末日。

4 _____ like Loki constantly tried to fool people.
   像洛基這樣的騙子一直試圖去欺騙人們。

5 _____ were huge monsters that lived underground.
   山精是住在地底下的巨大怪獸。

6 A _____ was a very small person who lived underground.
   侏儒是居住在地底下的小矮人。

7 The souls of warriors who died in battle lived in _____.
   戰亡將士的靈魂會住在瓦爾海拉。

8 The tales of Norse mythology were told in _____.
   《埃達經》講述北歐神話中的故事。

C

Read and Choose | 閱讀下列句子，並且選出最適當的答案。

1 Loki often tried to (trick | guard) others.

2 Four of the days of the week are (renamed | named) after Norse gods.

3 Every day, the warriors in Valhalla are (reincarnated | lived) to fight the next day.

4 When Thor (swung | hit) his hammer, thunderbolts flew and rain fell.

D

Look, Read, and Write | 看圖並且依照提示，在空格中填入正確答案。

1 ▶ the land where all the Norse gods lived

_____

3 ▶ the widely revered god in Norse mythology

_____

2 ▶ the end of the world in Norse mythology

_____

4 ▶ a host of female figures who collected the souls of dead warriors

_____

E

Read and Answer | 閱讀並且回答下列問題。 🔊 100

The Norse Gods

Norse mythology comes from northern Europe. The Norse were Vikings. They lived in the area that is Norway, Sweden, and Finland today. The Vikings loved to fight and make war. So their stories often are very violent.

There were many Norse gods. Odin was their leader. He was very wise. Odin always had two ravens. They were thought and memory. They told him everything that happened in the land.

Thor was the god of thunder. He was the most powerful of all the gods. He carried a great hammer that he often used to kill giants. Loki was the god of mischief and fire and was a half giant. He was also a trickster, so he caused many problems for the gods, especially Thor.

Frigg was Odin's wife and was also the goddess of marriage. And Freya was the goddess of love. There were also many other Norse gods and goddesses.

The gods lived at Asgard. They often had to fight their enemies, like frost giants and trolls. There are many stories about their deeds that people still enjoy reading.

Fill in the blanks.

1 Norse mythology comes from _____ countries.
2 The leader of the Norse gods was _____.
3 Loki often made problems for _____, the god of thunder.
4 The Norse gods all lived at _____.

Unit 26
Learning about Sentences 句子的學習

Key Words 🔊 101

01	**part of speech** [pɑrt əv spitʃ]	*(n.)* 詞類　*adverb (n.) 副詞　*pronoun (n.) 代名詞　*preposition (n.) 介系詞 Nouns, verbs, and adjectives are **parts of speech**. 名詞、動詞和形容詞屬於詞類。
02	**subject** [ˈsʌbdʒɪkt]	*(n.)* 主詞　*object (n.) 受詞；賓語 The **subject** of a sentence tells what the sentence is about. 句子的主詞陳述了它要說明的事情。
03	**predicate** [ˈprɛdɪkɪt]	*(n.)* 述語 The **predicate** of a sentence tells what the subject of a sentence is or does. 句子的述語說明了句中主詞的性質或狀態。
04	**conjunction** [kənˈdʒʌŋkʃən]	*(n.)* 連接詞　*coordinating/subordinating conjunction 並列／從屬連接詞 **Conjunctions** combine two sentences or phrases into one. 連接詞將兩個句子或片語併為一句。
05	**complete sentence** [kəmˈplit ˈsɛntəns]	*(n.)* 完整句子　*fragment (n.) 片段；不完整句子 A **complete sentence** has both a subject and a predicate. 一個完整句子要有主詞和述語。
06	**run-on sentence** [ˈrʌnɑn ˈsɛntəns]	*(n.)* 連寫句　*main/independent clause 主句／獨立子句 　　　　　　*dependent/subordinate clause 從屬子句 **Run-on sentences** are sentences that are too long and need either a comma or a conjunction. 連寫句是指句子太過冗長而且需要一個逗號或連接詞。
07	**tense** [tɛns]	*(n.)* 時態　*the present/past/future/perfect tense 　　　　　現在／過去／未來／完成式 The **tense** shows the time—past, present, or future—that the action in a sentence occurs. 時態顯示現在、過去或是未來，這也就是句中動作發生的時間。
08	**usage** [ˈjusɪdʒ]	*(n.)* 慣用法　*British/American usage 英／美語用法 **Usage** is the way that words are used in a language. 慣用法是指單詞用在語言文字中的方法。
09	**punctuation** [ˌpʌŋktʃʊˈeʃən]	*(n.)* 標點符號（= punctuation mark）　*exclamation mark 驚嘆號 Periods, commas, and question marks are all forms of **punctuation**. 句號、逗號以及問號都是標點符號的類型。
10	**agreement** [əˈgrimənt]	*(n.)* 一致　*in agreement 保持一致 The subject and verb must show **agreement** in every sentence. 每個句子中的主詞和動詞必須顯示一致。

complete sentence

conjunction　　　　past tense　　　period

Ben, Jane and Anne went to the beach last night.

comma　subject　　　　　predicate

Power Verbs 🔊 102

combine　合併
Conjunctions are used to **combine** two sentences. 連接詞用來合併兩個句子。

connect　連接
Conjunctions are used to **connect** two sentences. 連接詞用來連接兩個句子。

join　連接
Conjunctions are used to **join** two sentences. 連接詞用來連接兩個句子。

agree　一致
The subject and verb must always **agree** with each other.
主詞和動詞一定要彼此一致。

separate　分割
[ˈsɛpəˌret]
You may need to **separate** a run-on sentence into two sentences.
你可能要將這個連寫句分割為兩個句子。

divide　分隔
You may need to **divide** a run-on sentence into two sentences.
你可能要將這個連寫句分隔為兩個句子。

fix　修正
The easiest way to **fix** a run-on sentence is to divide it into two sentences.
修正連寫句最簡易的方法，就是將它分隔為兩個句子。

correct　修正
The easiest way to **correct** a run-on sentence is to divide it into two sentences.
修正連寫句最簡易的方法，就是將它分隔為兩個句子。

Word Families 🔊 103

present tense	現在式	*Study*, *watch*, and *play* are present tense verbs. study、watch、play 是現在式動詞。
past tense	過去式	*Did*, *went*, and *wrote* are past tense verbs. did、went、wrote 是過去式動詞。
future tense	未來式	Use *will* and *be going to* to make the future tense. 利用 will 和 be going to 造未來式的句子。
present perfect tense	現在完成式	The **present perfect tense** uses *have* or *has* plus the past participle. 現在完成式用「have／has＋過去分詞」。
past perfect tense	過去完成式	The **past perfect tense** uses *had* plus the past participle. 過去完成式用「had＋過去分詞」。
present continuous tense	現在進行式	The **present continuous tense** uses the *be* verb plus the present participle. 現在進行式用「be 動詞＋現在分詞」。

Checkup

A

Write | 請依提示寫出正確的英文單字和片語。

1	詞類	_____	9	標點符號	_____
2	主詞	_____	10	一致(n.)	_____
3	述語	_____	11	合併	_____
4	連接詞	_____	12	連接	c_____
5	完整句子	_____	13	一致(v.)	_____
6	連寫句	_____	14	分割	_____
7	時態	_____	15	分隔	_____
8	慣用法	_____	16	修正	f_____

B

Complete the Sentences | 請在空格中填入最適當的答案，並視情況做適當的變化。

complete sentence	usage	subject	punctuation	agreement
run-on sentence	tense	predicate	conjunction	part of speech

1 Nouns, verbs, and adjectives are _____ _____ _____.
名詞、動詞和形容詞屬於詞類。

2 The _____ of a sentence tells what the sentence is about.
句子的主詞陳述了它要說明的事情。

3 The _____ of a sentence tells what the subject of a sentence is or does.
句子的述語說明了句中主詞的性質或狀態。

4 _____ is the way that words are used in a language.
慣用法是指單詞用在語言文字中的方法。

5 A _____ _____ has both a subject and a predicate.
一個完整句子要有主詞和述語。

6 The subject and verb must show _____ in every sentence.
每個句子中的主詞和動詞必須顯示一致。

7 The _____ shows the time — past, present, or future — that the action in a sentence occurs. 時態顯示現在、過去或是未來，這也就是句中動作發生的時間。

8 _____ combine two sentences or phrases into one.
連接詞將兩個句子或片語併為一句。

C

Read and Choose | 閱讀下列句子，並且選出與鋪底字意思相近的答案。

1 Conjunctions are used to combine two sentences.
   a. agree   b. connect   c. complete

2 You may need to separate a run-on sentence into two sentences.
   a. join   b. fix   c. divide

3 The easiest way to fix a run-on sentence is to divide it into two sentences.
   a. correct   b. agree   c. separate

Look, Read, and Write | 看圖並且依照提示，在空格中填入正確答案。

1 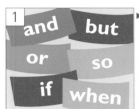 ▸ a word that connects words, phrases, and clauses in a sentence

_____

3

We went to the beach we had fun playing catch.

▸ a sentence that is too long and needs either a comma or a conjunction

_____

2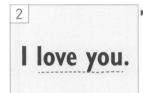

I love you.

▸ the part of a sentence that contains the verb and gives information about the subject

_____

4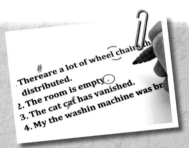

past present future

▸ a form of a verb that is used to show when an action happened

_____

E

Read and Answer | 閱讀並且回答下列問題。 ◉ 104

Understanding Sentences

All sentences must have a subject and a verb. Some sentences can be very short. For example, "I ate," is a complete sentence. Why? It has a subject and a verb. Other sentences can be very, very long.

People often make mistakes when making English sentences. One common mistake is the run-on sentence. Look at this sentence: "I went to the park I saw my friend." It's a run-on sentence. A run-on sentence is a combination of two sentences that either needs punctuation or a conjunction. Here's a complete sentence: " I went to the park, and I saw my friend."

All sentences need to have subject–verb agreement. It means that if the subject is singular, the verb must be singular. And if the subject is plural, the verb must be plural. Look at this sentence: "Jason like to play computer games." It's a wrong sentence. Why? It doesn't have subject–verb agreement. Here is the correct, complete sentence: "Jason likes to play computer games."

So watch out for run-on sentences, and always make sure your subjects and verbs agree. Then you'll be making lots of complete sentences.

What is NOT true?

1   All sentences must have a subject and a verb.

2   Run-on sentences have good grammar.

3   A singular subject needs a singular verb.

4   Subject–verb agreement is important in English.

Unit 27 The Art of the Middle Ages 中世紀藝術

Key Words 🔊 105

01 cathedral
[kəˈθidrəl]

(n.) 大教堂　*basilica (n.)（羅馬）長方形廊柱大廳或教堂　*chapel (n.) 禮拜堂
Cathedrals were enormous churches people built in the Middle Ages.
大教堂是人們在中世紀建造的宏偉教堂。

02 spire
[spaɪr]

(n.) 尖塔；尖頂（= steeple）　*church spire/steeple 教堂尖塔
Many cathedrals had spires that reached high in the air.
許多教堂擁有高聳的尖塔。

03 buttress
[ˈbʌtrɪs]

(n.) 拱壁　*flying buttress（教堂的）拱扶垛，拱柱
Buttresses were supports that kept the cathedrals from collapsing.
拱壁是防止教堂倒塌的支柱。

04 Gothic Age
[ˈgɑθɪk edʒ]

(n.) 哥德時代　*Gothic fiction 哥德小說（始於十八世紀的文學派別，描述以哥德時代為背景的恐怖故事）
The Gothic Age was the time when many cathedrals were built.
許多大教堂建造於哥德時期。

05 gargoyle
[ˈgɑrgɔɪl]

(n.) 滴水嘴（教堂上的怪獸狀石雕）
Gargoyles are stone statues of monsters that are often found on cathedrals. 滴水嘴是常出現在教堂的石像怪獸。

06 stained glass window
[ˈstend glæs ˈwɪndo]

(n.) 彩繪玻璃窗
The stained glass windows in cathedrals show many scenes from the Bible. 教堂裡的彩繪玻璃窗呈現許多《聖經》中的場景。

07 icon
[ˈaɪkɑn]

(n.) 聖像　*saint (n.) 聖徒　*iconography (n.)（宗教中表達思想的）象徵；意象
Icons were representations of images that were popular in the Middle Ages. 聖像是中世紀很受歡迎的代表性形象。

08 statuette
[ˌstætʃʊˈɛt]

(n.) 小雕像　*statue (n.) 雕像；雕塑
A statuette is a very tiny statue. 小雕像是非常小型的雕塑。

09 illuminated manuscript
[ɪˈluməˌnetɪd ˈmænjəˌskrɪpt]

(n.) 裝飾華美的手稿　*a manuscript of a novel 小說手稿
Monks made illuminated manuscripts by writing and drawing pictures in books. 修道士書寫並繪圖在書上藉以製作出裝飾華美的手稿。

10 tapestry
[ˈtæpɪstrɪ]

(n.) 壁毯；繡帷　*to be (all) part of life's rich tapestry 生活的插曲
Tapestries were carpets that had pictures on them and were often hung on walls. 壁毯是指有圖裝飾於表面且常被掛在牆上的毯子。

cathedral　spire

stained glass window　　illuminated manuscript

tapestry

inspire
驅使；激勵
Cathedrals **inspired** people to be more religious.
大教堂驅使人們變得更加虔誠。

emphasize
[ˈɛmfəˌsaɪz]
著重於
The designers of cathedrals **emphasized** their height.
大教堂的設計者著重於教堂的高度。

depict
[dɪˈpɪkt]
描畫；雕出
Stained glass windows often **depict** scenes from the *Bible*.
彩繪玻璃窗常描畫出《聖經》中的場景。

represent
[ˌrɛprɪˈzɛnt]
描繪；表現
Stained glass windows often **represent** scenes from the *Bible*.
彩繪玻璃窗常描繪出《聖經》中的場景。

hold up
支撐；支持
The buttresses **hold up** the cathedral. 拱壁支撐教堂。

support
支撐；支托
The buttresses **support** the cathedral. 拱壁支撐教堂。

Word Families 🔊 107

magnificent
[mægˈnɪfəsənt]
壯麗的；宏偉的
Medieval cathedrals were **magnificent** buildings. 中世紀大教堂是壯麗的建築物。

grand
雄偉的；堂皇的
Medieval cathedrals were **grand** buildings. 中世紀大教堂是雄偉的建築物。

majestic
[məˈdʒɛstɪk]
雄偉的；威嚴的
Medieval cathedrals were **majestic** buildings. 中世紀大教堂是雄偉的建築物。

majesty
[ˈmædʒɪstɪ]
雄偉；壯麗
The **majesty** of that building is impressive. 建築之雄偉令人讚歎。

dignity
[ˈdɪgnətɪ]
莊嚴；尊嚴
The **dignity** of that building is impressive. 建築之莊嚴令人敬佩。

grandeur
[ˈgrændʒɚ]
雄偉；壯觀
The **grandeur** of that building is impressive. 建築之雄偉令人難忘。

Famous European Cathedrals
著名歐洲大教堂

Notre Dame Cathedral 巴黎聖母院
Chartres Cathedral 沙特爾大教堂
Canterbury Cathedral 坎特伯里大教堂
Westminster Abbey 西敏寺
Orvieto Cathedral 奧維多大教堂

Checkup

A

Write | 請依提示寫出正確的英文單字和片語。

1　大教堂 ＿＿＿＿＿＿＿＿＿＿＿
2　尖塔；尖頂 ＿＿＿＿＿＿＿＿＿＿＿
3　拱壁 ＿＿＿＿＿＿＿＿＿＿＿
4　哥德時代 ＿＿＿＿＿＿＿＿＿＿＿
5　滴水嘴 ＿＿＿＿＿＿＿＿＿＿＿
6　聖像 ＿＿＿＿＿＿＿＿＿＿＿
7　小雕像 ＿＿＿＿＿＿＿＿＿＿＿
8　壁毯；繡帷 ＿＿＿＿＿＿＿＿＿＿＿

9　裝飾華美的手稿 ＿＿＿＿＿＿＿＿＿＿＿
10　彩繪玻璃窗 ＿＿＿＿＿＿＿＿＿＿＿
11　驅使；激勵 ＿＿＿＿＿＿＿＿＿＿＿
12　著重於 ＿＿＿＿＿＿＿＿＿＿＿
13　描畫；雕出 d＿＿＿＿＿＿＿＿＿
14　描繪；表現 r＿＿＿＿＿＿＿＿＿
15　支撐；支持 h＿＿＿＿＿＿＿＿＿
16　壯麗的；宏偉的 ＿＿＿＿＿＿＿＿＿＿＿

B

Complete the Sentences | 請在空格中填入最適當的答案，並視情況做適當的變化。

stained-glass Gothic Age	spire tapestry	statuette buttress	icon gargoyle	cathedral manuscript

1　Many cathedrals had ＿＿＿＿＿＿ that reached high in the air.
許多教堂擁有高聳的尖塔。

2　＿＿＿＿＿＿＿＿ were supports that kept the cathedrals from collapsing.
拱壁是防止教堂倒塌的支柱。

3　＿＿＿＿＿＿＿ were representations of images that were popular in the Middle Ages.
聖像是中世紀很受歡迎的代表性形象。

4　＿＿＿＿＿＿＿＿ were enormous churches people built in the Middle Ages.
大教堂是人們在中世紀建造的巨大教堂。

5　Monks made illuminated ＿＿＿＿＿＿＿＿＿ by writing and drawing pictures in books.
修道士書寫並繪圖在書上藉以製作出裝飾華美的手稿。

6　＿＿＿＿＿＿＿＿ were carpets that had pictures on them and were often hung on walls. 壁毯是指有圖裝飾於表面且常被掛在牆上的毯子。

7　The ＿＿＿＿＿＿ ＿＿＿＿＿ was the time when many cathedrals were built.
許多大教堂建造於哥德時期。

8　A ＿＿＿＿＿＿＿ is a very tiny statue. 小雕像是非常小型的雕塑。

C

Read and Choose | 閱讀下列句子，並且選出最適當的答案。

1　Cathedrals (represented｜inspired) people to be more religious.
2　Stained-glass windows often (depict｜support) scenes from the Bible.
3　The buttresses (hold｜build) up the cathedral.
4　The designers of cathedrals (represented｜emphasized) their height.

Look, Read, and Write | 看圖並且依照提示，在空格中填入正確答案。

 1
► a very large, usually stone, building for Christian worship

_____

 3
► a strange or ugly animal figure that sticks out from the roof of a building

_____

 2
► a structure made of stone or brick that sticks out from and supports a wall of a building

_____

 4
► windows in cathedrals that show many scenes from the Bible

_____

E

Read and Answer | 閱讀並且回答下列問題。 ● 108

Gothic Cathedrals

In the Middle Ages, religion was a very important part of people's lives. Almost everyone went to church on Sunday. So building churches was important. Some towns and cities built huge churches. They were called cathedrals. There were many different styles. One important style was Gothic. The Gothic Age lasted from around the twelfth to sixteenth centuries.

Westminster Abbey

Gothic cathedrals were enormous. Their builders made them to impress many people. So they look like they are reaching up into the sky. The reason that they are so high is that they have buttresses. These are supports that help the cathedrals stay up.

The cathedrals also had many stained glass windows. These showed scenes from the Bible. Also, they allowed a lot of light to enter the cathedral. Inside the cathedral, the ceilings were very high. This made them look even more impressive.

The outside of a cathedral often had many sculptures. These were called gargoyles. The gargoyles looked like monsters. They were used to ward off evil spirits.

Answer the questions.

1   What is another name for a huge church?   _____
2   What helped to support the cathedrals?   _____
3   What did stained glass windows show?   _____
4   What are gargoyles?   _____

The Art of Islam, Africa, and China 伊斯蘭、非洲和中國的藝術

Key Words 🔘 109

01 mosque
[mɑsk]

(n.) 清真寺（伊斯蘭教寺院）　*masjid (n.) 回教寺院

A mosque is where Muslims go to worship.
清真寺是伊斯蘭教徒做禮拜的地方。

02 dome
[dom]

(n.) 穹頂；穹窿　*domed stadium 巨蛋（體育場）

A dome is a rounded roof or ceiling on a building.
穹頂是指建築物上的圓形屋頂或是頂篷。

03 minaret
[ˋmɪnəˌrɛt]

(n.)（清真寺的）尖塔；叫拜樓

Minarets are tall towers that are connected to mosques.
尖塔是連接清真寺的高塔。

04 Islamic architecture
[ɪsˋlæmɪk ˋɑrkəˌtɛktʃə]

(n.) 伊斯蘭建築　*arabesque (n.) 阿拉伯式花紋（指伊斯蘭藝術中花葉交織的圖紋）

Domes and minarets are the main features of Islamic architecture.
穹頂和尖塔是伊斯蘭建築的主要特色。

05 terra cotta
[ˋtɛrə ˋkɑtə]

(n.) 赤土陶器　*Terracotta Army 兵馬俑

There are many terra cotta statues in Africa. 非洲有許多的赤陶雕像。

06 silk
[sɪlk]

(n.) 絲綢　*as smooth as silk 非常光滑　*Silk Road 絲路

Chinese artists often painted pictures on silk.
中國的藝術家常會在絲綢上繪製圖案。

07 scroll
[skrol]

(n.) 畫卷；卷軸　*the Dead Sea Scrolls《死海古卷》

Chinese artists used long scrolls to make pictures on.
中國的藝術家在長畫卷上繪製圖案。

08 calligraphy
[kəˋlɪgrəfɪ]

(n.) 書法　*Four Treasures of the Study 文房四寶

Calligraphy is the art of handwriting. 書法是一種書寫藝術。

09 pottery
[ˋpɑtərɪ]

(n.) 陶器；陶藝　*clay (n.) 陶土；黏土　*glaze (n.) 釉；釉料

The Chinese made excellent pottery. 中國人製作精美的陶器。

10 porcelain
[ˋpɔrslɪn]

(n.) 瓷器　*be made of/from porcelain 以瓷所製

Porcelain is a kind of pottery that is often white in color.
瓷器屬於陶器的一種，常以白色繪製。

mosque　dome　minaret

Terracotta Army

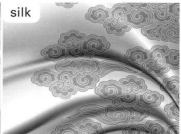

silk

calligraphy

Power Verbs 🔊 110

carve 雕刻
African artists **carved** beautiful sculptures with brass and terra cotta.
非洲藝術家用黃銅和赤土雕刻出美麗的雕塑品。

mold 塑造
Some African artists **molded** portrait masks with clay.
有些非洲藝術家用黏土塑造出肖像面具。

decorate 裝飾
[ˈdɛkə͵ret]
Some African masks are **decorated** in many colors.
有些非洲面具被裝飾上許多顏色。

stamp 壓印於
Chinese artists **stamped** their names on their work in red ink.
中國的藝術家將他們的名字，用紅色墨水壓印在他們的作品上。

Word Families 🔊 111

delicate 精緻的；精美的
[ˈdɛləkət]
Chinese silk paintings are very **delicate**. 中國的帛畫非常精緻。

fine 精美的；精巧的
Chinese silk paintings are very **fine**. 中國的帛畫非常精美。

Famous Examples of Islamic Architecture
著名伊斯蘭建築

Types of Pottery
陶器的種類

bowl 碗
vase 花瓶
plate 盤子
cup 杯子
saucer 茶碟

Alhambra
阿罕布拉宮

Dome of the Rock
圓頂清真寺

Taj Mahal
泰姬瑪哈陵

Sultan Ahmed Mosque
藍色清真寺

Checkup

Write | 請依提示寫出正確的英文單字和片語。

1	清真寺	9	陶器
2	穹頂；穹窿	10	瓷器
3	尖塔；叫拜樓	11	雕刻
4	伊斯蘭建築	12	塑造
5	赤土陶器	13	裝飾
6	絲綢	14	壓印於
7	畫卷；卷軸	15	雅緻的；精美的 d
8	書法	16	精美的；精巧的 f

B

Complete the Sentences | 請在空格中填入最適當的答案，並視情況做適當的變化。

minaret	porcelain	terra cotta	mosque	dome
scroll	pottery	Islamic architecture	calligraphy	silk

1   A _____ is where Muslims go to worship.
清真寺是伊斯蘭教徒做禮拜的地方。

2   There are many _____ _____ statues in Africa.
非洲有許多的赤陶雕像。

3   A _____ is a rounded roof or ceiling on a building.
穹頂是指建築物上的圓形屋頂或是頂篷。

4   _____ are tall towers that are connected to mosques.
尖塔是連接清真寺的高塔。

5   Domes and minarets are the main features of _____ _____.
穹頂和尖塔是伊斯蘭建築的主要特色。

6   Chinese artists used long _____ to make pictures on.
中國的藝術家在長畫卷上繪製圖案。

7   The Chinese made excellent _____. 中國人製作精美的陶器。

8   _____ is the art of handwriting. 書法是一種書寫藝術

C

Read and Choose | 閱讀下列句子，並且選出最適當的答案。

1   African artists (molded | carved) beautiful sculptures with brass and terra cotta.
2   Some African artists (built | molded) portrait masks with clay.
3   Some African masks are (decorated | delicate) in many colors.
4   Chinese artists (signed | stamped) their names on their work in red ink.

D

Look, Read, and Write | 看圖並且依照提示，在空格中填入正確答案。

 1

▸ a building for Islamic religious activities and worship

_____

 3

▸ a tall, thin tower on or near a mosque

_____

 2

▸ a reddish clay that is used for pottery and tiles

_____

 4

▸ the art of making beautiful handwriting

_____

E

Read and Answer | 閱讀並且回答下列問題。 112

Islamic Architecture

Islam began in the seventh century. Since then, there have been many styles of buildings designed by Muslims. They all combine to make up Islamic architecture.

In Islam, art is restricted. There should be no images of Allah-the god of Islam. Also, there should be no pictures of people either. So, many of Islam's most creative people became architects.

One of the main features of Islamic architecture is the minaret. These are tall towers. They are found in every mosque. There are usually four minarets at every mosque. There is one at each corner of the building. They can be very high towers.

Domes are also very popular features. Domes are rounded roofs of buildings. Many mosques have impressive domes.

As for famous buildings, there are many. The Dome of the Rock is in Jerusalem. It is one of the earliest examples of Islamic architecture. The Sultan Ahmed Mosque is in Istanbul, Turkey. It is another well-known building. And the Taj Mahal is located in India. Some say it is the most beautiful building in the entire world.

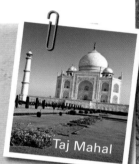
Taj Mahal

What is true? Write T(true) or F(false).

1 Islamic art allows images of Allah.   _____
2 Minarets are tall towers.   _____
3 Many mosques have domes.   _____
4 The Taj Mahal is in Jerusalem.   _____

The Elements of Music
Unit 29 音樂的元素

01	**musical notation** [ˈmjuzɪkḷ noˈteʃən]	*(n.)* 樂譜　*staff (n.) 五線譜（= stave）　*numbered musical notation 簡譜 Musical notation allows musicians to read and play music. 樂譜讓音樂家能閱讀並演奏樂曲。
02	**musical pitch** [ˈmjuzɪkḷ pɪtʃ]	*(n.)* 音高　*absolute/perfect pitch 絕對音感　*relative pitch 相對音感 The musical pitch is the tone of the music. 音高是指音樂的音調。
03	**tie** [taɪ]	*(n.)* 連結線 A tie is a curved line that ties the notes together. 連結線是連接音符的弧線。
04	**bar** [bɑr]	*(n.)* 符杠　*beat (n.) 節拍　*rhythm (n.) 節奏　*scale (n.) 音階 Sometimes a bar connects two or more eighth notes. 有時候一個符杠連接兩個以上的八分音符。
05	**dotted note** [ˈdɑtɪd not]	*(n.)* 附點音符　*note head 符頭　*stem (n.) 符桿　*flag (n.) 符尾 A dotted note means that the note should be increased by half. 附點音符表示將原本音符的音加長二分之一。
06	**measure** [ˈmɛʒɚ]	*(n.)* 小節　*measure signature 拍號（= time signature） Bar lines divide the music into measures. 小節線將樂曲分為數個小節。
07	**single bar line** [ˈsɪŋgḷ bɑr laɪn]	*(n.)* 小節線 Composers use a single bar line to mark the end of a measure. 作曲家用小節線來標記一個小節的結束。
08	**double bar line** [ˈdʌbḷ bɑr laɪn]	*(n.)* 終止線 Composers use a double bar line to mark the end of a piece of music. 作曲家用終止線來標記一首樂曲的結束。
09	**sharp** [ʃɑrp]	*(n.)* 升記號　*double sharp 重升記號　*accidental (n.) 變音記號 A sharp shows that a note should be played half a tone higher. 升記號表示演奏時音符要升高半個音。
10	**flat** [flæt]	*(n.)* 降記號　*double flat 重降記號　*natural (n.) 還原記號 A flat shows that a note should be played half a tone lower. 降記號表示演奏時音符要降低半個音。

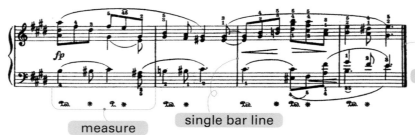

Musical Notation

double bar line

measure

single bar line

follow 跟隨
A musician **follows** the notes on the staff as he or she plays.
音樂家演奏時會跟隨五線譜上的音符。

raise 提高
Raise your voice to get a higher tone. 提高你的聲音來獲取較高的音調。

lower 降低
Lower your voice to get a lower tone. 降低你的聲音來獲取較低的音調。

hold 持續
A good singer can **hold** a note for several seconds.
優秀的歌手可以持續一個單音達好幾秒。

be held 持續
A whole note **is held** twice as long as a half note.
全音符持續的時間是二分音符的兩倍。

Word Families 🔊 115

legato 圓滑奏
[lɪˈgɑto]
Legato means the musicians should play the notes smoothly without breaks.
圓滑奏表示音樂家必須持續而圓滑地演奏，不得中斷。

staccato 斷奏
[stəˈkɑto]
Staccato means the musicians should play the notes with short, separate sounds. 斷奏表示音樂家必須演奏短而單獨的聲音。

beat 節拍
The musicians keep the **beat** while they play. 音樂家演奏時要保持節拍。

time 拍子
Musicians need to keep **time** to play the notes at the right time.
音樂家要跟上拍子才能完美演奏音符。

rhythm 節奏
The **rhythm** is the pattern of the beats in the music. 節奏是音樂中節拍的型態。

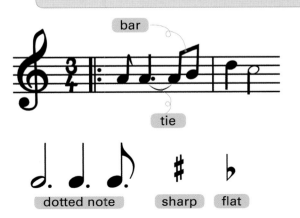

bar

tie

dotted note   sharp   flat

Musical Instructions 音樂指南

piano (*p*, soft) 弱的
pianissimo (*pp*, very soft) 極弱的
mezzo piano (*mp*, moderately soft) 中弱的
forte (*f*, loud) 強的
fortissimo (*ff*, very loud) 極強的
mezzo forte (*mf*, moderately loud) 中強的

Checkup

A

Write | 請依提示寫出正確的英文單字和片語。

1	樂譜	_____	9	小節線	_____
2	音高	_____	10	終止線	_____
3	連結線	_____	11	跟隨	_____
4	符杠	_____	12	提高	_____
5	附點音符	_____	13	降低	_____
6	小節	_____	14	持續	h_____
7	升記號	_____	15	圓滑奏	_____
8	降記號	_____	16	斷奏	_____

B

Complete the Sentences | 請在空格中填入最適當的答案，並視情況做適當的變化。

single bar line	dotted note	flat	bar	double bar line
musical notation	measure	tie	sharp	musical pitch

1 _____ _____ allows musicians to read and play music.
樂譜讓音樂家能閱讀並演奏樂曲。

2 A _____ is a curved line that ties the notes together.
連結線是連接音符的弧線。

3 A _____ _____ means that the note should be increased by half.
附點音符表示將原本音符的音加長二分之一。

4 Bar lines divide the music into _____. 小節線將樂曲分為數個小節。

5 Composers use a _____ _____ _____ to mark the end of a measure.
作曲家用小節線來標記一個小節的結束。

6 A _____ shows that a note should be played half a tone higher.
升記號表示演奏時音符要升高半個音。

7 Sometimes a _____ connects two or more eighth notes.
有時候一個符杠連接兩個以上的八分音符。

8 A _____ shows that a note should be played half a tone lower.
降記號表示演奏時音符要降低半個音。

C

Read and Choose | 閱讀下列句子，並且選出最適當的答案。

1 (Raise | Lower) your voice to get a higher tone.
2 A whole note is (hold | held) twice as long as a half note.
3 (Staccato | Legato) means the musicians should play the notes smoothly without breaks.
4 (Staccato | Legato) means the musicians should play the notes with short, separate sounds.

Look, Read, and Write | 看圖並且依照提示，在空格中填入正確答案。

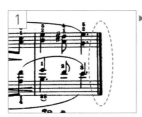 ▸ a bar line that marks the end of a piece of music

_____

 ▸ a note that is a semitone higher than the stated note

_____

 ▸ a note that indicates the note should be increased by half

_____

 ▸ a note that is a semitone lower than a stated note

_____

E

Read and Answer | 閱讀並且回答下列問題。 🔘 116

Musical Dynamics

When musicians play their instruments, they must do more than just read the notes and then play them. They must know the speed that they should play the music. And they must also know the dynamics. This means they must know if they should play softly or loudly. How do they know that? They can look for certain letters on their sheet music.

On the sheet music, they will see the letters _p_, _pp_, _mp_, _f_, _ff_, or _mf_. These letters are all related to musical dynamics. They indicate the softness or the loudness that the musician should play.

_p_ stands for piano. It means the music should be played softly. There are also _pp_ and _mp_. _pp_ means pianissimo, which stands for "very soft." And _mp_ means mezzo piano. This means "moderately soft."

Of course, some music should be played loudly. When a musician sees _f_, it means forte. That stands for "loud." Just like with soft music, there are two more degrees of loudness. The first is _ff_. That's fortissimo, which means "very loud." And there is _mf_. That's mezzo forte, which means "moderately loud."

Fill in the blanks.

1 Musicians must play their music either _____ or loudly.

2 Letters like _p_, _pp_, and _mp_ appear on _____ music.

3 _pp_ stands for _____.

4 Forte stands for "_____."

Understanding Music 了解音樂

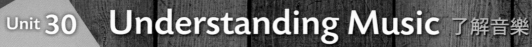

Key Words 🎧 117

01	**concert hall** [ˈkɑnsət hɔl]	*(n.)* 音樂廳　*auditorium (n.) 劇院；禮堂；音樂廳；觀眾席　*venue (n.) 會場 An orchestra typically performs in a **concert hall**. 管弦樂隊都在音樂廳裡表演。
02	**backstage** [ˈbækˈstedʒ]	*(n.)* 後臺　*backstage pass 後臺通行證　*to go on/off stage 登臺／下臺 The musicians wait **backstage** before they come out to perform. 音樂家出場表演前會在後臺等候。
03	**baton** [bæˈtn̩]	*(n.)* 指揮棒　*under the baton of sb. 在某人的指揮下 The conductor waves his **baton** as he conducts the orchestra. 指揮家帶領管弦樂隊時會揮動他的指揮棒。
04	**fugue** [fjug]	*(n.)* 賦格曲　*harmony (n.)（音樂中的）和聲 A **fugue** involves several instruments playing the same theme in turn. 在賦格曲中，數種樂器會依序演奏同一個主題。
05	**vocal range** [ˈvokl̩ rendʒ]	*(n.)* 音域　*falsetto (n.) 假音　*whistle register 哨音；海豚音 A person's **vocal range** is how high and low he or she can sing. 音域是指一個人能夠發出的最高音和最低音。
06	**high voice** [haɪ vɔɪs]	*(n.)* 高嗓音　*soprano (n.) 女高音　*tenor (n.) 男高音 A person with a **high voice** can sing high notes. 擁有高嗓音的人可以唱高音符。
07	**low voice** [lo vɔɪs]	*(n.)* 低嗓音　*alto/contralto (n.) 女低音　*bass (n.) 男低音 A person with a **low voice** can sing low notes. 擁有低嗓音的人可以唱低音符。
08	**chant** [tʃænt]	*(n.)* 禱文；吟誦　*Gregorian chant 格雷果聖歌（中世紀流行的無伴奏聖歌） Many monks sang **chants** without using any instruments. 許多僧侶吟誦禱文，不使用任何樂器。
09	**monotonous** [məˈnɑtənəs]	*(a.)* 無抑揚頓挫的；單調的　*a monotonous voice/job 單調的聲音／工作 Gregorian chants often have a **monotonous** sound. 格雷果聖歌通常沒有抑揚頓挫的聲音。
10	**tempo** [ˈtɛmpo]	*(n.)* 節奏；速度　*a change in tempo 節奏的變化　*up-tempo (a.) 快節奏的 The **tempo** is the speed of the music. 節奏是指音樂的速度。

concert hall

conductor

baton

chant

tune	調音
	Musicians **tune** their instruments to get them to play the right tones.
	音樂家為樂器調音來演奏正確的音。
adjust	調整；校正
	Musicians **adjust** their instruments to get them to play the right tones.
	音樂家調整樂器來演奏正確的音。
take turns	輪流
	Sometimes the musicians **take turns** playing their instruments.
	有時候音樂家會輪流演奏他們的樂器。
distinguish [dɪˋstɪŋgwɪʃ]	分辨
	Many listeners can distinguish between the different instruments that are playing.
	許多聽眾可以分辨不同的樂器演奏。
appreciate [əˋpriʃɪˏet]	欣賞
	Many listeners can appreciate the quality of the music being played.
	許多聽眾欣賞音樂演奏時的旋律。
chant	祝禱；吟誦
	The monks chant songs in a monotonous voice. 僧侶用平板無奇的聲音吟誦禱文。

Word Families 🔊 119

Women's Voices	女聲
soprano [səˋpræno]	女高音
	The highest female voice is called the soprano.
	聲域最高的女性稱為女高音。
mezzo soprano	女中音
	Most females sing in the mezzo-soprano voice.
	大部分的女性演唱女中音。
alto [ˋælto]	女低音
	The lowest female voice is called the alto. 聲域最低的女性稱為女低音。
Men's Voices	男聲
tenor [ˋtɛnɚ]	男高音
	The highest male voice is called the tenor. 聲域最高的男性稱為男高音。
baritone [ˋbærəˏton]	男中音
	Most males sing in the baritone voice. 大部分的男性演唱男中音。
bass	男低音
	The lowest male voice is called the bass. 聲域最低的男性稱為男低音。

Checkup

A

1	音樂廳	_____	9	無抑揚頓挫的；單調的 _____
2	後臺	_____	10	節奏；速度 _____
3	指揮棒	_____	11	調音 _____
4	賦格曲	_____	12	輪流 _____
5	音域	_____	13	分辨 _____
6	高嗓音	_____	14	欣賞 _____
7	低嗓音	_____	15	女中音 _____
8	禱文；吟誦	_____	16	男中音 _____

B

Complete the Sentences | 請在空格中填入最適當的答案，並視情況做適當的變化。

high voice	fugue	chant	tempo	concert hall
low voice	baton	backstage	monotonous	vocal range

1 An orchestra typically performs in a _____ _____.
管弦樂隊都在音樂廳裡表演。

2 The conductor waves his _____ as he conducts the orchestra.
指揮家帶領管弦樂隊時會揮動他的指揮棒。

3 The musicians wait _____ before they come out to perform.
音樂家出場表演前會在後臺等候。

4 A _____ involves several instruments playing the same theme in turn.
在賦格曲中，數種樂器會依序演奏同一個主題。

5 A person with a _____ _____ can sing low notes.
擁有低嗓音的人可以唱低的音符。

6 Many monks sang _____ without using any instruments.
許多僧侶吟唱禱文，不使用任何樂器。

7 The _____ is the speed of the music. 節奏是指音樂的速度。

8 Gregorian chants often have a _____ sound.
格雷果聖歌通常沒有抑揚頓挫的聲音。

C

Read and Choose | 閱讀下列句子，並且選出最適當的答案。

1 Musicians (turn | tune) their instruments to get them to play the right tones.

2 Many listeners can (distinguish | divide) between the different instruments that are playing.

3 Sometimes the musicians take (turns | tune) playing their instruments.

4 The monks (chant | can) songs in a monotonous voice.

D

Look, Read, and Write | 看圖並且依照提示，在空格中填入正確答案。

 ▸ a piece of music in which tunes are repeated in complex patterns

_____

 ▸ the range of how high and low people can sing

_____

 ▸ a woman or girl with a voice that can sing the highest notes

_____

 ▸ a man or boy with a voice that can sing the highest notes

_____

E

Read and Answer | 閱讀並且回答下列問題。 ⊙120

Handel and Haydn

Two of the greatest of all classical music composers were George Friedrich Handel and Joseph Haydn.

Handel lived during the Baroque Period in the eighteenth century. He was German. But he lived in England for a long time. Some of his music is very popular and well-known all around the world. He wrote _Water Music_ and _Music for the Royal Fireworks_. These are two easily recognizable pieces of music. But his most famous music by far is his _Messiah_. It is an oratorio that tells the life of Jesus Christ. From the _Messiah_, the most famous piece is the _Hallelujah_ chorus. Today, when orchestras play the _Hallelujah_ chorus, the audience always stands up. Why? When King George II of Great Britain first heard it, he stood up during that part.

Joseph Haydn was one of the best composers of the Classical Period. He composed hundreds of sonatas, symphonies, and string quartets. He also influenced many other composers. Beethoven was the greatest of all his students. Two of his best works are the _Surprise Symphony_ and _The Creation_, an oratorio.

What is NOT true?

1   Handel lived during the eighteenth century.
2   _Water Music_ is a famous piece of music by Handel.
3   Handel wrote the _Messiah_.
4   Joseph Haydn only wrote two pieces of music.

Review Test 6

A

Write | 請依提示寫出正確的英文單字和片語。

1	諸神的黃昏	_____	11 欺騙；欺詐	_____
2	諸神國度	_____	12 轉生	_____
3	述語	_____	13 一致(n.)	_____
4	連接詞	_____	14 合併	_____
5	大教堂	_____	15 驅使；激勵	_____
6	拱壁	_____	16 描畫；雕出	_____
7	伊斯蘭建築	_____	17 圓滑奏	_____
8	書法	_____	18 斷奏	_____
9	樂譜	_____	19 分辨	_____
10	指揮棒	_____	20 欣賞	_____

B

Choose the Correct Word | 請選出與鋪底字意思相近的答案。

1 Loki often tried to trick others.

   a. swing   b. fight   c. fool

2 Conjunctions are used to combine two sentences.

   a. agree   b. connect   c. complete

3 The easiest way to fix a run-on sentence is to divide it into two sentences.

   a. correct   b. agree   c. separate

4 Stained glass windows often depict scenes from the Bible.

   a. adjust   b. represent   c. hold

C

Complete the Sentences | 請在空格中填入最適當的答案，並視情況做適當的變化。

complete sentence	sharp	cathedral	Norse

1 _____ mythology tells stories from Scandinavian countries.
北歐神話中的故事來自古代斯堪地那維亞國家。

2 A _____ _____ has both a subject and a predicate.
一個完整句子要有主詞和述語。

3 _____ were enormous churches people built in the Middle Ages.
大教堂是人們在中世紀建造的宏偉教堂。

4 A _____ shows that a note should be played half a tone higher.
升記號表示演奏時音符要升高半個音。

Index

ANSWERS AND TRANSLATIONS

01 ● The West Region of the United States (p. 12)

A

1 bountiful   2 lush   3 dense   4 rain shadow
5 logging   6 deforestation   7 gold rush
8 traffic congestion   9 urban sprawl   10 Inuit
11 irrigate   12 deforest   13 log   14 cut down
15 be stuck in   16 overpopulate

B

1 bountiful   2 lush   3 rain shadow
4 deforestation   5 Logging   6 urban sprawl
7 Gold Rush   8 congestion

C

1 irrigate   2 deforested   3 stuck   4 cutting

D

1 rain shadow   2 gold rush   3 traffic congestion
4 Inuit

E　地震與森林大火

　　加州是美國最富裕的州之一，它擁有大量的土地以及高於其他州的人口，同時蘊藏豐富的天然資源。然而，並非一切都如此完美。加州有兩個主要的問題：地震以及森林大火。

　　聖安德烈斯斷層貫穿加州，基於此因，加州地震頻繁。其中有些地震非常強大。舉例來說，1906年舊金山發生過一次強震，它摧毀了眾多建築物並引起許多火災。超過3,000人命喪於此次災害。加州還有許多其他的強烈地震，有些人擔憂將來會發生一次「大地震」，他們相信這會帶來偌大的損害。

　　夏秋之際，加州大部分地區都很乾燥。因此，森林大火或是野火時常發生。這些火勢蔓延地很快，它們燒光了許多森林，也燒毀了人們的家園和建築物，它們常在消防隊員撲滅前就帶走許多人的性命。

填空

1 加州人口高於其他州。(people)
2 1906年舊金山發生了一次強震。(earthquake)
3 加州在夏秋之間常常是很乾燥的。(summer)
4 大火可能會燒毀森林、家園以及建築物。
　(Wildfires / Forest fires)

02 ● The Southwest Region of the United States (p. 16)

A

1 Sunbelt   2 precious   3 aquifer   4 aqueduct
5 petroleum   6 ranch   7 cattle drive
8 reservation   9 refinery   10 adobe   11 herd
12 drill   13 refine   14 vaquero   15 crude oil
16 petrochemical

B

1 precious   2 aqueducts   3 Aquifers   4 petroleum
5 cattle drive   6 reservations   7 refinery   8 Adobe

C

1 herd   2 refined   3 drilling   4 carry

D

1 Sunbelt   2 refinery   3 ranch   4 reservation

E　美國西南部地區

　　美國西南部地區涵蓋非常廣大的區域，但它卻只擁有少數幾個州。這些州包括亞利桑納州、新墨西哥州、德州以及奧克拉荷馬州，其中大部分的土地都非常乾燥。事實上，這些區域有許多的沙漠。正因如此，這裡的人時時刻刻都要節約用水。不過，這裡的土地也並非全是沙漠。科羅拉多河流經亞利桑納州；里約格蘭德河流經德州。此外，落磯山脈貫穿部分的亞利桑納州和新墨西哥州。亞利桑納州本身擁有多樣性的地理環境，它的土地多數屬於沙漠。而大峽谷位於此州的北部，所以北部大部分的地方都有山脈。同時，此區也擁有許多森林。德州也位在美國西南部地區，它大部分的土地都非常乾燥。然而德州許多地方盛產豐富的石油。石油工業為德州重大的產業，德州同時也是美國最大的產油州之一。

以下何者為非？(2)

1 美國西南部地區有許多沙漠。
2 奧克拉荷馬州和紐約位於西南部地區。
3 大峽谷位於亞利桑那州。
4 德州擁有豐富的石油。

03 ● The Southeast Region of the United States (p. 20)

A

1 delta   2 wetland   3 bayou   4 agriculture
5 cash crop   6 irrigation   7 Bible Belt
8 segregation   9 civil rights   10 boycott
11 empty into   12 segregate
13 integrate   14 tributary   15 source   16 fertile soil

B

1 wetland   2 Delta   3 bayous   4 cash crops
5 irrigation   6 Agriculture   7 civil rights
8 Segregation

C

1 empties   2 segregated   3 integrated
4 boycotted

D

1 wetland   2 cash crop   3 civil rights   4 boycott

E　民權運動

　　多年以來，美國南部的人擁有自己的非洲黑奴。在1860年代，美國因奴隸問題而引發了南北戰爭。戰爭期間，所有的奴隸都獲得自由。然而，黑人和白人之間仍存在許多問題。黑人依舊飽受歧視，這意味著他們並沒有受到平等的待遇。此外，南方的黑人與白人之間實行了種族隔離，所以他們在不同的餐廳吃飯並且上不同的學校，甚至在公車上都要坐不同的區域。

　　但是在1950年代，美國南方開始了民權運動。黑人開始要求平等的對待。其中最有名的領導人士就是馬丁路德‧金恩。黑人常在不同的地方進行聯合抵制，他們在禁止黑人飲食的餐廳靜坐抗議。金恩博士試圖尋求非暴力手段，然而警方以及其他人卻經常使用暴力來對待黑人。《民權法案》直到1964年才通過，保障了不論膚色，所有人的平等權。

* discrimination 歧視　**sit-in** 靜坐抗議

填空
1 南北戰爭的導因是奴隸問題。(Civil War)
2 在南方，黑人與白人實行了種族隔離政策。(segregated)
3 民權運動於1950年代開始。(1950s)
4 馬丁路德・金恩是民權運動的著名領導者。(Martin Luther King, Jr.)

Unit 04 ● The Northeast Region of the United States (p. 24)

A
1 coastal plain　2 mountain range　3 seaway
4 heritage　5 descendant　6 metropolitan
7 metropolis　8 megalopolis　9 foliage　10 bog
11 stretch　12 live off　13 commute　14 canal
15 bay　16 lock

B
1 Coastal Plain　2 foliage　3 bogs　4 seaway
5 mountain ranges　6 metropolitan　7 megalopolis
8 Heritage

C
1 stretch　2 lived　3 descendants　4 commute

D
1 mountain range　2 heritage　3 descendant
4 metropolis

E 來自東北部的短篇小說

　　許多來自歐州的首批移民者前往美國的東北部。他們大部分都是英國人。這些人定居於紐約和賓夕法尼亞州。這當中有很多人住在紐約的哈德遜河谷。美國有些偉大的文學家就是來自此區。

　　作家華盛頓・歐文寫了許多關於此區的小說，其中最有名的就屬《李伯大夢》。這個故事發生在紐約的卡茨基爾山。在故事中，李伯自行前往山上。在遇見一些鬼魂後，他沉睡了二十年。當李伯醒後回到村莊，卻發現人事已非。

　　歐文另一個著名的小說是《沉睡谷傳奇》，故事的背景仍設定在紐約州北部。這是一個關於無頭騎士的故事。這個男鬼魂沒有頭，而長著一個南瓜頭。

　　歐文所著的以上小說以及其他故事，在美國文化中非常重要。它們刻畫了美國東北部的早期生活。直至今日，它們仍是無數大人和小孩必讀的作品。

* depict 刻畫　**jack-o'-lantern** 南瓜頭

以下何者為非？(2)
1 許多英國人居住在紐約州北部。
2 華盛頓・歐文住在卡茨基爾山。
3《李伯大夢》是關於美國早期生活的小說。
4 無頭騎士的頭是個南瓜。

Unit 05 ● The Midwest Region of the United States (p. 28)

A
1 prairie　2 lake effect　3 breadbasket　4 grain
5 livestock　6 frontier　7 pioneer　8 assembly line
9 industrialization　10 reclamation　11 cultivate
12 industrialize　13 mass-produce　14 assemble
15 manufacture　16 compete with/against

B
1 lake effect　2 breadbasket　3 Grains　4 livestock
5 frontier　6 assembly line　7 industrialization
8 pioneers

C
1 cultivating　2 industrialize　3 manufacture
4 compete

D
1 prairie　2 lake effect　3 frontier　4 reclamation

E 美國中西部

　　美國中西部涵蓋了廣大的土地，它自俄亥俄州、密西根州以及印第安納州起，向西遠至南、北達科他州、內布拉斯加州以及堪薩斯州。中西部總共有十二個州。

　　事實上，中西部地區位於美國東部及中央地帶。但是在很久以前，美國比現在小很多。這個國家僅有的州全部皆臨大西洋岸，所以人們才稱他們的西邊的土地為中西部。

　　中西部的土地都大致相似，充滿了平原和草原。中西部的土地都非常平坦，山地不存在於此區。大部分的山丘只有幾百英尺高而已。然而，五大湖位於中西部，坐落於美國和加拿大之間。

　　現今，居住於中西部的居民通常從事工業或農業。在底特律及其他城市，汽車製造是一個巨大的工業。然而，那裡仍然有許多農夫，他們種植玉米、小麥以及其他穀物。同時他們也飼養豬隻和母牛。

* identical 完全相同的

閱讀並且回答下列問題
1 中西部有幾個州？(Twelve.)
2 中西部的地形為何？(It's very flat.)
3 什麼是五大湖？(The five huge lakes located between U.S. and Canada.)
4 中西部的哪一個城市製造汽車？(Detroit.)

Review Test 1

A
1 rain shadow　2 logging　3 petroleum
4 reservation　5 delta　6 cash crop　7 heritage
8 metropolitan　9 prairie　10 pioneer
11 irrigate　12 deforest　13 refine　14 crude oil
15 segregate　16 integrate　17 live off　18 commute
19 industrialization　20 reclamation

B
1 (b)　2 (b)　3 (c)　4 (b)

C
1 bountiful　2 aqueducts　3 civil rights
4 mountain ranges

Unit 06 • The Mountain States of the United States (p. 34)

A

1 Continental Divide 2 elevation 3 peak
4 timberline 5 gorge 6 wildfire
7 transcontinental 8 ghost town 9 whitewater
10 mountain chain 11 rise 12 span 13 climb
14 cliff dwelling 15 sparse 16 deserted

B

1 Continental Divide 2 peaks 3 elevation
4 mountain chain 5 transcontinental 6 timberline
7 whitewater 8 Ghost towns

C

1 rise 2 span 3 affects 4 sparse

D

1 timberline 2 gorge 3 wildfire 4 ghost town

E 黃石國家公園

美國最漂亮的地方之一就是黃石國家公園。它大部分位於懷俄明州，少部分位於蒙大拿州和愛達荷州。

多年以來，人們聽聞過西部美麗的土地，卻鮮少人真正見識過。然而在1800年代，人們開始造訪此地。此外，藝術家湯瑪斯‧莫蘭也曾來過黃石。他創作許多此區美景的畫作，這幫助黃石公園在1872年成為第一個國家公園。

許多不同的動物居住在黃石公園。北美野牛、狼、駝鹿、老鷹以及許多其他動物都生活於此。這裡大部分的土地都是森林，但也有些是平原、甚至有間歇泉。間歇泉將熱水噴至空氣中，其中最有名的間歇泉稱做「老忠實噴泉」。它因噴發時段固定而享有此名。

以下何者為「是」？請在空格中填入「T」或「F」。
1 黃石國家公園只位於懷俄明州。(F)
2 湯瑪斯‧莫蘭是個攝影師。(F)
3 黃石公園成為美國第一個國家公園。(T)
4 「老忠實噴泉」是黃石公園的間歇泉名稱。(T)

Unit 07 • Mountains, Rivers, and Deserts of the World (p. 38)

A

1 summit 2 majestic 3 backbone 4 extend
5 sea level 6 silt 7 arid 8 nomadic 9 rugged
10 river system 11 attempt 12 be attempted by
13 be accompanied by 14 dehydrate
15 Mount Everest 16 Sahara Desert

B

1 Rugged 2 majestic 3 extend 4 backbone
5 River system 6 Sea level 7 silt 8 nomadic

C

1 attempted 2 dehydrate 3 accompanied 4 K2

D

1 summit 2 sea level 3 rugged 4 arid

E 攀登聖母峰

聖母峰屬喜馬拉雅山脈群，位於尼泊爾、西藏和中國的邊界。其高8,848公尺，是世界上最高的山。人們稱它為「世界之頂」。

長久以來，許多人都想成為第一個攀上此山的人，但從沒有人到過山頂。許多人嘗試攀爬，不但無人成功，更有人喪命於此。

然而就在1953年，至少有兩個人成功了。他們是來自紐西蘭的艾德蒙‧西拉瑞爵士和雪巴的丹增‧諾蓋。雪巴人是來自西藏和尼泊爾的登山專家，他們常被雇用為前往喜馬拉雅山（特別是聖母峰）登山探險的嚮導。

那一個團隊有九個人，他們雇用了數百個搬運工和二十個雪巴人。他們花了數日才接近山頂附近。有些人離終點很近，卻無法抵達。最後在1953年5月29號，西拉瑞和諾蓋抵達了山頂。他們是第一批站在世界之頂的人。

以下何者為「是」？請在空格中填入「T」或「F」。
1 聖母峰是世界第一高山。(T)
2 艾德蒙‧西拉瑞於1953年攀登聖母峰。(T)
3 雪巴人來自紐西蘭。(F)
4 艾德蒙‧西拉瑞獨力登上聖母峰。(F)

Unit 08 • Asian Cultures (p. 42)

A

1 Hinduism 2 caste 3 Brahmin 4 Buddhism
5 Confucianism 6 Taoism 7 meditation
8 dynasty 9 gunpowder 10 Silk Road
11 make up one's mind 12 determine 13 set off
14 attain enlightment 15 compass 16 sacred

B

1 Hinduism 2 castes 3 Buddhism 4 Taoism
5 Brahmins 6 Confucianism 7 Meditation
8 dynasties

C

1 made 2 enlightened 3 meditates 4 sacred

D

1 caste 2 Hinduism 3 Confucianism 4 Silk Road

E 馬可波羅與絲路

中國和歐洲相距遙遠。今日，人們只要花幾個小時便可飛抵兩地。然而在過去，兩地往返需要幾個月或是幾年的時間。當人們由中國前往歐洲，他們會經過絲路。

絲路並非一條真的路，而是許多貿易路線所組合起來的。經由此道，人們可以由地中海前往太平洋。這條商道之所以稱做絲路，是因中國人經由此處將絲綢運送至西方。

絲路因馬可波羅而變得非常有名。他是一位義大利的探險家，和父親及舅舅一起離開義大利，至24年後才返回家鄉。他經由絲路抵達中國，途中經過許多冒險，甚至成為皇帝的顧問。當他返回義大利，他寫了一本《馬可波羅遊記》，這本書是關於他的遊歷，而且此書大受歡迎。

閱讀並且回答下列問題
1 在過去人們如何由中國前往歐洲？
  (They went on the Silk Road.)
2 絲路是什麼？(A large group of trade routes.)
3 誰利用絲路運送絲綢？(The Chinese.)
4 誰是馬可波羅？(An Italian adventurer.)

09 ● Europe in the Middle Ages (p. 46)

A
1 Byzantine Empire　2 medieval　3 feudalism
4 manor　5 knight　6 chivalry　7 noble　8 cathedral
9 Dark Ages　10 Crusade　11 collapse　12 split
13 reign　14 swear an oath　15 vassal　16 fief

B
1 medieval　2 Feudalism　3 manor　4 Chivalry
5 nobles　6 Dark Ages　7 Knights　8 Crusades

C
1 collapsed　2 split　3 reigned　4 swore

D
1 Byzantine Empire　2 chivalry　3 feudalism
4 Dark Ages

E　中世紀
　　羅馬帝國於476年瓦解，它被日耳曼人征服。在東方，拜占庭帝國仍存在，它就是東羅馬帝國。直至一千多年後，東羅馬帝國才於1453年被擊敗。

　　然而在西歐，西羅馬帝國瓦解後，黑暗時代來臨。黑暗時代一詞適用於羅馬帝國瓦解後的前三百年間或是整個中世紀。這段期間，只有少數人能夠閱讀和寫字。人們的生活非常艱苦，生活僅能糊口。大部分的人以農為業，生活過得非常簡單。

　　在中世紀期間，人們的生活沒有很大的改善。有些國王公平地對待他的臣民；但有些國王則非常殘酷。這些國王把他們的人民當成奴隸對待，並嚴加課稅。許多人死於飢餓或是疾病，黑死病在十四世紀奪走了幾乎歐洲半數人的性命。對大部分的人來說，中世紀是一場苦難。

* struggle 奮鬥

以下何者為非？(2)
1 羅馬帝國於476年瓦解。
2 拜占庭帝國在西歐。
3 黑暗時代出現在羅馬帝國瓦解之後。
4 許多中世紀時期的人們生活很苦。

10 ● The Civil War (p. 50)

A
1 slavery　2 secession　3 Union　4 Confederacy
5 rebellion　6 emancipation　7 blockade
8 attrition　9 ironclad　10 assassination　11 secede
12 break away　13 rebel　14 blockade
15 emancipate　16 surrender

B
1 slavery　2 Confederacy　3 Union　4 rebellion
5 attrition　6 secession　7 emancipation
8 assassination

C
1 secede　2 rebelled　3 emancipated
4 surrendered

D
1 slavery　2 blockade　3 emancipation
4 assassination

E　美國南北戰爭
　　南北戰爭是美國史上死傷最慘的戰爭。戰爭發生的原因有很多，主要是奴隸問題。南方有奴隸；北方則沒有。

　　南北戰爭發生於亞伯拉罕‧林肯成為總統後的1861年。當時北方人力充足，也擁有較多的鐵路和工業。但是南方的將領則比北方的出色。這場戰爭有過許多戰役。戰爭之初，南軍看似佔有優勢。但是在1863年，羅伯特‧E‧李將軍在蓋茲堡之役中大敗。隔天，南軍又敗於維克斯堡之役。在這之後，北軍開始勢如破竹。

　　聯邦軍的兩個將軍非常重要。威廉‧T‧謝爾曼將軍切斷了南軍。他的向海岸行軍計畫由亞特蘭大向沙凡那港市進軍，摧毀了許多南軍反抗的意志。尤利賽斯‧S‧格蘭特將軍帶領聯邦的軍隊打敗了南軍。李將軍最後向他投降。五天之後，約翰‧威爾克斯‧布斯刺殺了林肯總統。

* assassinate 刺殺

填空
1 南北戰爭發生在亞伯拉罕‧林肯就任總統時。
  (Civil War)
2 南方擁有比北方出色的將領。(generals)
3 謝爾曼將軍執行向海岸行軍計畫。(March)
4 戰爭結束後，約翰‧威爾克斯‧布斯刺殺了林肯總統。
  (John Wilkes Booth)

Review Test 2

A
1 timberline　2 elevation　3 majestic　4 sea level
5 caste　6 Confucianism　7 medieval　8 feudalism
9 slavery　10 secession　11 sparse　12 deserted
13 rugged　14 river system　15 meditate
16 sacred　17 Crusade　18 collapse　19 blockade
20 emancipate

B
1 (b)　2 (a)　3 (b)　4 (c)

C
1 Continental Divide　2 River system　3 Hinduism
4 manor

11 • Inquiry Skills and Science Tools (p. 56)

A

1 inquiry 2 scientific method 3 observation
4 inference 5 infer 6 investigation 7 hypothesis
8 experiment 9 conclusion 10 microscope
11 inquire 12 investigate 13 hypothesize
14 analyze 15 interpret 16 conclude

B

1 inquiry 2 observation 3 inference 4 infer
5 hypothesis 6 experiment 7 investigation
8 conclusion

C

1 (c) 2 (c) 3 (b)

D

1 scientific method / experiment 2 inference
3 hypothesis 4 microscope

E 科學探究方法

科學家有一個用來試圖獲知新事物的方法，稱做科學探究方法。

第一步是要提出問題。問題可以是「為什麼鳥會在冬天向南飛？」或者是「黃金需要多熱才會熔化？」。提出的問題可以是任何事情。

接下來，科學家會進行實驗。他們必須盡可能地瞭解研究主題。之後，科學家會形成一個假說。這會是一個有根據的猜測。例如「鳥在冬天向南飛是因為牠們會冷」或是「黃金在華氏200度會熔化」。現在科學家有了假說，就要對它進行檢測。他們通常會進行實驗來檢測假說。有些人在實驗室裡進行實驗；有些人則會在戶外進行。

實驗完成後，科學家會分析數據，並與假說加以比較。假說是正確還是錯誤的呢？就算是錯誤的假說，科學家也能從中學到許多。最後，他們會把結果寫下來。如此一來，其他人也可以從中獲益不少。

* educated 有根據的

填空
1 科學家使用科學探究方法來得知事情。(method)
2 假說是一個有根據的猜測。(hypothesis)
3 科學家在實驗室或是戶外進行實驗。(labs)
4 科學家在實驗完成後分析數據。(analyze)

12 • Classifying Living Things (p. 60)

A

1 organism 2 microorganism 3 protist
4 bacteria 5 fungus 6 vascular plant 7 cell
8 membrane 9 nucleus 10 cytoplasm 11 classify
12 divide 13 split 14 replicate
15 single-celled organism 16 multi-celled organism

B

1 organism 2 Protists 3 Microorganisms
4 Vascular plants 5 single-celled 6 nucleus
7 fungus 8 Cytoplasm

C

1 (c) 2 (c) 3 (b)

D

1 protist 2 vascular plant 3 cell
4 (cell) membrane

E 有機體

地球上有數百萬種的有機體。有機體是任何活著的生物。他們包含了動物、植物、真菌以及微生物。所有的有機體都由細胞組成。有些有機體只有一個細胞。有些則擁有數不盡的細胞。

微生物非常非常小。事實上，沒有顯微鏡是無法看到它們的。細菌和原生生物都是微生物，通常是單細胞生物。所以它們要維持的就只是個單一細胞生命。那麼它們要如何繁殖呢？它們將自己一分為二，這稱作無性生殖。

然而大多數的有機體屬於多細胞生物，所以它們可能僅有一些細胞或是擁有無數個細胞。多細胞生物擁有特定的細胞，這些細胞通常會進行專門的工作，它們可以用來抵禦疾病、繁殖、消化或是其他的特殊用途。

* asexual 無性生殖的 **asexual reproduction** 無性生殖

以下何者為「是」？請在空格中填入「T」或「F」。
1 地球上有一百萬個有機體。(F)
2 你需要顯微鏡來觀察微生物。(T)
3 多細胞生物僅有一個細胞。(F)
4 細胞有許多用途。(T)

13 • Heredity (p. 64)

A

1 evolution 2 adaptation 3 behavior 4 species
5 gene 6 genetic 7 inherited 8 heredity
9 sperm cell 10 egg cell 11 evolve 12 adapt
13 inherit 14 transfer 15 behave 16 characteristic

B

1 evolution 2 Behavior 3 Adaptations 4 species
5 Genes 6 Heredity 7 genetic 8 sperm cell

C

1 evolve 2 behave 3 transferred 4 Instinctive

D

1 evolution 2 heredity 3 gene 4 egg cell

E 遺傳

人們通常會與父母長得很像。他們也許會有相同的面孔、相同的髮色或是眼睛。他們也許會和父母一樣高或一樣矮。為什麼他們會長得如此相似呢？其答案在於遺傳。

遺傳是指由親代傳給後代的特徵，這發生的原因來自於基因，基因內有去氧核糖核酸。去氧核糖核酸是生命的基本架構，父母親雙方傳遞基因給後代，所以後代才會長得像父母親其中一人，或是與父母都很相似。

基因可分為顯性和隱性的，顯性基因帶給身體的影響比隱性基因來得大，隱性基因存在於體內，卻不會對身體有影響。然而顯性基因則會影響生物體。

基因不僅僅決定有機體的身體特徵，同時也決定了有機體的心理特徵。這其中也包含了智力、甚至是性格。

* dominant 顯性的　recessive 隱性的

閱讀並且回答下列問題
1 為什麼小孩長得像他們的父母？(Because of heredity.)
2 基因包含什麼？(DNA.)
3 基因的種類為何？
　(Dominant genes and recessive genes.)
4 哪一種基因會影響有機體？(Dominant genes.)

14 • The History of the Earth (p. 68)

A
1 eon　2 era　3 formation　4 dating　5 geology
6 topography　7 plate　8 fault　9 continental drift
10 collision　11 elapse　12 date　13 strike
14 collide with / crash into　15 shake　16 tremor

B
1 eon　2 era　3 dating　4 Topography　5 fault
6 formation　7 continental drift　8 collision

C
1 elapsed　2 date　3 colliding　4 tremors

D
1 geology　2 plate　3 fault　4 tsunami

E　地球的形成
　　太陽於數十億年前形成，巨大的岩石和氣體環繞著太陽系。最後約45億年前，這些物質開始形成行星，地球位於距離太陽的第三位。地球形成之初非常炙熱，數百萬年後開始冷卻。

　　隨著地球的冷卻，水蒸氣開始在大氣中形成，造就了地球表面雲層的產生。不久後，這些雲層開始落下大量的水於整個地球，這使地球的大洋、海、河流以及湖泊因此誕生。

　　但是45億年前的地球，和現今的地球長得不一樣。今日的地球有七塊大陸，以前卻不然，大陸的數量持續變動，曾經，整個地球僅只有一塊大陸。這是為什麼呢？板塊構造理論是一個線索。地殼由許多板塊組成，這些板塊是一片片巨大的陸塊，而且它們持續在移動。隨著地球年齡的增加，它們也緩慢得移動。今天，地球上有七塊大陸。在未來，陸塊也許會變多或是變少。

* plate tectonics 板塊構造理論

填空
1 地球於45億年前形成。(4.5 billion)
2 水蒸氣在地球開始冷卻時形成。(vapor)
3 今天地球上有七塊大陸。(continents)
4 因為板塊構造理論，地殼的板塊持續在移動。
　(plate tectonics)

15 • The Weather and Water Cycle (p. 72)

A
1 evaporation　2 condensation　3 weather map
4 humidity　5 air mass　6 cold front　7 warm front
8 isobar　9 wind speed　10 runoff　11 rise into
12 soak into / seep into　13 rate　14 storm surge
15 droplet　16 high pressure

B
1 evaporation　2 Condensation　3 humidity
4 runoff　5 air mass　6 cold front　7 isobar
8 wind speed

C
1 seeps　2 rated　3 moves　4 High

D
1 weather map　2 humidity　3 isobar　4 eye

E　水循環
　　地球上的水量是有限的。事實上，在這數十億年以來，水量一直沒有改變。不過，水通常以不同的形式出現，這些造就了水循環。

　　第一個環節為蒸發。這是指太陽溫度造成河水、湖水以及海水變為水蒸氣的過程，水蒸氣會上升到空氣中。

　　第二個環節是凝結。隨著水蒸氣的上升，空氣會跟著變冷。這導致水蒸氣變成微細的水滴。接下來，這些小水滴會聚在一起而形成雲。

　　第三個環節是降水。水滴會以某些形式在地表落下。最常見的降水是下雨。但是，天氣寒冷時，水滴可能以雪、凍雨或是冰的形式降下。

　　最後一個環節是匯流。當水降至地表，可能會流入河流、湖泊、海或是大洋。水也有可能進入土壤中，這些水會變成地下水。不過，水循環是生生不息的。

以下何者為「是」？請在空格中填入「T」或「F」。
1 地球的水量一直在變化。(F)
2 蒸發是水循環的第一個環節。(T)
3 水蒸氣是冰的一種形式。(F)
4 雨水、凍雨和雪都是降水的種類。(T)

Review Test 3

A
1 inquiry　2 inference　3 microorganism　4 protist
5 evolution　6 heredity　7 plate　8 fault
9 weather map　10 air mass　11 hypothesis
12 analyze　13 nucleus　14 cytoplasm　15 inherit
16 transfer　17 continental drift
18 collide with / crash into　19 soak into / seep into
20 rate

B
1 (c)　2 (c)　3 (a)　4 (b)

C
1 fungus　2 Genes　3 collision　4 runoff

16 • Changes in Matter (p. 78)

A
1 element 2 property 3 atom 4 molecule
5 particle 6 compound 7 solubility
8 physical change 9 chemical reaction 10 matter
11 take up 12 take place 13 dissolve
14 break down / break up 15 combine 16 react

B
1 Elements 2 Matter 3 atom 4 molecule
5 particle 6 chemical reaction 7 compound
8 properties

C
1 takes 2 physical 3 dissolve 4 react

D
1 atom 2 compound 3 solubility
4 physical change

E　物理變化與化學變化
　　物質通常會經過許多改變。主要的改變可分為兩種：物理變化和化學變化。

　　物理變化有許多種，它們通常牽涉到物質在固態、液態以及氣態上的改變。舉例來說，融化的冰變為水就是一種物理變化；沸騰的水變成水蒸氣也是一種物理變化。不過物理變化還是有其他可能的形式。譬如，將一些糖放入水中並攪拌它，糖會溶解，這就是物理變化。或是，單純把一張紙撕碎，這也是另一種物理變化。

　　化學變化則有所差別，它涉及到新混合物的生成。舉例來說，將鈉和氯結合會經過一個化學反應，反應的結果是鹽的生成。光合作用是另一種化學反應，水加上二氧化碳會變成糖加上氧氣。

* sodium 鈉　chlorine 氯

以下何者為非？(2)
1 物質會經受物理變化或是化學變化。
2 融化的冰變為水就是一種化學變化。
3 糖溶解於水中是一種物理變化。
4 光合作用是一種化學變化。

17 • Light and Heat (p. 82)

A
1 light wave 2 reflection 3 refraction 4 thermal
5 conduction 6 convection 7 radiation
8 conductivity 9 radiate 10 thermogram
11 transfer 12 pass through 13 see through
14 transparent 15 translucent 16 opaque

B
1 Light waves 2 Refraction 3 Reflection
4 conduction 5 convection 6 Thermal 7 radiate
8 thermograms

C
1 conduct 2 see 3 reflects 4 translucent

D
1 conduction 2 radiation 3 convection
4 conductivity

E　傳導、對流與輻射
　　熱是能量的一種形式，它可以由一處移動到另一處。熱移動的方式可分為三種：傳導、對流與輻射。

　　當熱接觸到物質，它也會使物質中的原子和分子移動。這些分子和原子接著碰到其他周遭的分子和原子們，它們也跟著移動。這就是傳導，也就是鍋柄會變熱的原因。鍋子本身被加熱，但鍋子中的分子接觸到鍋柄中的分子。它們也會使鍋柄變熱。

　　對流是熱移動的第二種形式。可在引力中移動的物質被加熱，就稱為對流。空氣、水和其他液體就屬於這種物質。烤箱就是利用對流來運作。烤箱中的線圈將空氣加熱，空氣上升的地方就能烹煮食物。空氣變涼後會下降。此時線圈再次加熱，空氣就會再次上升。

　　輻射是熱移動的第三種形式，它發生在熱能以波的形式移動時。太陽利用輻射加熱地表，並用波的形式將熱能送出。波會抵達地球並帶來熱能。

填空
1 熱是能量的一種形式。（energy）
2 傳導解釋了鍋柄變熱的原因。(Conduction)
3 由於對流，大部分的烤箱能烹煮食物。(convection)
4 太陽透過輻射加熱地表。(radiation)

18 • Circulation and Respiration (p. 86)

A
1 artery 2 vein 3 aorta 4 blood vessel
5 blood cell 6 platelet 7 blood pressure
8 heart rate 9 respiration 10 immune system
11 inhale 12 exhale 13 be immune to 14 resist
15 ventricle 16 atrium

B
1 Veins 2 Arteries 3 blood vessels 4 blood cells
5 Platelets 6 Blood pressure 7 respiration
8 immune system

C
1 inhale 2 exhale 3 respire 4 chambers

D
1 artery 2 vein 3 aorta 4 platelet

E　循環系統
　　循環系統能控制體內血液流動。它擁有許多部分，其中最重要的是心臟。然而，動脈和靜脈也會將血液流送至全身。

　　心臟可分為四個腔室。它們是左右心房和左右心室。首先，血液流入右心房，然後進入右心室和肺部。在肺部，氧氣會進入血液中。接著血液會回到心臟。血液通過左心房後，會由左心室流出心臟並進入主動脈。

主動脈是身體的主要動脈，它供給全身各處的血液。我們的身體有動脈和靜脈，它們被統稱為血管。這些血管帶著富氧血輸送至身體的每個地方。在被身體利用完後，血液會喪失氧氣。這時候其他的靜脈和動脈會將貧氧血帶回心臟，循環系統就會再次循環。

以下何者為非？(2)
1 循環系統控制血液的流動。
2 心臟有四個心室。
3 身體的主要動脈是主動脈。
4 血管運送血液至全身。

19 ● Electricity (p. 90)

A
1 static electricity　2 current electricity
3 series circuit　4 parallel circuit　5 charge
6 conductor　7 insulator　8 electromagnet
9 generator　10 hydroelectric　11 conduct
12 insulate　13 charge　14 closed circuit
15 potential energy　16 kinetic energy

B
1 charges　2 Static electricity　3 current electricity
4 parallel circuit　5 insulator　6 electromagnet
7 generator　8 Hydroelectric power

C
1 insulate　2 conduct　3 recharge　4 closed

D
1 conductor　2 insulator　3 static electricity
4 series circuit

E 導體與絕緣體
　　由於有導體的存在，電才能夠移動。有很多的材料都能使電自由移動。金和銀是非常好的導體，所以有些人利用它們製造金屬線。然而金和銀都很昂貴，因此人們用其他導體來製造金屬線。大部分的電線是由像銅這樣的導電金屬所構成。

　　還有哪些東西是導體呢？許多金屬都屬於導體，石墨就是其中之一。水是最佳的導體。這也就是為什麼在大雷雨中游泳是個壞主意。閃電會擊中水並傷害、甚至奪走人的性命。人體也是導體之一。人要對周遭的電加以小心就是這個原因。

　　當然，人可能會想阻止電的流動。為此，人們使用絕緣體，它們能阻斷電四處移動。那麼絕緣體有哪些呢？塑膠是非常好的絕緣體，紙和橡膠也是絕緣體，還有，玻璃和瓷器亦是絕緣體，這些材料都能有效阻止電的流動。

閱讀並且回答下列問題
1 導體有哪些？(Gold, silver, copper, graphite, metals, water, and the human body.)
2 導體的作用為何？(It lets electricity move freely.)
3 絕緣體的作用為何？(It stops the flow of electricity.)
4 絕緣體有哪些？(Plastics, paper, rubber, glass, and porcelain.)

20 ● Motion and Forces (p. 94)

A
1 force　2 motion　3 position　4 acceleration
5 inertia　6 friction　7 fulcrum　8 accelerate
9 velocity　10 gravity　11 gravitation　12 decelerate
13 attrack　14 pull　15 fall　16 law of motion

B
1 Force　2 Position　3 Velocity　4 inertia
5 Gravity　6 Gravitation　7 friction　8 Acceleration

C
1 accelerate　2 decelerate　3 attracts　4 fall

D
1 motion　2 velocity　3 acceleration　4 fulcrum

E 艾薩克・牛頓爵士
　　艾薩克・牛頓爵士生活在十七到十八世紀，他是史上最偉大的科學家之一。他研究光學、發明微積分，還發現重力和三大運動定律。

　　據說有一天牛頓坐在一棵蘋果樹下，被一顆落下的蘋果打中頭。因此他開始思考重力，他發現就是重力致使物體掉落到地面。

　　牛頓的三大運動定律對物理學非常重要。第一定律說明，未受到外力前，物體的運動狀態保持不變。這通常稱之為「慣性定律」。

　　第二運動定律稱為「加速度定律」。它通常被寫為「Ｆ＝ma」，這表示「作用力等於質量乘以加速度」。第二運動定律是三大運動定律中最重要的一個。

　　第三運動定律說明，在每一個作用力都存在著一個相等且相反的力。第三定律意味著所有的作用力會互相影響。

以下何者為「是」？請在空格中填入「T」或「F」。
1 艾薩克・牛頓爵士生活在二十世紀。(F)
2 牛頓發現了重力。(T)
3 第一運動定律是Ｆ＝ma。(F)
4 牛頓想出了三大運動定律。(T)

Review Test 4

A
1 element　2 atom　3 conduction　4 convection
5 artery　6 vein　7 series circuit　8 parallel circuit
9 inertia　10 friction　11 take up　12 dissolve
13 translucent　14 opaque　15 ventricle　16 atrium
17 generator　18 hydroelectric　19 velocity
20 gravity

B
1 (a)　2 (b)　3 (b)　4 (a)

C
1 Matter　2 Thermal　3 blood vessels　4 charges

21 ● Fractions and Decimals (p. 100)

A

1 improper fraction　2 mixed number
3 equivalent fraction　4 unit fraction
5 common factor　6 greatest common factor
7 common denominator　8 simplest form
9 lowest term　10 thousandth
11 reduce to one's lowest term
12 put in one's lowest term　13 round　14 round up
15 round down　16 be equivalent to

B

1 Improper fractions　2 mixed number
3 unit fraction　4 common factor　5 greatest
6 common denominator　7 simplest form
8 thousandth's

C

1 Reduce　2 lowest　3 up　4 equivalent

D

1 improper fraction　2 unit fraction
3 common factor　4 equivalent fraction

E 分數與小數的讀寫

　　你可以用數字或文字來表達分數與小數。它們有許多的表達方式。舉例來說，你可以把三分之二寫成 $\frac{2}{3}$。然而，分數在唸法上也有許多種。$\frac{1}{6}$ 可以唸成one-sixth或是one out of six。分數 $\frac{5}{8}$ 可以唸成 five divided by eight。

　　說到小數，它通常是由小數點左邊的數字開始一個一個唸。舉例來說，1.1唸作一點一；2.45唸作二點四五。然而有些小數是可以以分數的說法來唸。0.1唸作零點一或是十分之一；0.7唸作零點七或是十分之七。

　　有時候你可以用比較簡單的方式來書寫分數，這稱為最簡式。例如，分數 $\frac{4}{8}$ 的最簡式是 $\frac{1}{2}$；$\frac{3}{3}$ 的最簡式是 $\frac{1}{3}$。

　　最後，有時候你可以將分數寫成小數。分數 $\frac{2}{10}$ 可以寫成0.2；分數 $\frac{9}{10}$ 可以寫成0.9。這就是為什麼你可以將0.1讀作十分之一的原因。

閱讀並且回答下列問題

1 六分之一的寫法為何？($\frac{1}{6}$)
2 2.45的讀法為何？(Two point four five.)
3 $\frac{4}{8}$的最簡式為何？($\frac{1}{2}$)
4 $\frac{2}{10}$的小數形式為何？(0.2)

22 ● Lines, Rays, Angles, and Figures (p. 104)

A

1 plane　2 two-dimensional　3 segment　4 ray
5 endpoint　6 degree　7 acute angle
8 obtuse angle　9 right angle　10 straight angle
11 intersect

12 parallel　13 protractor　14 compass
15 perpendicular line　16 diagonal line

B

1 plane　2 two-dimensional　3 ray　4 segment
5 endpoint　6 acute angle　7 degrees
8 right angle

C

1 intersect　2 parallel　3 protractor　4 compass

D

1 acute angle　2 obtuse angle　3 right angle
4 straight angle

E 角度

　　當兩個線段交會在同一端點，會形成一個角度。角的大小會根據角度來測量。角可從0度到180度來衡量。角可分為四種，它們的種類取決於度數的大小。

　　平角的角度為180度，它可以形成一條線。

　　另一種角為銳角。它大於0度，小於90度。所有的三角形都至少有一個銳角，其中有許多三角形有三個銳角。

　　直角形成於兩垂直線相交時。這兩條線形成了一個90度的角，稱之為直角。正方形和長方形中的角度都為直角。有些三角形有一個直角，因此它們被稱為直角三角形。

　　最後一種角為鈍角。鈍角大於90度，小於180度。有些三角形有鈍角，但一個三角形不會有一個以上的鈍角。

以下何者為非？(3)
1 平角會形成一條線。
2 銳角介於0度到90度之間。
3 直角大於鈍角。
4 鈍角大於銳角。

23 ● Kinds of Polygons, Circles, and Triangles (p. 108)

A

1 polygon　2 quadrilateral　3 parallelogram
4 diagonal　5 chord　6 diameter　7 radius
8 equilateral　9 transformation　10 formula
11 construct　12 figure out　13 length　14 width
15 height　16 right triangle

B

1 polygon　2 quadrilateral　3 parallelograms
4 chord　5 Diameter　6 equilateral
7 Transformation　8 formula

C

1 construct　2 width　3 length　4 height

D

1 quadrilateral　2 equilateral triangle　3 diameter
4 radius

E 三角形

　　三角形為三個邊的幾何圖形，它可分為許多種類。三角形的種類決定於三角形的角度和邊長。

　　前三種三角形為銳角三角形、直角三角形和鈍角三角形。銳角三角形是指三角形的三個內角皆為銳角，所以每個角度都小於90度。直角三角形有一個為90度的內角，其他兩個內角都為銳角。最後，鈍角三角形有一個大於90度且小於180度的內角。它的其他兩個內角為銳角。

接下來，有三種三角形可以根據邊長來分類。它們是等邊三角形、等腰三角形以及不等邊三角形。等邊三角形的三個邊長皆相等，三個內角皆永遠為60度，所以它們也是銳角三角形。等腰三角形有兩個相等的邊長。不等邊三角形的三個邊長都不相等。

填空
1 三角形有三個邊。(three)
2 銳角三角形的每個內角都小於90度。(acute)
3 直角三角形有一個為90度的內角。(right)
4 等邊三角形的三個邊皆相等。(same)

24 ● Data and Graphs (p.112)

A
1 elapsed time 2 survey 3 diagram 4 chart
5 graph 6 mean 7 median 8 mode
9 frequency 10 probability 11 predict 12 conduct
13 make a prediction 14 organize 15 order
16 coordinate grid

B
1 Elapsed time 2 diagrams 3 mode 4 median
5 Frequency 6 mean 7 surveys 8 chart

C
1 (a) 2 (b) 3 (b)

D
1 circle graph 2 coordinate grid 3 probability
4 mean

E 蒐集和分配數據

人們時常會進行研究。他們研究一個主題並儘量蒐集相關資料。也許他們會想知道一個地區一整年的每日氣溫。或是學生一學期要閱讀的書量。首先，他們必需先決定他們想要何種資訊，接著才能蒐集數據。

然而，人們所蒐集的原始數據本身可能一無所用。所以必須要整理數據。常見的方法之一就是利用圖表來檢視數據所呈現的視覺化資料。舉例來說，研究員擁有每個學生閱讀書量的數據。他們可以把數據放到直條圖上，以便於分析。或者，也許他們知道一年每日的日平均溫度。他們可以把數據整理成圓形圖。此圖會顯示該區寒暖天數的百分比。藉由這些視覺輔助，他們能更易於解釋數據。

以下何者為非？(3)
1 數據是人們蒐集的資料。
2 人們用圖表來整理他們的資料。
3 直條圖用圓形來顯示數據。
4 圖表屬於視覺輔助。

Review Test 5

A
1 improper fraction 2 common factor
3 greatest common factor 4 acute angle
5 obtuse angle 6 right angle 7 quadrilateral
8 equilateral 9 mean 10 mode
11 put in one's lowest term 12 be equivalent to
13 perpendicular line 14 diagonal line
15 protractor 16 transformation 17 formula
18 right triangle 19 frequency 20 probability

B
1 (c) 2 (c) 3 (a) 4 (b)

C
1 two-dimensional 2 common denominator
3 parallelograms 4 diagrams

25 ● Norse Mythology (p. 118)

A
1 Norse 2 Asgard 3 Odin 4 Ragnarok
5 trickster 6 troll 7 dwarf 8 Valkyrie 9 Valhalla
10 Edda 11 trick 12 fool 13 swing 14 name after
15 reincarnate 16 Thor

B
1 Norse 2 Asgard 3 Ragnarok 4 Tricksters
5 Trolls 6 dwarf 7 Valhalla 8 Eddas

C
1 trick 2 named 3 reincarnated 4 swung

D
1 Asgard 2 Ragnarok 3 Odin 4 Valkyries

E 北歐眾神

北歐神話來自北歐。古北歐人曾是維京人，他們住在現今為挪威、瑞典以及芬蘭的區域。維京人喜愛打仗和製造戰爭，因此他們的故事都非常暴力。

北歐有許多的神，奧丁為他們的領導者。奧丁非常睿智。他身邊有兩隻渡鴉，分別代表思想與記憶。牠們告訴奧丁土地上發生的一切。

索爾是雷神，是諸神中最強大的一個。他擁有一根常用來殺死巨人的巨錘。洛基是奸詐之神與火神，同時是半個巨人。洛基也是個騙子，因此他替諸神帶來許多麻煩，特別是索爾。

弗麗嘉是奧丁的妻子，同時也是婚姻女神。芙蕾雅是愛之女神。北歐還有許多其他諸神。

眾神住在諸神國度。他們常要和像寒霜巨人和山精這樣的敵人戰鬥。至今人們仍喜愛閱讀關於諸神種種事蹟的故事。

* **mischief** 惡作劇 **deed** 行為；功蹟

填空
1 北歐神話來自古代斯堪地那維亞國家。(Scandinavian)
2 眾神的領導者為奧丁。(Odin)
3 洛基時常為雷神索爾帶來麻煩。(Thor)
4 北歐眾神住在諸神國度。(Asgard)

26 • Learning about Sentences (p. 122)

A
1 part of speech   2 subject   3 predicate
4 conjunction   5 complete sentence
6 run-on sentence   7 tense   8 usage
9 punctuation   10 agree   11 combine   12 connect
13 agree   14 separate   15 divide   16 fix

B
1 parts of speech   2 subject   3 predicate   4 Usage
5 complete sentence   6 agreement   7 tense
8 Conjunctions

C
1 (b)   2 (c)   3 (a)

D
1 conjunction   2 predicate   3 run-on sentence
4 tense

E 認識句子
　　所有的句子都有主詞和動詞。有的句子非常短。例如,「我吃過了」是一個完整的句子。為什麼呢?因為它有主詞和動詞。有些句子則可以非常長。

　　人們在造英文句子時,常會犯錯。常見的錯誤就是連寫句。看看這個句子「我去公園我看到我的朋友」。它就是一個連寫句。連寫句是指兩個需要標點符號或是連接詞來合併的句子。完整的句子應該是「我去公園,而且我看到我的朋友。」

　　所有的句子都需要主詞與動詞一致。這意味著主詞為單數,則動詞也要為單數形式;主詞為複數,則動詞也要為複數形式。看看這句子「Jason like to play computer games.」這是一個錯誤的句子。為什麼呢?因為此句中的主詞與動詞不一致。正確且完整的句子應該是「Jason likes to play computer games.」

　　所以要小心連寫句,並永遠確認主詞與動詞一致。你才能寫出許多完整的句子。

以下何者為非?(2)
1 所有的句子都有主詞和動詞。
2 連寫句擁有好的文法。
3 單數主詞搭配單數動詞。
4 主詞與動詞一致在英文中很重要。

27 • The Art of the Middle Ages (p. 126)

A
1 cathedral   2 spire   3 buttress   4 Gothic Age
5 gargoyle   6 icon   7 statuette   8 tapestry
9 illuminated manuscript   10 stained glass window
11 inspire   12 emphasize   13 depict   14 represent
15 hold up   16 magnificent

B
1 spires   2 Buttresses   3 Icons   4 Cathedrals
5 manuscripts   6 Tapestries   7 Gothic Age
8 statuette

C
1 inspired   2 depict   3 hold   4 emphasized

D
1 cathedral   2 buttress   3 gargoyle
4 stained glass window

E 哥德式教堂
　　中世紀時,宗教在人們生活中佔有很重要的地位。幾乎每個人星期天都會上教堂。因此建造教堂相當重要。有些城鎮建造巨大的教堂,稱作大教堂。大教堂有許多種不同的風格,哥德式是其中重要的一種。哥德時代大約從十二世紀持續到十六世紀。

　　哥德式教堂非常大。他們的建造者利用這樣的設計使許多人印象深刻。所以這些教堂都看似高聳直達天聽。他們如此高大的原因來自拱壁。拱壁是用來幫助支撐教堂的輔助物。

　　大教堂有許多彩繪玻璃窗,它們展示了來自《聖經》中的場景。同時,這些玻璃窗也讓許多光線射入教堂。大教堂內的天花板非常高,這讓教堂看起來更加令人欽佩。

　　大教堂外通常有許多雕像,它們被稱為滴水嘴。滴水嘴看起來像怪物,用來驅邪。

* ward off 避開

閱讀並且回答下列問題
1 巨大教堂的別稱為何?(Cathedral.)
2 什麼用來支撐大教堂?(Buttresses.)
3 彩繪玻璃窗展示了什麼?(Scenes from the Bible.)
4 滴水嘴是什麼?(Sculptures that look like monsters.)

28 • The Art of Islam, Africa, and China (p. 130)

A
1 mosque   2 dome   3 minaret
4 Islamic architecture   5 terra cotta   6 silk   7 scroll
8 calligraphy   9 pottery   10 porcelain   11 carve
12 mold   13 decorate   14 stamp   15 delicate
16 fine

B
1 mosque   2 terra cotta   3 dome   4 Minarets
5 Islamic architecture   6 scrolls   7 pottery
8 Calligraphy

C
1 carved   2 molded   3 decorated   4 stamped

D
1 mosque   2 terra cotta   3 minaret   4 calligraphy

E 伊斯蘭建築
　　伊斯蘭教於七世紀興起。自此,穆斯林便設計出許多風格的建築物,形成了伊斯蘭建築。

　　在伊斯蘭教中,藝術是受到限制的。不能有伊斯蘭教真主阿拉的圖像,同時,人們的圖像也不能出現。因此,許多伊斯蘭教最有創意的人都成為建築師。

　　伊斯蘭建築最主要的特色之一為尖塔。這些高大的塔樓出現在每一個清真寺中。每個清真寺通常都有四個尖塔,座落於建築物的角落。它們可以是非常高聳的塔樓。

穹頂也是非常著名的特色之一。穹頂是建築物上的圓形屋頂。許多清真寺都有令人讚歎的穹頂。

說到伊斯蘭教出名的建築物，可是多不勝數。位於耶路撒冷的圓頂清真寺，就屬伊斯蘭建築早期的代表作之一。座落於土耳其伊斯坦堡的藍色清真寺，也是非常著名的伊斯蘭建築。印度的泰姬瑪哈陵也是，有些人說它是世界上最漂亮的建築物。

以下何者為「是」？請在空格中填入「T」或「F」。
1 伊斯蘭藝術允許阿拉圖像的出現。(F)
2 尖塔是高大的塔樓。(T)
3 許多清真寺都有穹頂。(T)
4 泰姬瑪哈陵位於耶路撒冷。(F)

Unit 29 ● The Elements of Music (p. 134)

A
1 musical notation　2 musical pitch　3 tie　4 bar
5 dotted note　6 measure　7 sharp　8 flat
9 single bar line　10 double bar line　11 follow
12 raise　13 lower　14 hold　15 legato　16 staccato

B
1 Musical notation　2 tie　3 dotted note
4 measures　5 single bar line　6 sharp　7 bar
8 flat

C
1 Raise　2 held　3 Legato　4 Staccato

D
1 double bar line　2 dotted note　3 sharp　4 flat

E 音樂力度
　　當音樂家演奏樂器時，他們不僅僅只是閱讀樂符後然演奏。他們還要瞭解演奏樂器時的速度以及力度。力度表示他們必須要知道何時要輕柔地演奏或是響亮地演奏。然而他們是如何得知呢？音樂家可以從他們樂譜上的特定字母瞭解。

　　在活頁樂譜上，他們可以看到 p, pp ,mp, f, ff 或是 mf 這樣的字母。這些字母與音樂力度息息相關。他們顯示了音樂家要演奏的力度大小。

　　p 代表 piano，它表示音樂要輕柔地被演奏。另外還有 pp 和 mp。pp 為 pianissimo，意味著「極弱的」；mp 為 mezzo piano，表示「中弱的」。

　　當然，有時候音樂也要響亮地被演奏。當音樂家看見 f，那代表 forte，也就是「強的」。與輕音樂相同，響亮的力度也有其他兩種。ff 為 fortissimo，代表「極強的」；mf 為 mezzo forte，代表「中強的」。

填空
1 音樂家可以輕柔地或是響亮地演奏音樂。(softly)
2 p, pp 和 mp 這樣的字母出現在樂譜上。(sheet)
3 pp 代表 pianissimo。(pianissimo)
4 forte 代表「強的」。(loud)

Unit 30 ● Understanding Music (p.138)

A
1 concert hall　2 backstage　3 baton　4 fugue
5 vocal range　6 high voice　7 low voice　8 chant
9 monotonous　10 tempo　11 tune　12 take turns
13 distinguish　14 appreciate　15 mezzo soprano
16 baritone

B
1 concert hall　2 baton　3 backstage　4 fugue
5 low voice　6 chants　7 tempo　8 monotonous

C
1 tune　2 distinguish　3 turns　4 chant

D
1 fugue　2 vocal range　3 soprano　4 tenor

E 韓德爾與海頓
　　古典音樂作曲家中最有名的就屬格奧爾格‧弗里德里希‧韓德爾與約瑟夫‧海頓。

　　韓德爾生活在十八世紀的巴洛克時期。他是德國人，但他有很長的一段時間住在英國。他的一些創作非常受到歡迎並廣為世人所知。他創作了〈水上音樂〉與〈皇家煙火〉。這兩首是最為人所熟悉的樂曲。然而到目前為止，他最著名的樂曲就屬〈彌賽亞〉。這是訴說耶穌基督生命的神劇。〈彌賽亞〉中最出名的一首合唱曲為〈哈雷路亞〉。今日，當管弦樂隊演奏〈哈雷路亞〉合唱曲時，觀眾都會起立。為什麼呢？因為英國國王喬治二世第一次聽到此段音樂時，就站了起來。

　　約瑟夫‧海頓是古典時期最棒的作曲家之一。他創作了奏鳴曲、交響曲以及弦樂四重奏。海頓同時也影響了許多其他作曲家。貝多芬就是他最優秀的學生。他最出名的作品為〈驚愕交響曲〉與神劇〈創世紀〉。

以下何者為非？(4)
1 韓德爾生活在十八世紀。
2〈水上音樂〉是韓德爾的著名樂曲。
3 韓德爾創作了〈彌賽亞〉。
4 約瑟夫‧海頓只寫了兩首樂曲。

Review Test 6

A
1 Ragnarok　2 Asgard　3 predicate　4 conjunction
5 cathedral　6 buttress　7 Islamic architecture
8 calligraphy　9 musical notation　10 baton
11 trick　12 reincarnate　13 agreement
14 combine　15 inspire　16 depict　17 legato
18 staccato　19 distinguish　20 appreciate

B
1 (c)　2 (b)　3 (a)　4 (b)

C
1 Norse　2 complete sentence　3 Cathedrals
4 sharp

AMERICAN SCHOOL TEXTBOOK
VOCABULARY KEY

Workbook

GRADE **4**

Michael A. Putlack

FÜN學美國英語課本
各學科關鍵英單 二版

Unit 01

Listen to the passage and fill in the blanks.

🎧 121 | **Earthquakes and Forest Fires**

California is one of the richest states in America. It has a large amount of land. And it also has more people than any other state. It has plenty of 1._____, too. But everything is not perfect there. California has two major problems: earthquakes and forest fires.

The 2._____ runs through California. Because of it, the state gets many earthquakes. Some of them are very 3._____. For example, there was a strong earthquake in San Francisco in 1906. It destroyed many buildings. And it started 4._____ fires. Over 3,000 people died after it. There have also been many other strong earthquakes. Some people fear that the "big one" will hit someday. They think an earthquake will cause a huge amount of 5._____.

During summer and fall, much of California is dry. So forest fires, or 6._____, often start. These fires can 7._____ rapidly. They burn many forests. But they also can burn people's homes and buildings. They often kill people before 8._____ can put them out.

B **Read the passage above and answer the following questions.**

_____ 9. Another good title for this article would be _____.
   a California: The Richest State in America
   b The Most Highly Populated Area of the United States
   c The San Andreas Fault
   d Earthquakes and Forest Fires in the Western U.S

_____ 10. What do some people in California fear might happen one day?
   a A huge forest fire.   b A very large earthquake.
   c A long, dry season.   d A shortage of natural resources.

_____ 11. "The San Andreas Fault runs through California." In this sentence, "runs through" has a similar meaning to _____.
   a goes across   b jogs over
   c covers most of   d moves quickly past

Unit 02

A Listen to the passage and fill in the blanks.

 122   **The Southwest**

The American Southwest covers a very large area. But it only has a few states. It includes the states Arizona, New Mexico, Texas, and Oklahoma. Most of the land in these states is very dry. In fact, there are many 1._____ in these areas. Because of that, the people must practice water 2._____ all the time. But not all of the land there is desert. The Colorado River flows through Arizona. And the Rio Grande River flows through Texas. Also, the Rocky Mountains 3._____ parts of Arizona and New Mexico. Arizona itself has a very diverse 4._____. Much of its land is desert. But the Grand Canyon is in the northern part of the state. Much of the northern part of the state has 5._____. Also, there are many forests in this area. Texas is also a part of the Southwest. Much of the land is very dry. But many parts of Texas are rich with oil. The oil 6._____ is a huge business in Texas. It's one of the biggest 7._____ states in the entire country.

B Read the passage above and answer the following questions.

_____ 8. What is the main idea of this article?
  a The American Southwest is dry, mountainous, and hot.
  b Texas is an important state in the American Southwest.
  c Oil is the most important industry in the American Southwest.
  d The Colorado River flows through the American Southwest.

_____ 9. This article focuses on a _____.
  a state in the U.S
  b river
  c mountain range
  d region of the U.S

_____ 10. "Arizona itself has a very diverse geography." The word "diverse" means _____.
  a dangerous   b different
  c beautiful   d valuable

Unit 03

A **Listen to the passage and fill in the blanks.**

🎧 123 | **The Civil Rights Movement**

For many years, people in the South owned black African slaves. In the 1860s, the United States fought the Civil War because of 1._____. During the war, all of the slaves were freed. But there were still many problems between blacks and whites. There was a lot of 2._____ against blacks. This means they were not treated fairly. Also, blacks and whites in the South were 3._____. So they ate at separate restaurants. They went to separate schools. And they even sat in separate places on buses.

But in the 1950s, the Civil Rights Movement began in the South. Blacks began 4._____ equal treatment. The most famous leader of the movement was Martin Luther King, Jr. Blacks often organized 5._____ of different places. They had sit-ins at restaurants where they weren't allowed to eat. King tried to use 6._____. But the police and others often used violence against blacks. Still, in 1964, the Civil Rights Act was passed. It 7._____ equal rights for people of all colors

B **Read the passage above and answer the following questions.**

_____ 8. What is the main point in this article?
   a Martin Luther King Jr. launched the Civil Rights Movement.
   b Slavery used to be practiced in the U.S. before the Civil War.
   c The Civil Rights Movement achieved equal rights in the U.S.
   d Blacks and whites used to sit in different parts of the bus.

_____ 9. The article says that blacks demanded "equal" treatment. A word with the opposite meaning to equal is _____.
   a good   b similar
   c unfair   d same

_____ 10. Who was Martin Luther King Jr.?
   a The most famous leader of the Civil Rights Movement.
   b The first person to use nonviolence in politics.
   c An owner of several restaurants in the South.
   d A famous soldier in the U.S. Civil War.

Unit 04

A Listen to the passage and fill in the blanks.

🎧 124

Short Stories from the Northeast

Many of the first 1._____ from Europe went to the Northeast part of the United States. Most of them were English. They lived in New York and Pennsylvania. A lot of them lived in the Hudson River Valley area in New York. Some great American 2._____ comes from this area.

The writer Washington Irving wrote many stories about this area. One of the most 3._____ was *Rip van Winkle*. It 4._____ in the Catskill Mountains in New York. In the story, Rip goes off in the mountains by himself. After meeting some ghosts, he sleeps for twenty years. Then he 5._____, returns to his village, and sees how life has changed.

Another famous story by Irving was *The Legend of Sleepy Hollow*. It was also set in 6._____ New York. It involved the Headless Horseman, who was the ghost of a man with no head. Instead, he had a jack-o'-lantern for a head.

These stories and others by Irving became important in American culture. They 7._____ early life in the Northeast. And millions of children and adults have read them ever since.

B Read the passage above and answer the following questions.

_____ 8. This article focuses on _____.
- [a] American literature and the Northeast
- [b] *The Legend of Sleepy Hollow*
- [c] ghost stories from the Northeast
- [d] famous writers from the Northeast

_____ 9. What is Irving Washington's *The Legend of Sleepy Hollow* about?
- [a] A man who slept for 20 years.   [b] A headless ghost.
- [c] A jack-o'-lantern that could talk.   [d] A lonely horse.

_____ 10. The article says that these stories "depicted" early life in the Northeast.
To depict something means _____.
- [a] to miss   [b] to fear
- [c] to show   [d] to love

5

Unit 05

A Listen to the passage and fill in the blanks.

🎧 125 **The Midwest**

The American Midwest covers an 1._____ amount of land. It starts with Ohio, Michigan, and Indiana. It goes as far west as North and South Dakota, Nebraska, and Kansas. There are a total of twelve states in the Midwest.

Actually, the Midwest is in the east and central part of the country. But, a long time ago, the United States was much smaller. The only states in the country were beside the 2._____. So people called the lands west of them the Midwest.

The land in the Midwest is almost completely identical. It is full of 3._____ and prairies. The Midwest is very flat land. There are no mountains in it. Most hills only rise a few hundred feet high. However, the Great Lakes are in the Midwest. These are five huge lakes 4._____ between the U.S. and Canada.

Nowadays, people in the Midwest often work in industry or 5._____. In Detroit and other cities, making 6._____ is a huge business. However, there are also many farmers. They grow corn, wheat, and other 7._____. And they also raise pigs and cows.

B Read the passage above and answer the following questions.

_____ 8. This article is mainly about _____.
- a the Great Lakes, landscape and settlement of the Midwest
- b the people occupations of the people who live in the Midwest
- c the location, landscape, industry, and agriculture of the Midwest
- d the history, mountains and farms of the Midwest

_____ 9. "The land in the Midwest is almost completely identical." The opposite meaning of the word "identical" is _____.
- a similar
- b alike
- c changed
- d varied

_____ 10. According to the article, most people in the Midwest _____.
- a are farmers
- b work in the automobile industry
- c raise cows and pigs
- d work in industry or agriculture

Unit 06

A Listen to the passage and fill in the blanks.

🎧 126 **Yellowstone National Park**

One of the most beautiful places in the U.S. is Yellowstone National Park. It is located 1._____ in Wyoming. But parts of it are in Montana and Idaho, too.

For many years, people had 2._____ about a beautiful land in the west. But few ever saw it. Then more people began visiting the area in the 1800s. Also, the 3._____ Thomas Moran visited Yellowstone. He made many beautiful 4._____ of the region. This helped Yellowstone to become the first national park in 1872.

Many different animals live in Yellowstone. 5._____, wolves, elk, eagles, and lots of other animals live there. Much of the land is forest. But there are also plains. And there are even 6._____ there. Geysers shoot hot water into the air. The most famous geyser is called Old Faithful. It has this name because it 7._____ on a regular schedule all the time.

B Read the passage above and answer the following questions.

_____ 8. "Also, the artist Thomas Moran visited Yellowstone. He made many beautiful landscapes of the region. This helped Yellowstone to become the first national park in 1872." What does the word "this" refer to?
  a The artist Thomas Moran.
  b Moran's visit to Yellowstone.
  c The landscapes Moran made.
  d Yellowstone becoming a national park.

_____ 9. "The most famous geyser is called Old Faithful." The opposite of the word "faithful" is _____.
  a loyal   b unreliable
  c dependable   d uncertain

_____ 10. This passage centers on _____.
  a Yellowstone National Park in the 1800's
  b The development of Yellowstone National Park
  c Old Faithful as the biggest attraction in the park
  d The beauty of Yellowstone National Park

Unit 07

A Listen to the passage and fill in the blanks.

Climbing Mount Everest

Mount Everest is in the Himalaya Mountains. It is located near the 1._____ of Nepal, Tibet, and China. At 8,848 meters high, it is the highest mountain in the world. People call it "The Top of the World."

For years, people wanted to be the first to climb the mountain. But no one could get to the top. Many people 2._____, but none of them succeeded. Some of them even died.

But, in 1953, at last two men were 3._____. They were Sir Edmund Hilary and Tenzing Norgay. Hilary was from New Zealand. Norgay was a Sherpa. Sherpas are expert mountain 4._____ from Tibet and Nepal. They are often employed as guides for mountaineering 5._____ in the Himalayas, particularly Mt. Everest.

There were nine people on the team. They also had hundreds of 6._____ and twenty Sherpas. It took them several days to get near the top. Some men came very 7._____. But they couldn't get there. Finally, on May 29, 1953, Hilary and Norgay got to the top of the mountain. They were the first people to stand on top of the world!

B Read the passage above and answer the following questions.

_____ 8. What is this article mainly about?
- a Sherpas from Tibet and Nepal.
- b Tibetan and Nepalese mountaineers.
- c The location of Mount Everest.
- d The first people to climb Mount Everest.

_____ 9. According to the article, what are "Sherpas"?
- a People who carry items for mountain climbers.
- b People who have already reached the top of Mt. Everest.
- c Expert mountain climbers from Tibet and Nepal.
- d Expert porters from New Zealand.

_____ 10. "They are often employed as guides for mountaineering expeditions in the Himalayas, particularly Mt. Everest." Another word for "particularly" is _____.
- a always
- b especially
- c only
- d sometimes

A Listen to the passage and fill in the blanks.

🎧 128 **Marco Polo and the Silk Road**

China and 1._____ are very far from each other. Today, people can fly between the two in a few hours. But in the past, it took months or years to go from one place to the other. When people traveled from China to Europe, they went on the Silk Road.

The Silk Road was not a real road. It was a large group of 2._____. But, by following it, people could get from the Mediterranean Sea to the 3._____. It was called the Silk Road because the Chinese 4._____ silk to the west on it.

The Silk Road became very famous because of Marco Polo. He was an Italian 5._____. With his father and uncle, he left Italy and 6._____ twenty-four years later. He had taken the Silk Road to China. He had many adventures. He even became an advisor to the 7._____. When he came back, he wrote a book, *The Travels of Marco Polo*, about his travels and became very famous.

B Read the passage above and answer the following questions.

_____ 8. When people traveled the Silk Road, how long did it take?

      a A few hours.

      b Months or years.

      c Days or weeks.

      d Years or decades.

_____ 9. "It was called the Silk Road because the Chinese transported silk to the west of it." A word with a similar meaning to "transported" is _____.

      a moved   b sailed

      c flew   d sold

_____ 10. What is the main purpose of this article?

      a Many people stopped travelling the Silk Road.

      b It took a long time to construct the Silk Road.

      c Most people traveled the Silk Road by car.

      d The Silk Road was an important trade route between Europe and China.

Unit 09

Listen to the passage and fill in the blanks.

🎧 129 | **The Middle Ages**

The Roman Empire fell in 476. It was 1._____ by Germanic invaders. In the east, there was still the 2._____. It was the eastern part of the Roman Empire. It lasted for almost 1,000 more years. It was finally defeated in 1453.

But in Western Europe, after the fall of the Western Roman Empire, the 3._____ began. This term is sometimes applied to the first 300 years after the fall of Rome and sometimes to the whole Middle Ages. During this time, only a few people could read and write. The people had hard lives. They often just struggled to 4._____. Most people farmed the land. Their lives were very simple then.

Throughout the Middle Ages, there were very slow 5._____ in people's lives. Some kings ruled their lands fairly. Others were very harsh. They treated their people like 6._____. And they taxed them very much. Many people died of 7._____. Others died because of diseases. The 8._____ killed almost half of the people in Europe in the fourteenth century. The Middle Ages were a very difficult time for most people.

B **Read the passage above and answer the following questions.**

_____ 9. According to the article, how were many people treated by kings during the Middle Ages?
- a Like invaders.
- b Very well.
- c Poorly.
- d Like farmers.

_____ 10. The best alternate title for this article would be _____.
- a The Germanic Take-Over of the Roman Empire
- b The Black Death
- c The Byzantine and Roman Empires
- d The Dark Ages

_____ 11. "Some kings ruled their lands fairly. Others were very harsh." An opposite of the word "harsh" is _____.
- a bad
- b gentle
- c ordinary
- d excellent

Unit 10

Listen to the passage and fill in the blanks.

🎧 130 | **The American Civil War**

The Civil War was the 1._____ war in American history. It was fought for many reasons. One big reason was 2._____. The South had slaves. The North did not.

The Civil War began after Abraham Lincoln became president. It started in 1861. The North had more men. It also had more 3._____ and more industries. But the South had better generals than the North. There were many 4._____ during the war. At first, the South seemed to be winning the war. But, in 1863, General Robert E. Lee lost at Gettysburg. The next day, the South lost the Battle of Vicksburg. The North began winning after that.

Two Union generals were very important. General William T. Sherman 5._____ the South. His March to the Sea from Atlanta to 6._____ the of Savannah destroyed much of the South's will to fight. General Ulysses S. Grant led the Union forces. He finally defeated the South, so General Lee 7._____ to him. Five days later, John Wilkes Booth 8._____ President Lincoln.

B **Read the passage above and answer the following questions.**

_____ 9. What is the main idea of the article?
- a How Abraham Lincoln was assassinated.
- b Slavery in America.
- c The battles of Gettysburg and Vicksburg.
- d The war between the North and the South.

_____ 10. Who killed President Lincoln?
- a General William T. Sherman.
- b General Robert E. Lee.
- c Slaves from the South.
- d John Wilkes Booth

_____ 11. "His March to the Sea from Atlanta to the port of Savannah destroyed much of the South's will to fight." In this sentence, the word "will" means _____.
- a desire
- b ability
- c power
- d request

Unit 11

Listen to the passage and fill in the blanks.

🎧 131 | **The Scientific Method of Inquiry**

Scientists have a 1._____ they use when they are trying to learn something new. It is called the scientific method of inquiry.

The first step is to ask a question. It could be "Why do birds fly south for the winter?" Or it could be "How much heat does it take for gold to melt?" It could be about anything.

Then, the scientist must do 2._____. He or she should learn as much about the topic as possible. Next, the scientist makes a 3._____. This is an educated guess. It could be "Birds fly south for the winter because they are cold." Or it could be "Gold melts at 200 degrees 4._____." Now, the scientist has a hypothesis, so it must be tested. Scientists do this by 5._____ experiments. Some do experiments in labs, and others do them outdoors.

After the experiments are complete, the scientist must 6._____ the data. Then he should compare it with the hypothesis. Was the hypothesis right or wrong? Even with a wrong hypothesis, scientists can still learn a lot. Finally, they should write about their 7._____. That way, other people can learn, too.

B **Read the passage above and answer the following questions.**

_____ 8. What is the first step in the scientific method?
  a Make a hypothesis.   b Ask a question.
  c Do experiments.   d Do research.

_____ 9. Which of the following statements is FALSE?
  a Scientists don't learn anything if their hypotheses are wrong.
  b Scientists using the scientific method must look at their data.
  c Scientists must do experiments as part of the scientific method.
  d Scientists make educated guesses before conducting experiments.

_____ 10. Another good title for this article is _____.
  a How Scientists Find Answers to Inquiries
  b Creating Accurate Hypotheses
  c Scientists and the Analysis of Data
  d Completing Experiments in Labs and Outdoors

Unit 12

Listen to the passage and fill in the blanks.

🎧 132 | **Organisms**

There are millions of types of organisms on the Earth. An organism is any
1._____ that is alive. These include animals, plants, 2._____,
and microorganisms. All organisms are made of cells. Some have just one
cell. Others have billions and billions of them.

Microorganisms are very, very small. In fact, you can't even see them without
a 3._____. Bacteria and protists are microorganisms. These are often
4._____. So everything they need to survive is in a single cell. How
do they reproduce? They simply 5._____ themselves in half. This is
called asexual reproduction.

But most organisms are multi-celled. So they may have a few cells.
Or they could have trillions of them. Multi-celled organisms have
6._____ cells. These cells often do one specific thing. They could
be used to defend the organism from disease. They could be used for
7._____. They could be used for digestion. Or they could be used for
many other purposes.

B **Read the passage above and answer the following questions.**

_____ 8. What is this article mainly about?
- a Microorganisms and multi-celled organisms.
- b Specialized cells and their functions.
- c Asexual reproduction of microorganisms.
- d Using microscopes to see protists and bacteria.

_____ 9. How many cells are in bacteria?
- a Billions and billions.   b One.
- c Trillions.   d A few.

_____ 10. "Multi-celled organisms have specialized cells. These cells often do one
specific thing. They could be used to defend the organism from disease."
In this sentence, "they" refers to _____.
- a organisms   b disease
- c multi-celled organisms   d specialized cells

13

Listen to the passage and fill in the blanks.

🎧 133 | **Heredity**

People often look very 1._____ to their parents. They might have the same face. Or they have the same color hair or eyes. They might be tall or short like their parents. Why do they look this way? The answer is heredity.

Heredity is the passing of 2._____ from a parent to his or her offspring. This happens because of genes. Genes 3._____ DNA. DNA is the basic building block for life. Both parents 4._____ their genes to their offspring. So the offspring may 5._____ the mother, father, or both.

There are dominant and recessive genes. Dominant genes affect the body more than recessive genes. Recessive genes exist in a body. But they do not 6._____ it. Dominant genes, however, affect the organism.

Genes do not just 7._____ an organism's physical characteristics. They also determine the organism's mental characteristics. This can include 8._____. And it may even affect personality, too.

B **Read the passage above and answer the following questions.**

_____ 9. According to the article, the body is not affected by _____.
     a heredity   b recessive genes
     c characteristics   d DNA

_____ 10. "Heredity is the passing of traits from a parent to his or her offspring."
       The word "offspring" means the same as _____.
     a relatives   b children
     c parents   d ancestors

_____ 11. This article is mostly about _____.
     a DNA
     b mental and physical characteristics
     c genes
     d parents and their children

Unit 14

A Listen to the passage and fill in the blanks.

🎧 134 **The Formation of the Earth**

Billions of years ago, the sun formed. There was a huge disk of rocks and gases in the solar system. Eventually, these rocks and gases began to form 1._____. This was about 4.5 billion years ago. Earth was the third planet from the sun. At first, the Earth was 2._____ hot. But, over millions of years, it began to cool down.

As the Earth cooled, water vapor started forming in the 3._____. This caused the creation of clouds all over the planet. Soon, the clouds began 4._____ huge amounts of water all over the planet. This caused the creation of the Earth's oceans, seas, rivers, and lakes.

But the Earth 4.5 billion years ago looked different from the Earth of today. Today, there are seven 5._____. In the past, this was not true. There have been different numbers of continents. Once, there was just one continent on the whole planet. Why? One clue is the theory of plate 6._____. There are many plates that make up the Earth's 7._____. These plates are huge pieces of land. And they are 8._____ moving. As the Earth ages, the plates slowly move around. Today, there are seven continents. In the future, perhaps there will be more or less.

B Read the passage above and answer the following questions.

_____ 9. Which of the following sentences is FALSE?
- a The sun was formed billions of years ago.
- b Seven continents were formed 4.5 billion years ago.
- c The earth's plates are constantly moving.
- d There are many plates that make up Earth's crust.

_____ 10. This article is mainly about how _____.
- a water formed on Earth over a period of time
- b the Earth has developed over billions of years
- c plate tectonics explains Earth's formation
- d planets developed within the solar system

_____ 11. "One clue is the theory of plate tectonics." The word "clue" is closest in meaning to _____.
- a guess   b answer
- c idea   d hint

15

Unit 15

A **Listen to the passage and fill in the blanks.**

🎧 135 **The Water Cycle**

There is a 1._____ amount of water on the Earth. In fact, for billions of years, the amount of water has not changed. However, water can often 2._____ in many different forms. These all make up the water cycle.

The first stage is 3._____. This happens when the sun's heat on rivers, lakes, seas, and oceans causes water to turn into water vapor. The water vapor then rises into the air.

The second stage is 4._____. As water vapor rises, the air gets colder. This causes the water vapor to turn into tiny water droplets. These droplets come together to form clouds.

The third stage is 5._____. The water droplets fall to the ground in some form. The most common kind of precipitation is rain. But, in cold weather, snow, sleet, or ice may fall instead.

The final stage is 6._____. When water falls to the ground, it may flow into rivers, lakes, seas, or oceans. Or it may go down into the ground. There, it becomes 7._____. But the water cycle goes on and on.

B **Read the passage above and answer the following questions.**

_____ 8. Which of the following statements is TRUE?
- a Condensation happens right after precipitation.
- b The amount of water on Earth never changes.
- c Precipitation is when water vapor rises.
- d As water vapor rises, the air gets warmer.

_____ 9. Another good title for this article is _____.
- a Nature's Water-Recycling Process
- b How to Make It Rain
- c Reasons Why Water Is So Important
- d The History of the Water Cycle

_____ 10. "The water droplets fall to the ground in some form. The most common kind of precipitation is rain. But, in cold weather, snow, sleet, or ice may fall instead." In this part of the article, what "may fall instead" of snow, sleet, or ice?
- a Precipitation.   b Cold weather.
- c Droplets.   d Rain.

16

A Listen to the passage and fill in the blanks.

🎧 136 **Physical and Chemical Changes**

Matter often 1._____ many changes. There are two main types of changes. They are physical and chemical changes.

There are a lot of physical changes. They can often involve changing a 2._____ into a solid, a liquid, or a gas. For instance, melting ice to get water is a physical change. And boiling water to get water 3._____ is another one. But it is also possible to make physical changes in other ways. For instance, put some sugar in water and then stir it. The sugar 4._____. That is a physical change. Or, simply 5._____ a piece of paper. That is another physical change.

Chemical changes are different. Chemical changes involve the forming of a new 6._____. For instance, if sodium and chlorine come together, they undergo a 7._____. The result is the creation of salt. Photosynthesis is another chemical reaction. Water and carbon dioxide change into sugar and 8._____.

B Read the passage above and answer the following questions.

_____ 9. What is closest to the main point the author wants to make in this article?
   a Matter doesn't often undergo changes.
   b Water is required for all changes.
   c Matter can undergo two types of changes.
   d A chemical change is also called a chemical reaction.

_____ 10. Which of the following is an example of a chemical change?
   a Ice melting.   b Sugar dissolving in water.
   c Paper tearing.   d Photosynthesis.

_____ 11. "Or, simply tear up a piece of paper." The word "tear" in this sentence
      means _____.
   a to rip   b to squeeze into a ball
   c to put in water   d to write

A Listen to the passage and fill in the blanks.

137 **Conduction, Convection, and Radiation**

Heat is a form of 1._____. It can move from place to place. There are three ways it can move: conduction, convection, and radiation.

When heat touches matter, it makes the atoms and 2._____ in that matter move, too. These atoms and molecules then touch other nearby ones. They start moving, too. This is 3._____, and it's the reason why the pot handle gets hot. The pot itself is being heated, but the molecules on the pot touch those on the handle. They make the handle hot, too.

Convection is the second way that heat moves. Convection happens when something that can move becomes heated in 4._____. This can be air, water, or some other 5._____. Ovens work by convection. Coils in the oven heat the air. The air rises, where it cooks the food. The air then cools, so it goes down. Then the coils heat it again, so it rises once more.

Radiation is the third way that heat moves. This occurs when heat moves as 6._____. The sun heats the 7._____ by radiation. The sun sends out heat in the form of waves. The waves reach the Earth, where they provide heat.

B Read the passage above and answer the following questions.

_____ 8. Which statement best expresses the main idea of this article?

   a There are three different ways that heat can travel.
   b Conduction is the most common method of heat transfer.
   c Conduction and convection need a lot of energy.
   d Radiation can be very dangerous sometimes.

_____ 9. Which of the following best describes the process of radiation?

   a Heat touches matter and causes it to move.
   b Heat transfers to cooler spaces in a cycle.
   c Heat slowly releases and disappears.
   d Heat moves as waves without any matter.

_____ 10. "When heat touches matter, it makes the particles in that matter move."

   A "particle" is a _____.

   a large circular object   b tiny thing that makes up matter
   c type of electricity   d rush of heated air

Unit 18

Listen to the passage and fill in the blanks.

🎧 138 | **The Circulatory System**

The circulatory system is the part of the body that controls the 1._____ of blood. It has many parts. The most important is the heart. However, there are also artery and 2._____ that send blood throughout the body.

The heart has four chambers. They are the left and right atria and the left and right 3._____. First, blood flows into the right atrium. Then it goes to the right ventricle and into the lungs. In the lungs, 4._____ is added to the blood. Then the blood returns to the heart. It goes into the left atrium and then into the left ventricle. From there, it leaves the heart by going to the 5._____.

The aorta is the body's main 6._____. It feeds blood to the rest of the body. The body has both arteries and veins. Together, they are called 7._____. These blood vessels take oxygen-rich blood and 8._____ it everywhere in the body. The body then uses the blood, which loses its oxygen. Then, other veins and arteries take the oxygen-depleted blood back to the heart, and the 9._____ begins again.

B **Read the passage above and answer the following questions.**

_____ 10. What is the main idea of the article?
- a The heart is the most important part of the circulatory system.
- b The circulatory system controls blood flow in our bodies.
- c The heart has four important chambers to help it beat.
- d The human body needs veins and arteries to survive.

_____ 11. In which part of the body is oxygen added to blood?
- a The lungs.
- b The heart.
- c The left ventricle.
- d The right ventricle.

_____ 12. "Then, other veins and arteries take the oxygen-depleted blood back to the heart, and the cycle begins again." In this sentence, "oxygen-depleted blood" means the blood _____.
- a has too much oxygen
- b needs less oxygen
- c has the perfect amount of oxygen
- d needs more oxygen

A Listen to the passage and fill in the blanks.

🎧 139 | **Conductors and Insulators**

Electricity can move thanks to conductors. These are 1._____ that let electricity move freely. Gold and silver are very good conductors. Some people make wires out of them. But they are both 2._____. So, people often use other conductors to make wires. Most electrical wires are made from a conducting metal, such as 3._____.

What are some other conductors? Lots of metals are conductors. So is 4._____. Water is an excellent conductor. That's why it's a bad idea to go swimming in 5._____. Lightning can strike the water and hurt or even kill a person. The human body is also a conductor. That's why people need to be careful around electricity.

Of course, people may want to stop the flow of electricity. To do this, people use 6._____. They prevent electricity from moving from place to place. What are some of them? Plastics are very good insulators. Paper and 7._____ are also insulators. And glass and 8._____ are two more insulators. These materials are all useful for stopping the flow of electricity.

B Read the passage above and answer the following questions.

_____ 9. According to the article, most wires aren't made from silver or gold because they are _____.

a poor conductors   b insulators
c expensive   d difficult to make

_____ 10. "Lightning can strike the water and hurt or even kill a person." In this sentence, "strike" means _____.

a cancel   b hit
c cross   d damage

_____ 11. This article is mainly about _____.

a electricity and insulators
b the dangers of electricity
c how electricity can be controlled
d the risks of thunderstorms

Unit 20

A Listen to the passage and fill in the blanks.

Sir Isaac Newton

Sir Isaac Newton lived in the seventeenth and eighteenth centuries. He was one of the greatest 1._____ who ever lived. He worked with light. He invented calculus. And he also discovered 2._____ and the three laws of motion.

Supposedly, Newton was sitting under an apple tree one day. An apple fell and hit him on the head. So he started thinking about gravity. He realized that it was gravity that caused 3._____ to fall to the ground.

Newton's three laws of motion are 4._____ important to physics. The first law says that the state of motion of an object does not change until a force is applied to it. It is often called the *law of* 5._____.

The second law of motion is called the *law of* 6._____. It is often written as F = ma. That means "force equals mass times acceleration." This is the most important of the three laws.

The third law says that for every 7._____, there is an equal and opposite reaction. The third law means that all forces are 8._____.

B Read the passage above and answer the following questions.

_____ 9. What did Newton discover when an apple fell from a tree and hit him on the head?

      [a] Calculus.   [b] Physics.

      [c] Science.   [d] Gravity.

_____ 10. Most of the article is about _____.

      [a] the background of Newton's life

      [b] the three laws of motion

      [c] the way gravity works

      [d] the invention of calculus

_____ 11. "The first law says that the state of motion of an object does not change until a force is applied to it." The opposite of the word "applied" is _____.

      [a] attached   [b] removed

      [c] hidden   [d] affected

Unit 21

Listen to the passage and fill in the blanks.

🎧 141 | **Reading and Writing Fractions and Decimals**

You can write both fractions and decimals as numbers and 1._____.
There are many ways to do this. For example, write the fraction two-thirds as
$\frac{2}{3}$. However, there are other ways to say fractions. You can say that $\frac{1}{6}$ is
2._____ or one out of six. And the fraction $\frac{5}{8}$ could be five
3._____ by eight.

As for decimals, usually just say the 4._____ numbers to the right of
the 5._____. For example, 1.1 is one point one. 2.45 is two point four
five. However, for some decimals, you can say them as fractions. 0.1 is zero
point one or one-tenth. 0.7 is zero point seven or seven-tenths.

Sometimes, you can write a fraction in easier 6._____. This is called
its simplest form. For instance, think about the fraction $\frac{4}{8}$. In its simplest
form, it is $\frac{1}{2}$. And the simplest form of $\frac{3}{9}$ is $\frac{1}{3}$.

Finally, you can sometimes write 7._____ as decimals. The fraction
$\frac{2}{10}$ can be 0.2. The fraction $\frac{9}{10}$ can be 0.9. This is why you can read the
decimal 0.1 as one-tenth.

B **Read the passage above and answer the following questions.**

_____ 8. Which statement best expresses the main idea of this article?
- a Fractions can help us understand advanced math.
- b Fractions are not the same thing as decimals.
- c Decimals are easier to use than fractions.
- d There are many ways to write fractions and decimals.

_____ 9. Another way of writing nine-tenths is _____.
- a 0.1
- b 0.5
- c 9.0
- d 0.9

_____ 10. "You can write both fractions and decimals as numbers and words." The
word "fractions" means _____.
- a parts of a whole
- b teams or sides
- c numbers over 100
- d types of experiments

Unit 22

Listen to the passage and fill in the blanks.

🎧 142 | **Angles**

When two line 1._____ meet at the same endpoint, they form an angle. The size of an angle is measured in 2._____. An angle can measure anywhere from 0 to 180 degrees. There are four different kinds of angles. What type they are depends on how many degrees they have.

A straight angle measures 180°. A straight angle forms a 3._____.

The next kind of angle is an 4._____. This angle measures more than 0° but less than 90°. All triangles have at least one acute angle, and many have three of them.

A right angle occurs when two 5._____ lines intersect. These two lines form a ninety-degree angle. This is called a right angle. All of the angles in a square or rectangle are right angles. Some triangles have one right angle, so they are called 6._____.

The last kind of angle is an obtuse angle. An obtuse angle is more than 90° but less than 180°. Some triangles have obtuse angles, but a triangle can never have more than one 7._____.

B **Read the passage above and answer the following questions.**

_____ 8. What is the main point of this passage?
  a It explains some ideas about triangles.
  b It shows what happens when two line segments meet.
  c It talks about how a right angle is formed.
  d It explains what an obtuse angle is.

_____ 9. "What type they are depends on how many degrees they have." Which of the following means the same as "depends on"?
  a Relies on.   b Catches on.
  c Drops off.   d Falls out.

_____ 10. Which of the following statements about an obtuse angle is true?
  a It forms a straight line.   b It is equal to 90 degrees.
  c It is less than 90 degrees.   d It is less than 180 degrees.

Unit 23

A **Listen to the passage and fill in the blanks.**

🎧 143 **Triangles**

Triangles are 1._____ figures that have three sides. There are several kinds of triangles. They depend on the type of angles in the triangles and the 2._____ of the sides of the triangles.

The first three types of triangles are acute, right, and obtuse triangles. An acute triangle is one where all three angles in the triangle are acute. So each angle is less than 90°. A right triangle has one angle that is 90°. And the other two angles are acute. Finally, an obtuse triangle has one angle that is more than 90° but less than 180°. The other two angles in it are 3._____.

Next, there are three types of triangles that are 4._____ by the length of the triangles' sides. They are equilateral, isosceles, and scalene triangles. Equilateral triangles have three sides that are the same length. All three angles are always 60°, so they are also acute triangles. Isosceles triangles have two sides with 5._____ length. And all three sides in a 6._____ triangle are of different lengths.

B **Read the passage above and answer the following questions.**

_____ 7. According to the passage, an acute triangle _____.

　　　a contains no acute angles
　　　b contains two acute angles
　　　c contains three acute angles
　　　d contains one acute angle

_____ 8. This passage focuses on _____.

　　　a different kinds of triangles　　b how many sides a triangle has
　　　c different uses of triangles　　d the history of triangles

_____ 9. "Next, there are characterized by the length of the triangles' sides."
　　　Which of the following means the same as "characterized"?

　　　a Traded.　　　　　　　　b Watched.
　　　c Studied.　　　　　　　　d Defined.

24

A Listen to the passage and fill in the blanks.

🎧 144   **Collecting and Organizing Data**

People often 1._____ research. They may research a topic and find as much information as they can about it. Perhaps they want to know the daily temperature in a region for an entire year. Or maybe they want to know how many books students read during a semester. First, they decide what 2._____ they want. Then they collect the data.

But the 3._____ they collect could be useless by itself. So they need to organize it. One common way to organize data is to use charts and 4._____. This lets people see the visual results of their data. For example, perhaps the researchers have some data on how many books each student reads. They can put that data onto a 5._____. This will let them analyze it more easily. Or, maybe they know the average temperature for each day of the year. They can organize it into a circle graph. This will show them the 6._____ of hot, warm, cool, and cold days the area gets. By using these visual aids, they can 7._____ their data much more easily.

B Read the passage above and answer the following questions.

_____ 8. "Then they collect the data." The word "data" in this sentence has the same meaning as _____.

    a graph   b chart
    c information   d percentage

_____ 9. This article provides examples of _____.

    a how to get data from students
    b ways to design good charts
    c commonly used graphs
    d the only ways to interpret data

_____ 10. According to the article, which of the following sentences is TRUE?

    a Graphs can help researchers analyze data.
    b Raw data can be analyzed easily without organization.
    c People usually analyze data, and then organize it.
    d Most researchers don't use visual bar graphs.

A **Listen to the passage and fill in the blanks.**

🎧 145　**The Norse Gods**

Norse 1._____ comes from northern Europe. The Norse were Vikings. They lived in the area that is Norway, Sweden, and Finland today. The Vikings loved to fight and make war. So their stories often are very 2._____.

There were many Norse gods. Odin was their leader. He was very wise. Odin always had two 3._____. They were thought and memory. They told him everything that happened in the land.

Thor was the god of 4._____. He was the most powerful of all the gods. He carried a great 5._____ that he often used to kill giants. Loki was the god of mischief and fire and was a half giant. He was also a 6._____, so he caused many problems for the gods, especially Thor. Frigg was Odin's wife and was also the goddess of 7._____. And Freya was the goddess of love. There were also many other Norse gods and goddesses.

The gods lived at 8._____. They often had to fight their enemies, like frost giants and 9._____. There are many stories about their deeds that people still enjoy reading.

B **Read the passage above and answer the following questions.**

_____ 10. This article focuses on _____.
　　　ⓐ the descriptions of some Norse gods
　　　ⓑ the violence created by Norse gods
　　　ⓒ the location of Norse gods
　　　ⓓ the popularity of Norse gods in stories

_____ 11. "They lived in the area that is Norway, Sweden, and Finland today. The Vikings loved to fight and make war. So their stories often are very violent." In this sentence, "their" refers to _____.
　　　ⓐ Northern European mythology
　　　ⓑ modern Norwegians, Swedes, and Finns
　　　ⓒ authors who write about the Norse
　　　ⓓ the Vikings who lived in Northern Europe

_____ 12. Which of the following sentences is TRUE?
　　　ⓐ Odin was the leader of the Norse gods.
　　　ⓑ Odin was the goddess of marriage.
　　　ⓒ There weren't many Norse goddesses.
　　　ⓓ Thor was the goddess of love.

Unit 26

A **Listen to the passage and fill in the blanks.**

🎧 146   **Understanding Sentences**

All sentences must have a 1._____ and a verb. Some sentences can be very short. For example, "I ate," is a complete sentence. Why? It has a subject and a verb. Other sentences can be very, very long.

People often make mistakes when making English sentences. One common mistake is the 2._____. Look at this sentence: "I went to the park I saw my friend." It's a run-on sentence. A run-on sentence is a combination of two sentences that either needs 3._____ or a conjunction. Here's a complete sentence: " I went to the park, and I saw my friend."

All sentences need to have subject–verb 4._____. It means that if the subject is singular, the verb must be singular. And if the subject is plural, the verb must be plural. Look at this sentence: "Jason like to play computer games." It's a wrong sentence. Why? It doesn't have subject–verb agreement. Here is the 5._____, complete sentence: "Jason likes to play computer games."

So 6._____ for run-on sentences, and always make sure your subjects and verbs agree. Then you'll be making lots of 7._____.

B **Read the passage above and answer the following questions.**

_____ 8. Which of the following sentences is TRUE?

     a All sentences need a verb and a conjunction.
     b All sentences need a comma and a subject.
     c All sentences need a subject and a verb.
     d All sentences need a subject and a conjunction.

_____ 9. This article is mainly about _____.

     a the correct punctuation of sentences
     b how to write good sentence subjects
     c subject-verb agreement and run-on sentences
     d how to punctuate subject-verb agreement

_____ 10. "One common mistake is the run-on sentence." A word that means the same as "mistake" as it is used in this sentence is _____.

     a correction   b error
     c misunderstanding   d surprise

Listen to the passage and fill in the blanks.

🎧 147 | **Gothic Cathedrals**

In the Middle Ages, religion was a very important part of people's lives. Almost everyone went to church on Sunday. So building churches was important. Some towns and cities built huge churches. They were called 1._____. There were many different styles. One important style was Gothic. The 2._____ lasted from around the twelfth to sixteenth centuries.

Gothic cathedrals were enormous. Their builders made them to impress many people. So they look like they are 3._____ into the sky. The reason that they are so high is that they have 4._____. These are supports that help the cathedrals stay up.

The cathedrals also had many 5._____. These showed scenes from the Bible. Also, they allowed a lot of light to enter the cathedral. Inside the cathedral, the 6._____ were very high. This made them look even more impressive.

The outside of a cathedral often had many sculptures. These were called gargoyles. The gargoyles looked like monsters. They were used to 7._____ evil spirits.

B **Read the passage above and answer the following questions.**

_____ 8. Which of the sentences about the article is TRUE?
 a There was only one style of cathedral in the Middle Ages.
 b Not very many people went to church on Sunday in the Middle Ages.
 c Cathedrals had only a few windows, so they were dark inside.
 d In the Middle Ages, religion was an important part of people's lives.

_____ 9. "Their builders made them to impress many people." The word "impress" is similar in meaning to _____.
 a shock   b encourage
 c amaze   d convince

_____ 10. Another good title for this article is _____.
 a Gothic Architecture of Cathedrals in the Middle Ages
 b The Use of Gargoyles in Middle-Age Architecture
 c How to Build a Catholic Church in the Middle Ages
 d Attracting New Church Members with Cathedrals

Unit 28

A Listen to the passage and fill in the blanks.

 148 | **Islamic Architecture**

Islam began in the seventh century. Since then, there have been many styles of buildings designed by 1._____. They all combine to make up Islamic architecture.

In Islam, art is restricted. There should be no images of Allah–the god of Islam. Also, there should be no pictures of people either. So, many of Islam's most creative people became 2._____.

One of the main features of Islamic architecture is the 3._____. These are tall towers. They are found in every mosque. There are usually four minarets at every 4._____. There is one at each corner of the building. They can be very high towers.

Domes are also very popular features. Domes are 5._____ roofs of buildings. Many mosques have 6._____ domes.

As for famous buildings, there are many. The Dome of the Rock is in Jerusalem. It is one of the earliest examples of Islamic architecture. The Sultan Ahmed Mosque is in Istanbul, Turkey. It is another 7._____ building. And the Taj Mahal is located in India. Some say it is the most beautiful building in the entire world.

B Read the passage above and answer the following questions.

_____ 8. "In Islam, art is restricted." The word "restricted" is similar in meaning to _____.

    a controlled   b illegal
    c beautiful   d respected

_____ 9. According to the article, which of the following statements is TRUE?

    a There are usually four domes at every mosque.
    b The Dome of the Rock is a modern mosque.
    c There should be no images of Allah in a mosque.
    d The Taj Mahal is in Istanbul, Turkey.

_____ 10. This article is mainly about _____.

    a domes and minarets   b famous mosques
    c Islamic art inside mosques   d buildings designed by Muslims

Unit 29

Listen to the passage and fill in the blanks.

🎧 149 | **Musical Dynamics**

When musicians play their instruments, they must do more than just read the 1._____ and then play them. They must know the 2._____ that they should play the music. And they must also know the dynamics. This means they must know if they should play softly or loudly. How do they know that? They can look for 3._____ letters on their sheet music.

On the sheet music, they will see the letters *p*, *pp*, *mp*, *f*, *ff*, or *mf*. These letters are all 4._____ musical dynamics. They indicate the softness or the loudness that the musician should play.

p stands for piano. It means the music should be played softly. There are also *pp* and *mp*. *pp* means 5._____, which stands for "very soft." And *mp* means mezzo piano. This means "moderately soft."

Of course, some music should be played loudly. When a musician sees *f*, it means 6._____. That stands for "loud." Just like with soft music, there are two more 7._____ of loudness. The first is *ff*. That's fortissimo, which means "very loud." And there is *mf*. That's mezzo forte, which means "moderately loud."

B **Read the passage above and answer the following questions.**

_____ 8. Which statement is closest to the main idea of the passage?
- a The piano is a very difficult instrument to learn if you cannot read sheet music.
- b When musicians play their instruments, they only have to read the musical notes.
- c Certain letters on sheet music indicate how loudly or softly it should be played.
- d Dynamics show how quickly or slowly the piece of music should be played.

_____ 9. "That's mezzo forte, which means 'moderately loud.'" Which of the following words is closest in meaning to "moderately"?
- a Reasonably.
- b Quietly.
- c Carefully.
- d Extremely.

_____ 10. How many different letter codes for musical dynamics are described in the passage?
- a Two.
- b Four.
- c Six.
- d Eight.

Unit 30

 A Listen to the passage and fill in the blanks.

🎧 150 | **Handel and Haydn**

Two of the greatest of all classical music 1._____ were George Friedrich Handel and Joseph Haydn.

Handel lived during the Baroque Period in the eighteenth century. He was German. But he lived in 2._____ for a long time. Some of his music is very popular and well-known all around the world. He wrote *Water Music* and *Music for the Royal Fireworks*. These are two easily 3._____ pieces of music. But his most famous music by far is his *Messiah*. It is an oratorio that tells the life of Jesus Christ. From the *Messiah*, the most famous piece is the *Hallelujah* 4._____. Today, when orchestras play the *Hallelujah* chorus, the 5._____ always stands up. Why? When King George II of Great Britain first heard it, he stood up during that part.

Joseph Haydn was one of the best composers of the Classical Period. He composed hundreds of sonatas, 6._____, and string quartets. He also influenced many other composers. Beethoven was the 7._____ of all his students. Two of his best works are the *Surprise Symphony* and *The Creation*, an oratorio.

B Read the passage above and answer the following questions.

_____ 8. The Hallelujah chorus comes from which piece of music?
- [a] The Surprise Symphony.
- [b] The Messiah.
- [c] The Creation.
- [d] Water Music.

_____ 9. "These are two easily recognizable pieces of music." Which of the following words is closest in meaning to "recognizable"?
- [a] Identifiable.
- [b] Repeated.
- [c] Confusing.
- [d] Wonderful.

_____ 10. Which of the following statements is TRUE, according to the passage?
- [a] Haydn and Beethoven were friends.
- [b] Haydn and Beethoven were cousins.
- [c] Beethoven was Haydn's student.
- [d] Haydn was Beethoven's student.

Answer Key

Unit 01
1. natural resources 2. San Andreas Fault
3. powerful 4. numerous 5. damage 6. wildfires
7. spread 8. firefighters 9. d 10. b 11. a

Unit 02
1. deserts 2. conservation 3. go through 4. geography
5. mountains 6. industry 7. oil-producing 8. a 9. d 10. b

Unit 03
1. slavery 2. discrimination 3. segregated 4. demanding
5. boycotts 6. nonviolence 7. guaranteed 8. c 9. c 10. a

Unit 04
1. settlers 2. literature 3. famous 4. takes place
5. wakes up 6. upstate 7. depicted 8. a 9. b 10. c

Unit 05
1. enormous 2. Atlantic Ocean 3. plains 4. located
5. agriculture 6. automobiles 7. grains 8. c 9. d 10. d

Unit 06
1. mostly 2. heard 3. artist 4. landscapes
5. Bison 6. geysers 7. erupts 8. c 9. b 10. d

Unit 07
1. border 2. tried 3. successful 4. climbers
5. expeditions 6. porters 7. close 8. d 9. c 10. b

Unit 08
1. Europe 2. trade routes 3. Pacific Ocean
4. transported 5. adventurer 6. returned
7. emperor 8. d 9. d 10. d

Unit 09
1. conquered 2. Byzantine Empire 3. Dark Ages
4. survive 5. improvements 6. slaves
7. starvation 8. Black Death 9. c 10. d 11. b

Unit 10
1. bloodiest 2. slavery 3. railroads 4. battles
5. cut through 6. port 7. surrendered 8. assassinated
9. d 10. d 11. a

Unit 11
1. method 2. research 3. hypothesis 4. Fahrenheit
5. conducting 6. analyze 7. results 8. b 9. a 10. a

Unit 12
1. creature 2. fungi 3. microscope 4. one-celled organisms
5. divide 6. specialized 7. reproduction 8. a 9. b 10. d

Unit 13
1. similar 2. traits 3. contain 4. pass on 5. resemble
6. affect 7. determine 8. intelligence 9. b 10. b 11. c

Unit 14
1. planets 2. extremely 3. atmosphere 4. dropping
5. continents 6. tectonics 7. crust 8. constantly 9. b
10. b 11. d

Unit 15
1. limited 2. appear 3. evaporation 4. condensation
5. precipitation 6. collection 7. groundwater 8. b 9. a 10. c

Unit 16
1. undergoes 2. substance 3. vapor 4. dissolves
5. tear up 6. compound 7. chemical reaction
8. oxygen 9. c 10. d 11. a

Unit 17
1. energy 2. molecules 3. conduction 4. gravity 5. liquid
6. waves 7. Earth 8. a 9. d 10. b

Unit 18
1. flow 2. veins 3. ventricles 4. oxygen 5. aorta
6. artery 7. blood vessels 8. transport 9. cycle 10. b
11. a 12. d

Unit 19
1. materials 2. expensive 3. copper 4. graphite
5. thunderstorms 6. insulators 7. rubber 8. porcelain
9. c 10. b 11. a

Unit 20
1. scientists 2. gravity 3. objects 4. incredibly 5. inertia
6. acceleration 7. reaction 8. interactions 9. d 10. b 11. b

Unit 21
1. words 2. one-sixth 3. divided 4. individual
5. decimal point 6. terms 7. fractions 8. d 9. d 10. a

Unit 22
1. segments 2. degrees 3. line 4. acute angle 5. perpendicular
6. right triangles 7. obtuse angle 8. a 9. a 10. d

Unit 23
1. geometrical 2. lengths 3. acute 4. characterized
5. equal 6. scalene 7. c 8. a 9. d

Unit 24
1. conduct 2. information 3. raw data 4. diagrams
5. bar graph 6. percentage 7. interpret 8. c 9. c 10. a

Unit 25
1. mythology 2. violent 3. ravens 4. thunder 5. hammer
6. trickster 7. marriage 8. Asgard 9. trolls 10. a 11. d 12. b

Unit 26
1. subject 2. run-on sentence 3. punctuation
4. agreement 5. correct 6. watch out
7. complete sentences 8. c 9. c 10. b

Unit 27
1. cathedrals 2. Gothic Age 3. reaching up
4. buttresses 5. stained glass windows 6. ceilings
7. ward off 8. d 9. c 10. a

Unit 28
1. Muslims 2. architects 3. minaret 4. mosque
5. rounded 6. impressive 7. well-known 8. a 9. c 10. d

Unit 29
1. notes 2. speed 3. certain 4. related to 5. pianissimo
6. forte 7. degrees 8. c 9. a 10. c

Unit 30
1. composers 2. England 3. recognizable
4. chorus 5. audience 6. symphonies 7. greatest 8. b
9. a 10. c

2 1. the   2. the   3. ✗   4. the   5. ✗, ✗   6. ✗

Unit 11   p. 29

1 1. the city   2. the violin   3. church
4. university   5. court
6. hospital（美式：the hospital）
2 1. the   2. ✗   3. the, the, the   4. ✗   5. ✗, ✗
6. the   7. the   8. ✗

Unit 12   p. 31

1 1. work   2. tennis   3. winter   4. math
5. home
2 1. ✗   2. ✗, the   3. ✗, ✗   4. ✗   5. ✗   6. ✗
3 The answers may vary.

Unit 13   p. 33

1 1. Catherine's key, Catherine's
2. Kiki's collar, Kiki's
3. Shakespeare's pen and ink, Shakespeare's
4. Tim Cook's briefcase, Tim Cook's
5. the wizard's magic wand, the wizard's
6. Kevin Durant's basketball, Kevin Durant's
2 1. student's, aunt's, Jeff's, tank's
2. Jennifer's, bottle's, lion's, kid's
3. Alice's, dish's, ox's, tax's

Unit 14   p. 35

1 1. the student's schoolbag
2. Jenny's iPad
3. Grandpa's newspaper
4. David's laptop
5. my sister's headphones
6. my brother's umbrella
7. the manager's cell phone
8. my mother's scarf
9. Liz's book
2 1. the light of the sun
2. the pile of trash
3. the keyboard of the computer
4. the speech of the president
5. the ninth symphony of Beethoven

Unit 15 Review Test   p. 37

1 1. C   2. C   3. C   4. U   5. U   6. C   7. U   8. C
9. U   10. C   11 U   12. C   13. U   14. C   15. U
2 1. rats   2. dishes   3. watches   4. jelly candies
5. holidays   6. calves   7. Elves   8. teeth
9. fish   10. diaries
3 1. a carrot   2. a carrot   3. Carrots   4. a lion
5. the lion   6. Lions   7. sugar   8. the sugar
9. a banana   10. the banana   11. the keyboard
12. a keyboard   13. Music   14. the music
4 1. the suburbs   2. car   3. football   4. TV

5. home   6. dinner   7. bed   8. an Egyptian
9. the Nile River   10. Egyptians   11. Brazil
12. the Amazon River   13. new sources
14. scientists   15. tourists
5 1. a camera   2. potatoes   3. hair   4. a box
5. a loaf   6. lots of snow   7. is   8. are   9. Is
6 1. Ⓐ Ned's suitcase
Ⓑ the suitcase of Ned
2. Ⓐ my father's jacket
Ⓑ the jacket of my father
3. Ⓐ my sister's colored pencils
Ⓑ the colored pencils of my sister
4. Ⓐ ✗
Ⓑ the corner of the bathroom
5. Ⓐ Edward's brother
Ⓑ the brother of Edward
6. Ⓐ ✗
Ⓑ the end of the vacation
7 1. **a bottle of:** soy sauce, wine, lotion
2. **a jar of:** pickles, peanut butter, strawberry jam
3. **a piece of:** luggage, cheese, jewelry
4. **a can of:** tuna, shaving cream, soda
5. **a bowl of:** grapes, salad, rice
6. **a tube of:** watercolor, cleansing foam, ointment
7. **a pot of:** tea, coffee, soup
8. **a packet of:** potato chips, ketchup, cookies
8 （例子僅供參考）
1. ✓：the Shed Aquarium, the Field Museum
2. ✓：the Hilton Hotel, the Metro Café
3. ✗：Monday, Tuesday
4. ✓：the New Wave Cinema, the Varsity Multiplex
5. ✓：the Pacific Ocean, the Aegean Sea
6. ✗：Sri Lanka, Europe
7. ✓：Jennifer Lawrence, Justin Timberlake
8. ✗：Madison Avenue, Hollywood Boulevard
9. ✗：March, May
10. ✗：Spaniards, Japanese
11. ✓：the Concord River, the River Thames
12. ✗：Tuxedo Junction, Long Island City

Unit 16   p. 43

1 1. I   2. You   3. She   4. It   5. It   6. We
7. They   8. She   9. He
2 1. They   2. He   3. She   4. He   5. She
6. He   7. It   8. We

Unit 17   p. 45

1 1. I like him. / I don't like him.
2. I like it. / I don't like it.

3

3. I like it. / I don't like it.
4. I like it. / I don't like it.
5. I like them. / I don't like them.
6. I like her. / I don't like her.

2 1. us   2. us   3. him   4. me   5. him   6. her
7. them   8. it   9. him   10. us   11. him   12. us

Unit 18   p. 47

1 1. My   2. our   3. his   4. her   5. their
6. their   7. Our   8. his, her, their

2 1. your, hers   2. my, your   3. your, mine
4. its   5. Yours

Unit 19   p. 49

1 1. There aren't any eggs.
2. There's some meat.
3. There isn't any ice.
4. There are some bottled waters.
5. There are some vegetables.
6. There isn't any milk.

2 1. There's no space.
2. We haven't got any newspapers.
3. She's got no money.
4. There aren't any boxes.
5. I haven't got any blank disks.
6. He doesn't have any bonus points.

3 1. some   2. some   3. any   4. some
5. no   6. any

Unit 20   p. 51

1 1. How many televisions do you want?
2. How many cell phone batteries do you want?
3. How many cameras do you want?
4. How much detergent do you want?
5. How many lightbulbs do you want?
6. How many air conditioners do you want?
7. How many water filters do you want?

2 1. too much   2. too much   3. too many
4. too many   5. too much   6. too much
7. enough

Unit 21   p. 53

1 （此題答案可有變化，僅供參考）
1. There are a lot of bananas.
2. There are many books.
3. There are a lot of masks.
4. There isn't much beer.
5. There are a few sandwiches.
6. There are a lot of gift boxes.
7. There are many candles.
8. There are a few passion fruits.

2 1. much   2. a few   3. Little / A little
4. a lot of   5. many / a lot of   6. a little

Unit 22   p. 55

1 1. one, one, one   2. one, one, one
3. ones, ones, one, ones, one

Unit 23   p. 57

1 1. someone, anyone, anyone
2. anyone, someone
3. someone, someone, someone
4. anyone, anyone, someone, anyone
5. Someone, anyone

2 1. go   2. to talk   3. Someone   4. someone
5. anyone   6. to keep   7. someone

Unit 24   p. 59

1 1. anything to eat   2. anything to drink
3. anywhere to go   4. something to do

2 1. anything, anything   2. to hide
3. something   4. something
5. anywhere   6. to read
7. anywhere, anything, to do

Unit 25   p. 61

1 1. There is nobody at the office.
2. There is no one leaving today.
3. There is nothing to feed the fish.
4. There is nowhere to buy envelops around here.
5. There isn't anybody here who can speak Japanese.
6. There isn't anyone that can translate your letter.
7. There isn't anything that will change the manager's mind.
8. There isn't anywhere we can go to get out of the rain.

2 1. I have nowhere to go. / I don't have anywhere to go.
2. No one believed me.
3. Everything is ready. Let's go.
4. There is nothing to eat.
5. I never want to hurt anybody.
6. Everyone in this room will vote for me.
7. Did you see my glasses? I can't find it anywhere.
8. Anyone who doesn't support this idea please raise your hand.

Unit 26   p. 63

1 1. This   2. These   3. this   4. That   5. Those
6. these

2 1. this 2. that 3. those 4. these
5. that 6. this 7. Those 8. these
9. That 10. those

Unit 27 p. 65

1 1. myself 2. yourself 3. itself 4. himself
5. herself 6. yourself 7. ourselves
8. themselves

2 1. each other 2. themselves 3. themselves

Unit 28 Review Test p. 67

1 1. my 2. I 3. mine 4. me 5. My 6. I
7. me 8. mine

2 1. My, your 2. I, Our 3. her 4. my
5. he, her 6. I, mine, you, mine
7. their, ours 8. it 9. It, them
10. Their, They, it 11. your, It, mine

3 1. wine / green peppers
2. bread / cookies 3. sugar 4. toothpaste
5. candy 6. grapes 7. fish / goats
8. medicine 9. chocolate cakes / fruit tarts
10. soup / soda 11. garlic 12. notebooks

4 1. We have any rice. **some**
2. Are there any spoons in the drawer? **OK**
3. There isn't some orange juice in the refrigerator. **any**
4. Are there any cookies in the box? **OK**
5. Could I have any coffee, please? **some**
6. Would you like some ham? **OK**
7. We have lots of fruit. Would you like any? **some**
8. I already had some fruit at home. I don't need some now. **any**
9. There aren't some newspapers. **any**
10. There are any magazines. **some**

5 1. Who are these boxes for, the **ones** you are carrying?
2. Do you like the red socks or the yellow **ones**?
3. My cubicle is the **one** next to the manager's office.
4. I like the pink hat. Which **one** do you like?
5. Our tennis balls are the **ones** stored over there.

6 1. B 2. B 3. B 4. A 5. B
6. A 7. A 8. A 9. A 10. B

7 1. everywhere 2. nowhere 3. anywhere
4. somewhere 5. no one 6. anyone
7. Someone 8. Everyone 9. something
10. anything 11. nothing 12. everything
13. everybody 14. anybody 15. somebody
16. nobody

8 1. someone 2. No one 3. anyone

4. Everyone 5. No one 6. somewhere
7. anywhere 8. nowhere 9. everywhere
10. somewhere 11. something 12. anything
13. nothing 14. everything

9 1. A 2. A 3. C 4. B 5. B 6. A

10 1. My brother made himself sick by eating too much ice cream. **OK**
2. My sister made himself sick by eating two big pizzas. **herself**
3. The dog is scratching itself. **OK**
4. I jog every morning by me. **myself**
5. You have only yourself to blame. **OK**
6. We would have gone there us but we didn't have time. **ourselves**
7. He can't possibly lift that sofa all by himself. **OK**
8. Do you want to finish this project by yourself or do you need help? **OK**
9. I helped him. He helped me. We helped ourselves. **each other**
10. Don't fight about it. You two need to talk to each other if you are going to solve this problem. **OK**

11 1. a little 2. a few 3. enough 4. a lot of
5. enough 6. a lot 7. little 8. Few
9. enough 10. many 11. a few 12. a lot of
13. too many 14. enough

Unit 29 p. 75

1 1. is 2. am 3. is 4. is 5. is 6. is 7. are
8. are 9. am 10. is 11. are 12. are
13. is 14. are

2 (此題答案可能不同，僅供參考)
1. am 2. am 3. am not 4. is 5. are
6. isn't 7. are 8. are

3 1. Karl is Canadian. He is a violinist.
2. Dominique is Italian. He is a chef.
3. Hiroko is Japanese. She is a drummer.
4. Lino is French. He is a businessman.
5. Jane is Chinese. She is a singer.
6. Mike is American. He is a policeman.

Unit 30 p. 77

1 1. There isn't 2. There are 3. There isn't
4. There are 5. There is 6. There is
7. There is 8. There isn't 9. There isn't
10. There are 11. There isn't 12. There are
13. There aren't 14. There is 15. There isn't
16. There are

2 (此題答案可能不同，僅供參考)
1. is, It is 2. isn't, it 3. is, It is
4. are, They are 5. are, They are 6. is, It is

Unit 31   p. 79

1 1. She's got a hamster. 2. She's got a parrot.
3. They've got a cat. 4. He's got a dog.
5. She's got a snake. 6. He's got a pig.

2 1. Has your family got a cottage on Lake Michigan?
2. Have you got your own room?
3. Have you got your own closet?
4. How many cups have you got?
5. How many TVs has your family got?
6. How many cars has your brother got?

Unit 32   p. 81

1 1. eats 2. drinks 3. walks 4. runs
5. paints 6. buries 7. watches
8. carries 9. unboxes 10. crunches
11. tries 12. chases 13. cuts 14. goes
15. fixes 16. teaches

2 **Bobby:** I **cook** simple food every day. I usually **heat** food in the microwave oven. I often **make** sandwiches. I sometimes **pour** hot water on fast noodles. However, I **don't wash** dishes.
Jenny: I usually **get up** at 6:00 in the morning. I **eat** breakfast at 6:30. I **leave** my house at 7:00. I **walk** to the bus stop. I **take** the 7:15 bus. I always **get** to work at 8:00. I **have** lunch at 12:30. I **leave** work at 5:30. I **take** the bus home. I **arrive** at my home about 6:30. I **eat** dinner at 7:00. I often **fall asleep** after the 11:00 news ends.

3 1. cuts 2. tightens 3. makes 4. moves
5. pounds 6. pushes

Unit 33   p. 83

1 1. talking 2. caring 3. staying 4. sleeping
5. jogging 6. eating 7. making 8. robbing
9. advising 10. dying 11. spitting
12. staring 13. waiting 14. clipping
15. swimming 16. crying 17. lying
18. planning 19. throwing 20. speaking

2 1. is walking 2. is buying 3. is shining
4. is playing 5. are picnicking 6. is lying
7. are running 8. is eating 9. is sitting

Unit 34   p. 85

1 1. driving 2. leaves 3. designs 4. ends
5. drinks 6. is thinking 7. goes 8. wishes

2 1. **Q:** Do you often listen to music?
A: Yes, I do. I often listen to music.
2. **Q:** Are you watching TV at this moment?
A: Yes, I am. I'm watching TV at this moment. / No, I'm not. I'm not watching TV at this moment.

3. **Q:** Is it hot now?
A: Yes, it is. It is hot now. / No, it isn't. It isn't hot now.
4. **Q:** Is it often hot this time of year?
A: Yes, it is. It is often hot this time of year. / No, it isn't. It isn't often hot this time of year.
5. **Q:** Do you drink coffee every day?
A: Yes, I do. I drink coffee every day. / No, I don't. I don't drink coffee every day.
6. **Q:** Are you drinking tea right now?
A: Yes, I am. I'm drinking tea right now. / No, I'm not. I'm not drinking tea right now.

Unit 35   p. 87

1 1. am eating, hate 2. is eating, likes
3. loves 4. likes 5. are making, know
6. Do, mean 7. seem, are, doing
8. Are, going, Do, need
9. is carrying, belongs 10. Do, understand
11. remembers

2 1. I am owning my own house. **own**
2. This book belongs to Mary. **OK**
3. Mother is believing your story. **believes**
4. I often forget names. **OK**
5. I am having a snack. **OK**
6. The man is recognizing you. **recognized**
7. The story is needing an ending. **needs**
8. You are seeming a little uncomfortable. **seem**
9. Are you feeling sick? **OK**
10. Do you have got a swimsuit? **have**

Unit 36 Review Test   p. 89

1 1. changes, changing 2. visits, visiting
3. turns, turning 4. jogs, jogging
5. mixes, mixing 6. cries, crying
7. has, having 8. cuts, cutting
9. fights, fighting 10. feels, feeling
11. ties, tying 12. applies, applying
13. jumps, jumping 14. enjoys, enjoying
15. steals, stealing 16. swims, swimming
17. sends, sending 18. tastes, tasting
19. finishes, finishing 20. studies, studying

2 1. **Q:** What is your favorite TV show?
A: The Simpsons.（參考答案）
2. **Q:** What is your favorite movie?
A: The Godfather.（參考答案）
3. **Q:** Who is your favorite actor?
A: Johnny Depp.（參考答案）
4. **Q:** Who is your favorite actress?
A: Nicole Kidman.（參考答案）
5. **Q:** What is your favorite food?

A: Hamburgers.（參考答案）
6. Q: What is your favorite juice?
   A: Orange juice.（參考答案）
7. Q: Who are your parents?
   A: Mike and Jennifer.（參考答案）
8. Q: Who are your brothers and sisters?
   A: James, David, and Alice.（參考答案）

3. 1. Q: Is Seoul in Vietnam?
   A: No, Seoul is in Korea.
   2. Q: Are Thailand and Vietnam in East Asia?
   A: No, they are in Southeast Asia.
   3. Q: Is Hong Kong in Japan?
   A: No, Hong Kong is in China.
   4. Q: Are Beijing and Shanghai in China?
   A: Yes, they are in China.
   5. Q: Is Osaka in Taiwan?
   A: No, Osaka is in Japan.
   6. Q: Are Tokyo, Osaka, and Kyoto in Japan?
   A: Yes, they are in Japan.

4. 1. Q: Are there any men's shoe stores?
   A: Yes, there are.
   2. Q: Is there a wig store?
   A: No, there isn't.
   3. Q: Is there a computer store?
   A: No, there isn't.
   4. Q: Are there two bookstores?
   A: No, there aren't.
   5. Q: Are there any women's clothing stores?
   A: Yes, there is (one).
   6. Q: Are there any women's shoe stores?
   A: Yes, there is (one).
   7. Q: Are there three music stores?
   A: No, there aren't.
   8. Q: Is there a jewelry store?
   A: Yes, there is.

5. 1. is 2. am 3. have 4. are 5. has
   6. are 7. am 8. are 9. are 10. am

6. 1. Q: Are you a university student?
   A: Yes, I am. / No, I'm not.
   2. Q: Are you a big reader?
   A: Yes, I am. / No, I'm not.
   3. Q: Is your birthday coming soon?
   A: Yes, it is. / No, it isn't.
   4. Q: Is your favorite holiday Chinese New Year?
   A: Yes, it is. / No, it isn't.

7. （參考答案）
· There is an alarm clock on the dresser.
· There are two pillows on the bed.
· There is a chair in the room.
· There is a candle on the dresser.
· There is a pen and a bottle of ink on the dresser.
· There are some books on the shelf.
· There is a light hanging from the ceiling.

· There is a dresser in the room.
· There is a bed in the room.

8. 1. Do 2. work 3. don't 4. work 5. Does
   6. work 7. works 8. Does 9. work
   10. doesn't 11. work 12. works

9. 1. Q: Do you watch many movies?
   A: Yes, I do. I watch many movies. / No, I don't. I don't watch many movies.
   2. Q: Does your mother work?
   A: Yes, she does. She works. / No, she doesn't. She doesn't work.
   3. Q: Does your father drive a car to work?
   A: Yes, he does. He drives a car to work. / No, he doesn't. He doesn't drive a car to work.
   4. Q: Does your family have a big house?
   A: Yes, we do. My family has a big house. / We have a big house. / No, we don't. We don't have a big house. / My family doesn't have a big house.
   5. Q: Do your neighbors have children?
   A: Yes, they do. They have children. / No, they don't. They don't have children.
   6. Q: Do you have a university degree?
   A: Yes, I do. I have a university degree. / No, I don't. I don't have a university degree.

10. 1. do you like to be called
   2. do you come from
   3. do you go to the café
   4. do you drink at the café
   5. do you go home
   6. do you go home
   7. do you have to be at school

11. 1. Peter has got a good car. 2. ✗
   3. Wendy has got a brother and a sister.
   4. The Hamiltons have got two cars.
   5. Ken has got a lot of good ideas.
   6. ✗ 7. I have got the answer sheet.

12. 1. is fixing 2. is delivering
   3. is changing 4. is talking 5. are using
   6. are working

13. 1. I am going 2. stop 3. He often has
   4. is having 5. wants 6. is having
   7. I'm thinking 8. I have got
   9. I don't believe 10. I can hear

14. 1. We aren't tired. Are we tired?
   2. You aren't rich. Are you rich?
   3. There isn't a message for Jim. Is there a message for Jim?
   4. It isn't a surprise. Is it a surprise?
   5. They haven't got tickets. Have they got tickets?
   6. You haven't got electric power. Have you got electric power?

7. She doesn't work out at the gym.
   Does she work out at the gym?
8. He doesn't usually drink a fitness shake for breakfast.
   Does he usually drink a fitness shake for breakfast?
9. We aren't playing baseball this weekend.
   Are we playing baseball this weekend?
10. He doesn't realize this is the end of the vacation.
    Does he realize this is the end of the vacation?

Unit 37   p. 97

1 1. was, is   2. was , is   3. is, was   4. is, was
5. is, was   6. was, is   7. were, are
8. were, are   9. are, were   10. were, are
11. were, are   12. were, are

2 1. **Were** you busy yesterday?
   Yes, I was. I was very busy yesterday. / No, I wasn't. I wasn't very busy yesterday.
2. **Were** you at school yesterday morning?
   Yes, I was. I was at school yesterday morning. / No, I wasn't. I wasn't at school yesterday morning.
3. **Was** yesterday the busiest day of the week?
   Yes, it was. It was the busiest day of the week. / No, it wasn't. It wasn't the busiest day of the week.
4. **Was** your father in the office last night?
   Yes, he was. He was in the office last night. / No, he wasn't. he wasn't in the office last night.
5. **Were** you at your friend's house last Saturday?
   Yes, I was. I was at my friend's house last Saturday. / No, I wasn't. I wasn't at my friend's house last Saturday.
6. **Was** your mother at home at 8 o'clock yesterday morning?
   Yes, she was. She was at home at 8 o'clock yesterday morning. / No, she wasn't. She wasn't at home at 8 o'clock yesterday morning.
7. **Were** you in bed at 11 o'clock last night?
   Yes, I was. I was in bed at 11 o'clock last night. / No, I wasn't. I wasn't in bed at 11 o'clock last night.
8. **Were** you at the bookstore at 6 o'clock yesterday evening?
   Yes, I was. I was at the bookstore at 6 o'clock yesterday evening. / No, I wasn't. I wasn't at the bookstore at 6 o'clock yesterday evening.

Unit 38   p. 99

1 1. walked   2. ran   3. coughed   4. wrote
5. ate   6. dropped   7. asked   8. picked
9. showed   10. drank   11. waited
12. typed   13. married   14. flied   15. went
16. used   17. joined   18. played   19. looked
20. liked   21. sent   22. jogged

2 1. counted   2. attended   3. received
4. used   5. checked   6. put

Unit 39   p. 101

1 1. Did, had, didn't have   2. Did, have, did
3. did, have, had

2 1. Q: Did you see your friends last night?
   A: Yes, I did. I saw my friends last night. / No, I didn't. I didn't see my friends last night.
2. Q: Did you go to a movie last weekend?
   A: Yes, I did. I went to a movie last weekend. / No, I didn't. I didn't go to a movie last weekend.
3. Q: Did you play basketball yesterday?
   A: Yes, I did. I played basketball yesterday. / No, I didn't. I didn't play basketball yesterday.
4. Q: Did you graduate from university last year?
   A: Yes, I did. I graduated from university last year. / No, I didn't. I didn't graduate from university last year.
5. Q: Did you move out of your parents' house last month?
   A: Yes, I did. I moved out of my parents' house last month. / No, I didn't. I didn't move out of my parents' house last month.

3 1. was   2. saw   3. was   4. pondered
5. succeeded

Unit 40   p. 103

1 1. were decorating   2. was hanging
3. was draping   4. was arranging
5. was putting   6. was unpacking
7. was putting

2 1. Q: **What was she doing** when the phone rang?
   A: **She was sleeping soundly.**
2. Q: **What was he doing** while walking?
   A: **He was talking on the phone.**
3. Q: **What was he doing** while watching TV during breakfast?
   A: **He was drinking coffee.**

Unit 41   p. 105

1 1. eaten 2. seen 3. written 4. gone
5. loved 6. come 7. fought 8. read
9. got/gotten 10. left 11. brought 12. lent
13. cost 14. lost 15. hit 16. paid
17. found 18. taken 19. rung 20. spoken

2 1. has eaten 2. has taught 3. has arrived
4. has won 5. has stolen 6. has written

3   Clive grew up in the country. He moved to the city in 2010. He **has lived** there since then.

He **has worked** in an Italian restaurant for a year and half. He met his wife in the restaurant. They got married last month, and she moved in to his apartment. They **have become** a happy couple, but they **haven't had** a baby yet.

Unit 42   p. 107

1 1. have been, since 2. have built, for
3. for 4. have piloted 5. have worked, for
6. have dreamed 7. have wondered
8. Since, have started

2 1. Q: Have you ever eaten a worm?
A: Yes, I have. I have eaten a worm. / No, I haven't. I haven't eaten a worm.
2. Q: Have you ever been to Japan?
A: Yes, I have. I have been to Japan./ No, I haven't. I haven't been to Japan.
3. Q: Have you ever swum in the ocean?
A: Yes, I have. I have swum in the ocean. / No, I haven't. I haven't swum in the ocean.
4. Q: Have you ever cheated on an exam?
A: Yes, I have. I have cheated on an exam. / No, I haven't. I haven't / I have never cheated on an exam.

Unit 43   p. 109

1 1. has loved 2. has been 3. stayed
4. went surfing 5. liked 6. discovered
7. rented 8. learned 9. visited
10. has enjoyed 11. has fished 12. visited
13. has gone 14. has talked

2 1. has he been 2. was 3. has he been
4. Did he go 5. Did he stay
6. Has he visited 7. When was

Unit 44 Review Test   p. 111

1 1. drove, driven 2. went, gone 3. ate, eaten
4. wrote, written 5. thought, thought
6. kept, kept 7. drank, drunk 8. slept, slept
9. made, made 10. stood, stood
11. bought, bought 12. sang, sung
13. did, done 14. hid, hid/hidden
15. fell, fallen 16. said, said 17. gave, given
18. sat, sat 19. shot, shot 20. taught, taught

2 1. I **sailed** on a friend's boat last weekend.
→ **I didn't sail on a friend's boat last weekend.**
→ **Did I sail on a friend's boat last weekend?**
2. I **saw** the seals on the rocks.
→ **I didn't see the seals on the rocks.**
→ **Did I see the seals on the rocks?**
3. We **fed** the seagulls.
→ **We didn't feed the seagulls.**
→ **Did we feed the seagulls?**
4. The seagull **liked** the bread we threw to it.
→ **The seagull didn't like the bread we threw to it.**
→ **Did the seagull like the bread we threw to it?**
5. We **fished** for our dinner.
→ **We didn't fish for our dinner.**
→ **Did we fish for our dinner?**
6. My friend **cooked** our dinner in the galley of the boat.
→ **My friend didn't cook our dinner in the galley of the boat.**
→ **Did my friend cook our dinner in the galley of the boat?**
7. We **ate** on deck.
→ **We didn't eat on deck.**
→ **Did we eat on deck?**
8. We **passed** the time chatting and watching the water.
→ **We didn't pass the time chatting and watching the water.**
→ **Did we pass the time chatting and watching the water?**

3 1. called, ordered, played, brushed
2. fixed, hiked, walked, marched
3. started, landed, carted, handed

4 Catherine **got** up at 5:00. She **took** a shower. Then she **made** a cup of strong black coffee. She **sat** at her computer and **checked** her email. She **answered** her email and **worked** on her computer until 7:30. At 7:30, she **ate** a light breakfast. After breakfast, she **went** to work. She **walked** to work. She **bought** a cup of coffee and a newspaper on her way to work. She **arrived** promptly at 8:30 and **was** ready to start her day at the office.

5 1. was snowing, went 2. fell, had
3. were walking, saw 4. saw, said
5. fell 6. broke, fell 7. was feeding, heard
8. woke, realized 9. started

6 1. **Q:** Have they picked up the flyers yet?
   A: Yes, they have. They have already picked up the flyers.
2. **Q:** Have they put out order pads yet?
   A: Yes, they have. They have already put out order pads.
3. **Q:** Have they gotten pens with their company logo yet?
   A: No, they haven't. They haven't gotten pens with their company logo yet.
4. **Q:** Have they set up the computer yet?
   A: No, they haven't. They haven't set up the computer yet.
5. **Q:** Have they arranged flowers yet?
   A: Yes, they have. They have already arranged flowers.
6. **Q:** Have they unpacked boxes yet?
   A: No, they haven't. They haven't unpacked boxes yet.

7 （答案略）

8 1. was   2. was, was   3. had
   4. bought   5. slept   6. have gone
   7. kept, died   8. registered
   9. Have, finished, haven't finished
   10. was cooking   11. did

9 1. B   2. B   3. B   4. A   5. A   6. A   7. A
   8. A   9. B

Unit 45 p. 117

1 1. Who **is going** on vacation?
   → **Mark and Sharon are going on vacation.**
2. When **are** Mark and Sharon **going** on vacation?
   → **They are going on vacation on May 18ᵗʰ.**
3. Where **are** they **departing** from?
   → **They are departing from Linz.**
4. Where **are** they **flying** to?
   → **They are flying to Budapest.**
5. What time **are** they **departing**?
   → **They are departing at 15:30.**
6. What time **are** they **arriving** at their destination?
   → **They are arriving at their destination at 17:30.**
7. What airline **are** they **taking**?
   → **They are taking Aeroflot Airlines.**
8. What flight **are** they **taking**?
   → **They are taking Flight 345.**

Unit 46 p. 119

1 1. No, he isn't. He is going to use a laptop.
2. Yes, she is. She's going to buy some vegetables.
3. Yes, she is. She's going to take a nap with her teddy bear.
4. No, they aren't. They're going to drink some orange juice.
5. No, they aren't. They are going to buy some books.
6. No, she isn't. She's going to give the customers a key.

2 1. I'm going to eat at a restaurant. / I'm not going to eat at a restaurant.
2. I'm going to watch a baseball game. / I'm not going to watch a baseball game.
3. I'm going to read a book. / I'm not going to read a book.
4. I'm going to play video games. / I'm not going to play video games.
5. I'm going to write an email. / I'm not going to write an email.

Unit 47 p. 121

1 1. Will scientists clone humans in 50 years?
   Scientists will clone humans in 50 years.
   Scientists won't clone humans in 50 years.
2. Will robots become family members in 80 years?
   Robots will become family members in 80 years.
   Robots won't become family members in 80 years.
3. Will doctors insert memory chips behind our ears?
   Doctors will insert memory chips behind our ears.
   Doctors won't insert memory chips behind our ears.
4. Will police officers scan our brains for criminal thoughts?
   Police officers will scan our brains for criminal thoughts.
   Police officers won't scan our brains for criminal thoughts.

2 1. I think I'll live in another country.
   Perhaps I'll live in another country.
   I doubt I'll live in another country.
2. I think my sister will learn how to drive.
   Perhaps my sister will learn how to drive.
   I doubt my sister will learn how to drive.
3. I think Jerry will marry somebody from another country.
   Perhaps Jerry will marry somebody from another country.
   I doubt Jerry will marry somebody from another country.
4. I don't think Tammy will go abroad again.
   Perhaps Tammy will not go abroad again.
   I doubt Tammy will go abroad again.

Unit 48　　　　　　p. 123

1 1. Are you going to the bookstore tomorrow?
2. Janet is going to help Cindy move in to her new house.
3. Are you playing baseball this Saturday?
4. He will cook dinner at 5:30.
5. She will fall into the water.
6. I'm going to give him a call tonight.
7. When are you going to get up tomorrow morning?
8. I'm driving to Costco this afternoon.

2 1. is leaving　2. will melt　3. will quit
4. am going to quit　5. will eat　6. is having
7. am going to find, am going to make
8. will rain

Unit 49 Review Test　　　p. 125

1 1. I **am going** out for lunch tomorrow.
→ **I am not going out for lunch tomorrow.**
→ **Am I going out for lunch tomorrow?**
2. I **am planning** a birthday party for my grandmother.
→ **I'm not planning a birthday party for my grandmother.**
→ **Am I planning a birthday party for my grandmother?**
3. She **is going** to take the dog for a walk after dinner.
→ **She isn't going to take the dog for a walk after dinner.**
→ **Is she going to take the dog for a walk after dinner?**
4. Mike **is planning** to watch a baseball game later tonight.
→ **Mike isn't planning to watch a baseball game later tonight.**
→ **Is Mike planning to watch a baseball game later tonight?**
5. Dr. Johnson **is meeting** a patient at the clinic on Saturday.
→ **Dr. Johnson isn't meeting a patient at the clinic on Saturday.**
→ **Is Dr. Johnson meeting a patient at the clinic on Saturday?**
6. Jack and Kim **are applying** for admission to a technical college.
→ **Jack and Kim aren't applying for admission to a technical college.**
→ **Are Jack and Kim applying for admission to a technical college?**
7. I **am thinking** about having two kids after I get married.
→ **I'm not thinking about having two kids after I get married.**
→ **Am I thinking about having two kids after I get married?**
8. Josh **is playing** basketball this weekend.
→ **Josh isn't playing basketball this weekend.**
→ **Is Josh playing basketball this weekend?**
9. My little brother **is planning** to sleep late on Sunday morning.
→ **My little brother isn't planning to sleep late on Sunday morning.**
→ **Is my little brother planning to sleep late on Sunday morning?**
10. Father and I **are working** out at the gym on Sunday.
→ **Father and I aren't working out at the gym on Sunday.**
→ **Are Father and I working out at the gym on Sunday?**

2 1. F　2. C　3. C　4. C　5. C　6. F　7. F　8. C

3 1. What **are** you **going to do** tomorrow night?
I'm going to do some shopping tomorrow night.
2. When **are** you **going to leave**?
I'm going to leave at 9 a.m.
3. **Is** he **going to call** her later?
Yes, he is going to call her later.
4. What **are** you **going to say** when you see him?
I'm going to tell him the truth.
5. **Are** they **going to study** British Literature in college?
No, they are going to study Chinese Literature in college.
6. **Is** your family **going to have** a vacation in Hawaii?
No, my family is going to have a vacation in Guam.

4 1. I think I'll take a nap.
2. I think I'll turn on a light.
3. I think I'll check my voicemail.
4. I think I'll eat them right away.
5. I think I'll pay it at 7-Eleven.
6. I think I'll buy him a gift.
7. I think I'll visit her in the hospital.
8. I think I'll bring my umbrella.

5 1. ✓　2. ✗　I think it'll rain soon.　3. ✓
4. ✗ I'm sure you won't get called next week.
5. ✓　6. ✗ Is Laura going to work?　7. ✓
8. ✗ In the year 2100, people will live on the moon.
9. ✗ What are you doing next week?

6 1. A　2. A　3. A　4. A

7 1. I won't be watching the game on Saturday afternoon.
Will I be watching the game on Saturday afternoon?

11

2. You aren't going to visit Grandma Moses tomorrow.
   Are you going to visit Grandma Moses tomorrow?
3. She isn't planning to be on vacation next week.
   Is she planning to be on vacation next week?
4. We aren't going to take a trip to New Zealand next month.
   Are we going to take a trip to New Zealand next month?
5. He won't send the tax forms soon.
   Will he send the tax forms soon?
6. It won't be cold all next week.
   Will it be cold all next week?

8 1. A 2. A 3. B 4. C 5. A 6. B 7. B
   8. A 9. C 10. A 11. C 12. B

Unit 50 p. 131

1 1. watch 2. to play 3. fly 4. to give
   5. going / to go 6. to win 7. hear 8. play
   9. go 10. to be 11. to meet

2 1. to pay the bill
   2. to quit drinking and smoking
   3. make good coffee
   4. look very happy; to wear clothes
   5. to work 10 hours a day
   6. to buy some red peppers

Unit 51 p. 133

1 1. to finish 2. go 3. sit 4. to fly 5. to join
   6. to call 7. to call 8. make / to make
   9. to have 10. to throw 11. to sit

2 1. to get the sausage on the plate
   2. take a look at your answers
   3. to climb a tree
   4. to eat on a train
   5. to bake cookies
   6. to study for the exam
   7. to read a story to you
   8. to finish the paper today

Unit 52 p. 135

1 1. playing soccer 2. making clothes
   3. blowing bubbles 4. singing a song
   5. drawing on canvas 6. biking
   7. waiting for his master
   8. walking in the rain

2 1. call / to call 2. to avoid 3. drinking
   4. getting up / to get up 5. swimming
   6. sharing 7. going 8. living 9. running
   10. going / to go 11. meeting 12. eating

Unit 53 p. 137

1 1. a library to borrow books
   2. a history museum to see artifacts
   3. the aquarium to see the fish
   4. an art gallery to look at paintings
   5. the amusement park for fun
   6. a zoo to see the animals

2 1. for carrying liquid cement
   2. for putting out fires
   3. for towing cars and trucks
   4. for taking the sick or wounded to the hospital
   5. for pushing soil and rocks

Unit 54 Review Test p. 139

1 1. surf 2. to surf 3. surfing / to surf, surfing
   4. ski 5. to ski 6. skiing 7. drive
   8. drive / to drive 9. driving 10. to drive

2 1. My parents went out for a walk.
   2. Mr. Lyle went to the front desk for his package.
   3. I have to get everything ready for the meeting.
   4. I jog every day to stay healthy.
   5. I walked into the McDonald's on Tenth Street to buy two cheeseburgers.

3 1. C 2. A 3. B 4. A 5. C 6. B 7. C
   8. B 9. C 10. B 11. B 12. B 13. B
   14. B 15. C

4 1. the beach to play beach volleyball
   2. the water to get the ball
   3. the supermarket for some milk
   4. the opera house for a concert
   5. the store to buy a gift
   6. my friend's house to see her new doll house
   7. the dentist's for a dental checkup
   8. the Starbucks for a cup of latté
   9. the stadium to watch a baseball game
   10. the market to buy some pumpkins

5 1. ✓ 2. ✗ I should visit my sister.
   3. ✗ Let's go to see a movie. 4. ✓
   5. ✓ 6. ✗ I want you to call me next week.
   7. ✗ Would you like me to call you next week?
   8. ✓ 9. ✗ When you finish playing cards, call me.
   10. ✗ I go swimming every morning at 6:00.
   11. ✓
   12. ✗ Most people love to go on a vacation. / Most people love going on a vacation.
   13. ✓
   14. ✗ Kelly went to see the doctor to have a checkup.
   15. ✓

Unit 55   p. 143

1 1. go bowling   2. go swimming   3. go skiing
4. go sailing   5. go camping   6. go skating
2 1. has gone   2. go for   3. have gone by
4. going   5. going for   6. went on   7. went

Unit 56   p. 145

1 1. to finish   2. to listen   3. to fix   4. done
5. cut   6. washed
2 a shower, a walk, a nap, a look, a note, a
picture, a shortcut, a chance, a seat
3 1. Get on, get off   2. took   3. get over
4. Take off   5. take part in
6. gotten together   7. of

Unit 57   p. 147

1 1. a favor   2. a mistake   3. good   4. his best
5. a wish   6. a speech   7. the decision
2 1. do   2. make   3. made   4. do   5. made of
6. made from   7. good   8. made of   9. fly
10. sad

Unit 58   p. 149

1 1. He had the pants shortened.
2. Yvonne had her son mop the floor.
3. She had the car washed.
4. She had her husband replace the lightbulb.
5. He had the paper folded.
6. She had the box packed with books and
sent to the professor.
7. He had his students read thirty pages of
the book a day.
8. I'm going to have this gift wrapped.
2 1. have your baby
2. have something to do with
3. has nothing to do with
4. have a look
5. have a good time
6. having a haircut

Unit 59 Review Test   p. 151

1 1. A   2. C   3. A   4. B   5. A   6. B   7. B   8. C
9. C   10. A   11. C   12. C   13. A   14. C
2 1. is made from   2. went for   3. get along
4. took part in   5. go on   6. took place
7. Get over   8. is made of
3 1. finish   2. to change   3. finished   4. clean
5. apologize   6. work   7. done   8. painted
9. to remove   10. explain   11. repaired
4 1. Did you **have** your hair cut last week?
→ **Yes, I did. I had my hair cut last week.
/ No, I didn't. I didn't have my hair cut
last week.**

2. Do you have to **do** a lot of homework
tonight?
→ **Yes, I do. I have to do a lot of homework
tonight. / No, I don't. I don't have to do
a lot of homework tonight.**
3. Does your family **go** on a picnic every
weekend?
→ **Yes, we do. We go on a picnic every
weekend. / No, we don't. We don't go
on a picnic every weekend.**
4. Do you like to **take** pictures of dogs and
cats?
→ **Yes, I do. I like to take pictures of dogs
and cats. / No, I don't. I don't like to
take pictures of dogs and cats.**
5. Do you **take** care of your little sister when
your parents are out?
→ **Yes, I do. I take care of my little sister
when my parents are out. / No, I don't.
I don't take care of my little sister when
my parents are out.**
6. Do you like to **go** camping on your
summer vacation?
→ **Yes, I do. I like to go camping on my
summer vacation. / No, I don't. I don't
like to go camping on my summer
vacation.**
7. Do you **do** the dishes every day?
→ **Yes, I do. I do the dishes every day. /
No, I don't. I don't do the dishes every
day.**
8. Do you **take** a shower in the morning?
→ **Yes, I do. I take a shower in the
morning. / No, I don't. I don't take a
shower in the morning.**
9. Do you **go** crazy with your homework
every day?
→ **Yes, I do. I go crazy with my homework
every day. / No, I don't. I don't go crazy
with my homework every day.**
10. Do you **make** a lot of mistakes?
→ **Yes, I do. I make a lot of mistakes. / No,
I don't. I don't make a lot of mistakes.**
11. Have you ever **had** the dentist fill a cavity?
→ **Yes, I have. I have had the dentist fill a
cavity. / No, I haven't. I haven't had the
dentist fill a cavity.**
5 **do:** exercise, the laundry, the shopping
take: a nap, a bath, a break
make: friends, a wish, money

Unit 60   p. 155

1 1. Chris can play the guitar.
2. Chris can't play the drums.
3. Chris can't play the piano.

13

4. Chris can play the flute.

5. Chris can play the violin.

6. Chris can't play the saxophone.

2 1. Yes, I can. I can speak English.
/ No, I can't. I can't speak English.

2. Yes, I can. I can read German.
/ No, I can't. I can't read German.

3. Yes, I can. I can hang out with my friends on the weekend. / No, I can't. I can't hang out with my friends on the weekend.

4. Yes, I can. I can run very fast.
/ No, I can't. I can't run very fast.

5. Yes, she can. She can cook Mexican food. / No, she can't. She can't cook Mexican food.

6. No, it can't. A dog can't fly.

7. No, it can't. A pig can't climb a tree.

8. No, we can't. We can't speak loudly in the museum.

Unit 61 p. 157

1 1. could paint pictures

2. could write calligraphy

3. could sculpt figures

4. could shoot photographs

5. could make pots

6. could paint landscapes

2 1. Yes, I could. I could play the piano when I was twelve. / No, I couldn't. I couldn't play the piano when I was twelve.

2. Yes, I could. I could swim when I was twelve. / No, I couldn't. I couldn't swim when I was twelve.

3. Yes, I could. I could use a computer when I was twelve. / No, I couldn't. I couldn't use a computer when I was twelve.

4. Yes, I could. I could read novels in English when I was twelve. / No, I couldn't. I couldn't read novels in English when I was twelve.

5. Yes, I could. I could ride a bicycle when I was twelve. / No, I couldn't. I couldn't ride a bicycle when I was twelve.

Unit 62 p. 159

1 1. must finish 2. mustn't smoke

3. had to clean 4. mustn't fight

5. must come 6. must finish

7. had to break 8. mustn't eat

9. must behave 10. had to run

2 1. You must hurry.

2. You must go to bed.

3. You must eat something.

4. You must drink something.

5. You must be careful.

6. You mustn't fight with them.

7. You mustn't lose it.

Unit 63 p. 161

1 1. She has to pack products.

2. She has to work on the computer.

3. She has to answer the phone.

4. She has to make copies.

2 1. doesn't have to deliver the mail.

2. don't have to make coffee.

3. doesn't have to show up every day.

4. doesn't have to fax documents.

Unit 64 p. 163

1 （答案略）

2 1. You mustn't smoke

2. You don't have to pay cash

3. You mustn't skateboard

4. You mustn't talk on a cell phone

5. You don't have to pay full price

Unit 65 p. 165

1 1. may/might block the shot

2. may/might hit a home run

3. may/might win the set

4. may/might score a touchdown

5. may/might win the race

6. may/might clear the bar

2 1. We may go to the seashore tomorrow.

2. I might take you on a trip to visit my hometown.

3. We may pick up Grandpa on the way.

4. We might visit my sister in Sydney next year.

5. My sister may bring her husband and baby to visit us instead.

6. We might go to Hong Kong for the weekend.

7. You may go to a boarding school in Switzerland.

8. Or you might go to live with your grandparents.

Unit 66 p. 167

1 1. shouldn't eat 2. should yield

3. shouldn't cheat 4. should respect

5. shouldn't arrive 6. should work

7. shouldn't feed 8. should take

2 1. →Should I call the director about the resume I sent?

→Do you think I should call the director about the resume I sent?

2. →Should I bring a gift with me?
   →Do you think I should bring a gift with me?
3. →Should Mike go on a vacation once in a while?
   →Do you think Mike should go on a vacation once in a while?
4. →Should we visit our grandma more often?
   →Do you think we should visit our grandma more often?
5. →Should I ask Nancy out for a date?
   →Do you think I should ask Nancy out for a date?
6. →Should Sally apply for that job in the restaurant?
   →Do you think Sally should apply for that job in the restaurant?

Unit 67　p. 169

1 1. →May I get two more shirts just like this one?
   →Could I get two more shirts just like this one?
   →Can I get two more shirts just like this one?
2. →May I have three pairs of socks similar to these?
   →Could I have three pairs of socks similar to these?
   →Can I have three pairs of socks similar to these?
3. →May I have a tie that goes with my shirt?
   →Could I have a tie that goes with my shirt?
   →Can I have a tie that goes with my shirt?
4. →May I pay with a credit card?
   →Could I pay with a credit card?
   →Can I pay with a credit card?
2 1. May I speak to Dennis?
2. May I borrow your father's drill?
3. Could you move these boxes for me?
4. Could you turn up the heat?
5. Can I put my files here?

Unit 68　p. 171

1 1. →Would you like some fruit salad?
   →Would you like me to make some fruit salad?
   →I'll make some fruit salad for you.
   Shall I make some fruit salad for you?
2. →Would you like some tea?
   →Would you like me to make some tea?
   →I'll make some tea for you.
   →Shall I make some tea for you?

3. →Would you like some orange juice?
   →Would you like me to squeeze some orange juice?
   →I'll squeeze some orange juice for you.
   →Shall I squeeze some orange juice for you?
4. →Would you like some pudding?
   →Would you like me to make some pudding?
   →I'll make some pudding for you.
   →Shall I make some pudding for you?
2 1. Would you like to go fishing
2. Would you like to play basketball
3. Would you like to go hiking
4. Would you like to go to the beach
5. Would you like to have some pizza

Unit 69　p. 173

1 1. →Shall we play another volleyball game?
   →Why don't we play another volleyball game?
   →How about playing another volleyball game?
   →Let's play another volleyball game.
2. →Shall we go on a picnic?
   →Why don't we go on a picnic?
   →How about going on a picnic?
   →Let's go on a picnic.
3. →Shall we eat out tonight?
   →Why don't we eat out tonight?
   →How about eating out tonight?
   →Let's eat out tonight.
4. →Shall we take a walk?
   →Why don't we take a walk?
   →How about taking a walk?
   →Let's take a walk.
5. →Shall we go to Bali this summer?
   →Why don't we go to Bali this summer?
   →How about going to Bali this summer?
   →Let's go to Bali this summer.
6. →Shall we have Chinese food for dinner?
   →Why don't we have Chinese food for dinner?
   →How about having Chinese food for dinner?
   →Let's have Chinese food for dinner.

Unit 70 Review Test　p. 175

1 1. Q: Can you boil tea eggs?
   A: Yes, I can. I can boil tea eggs. / No, I can't. I can't boil tea eggs.
2. Q: Can you purée tomatoes?
   A: Yes, I can. I can purée tomatoes. / No, I can't. I can't purée tomatoes.
3. Q: Can you deep fry French fries?
   A: Yes, I can. I can deep fry French fries. / No, I can't. I can't deep fry French fries.

15

4. **Q:** Can you grill hamburgers?
   A: Yes, I can. I can grill hamburgers. / No, I can't. I can't grill hamburgers.
5. **Q:** Can you bake muffins?
   A: Yes, I can. I can bake muffins. / No, I can't. I can't bake muffins.
6. **Q:** Can you make coffee?
   A: Yes, I can. I can make coffee. / No, I can't. I can't make coffee.
7. **Q:** Can you fry an egg?
   A: Yes, I can. I can fry an egg. / No, I can't. I can't fry an egg.
8. **Q:** Can you steam a bun?
   A: Yes, I can. I can steam a bun. / No, I can't. I can't steam a bun.

2 1. do, have to   2. Does, have to
3. Do, have to   4. Do, have to
5. Does, have to   6. do, have to

3 1. May I   2. Can I / May I   3. Could you
4. Shall I   5. Would you   6. I'll
7. How about   8. Would you

4 1. Would you like something to drink?
2. Would you like an alcoholic beverage?
3. Would you like some juice?
4. Would you like a cup of coffee or tea?
5. Would you like a bag of nuts?

5 1. I can't walk to work.
2. Susie couldn't dance all night.
3. I don't have to go to Joe's house tonight.
4. I don't have to go to see the doctor tomorrow.
5. I may not go on a vacation in August.
6. I might not go see the Picasso exhibit at the museum.
7. My friend can't sit in the full lotus position.
8. I can't finish all my homework this weekend.
9. I don't have to stop eating beans.
10. John doesn't have to see Joseph.
11. The turtle may not win the race against the rabbit.
12. My friend Jon shouldn't get a different job.

6 1. Can you fry an egg?
2. Could Paul swim out to the island?
3. Must John go to Japan? / Does John have to go to Japan?
4. Does Abby have to go to the studio?
5. Can George play the guitar?
6. Must David finish his homework before he goes outside to play?
7. Do they have to cross the road?
8. Do I have to give away my concert tickets?
9. Does Joan have to stay at home tomorrow night?

7 1. A   2. A   3. C   4. A   5. A   6. A   7. A
8. C   9. B   10. B

8 1. A   2. D   3. H   4. C   5. F   6. B   7. G   8. E

9 1. must be   2. must visit
3. must be, must eat   4. must pay
5. mustn't play

10 1. may have, should not eat
2. may listen, should not download
3. may have, should not put
4. may drive, may not find
5. may call, may not answer
6. may watch, must not try

11 1. should give   2. shouldn't feed
3. should adopt   4. shouldn't give
5. should spend   6. should take

Unit 71 p. 183

1 1. James isn't playing with his new iPhone.
2. Vincent doesn't own a shoe factory.
3. They didn't go to a concert last night.
4. I don't enjoy reading.
5. I can't ride a unicycle.
6. Summer vacation won't begin soon.
7. I didn't have a nightmare last night.
8. I'm not from Vietnam.

2 1. Sue watched the football game on TV last night.
2. Rick can speak Japanese.
3. Phil and Jill were at the office yesterday.
4. I could enter the house this morning.
5. Joseph likes spaghetti.
6. They are drinking apple juice.
7. She is going shopping tomorrow.
8. I will tell Sandy.

Unit 72 p. 185

1 1. Is Jerry good at photography?
2. Doesn't Jane believe what he said?
3. Did he ever show up at the party?
4. Does Johnny get up early every day?
5. Will I remember you?
6. Did Julie ask me to give her a ride yesterday?
7. Was she surprised when he called?
8. Is he going to buy a gift tomorrow?

2 1. What are you watching on the Internet?
2. What are you interested in?
3. Who is that man?
4. Who is your favorite musician?
5. What is he looking at?
6. Who is writing an email?

Unit 73   p. 187

1 1. Who ate my slice of pizza?
   What did Johnny eat?
2. Who consulted Lauren first?
   Who did the boss consult first?
3. Who helped cook the fish?
   What did Tom help cook?
4. Who broke the vase?
   What did my dog break?
5. Who is making food for the baby?
   Who is Mom making food for?
6. Who is standing next to Allen?
   Who is Denise standing next to?

Unit 74   p. 189

1 **which:** this one, the blue shirt, the large one, the taller man
where: Italy, the office, the mall, the garage
when: tomorrow, last December, in 2022, next month
whose: Amber's, my brother's, Ms. Smith's, the cat's
2 1. When   2. Where   3. Which   4. Whose
5. Where   6. When   7. Whose   8. When
9. Which   10. When

Unit 75   p. 191

1 1. How old   2. How tall   3. How much
4. How many   5. How   6. How often
7. How long   8. How old   9. How
10. How tall   11. How much   12. How often
13. How long   14. How

Unit 76   p. 193

1 1. can't I   2. aren't you   3. do I   4. can't I
5. do you   6. have I   7. didn't you
8. did you   9. did you   10. haven't you
11. do you   12. do you
2 1. aren't you   2. is he   3. can you
4. won't she   5. didn't I   6. does she
7. isn't it   8. aren't I   9. isn't it   10. did he

Unit 77   p. 195

1 1. ✓   2. -   3. ✓   4. -   5. ✓   6. ✓   7. -
8. ✓   9. -   10. ✓
2 1. Paul, close that door.
2. Don't go out at midnight.
3. Don't throw garbage into the toilet.
4. Go buy some eggs now.
5. Don't be mad at me.
6. Take a No. 305 bus to the city hall.
7. Be careful not to wake up the baby.
8. Don't worry about so many things.

9. Relax.
10. Do your homework right now.

Unit 78 Review Test   p. 197

1 1. N   2. A   3. N   4. Q   5. N   6. Q   7. A
8. Q   9. Q   10. A
2 1. When   2. Where   3. Who   4. How
5. Who   6. Where   7. When   8. How
9. Why   10. Why   11. Which   12. What
13. Which   14. What   15. Whose   16. Whose
3 1. Who is visiting Charles?
2. Who is Eve visiting?
3. Who wants to meet Cathy?
4. Who does Cathy want to meet?
5. What took Mary such a long time?
6. What did he take with him?
7. Who is Keith dating?
8. What crashed?
9. Who answered the phone?
10. Who wants to marry Jenny?
11. What does Dennis want to buy?
12. Who wants to buy a new cell phone?
13. Who wants to eat peanuts?
14. What does Sylvia want to eat?
4 1. isn't it?   2. is it?   3. aren't they?
4. are we?   5. didn't you?   6. did you?
7. wasn't it   8. was it?   9. didn't you?
5 1. Who is Chris calling?
2. What does Irene want to do?
3. Who wants to stay for dinner?
4. Who finished the last piece of cake?
5. Who invented the automobile?
6. Whose dirty dishes are these on the table?
7. Which side of the road do you drive on?
8. Rupert likes history, doesn't he?
9. They drive a minivan, don't they?
6 **Bob:** How can I get to the station?
Eve: **Go** straight down this road. **Walk** for fifteen minutes and you will see a park.
Bob: So the station is near the park?
Eve: Yes. **Turn** right at the park and **walk** for another five minutes. **Cross** the main road. The station will be at your left. You won't miss it.
Bob: That's very helpful of you.
Eve: **Be** sure not to take any small alleys on the way.
Bob: I won't. Thank you very much.
Eve: You're welcome.
7 1. Eddie isn't a naughty boy.
   Is Eddie a naughty boy?
2. Jack doesn't walk to work every morning.
   Does Jack walk to work every morning?

3. Sammi didn't visit Uncle Lu last Saturday.
Did Sammi visit Uncle Lu last Saturday?
4. She won't be able to finish the project next week.
Will she be able to finish the project next week?
5. My boss isn't going to Beijing tomorrow.
Is my boss going to Beijing tomorrow?
6. Joe hasn't seen the show yet.
Has Joe already seen the show?

Unit 79 p. 201

1 1. come along   2. work out   3. hang out
4. taken off   5. stay up   6. moving in
7. Come in
2 1. true   2. out   3. up   4. up   5. in   6. down
7. off   8. down   9. up   10. up   11. on   12. up

Unit 80 p. 203

1 1. set off
→ Dick and Byron set the fire crackers off.
→ Dick and Byron set them off.
2. take off
→ Don't take the price tag off in case we have to return the sweater.
→ Don't take it off in case we have to return the sweater.
3. turn down
→ Don't turn the offer down right away.
→ Don't turn it down right away.
4. throw away
→ We don't throw bottles away if they can be recycled.
→ We don't throw them away if they can be recycled.
5. fill out
→ You need to fill the form out and attach two photos.
→ You need to fill it out and attach two photos.
6. try on
→ Would you like to try these shoes on?
→ Would you like to try them on?
7. turn off
→ Could you turn the radio off? I don't want to listen to it.
→ Could you turn it off? I don't want to listen to it.
8. call off
→ I'll have to call the meeting off.
→ I'll have to call it off.
9. brought up
→ Lucy brought her son up by herself.
→ Lucy brought him up by herself.

Unit 81 p. 205

1 1. look after   2. Watch out for   3. catch up with
4. put up with   5. come across
6. fed up with   7. run down   8. get over
2 1. on, off   2. in/into   3. into   4. to   5. out of
6. of   7. for   8. on   9. to   10. in   11. for

Unit 82 Review Test p. 207

1 1. wake, up   2. hang out   3. take off, get on
4. hand in   5. threw away   6. move in
7. Get in   8. Keep away from   9. fill out
10. getting along with   11. keep up with
12. pick up   13. grew up   14. brought up
15. working out   16. call off   17. hung up
18. try on
2 1. looking for   2. Look up   3. look after
4. Look out   5. turn down   6. turn on
7. turn down   8. turn off   9. take out
10. Take off   11. take off   12. take after
13. put on   14. put out   15. put off
16. put away   17. go on   18. went off
19. went out

Unit 83 p. 209

1 1. old pants   2. new pants   3. soft chair
4. hard chair   5. big dog   6. small dog
7. curved road   8. straight road
2 1. He lives in a small town.
2. She has blue eyes.
3. The lamb stew smells good.
4. I have two lovely kids.
5. My teddy bear is cute.

Unit 84 p. 211

1 1. suddenly   2. really   3. early   4. quickly
5. well   6. finally   7. fast   8. lazily
9. entirely   10. gently   11. luckily
12. cheaply   13. probably   14. specially
15. cheerfully   16. deeply   17. merrily
18. clean   19. simply   20. angrily
2 1. He answered clearly.
2. He sings badly.
3. He arrived at school late. / He arrived late for school.
4. She paints well.
5. She learns fast.
6. He works noisily.
7. She translates professionally.
8. The earth trembled terribly.
9. She reads fast.
10. She shops frequently.

Unit 85 p. 213

1 1. My parents live over there.
2. They bought the house over 20 years ago.
3. My dad pays the mortgage to the bank on the first day of each month.
4. He went downstairs to check the mailbox.
5. No packages were delivered to Wendy's house this morning.
6. Jack and Jimmy are going to meet at the café this afternoon.

2 1. I left the bag in the cloakroom at 4:30 yesterday.
2. I last saw him at Teresa's birthday party on January 22nd.
3. I bought that book at the bookstore around the corner last week.
4. I go swimming at the health club on Sundays.
5. I learned to dive at the Pacific Diving Club three years ago.
6. I ate lunch at Susie's Pizza House at 12:30 yesterday.

Unit 86 p. 215

1 1. He never misses the mortgage payment.
2. He is always the first customer in the morning.
3. He walks to work every day.
4. The water overflowed quickly. /
The water quickly overflowed.
5. The volcano exploded suddenly. /
The volcano suddenly exploded.
6. There have been many burglaries lately.
7. That changed their minds entirely.

2 （答案略）

Unit 87 p. 217

1 1. bigger, biggest   2. taller, tallest
3. closer, closest   4. faster, fastest
5. sadder, saddest   6. cuter, cutest
7. spicier, spiciest   8. thinner, thinnest
9. better, best   10. more, most
11. larger, largest   12. later, latest
13. busier, busiest   14. simpler, simplest
15. tinier, tiniest   16. worse, worst
17. more useful, most useful   18. less, least
19. quieter, quietest   20. higher, highest

2 （答句之答案略）
1. the cutest   2. the most hardworking
3. the funniest   4. the most boring
5. the most friendly   6. the tallest
7. the smartest   8. the most creative

Unit 88 p. 219

1 1. Ken is shorter than Jim.
2. Ken is more professional than Jim.
3. Ken is fatter than Jim.
4. Jim is taller than Ken.
5. Jim is more casual than Ken.
6. Ken is more business-like than Jim.
7. Ken is more intense than Jim.
8. Jim is more lighthearted than Ken.

2 1. ✗ Mt. Everest is the highest mountain in the world.
2. ✗ The Japan Trench is deeper than the Java Trench, but the Mariana Trench is the deepest.
3. ✗ Africa is not as large as Asia.
4. ✗ Blue whales are the largest animal in the world.
5. ✓
6. ✗ China is not as democratic as the United States.
7. ✗ The Burj Dubai is taller than Taipei 101.
8. ✓

Unit 89 p. 221

1 1. too noisy   2. too many   3. too dark
4. too busy   5. too talkative

2 1. It was too noisy for Charlie to talk on the phone.
2. There were too many phone calls for Amy to take a coffee break.
3. It was too dark for Andrew to see the keyboard very well.
4. Jessica was too busy to help her colleagues with their work.
5. Tony's colleagues were too talkative for him to concentrate on his work.

Unit 90 Review Test p. 223

1 1. He is/looks strong.   2. He is/looks weak.
3. It is/looks tall.   4. She is/looks short.
5. He is/looks fat.   6. She is/looks healthy.
7. She is/looks happy.
8. She is/looks thoughtful.

2 1. clear   2. dearly   3. fair   4. just   5. wide
6. quickly   7. wrongly   8. slowly
9. carefully

3 1. He is a handsome guy.
2. That guy is handsome.
3. Ned takes the subway to his office.
4. Penny is always ready to take a break.
5. Dennis is a terrible driver.
6. Dennis drives terribly.
7. I'm too excited to wait.

8. This bag isn't big enough for these gifts.
9. Do you work here in this building?
10. Does Larry fight with his brother every day?
11. Did we meet at the Italian restaurant last Monday night?
12. Does Mr. Harrison always eat lunch at the same time?
13. Is Greg usually late for his tennis date?
14. Does Frederica go to the spa every week?
15. Are you sometimes too tired to get up in the morning?

4 1. every day   2. twice a week   3. often
4. sometimes   5. never

5 1. every Sunday   2. six times a month
3. always   4. every week   5. every weekend

6 1. ✗ I see two tall guys.
2. ✓
3. ✗ Tony is taller than David.
4. ✗ Who is the tallest guy in the room?
5. ✓
6. ✗ James is better at math than Robert.
7. ✗ Irving is a happy guy.
8. ✗ Janice speaks English very well.

7 1. quietly   2. joyfully   3. eagerly   4. slowly

8 1. Mt. Fuji isn't as tall as Mt. Everest.
2. Brazil isn't as big as Russia.
3. Madagascar isn't as big as Greenland.
4. Jakarta isn't as prosperous as Seoul.
5. Manila isn't as densely populated as Tokyo.
6. France isn't as small as Switzerland.
7. Iceland isn't as far south as Spain.
8. Italy isn't as far north as Germany.
9. Canada isn't as hot as Mexico.
10. Egypt isn't as cold as Sweden.

9 1. sweeter than   2. warmer than
3. hotter than   4. the coldest   5. the biggest
6. the tallest   7. as terrible as   8. as fast as
9. as high as

10 1. too hard / hard enough
2. too late
3. too salty / salty enough
4. too spicy / spicy enough
5. too blunt / blunt enough
6. too loud / loud enough
7. too expensive
8. too slow

Unit 91   p. 229

1 1. on   2. in   3. at   4. in   5. in   6. on
7. on   8. on   9. on

Unit 92   p. 231

1 1. in   2. at   3. in   4. in
2 1. in   2. on   3. on   4. at   5. in   6. in

Unit 93   p. 233

1 1. behind   2. next to   3. in   4. on
5. against, near   6. next to   7. in front of
8. on   9. under   10. over   11. between
12. against

Unit 94   p. 235

1 1. out of   2. into   3. up   4. on   5. around
6. out of   7. along   8. across   9. through
10. past   11. down   12. off

Unit 95   p. 237

1 **in:** the morning, the evening
on: Friday afternoons, National Day, the weekend, Sundays, Monday, Christmas Day
at: Christmas, night, 6 o'clock

2 1. at   2. on   3. in   4. at   5. on   6. on
7. at   8. on   9. on   10. on

Unit 96   p. 239

1 **in:** winter, October, 1998, the fall
on: May 5, June 27
✗: this weekend, tomorrow afternoon, next summer, yesterday morning, last month

2 1. in   2. on   3. in   4. on   5. in   6. ✗   7. ✗
8. on   9. in   10. in

Unit 97   p. 241

1 （答案略）
2 1. since   2. since   3. for   4. for   5. since
6. since   7. since   8. for   9. for   10. since
11. for   12. since
3 （答案略）

Unit 98 Review Test   p. 243

1 1. behind   2. from   3. under   4. down
5. off   6. out of
2 1. in   2. on   3. on   4. on   5. into   6. out of
7. into   8. on   9. between   10. behind
11. over   12. in   13. along   14. past   15. in
16. against   17. near   18. under   19. to
20. down
3 1. on   2. on   3. at   4. at   5. at   6. to   7. in
8. in   9. at   10. on   11. in
4 1. on   2. at   3. on   4. in   5. at   6. on
7. on   8. at, on   9. in, on   10. in   11. in

20

5 1. under, on 2. in 3. in front of 4. behind
  5. near 6. opposite 7. next to 8. between
6 1. for 2. for 3. since 4. ago 5. for
  6. for 7. ago 8. for 9. since
7 1. Dana left an hour ago.
  2. Nancy walked out of the office thirty-five minutes ago.
  3. Victor called three hours ago.
  4. Julie came four days ago.
  5. It happened a month ago.
  6. We saw her a year ago.
8 1. ago 2. left 3. for 4. for 5. since
  6. since

Unit 99 p. 249

1 1. I like soda and potato chips.
  2. Do you want to leave at night or in the morning?
  3. I can't cook, but I can barbecue.
  4. I have been to Switzerland and New Zealand.
  5. She isn't a ballet dancer, but she is a great hip hop dancer.
  6. Tom says he is rich, but he always borrows money from me.
  7. Will you come this week or next week?
  8. Shall we sit in the front or in the back?
  9. I read comic books and novels.
  10. Do you like to eat German food or French food?

Unit 100 p. 251

1 1. If he lifts weights, he will build up his muscles.
  2. If she skips dessert, she will stay slim.
  3. If she often goes jogging, she will increase her stamina.
  4. If she reads widely, she'll learn lots of things.
  5. If he practices writing, he'll improve his communication skills.
  6. If he practices public speaking, he'll become self-confident.
2 1. When she finishes stretching, she'll start jogging.
  2. When she gets tired, she'll rest on a bench.
  3. When she gets home, she'll eat breakfast.

Unit 101 Review Test p. 253

1 1. because my car broke down
  2. because my boss needed me to work late in the office
  3. so I could finish my report
  4. because I had to bake cookies

  5. because my dog was sick
  6. so I could see my favorite TV show
  7. because I had to take a sick friend to the hospital
  8. because I had to help my mom clean the house
2 1. and 2. but 3. or 4. and 5. but 6. or
  7. and 8. but 9. or 10. or
3 1. when 2. if 3. when 4. if 5. when
  6. if 7. When 8. If 9. when 10. If
4 1. When, will wear 2. If, will ask 3. when, ask
  4. If, will take 5. if, tell 6. When, will give
5 1. after, before 2. before 3. after
  4. before 5. after

Unit 102 p. 255

1 1. nine 2. thirteen 3. seventy-eight
  4. one hundred and forty-one
  5. three hundred and eighty-five
  6. seven thousand, and sixty-four
  7. nine thousand, eight hundred and fifty-six
  8. ten thousand, two hundred and thirty-one
  9. one million, thirty-two thousand, five hundred and forty
  10. six million, eight hundred and thirty-seven thousand, six hundred and fifty
  11. forty million
  12. twelve million, four hundred and fifty-two thousand, six hundred and eighty-nine
2 1. nine one one
  2. eight seven eight six, five two three nine
  3. three one eight, dash, nine two six, dash, five two seven three
  4. zero zero three, dash, one, dash, two five zero, dash, seven six four, dash, five three two zero
  5. zero two, dash, three two seven six, dash, nine three seven zero
  6. zero nine three two, dash, five four zero, dash, six nine six
  7. two three six four, dash, five eight three nine, extension twelve

Unit 103 p. 257

1 1. the first 2. the third 3. the fourth
  4. the sixteenth 5. the twenty-ninth
  6. the thirty-second 7. the thirty-fifth
  8. the thirty-seventh 9. the forty-second
  10. the forty-fourth

Unit 104 p. 259

1 1. Mr. Simpson is meeting Ms. Miller on Monday.

2. Mr. Simpson is visiting his grandma on Tuesday.
3. Mr. Simpson is going shopping on Wednesday.
4. Mr. Simpson is having dinner with Tom on Thursday.
5. Mr. Simpson is picking up Peter at the airport on Friday.
6. Mr. Simpson is playing basketball on Saturday.
7. Mr. Simpson is going to the movies on Sunday.

2 1. the twentieth of May, nineteen ninety-nine
2. the nineteenth of June, nineteen ninety-six
3. the first of March, two thousand eighteen
4. the eleventh of October, fifteen oh two
5. the twenty-sixth of February, two thousand ten
6. the thirty-first of December, eighteen seventy-six

Unit 105   p. 261

1 1. D 2. E 3. A 4. F 5. C 6. B
2 1. It's a quarter past nine. It's nine fifteen.
2. It's three o'clock. / It's 3 p.m. / It's 3 a.m.
3. It's half past three. It's three thirty.
4. It's a quarter to three.
It's fifteen minutes to three.
It's two forty-five.
5. It's seven oh two.
It's two minutes past seven.
6. It's five thirty-nine.
It's twenty-one minutes to six.
7. It's ten nineteen.
It's nineteen minutes past ten.

Unit 106 Review Test   p. 263

1 1. January, February 2. Sunday 3. March
4. August 5. Sunday 6. Thursday
7. Friday 8. July, August, September
9. Thursday, November 10. May, June

2 1. the twenty-fifth of December
2. the thirty-first of December
3. the first of January
4. the fourteenth of February
5. the fifth of May
6. the seventh of July
7. the fifteenth of August
8. the thirty-first of October
9. the twenty-nine of February

3 1. eight nine three zero seven six three five
2. zero two, dash, three four seven eight nine seven one one
3. eight eight six, dash, two, dash, one one five, dash, six seven three zero

4. four five six one eight nine three two, extension one one two
5. zero nine six five three two one five seven eight
6. the twenty-eighth of March / March (the) twenty-eighth
7. the fourth of July / July (the) fourth
8. the first of January / January (the) first
9. the eighteenth of September / September (the) eighteenth
10. fourteen fifty-nine
11. nineteen thirty-eight
12. two thousand nine
13. two thousand twenty

Progress Test

Part 1   p. 264

1 1. C 2. C 3. C 4. C 5. U 6. C 7. U 8. U
9. U 10. C 11. C 12. U 13. U 14. C 15. C
16. U 17. U 18. U 19. U 20. U
2 1. giraffes 2. dishes 3. oxen 4. lives
5. ducks 6. churches 7. sizes 8. erasers
9. geese 10. televisions 11. pencils
12. oases 13. cherries 14. species
15. libraries 16. data 17. sheep 18. fairies
19. deer 20. witches
3 1. a 2. the 3. a 4. an 5. a 6. An 7. a
8. An, the 9. an 10. the 11. an 12. The
13. a 14. the 15. an 16. a 17. the
18. the, a
4 1. bottles 2. box 3. tube 4. cups 5. carton
6. jar 7. can 8. bowl 9. glass 10. head
5 1. traffic 2. furniture 3. scissors 4. milk
5. tea 6. coffee
6 1. ✗ 2. the 3. the 4. ✗ 5. the 6. The
7. ✗ 8. ✗ 9. the 10. the, the 11. ✗, ✗
12. ✗ 13. the 14. ✗, ✗
7 1. ✗ Calvin is a cool little kid.
2. ✗ Our vacation starts on Friday, January 20th.
3. ✓
4. ✗ The nearest airport is in Canberra.
5. ✗ The Museum of Modern Art in New York is 50 years old.
6. ✗ The Great Wall of China is pretty amazing.
8 1. Jane's hat 2. my grandparents' house
3. the side of the road
4. Beethoven's Fifth Symphony
5. the price tags of the products
6. the ruins of ancient civilizations

9 1. ✓   2. ✓
  3. ✗ Are you watching TV or doing homework?
  4. ✓
  5. ✗ Helen has decided to learn the piano.
  6. ✗ The closest star to us is the Sun.

Part 2 — p. 267

1 1. I 2. you 3. You 4. We 5. he 6. They
  7. she 8. it
2 1. me 2. you 3. him 4. her 5. it 6. us
  7. You 8. them 9. ours 10. my 11. yours
  12. yours 13. yours 14. mine 15. hers
3 1. my 2. our 3. its 4. their 5. her 6. his
  7. your
4 1. some 2. any 3. any 4. some 5. any
  6. any 7. some 8. some 9. any 10. any
  11. some 12. some 13. any 14. any 15. any
  16. some 17. any 18. any 19. some
  20. some 21. any 22. some 23. any
5 1. any 2. some 3. no 4. any 5. some
  6. some 7. No 8. some 9. Any 10. some
6 1. A 2. C 3. B 4. C 5. A 6. B
7 1. little 2. a few 3. little 4. A little
  5. a few 6. a few 7. a few 8. a little
8 1. one, a glass of juice 2. ones, ties
  3. one, pair of shoes 4. one, jacket
9 1. Everybody / Everyone 2. anybody / anyone
  3. anything 4. somebody / someone
  5. something 6. nowhere
  7. Nobody / No one 8. anywhere 9. nothing
10 1. that 2. this 3. these 4. that 5. those
11 1. himself 2. herself 3. ourselves
  4. themselves 5. myself 6. yourself

Part 3 — p. 270

1 1. am 2. is 3. is 4. am 5. am 6. are
  7. is 8. are 9. is 10. am 11. is
2 1. Is there 2. There are 3. It is 4. Are there
  5. it is 6. there is
3 1. have got 2. haven't got
  3. Have, got, have 4. have got, haven't got
4 1. work 2. take 3. commutes 4. do, get
  5. don't drive, don't know 6. Do, go
  7. takes
5 1. are, doing 2. is ringing 3. am, cooking
  4. is looking 5. Are, working
  6. am planning
6 1. B 2. B 3. C 4. C 5. A 6. C 7. B
  8. B 9. A
7 1. ✗ I want something to eat.
  2. ✗ I love that dress you are wearing.
  3. ✓

4. ✗ I think you are right about Jim.
5. ✓
6. ✗ I saw some new shopping bags in your closet.

Part 4 — p. 272

1 1. Were, were 2. Was, wasn't 3. Was, was
  4. Were, weren't
2 1. Did 2. go 3. met 4. happened 5. ate
  6. talked 7. did 8. do 9. stayed
  10. behaved 11. meant 12. was
3 1. was standing 2. was sitting 3. pulled up
  4. grabbed 5. noticed
  6. was looking / looked 7. started
  8. opened 9. began 10. discovered
4 1. has been 2. Have, attended 3. has had
  4. has left 5. has been
5 1. opened 2. have had 3. Have you been
  4. Did you go

Part 5 — p. 273

1 1. Are 2. seeing 3. am seeing 4. am going
  5. Are 6. coming 7. am meeting 8. Are
  9. taking 10. am visiting
2 1. am going to sleep 2. are, going to visit
  3. Are, going to quit 4. are, going to move
  5. Are, going to live
3 1. will wonder 2. won't date 3. will send
  4. will screen 5. won't respond

Part 6 — p. 274

1 1. use 2. to use 3. to use / using 4. finish
  5. call 6. to see 7. stuff / to stuff 8. to start
  9. starting 10. to send 11. to learn
  12. to learn 13. playing 14. to turn
  15. holding
2 1. for 2. for 3. to 4. to

Part 7 — p. 275

1 1. shopping 2. started 3. to fix 4. do
  5. deliver 6. mailed 7. to walk
2 1. a swim 2. a trip 3. taking 4. of
  5. from 6. have 7. do, do 8. place

Part 8 — p. 275

1 1. can 2. can 3. can 4. can't 5. Can you
2 1. ✓ 2. ✓
  3. ✗ If I could I would, but I can't so I won't.
  4. ✗ He could climb up trees when he was young, but he couldn't get down.
  5. ✓
3 1. must tell 2. must pay 3. mustn't eat
  4. must call

4. 1. shouldn't make 2. should leave
   3. should see 4. should ask
5. 1. must / have to 2. must 3. has to
   4. has to 5. have to 6. must
6. 1. Can you check the balance in my account?
   2. Could I please transfer $20,000?
   3. Could you go over the charges for an electronic fund transfer?
   4. May I use your pen to fill out this form?
   5. May I have some extra copies of this EFT form?
   6. Would you like me to give the baby a bath?
   7. Would you like to take a break while I watch the baby?
   8. I'll change the baby's diaper for you.
   9. Should I warm up some milk for your baby?
   10. Should I put the baby down for a nap?
7. 1. Let's 2. Why don't we 3. shall
   4. How about 5. shall 6. How about
   7. Why don't we

Part 9   p. 278

1. 1. Who 2. What 3. Which 4. Whose
   5. Where 6. When 7. Why 8. How
   9. How old 10. How often
2. 1. What are you doing?
   2. What is the movie about?
   3. What happened to the daughter?
   4. What happens at the end of the movie?
3. 1. aren't you 2. isn't it 3. can he 4. am I
   5. don't you 6. didn't he
4. 1. Call 2. Move 3. come, sit 4. Don't take
   5. Don't forget 6. pass

Part 10   p. 279

1. 1. B 2. C 3. A 4. A 5. B 6. B 7. A 8. A
2. 1. to 2. from 3. to 4. for 5. with 6. for

Part 11   p. 279

1. 1. too sweet 2. loud enough 3. too bitter
   4. very
2. 1. ✓ 2. ✗ It's a fast computer. 3. ✓
   4. ✗ The machine is light.
3. 1. I leave at 10:00.
   2. Pick me up at my house at 7:00.
   3. Greg always dresses up to go dancing.
   4. Teddy is never the first to arrive.
   5. The kids were playing at the park yesterday.
   6. She ran to the car quickly five minutes ago. / She quickly ran to the car five minutes ago.

4. 1. nicer, nicest 2. smaller, smallest
   3. sadder, saddest 4. busier, busiest
   5. prettier, prettiest 6. better, best
   7. worse, worst 8. more, most
   9. more important, most important
   10. more popular, most popular
   11. more successful, most successful
   12. more boring, most boring
5. 1. smooth 2. smoothly 3. awful
   4. earnest 5. incredibly 6. artificially
6. 1. bad 2. worse 3. worst 4. tight
   5. tighter 6. tightest 7. important
   8. more important 9. most important

Part 12   p. 281

1. 1. on, in 2. on 3. at, at 4. at, in
   5. in, at/in 6. at, in
2. 1. at, at 2. in, at 3. on 4. on, in 5. ✗, ✗
3. 1. near, in front of 2. next to, opposite
   3. into, out of 4. to, off 5. up, down
   6. through, across 7. over, under
   8. past, around, between 9. to, from
4. 1. ✗ They left for lunch an hour ago. 2. ✓
   3. ✓ 4. ✗ I have been shopping for an hour.
   5. ✓ 6. ✓

Part 13   p. 282

1. 1. when 2. if/when 3. if 4. When
   5. When 6. If
2. 1. and 2. and 3. but 4. or 5. because
   6. so
3. 1. because 2. so 3. because 4. because
   5. so 6. because 7. so 8. because
   9. so 10. because

Part 14   p. 283

1. 1. thirty-four
   2. one hundred and forty-three
   3. one thousand, eight hundred, and ninety-five
   4. eight thousand
   5. zero three, three four five nine eight four three one
   6. ninth and tenth
   7. the twentieth of April / April (the) twentieth
   8. eight o'clock
   9. eight thirty / half past eight / thirty minutes past eight
   10. eight oh eight / eight minutes past eight
   11. eight forty-five / fifteen to nine / a quarter to nine
2. 1. Monday, Tuesday 2. January, February
   3. weekend 4. autumn/fall 5. in, at